I0691781

Like the Days of Noah

A Christian Fantasy

Tara La Sean

That Girl! Publishing, LLC

ISBN-13: 978-0692264966

ISBN-10: 0692264965

This book is dedicated to the memory of Cassundra Y. Davie who was more than just my best friend and sister, but my very own Mama Bear.

November 6, 1958- October 29, 2008

Acknowledgments

First giving honor to God and His Son Jesus, Who is the head of my life. Truly I thank Him for the gift of salvation! I am also grateful for Him giving me the ability to bring this story to life, for without Him I can do nothing.

I would also like to thank Bridget Hooks who, after hearing a little of the dream that inspired this story, used some of her own "Mama Bear" tactics and *made* me write it. **Message-** Sometimes God uses something as simple as lunch with a friend to start you on a journey!

A special thanks to my pastor and his wife, Raymond and Lena Like for their encouragement and prayers, as well as Valerie "my favorite *sustah* Val" Like and my God's Grace family. Many thanks go out to "the Donnas" at That Girl! Publishing. Donna "Friend" Hughes for all of her support throughout this process, and Donna "Shortcake" Luellen for reading every draft and making me believe this story was "the bomb.com!" I also want to thank Michelle Lewis of Aroused By Art for designing the cover.

A *very* special thanks goes out to Traci and Cedric Kimes, Suzette Steptoe, Ebony Davie, Charlene Teaser-Polk, Kameel Polk, Debbie Roberts and Imani Covington for their financial support during this process. And finally, to all of my friends and family on Facebook and Twitter who have supported me and kept me encouraged; THANK YOU ALL!

Tara La Sean

Pronunciation guide:

I hope this helps give you an idea of how to pronounce the names of the characters!

1. Kafeel (Kah-feel) Arabic word meaning provider or responsible for.

2. Carienne (Kah-rain) Egyptian word meaning water.

3. Jahmil (Ya-mill) Arabic word. To pick up, lift or carry.

4. Tehillah (Tuh-hay-luh) Hebrew word for praising the Lord in song.

5. Laqat (Law-QAHT) Hebrew word for gather or collect.

6. Imani (Ee-mah-nee) Swahili word for faith.

7. Myla (My-lah) Latin word for mild and merciful.

8. Magali (Muh-gah-lee) Spanish name meaning "pearl". Also means artistic girl.

9. Princess: French word meaning the daughter of a King

10. Bridget: Irish word for a strong and protective woman. In mythology she is the goddess of fire, wisdom and poetry.

11. Lanaia (La-Nie-uh) No origin. Made it up.

12. Daieh (Die-yeh) No origin. Made it up.

13. Dakkar (Duh-car) No direct origin. Name of West African city of Dakar.

14. Anuka (Ah-nu-kah) No origin. Made it up.

15. Mmoju (Mo-jew) No origin. Made it up.

16.   Anjelita Azul (On-hell-ee-tah; Ah-zool) Spanish for little blue angel.

17. Cilfure (Sill-fure-ay) No direct origin. It is an anagram.

18. Abuela (Ahb-way-lah) Spanish word for grandmother.

19. Binah (Bin-Nah) No origin. Made it up.

20. Haku (Ha-koo) No origin. Made it up.

21. Chaverah (Cha-ver-ah) Hebrew Word for friend.

22. Tefilah (Te-fie-lah) Hebrew word for prayer.

23. Esperanza (Es-per-ahn-zuh) Spanish for hope.

24. Tookey (Too-kee) No origin. Made it up.

25. Badee (Bah-dee) No origin. Made it up.

26. Cassa (Kah-suh) No origin. Made it up.

27. Nadah (Nah-dah) No origin. Made it up.

28. Jaffee (Jah-fee) No origin. Made it up

29. Loah (Low-ah) No origin. Made it up

30. Tenee (Ten-nee) No origin. Made it up

31. Tió (Tee-oh) Spanish for uncle.

32. Hermano (Err-mah-no) Spanish for brother.

33. Sobrina (So-bree-nah) Spanish for niece.

34. Morenita (Moor-eh-nee-tah) Spanish for little dark lady.

35. Querida (Ker-ee-dah) Spanish for sweetheart.

Prologue

Clark Air Force Base, Philippines

Two Months Ago

"Sir," the young officer said hesitantly. "We have a problem with Operation Condor."

"What kind of a problem?" came the irritated senior officer's reply.

"He's gone, sir. Escaped."

"What do you mean he's escaped!? For Chrissakes man, he was kept in a secure facility 50 floors below ground! There was supposed to be round-the-clock security and cameras on him at all times!"

"Yes sir, there was. But apparently the subject has abilities we were not aware of. He was in his bunker one minute; then he was gone. The surveillance footage shows that he stood up, walked to a wall, and went through it."

Five years ago, Captain Robert Chaffe would have laughed at the ridiculousness of what he was saying to Major General Riley. But five years ago, he hadn't known that anomalies like this existed. At the time he was just another promising pilot barely holding the rank of Quarter-Master Sergeant. He remembered being excited to learn that he'd been hand-picked for a special project that would guarantee him a fast-track to becoming a colonel or possibly a general. Already he'd been promoted to captain. But now, the increases in rank and pay did not compensate for all he'd seen and done over the past few years. Things that he knew would follow him to his grave.

After a brief pause, John Riley responded to the captain. "I don't care what you have to do. I don't care what it takes or what it costs; bring him back; dead or alive and preferably *dead*. This might get ugly, so bring in the locals if he makes it to the States. That way, if they kill him, our hands are clean."

Riley stood in his plush office and slammed his phone down as he let a curse fly from his lips. He had spent the past 25 years getting to this point. Years of tracking down what many people thought was a myth. He'd nearly been laughed out of the Air Force when, at the age of 32 he'd been flying into Senegal and had nearly collided with a man who was flying. Not in a craft; but of his own power. Before he could respond and bring the man down; he was gone.

His account of the incident brought with it humiliating psychiatric evaluations, the ridicule of his peers, and the estrangement of his wife. Worst of all, he had been grounded indefinitely. Using his psychiatric leave to his benefit, he'd spent the next two years and every cent he had scouring every inch of Senegal and the surrounding areas for any mention of a man who could fly. It was not until he'd returned to the States that he'd come across African myths about people who had the ability to fly.

Three years later, he was visited on base by a man who'd introduced himself simply as Mr. Cilfure. The tall, strikingly handsome man said he wanted to hear his account of what happened firsthand. Leery at first, Riley told his story again, and after that, was fully reinstated. The ban was lifted, and contingent upon a refresher flight course, he was granted full permission to fly. Over the next few years, he was also promoted from captain to major general. He hadn't heard from Mr. Cilfure again during that time, but exactly 10 years from the day that Riley had his first encounter in Senegal, Mr. Cilfure showed up again. And when he did, everything changed.

Chapter One: Gifts From the Sea

September 9th, 15 years ago

"BEEP, BEEP, BEEP, BEEP..." The alarm sounded at exactly 4:45am. Barbara Cotton turned over, hit the snooze button on the clock and stretched out her 5'2" frame before nestling back into the covers. There had been a fierce storm last night and she had spent a good portion of the night praying. Having grown up in the coastal areas of the American southeast, she was accustomed to tropical storms and often prayed through them for the safety of her family, friends and the men and women who were out to sea. After only a couple hours of sleep, the alarm signaling the start of a new day was not a welcomed sound. Five minutes later, the annoying sound of her alarm made her mumble to herself "Alright, alright; I'm up."

The 42-year-old woman swung her legs over the edge of the bed and stood. Although she always grumbled about getting up so early, she absolutely loved her morning ritual. Within 20 minutes, she had attended to her morning needs and donned a pair of powder blue Under Armour capris and matching crew-shirt along with her clean, white tennis shoes. She started to admonish herself for spending so much on workout clothes, but she found them to be perfect for her morning missions. She grabbed the matching sweat-jacket and her cell phone and headed out.

Two years ago she had purchased the small house on the edge of Cape Romain in South Carolina. Known mostly for its wildlife refuge, she found the quiet and tranquility sublime; unlike her native Miami, Florida with its cacophony of noise and throngs of people. As she headed out the door to enjoy her morning walk and commune with God, Barbara smiled inwardly as she prepared to "wake up the sun."

As usual, she began with the Serenity Prayer. Although she had never had any addictions personally, she found the simple recitation powerful, poignant, and an excellent way to begin her dialogue with the Most High. As she walked northeast along the beach, Barbara noticed the debris and dead fish washed ashore by the storm, and began singing softly in her clear, alto voice. Today, she began singing the title track "*Yes Lord*" of her favorite gospel singer, Patrice MucCular's latest CD. She found the singer's unique sound to be one she worked to emulate as she stretched her range from alto to soprano to match the notes.

Just as she began the hook of the song, she stopped short. She swore she heard someone or something singing with her. Quiet now, she strained her ears and listened. Amidst the sounds of the waves lapping against the shore, she heard a faint whimper. Curious now, she trained her hearing to the sound and moved quietly towards it. A few yards up the beach she found the source of the noise and gasped.

There on the beach, all alone, was a naked baby. As a licensed nurse, she immediately checked the babe for injuries. Aided by only the waning moonlight and the glowing face of her cell phone, she quickly determined that aside from being alone, the child appeared to be healthy. She scanned the beach for signs of a parent or someone else the child might have been with. Not seeing anyone, she used her cell phone and dialed for help.

Within minutes the local police and an ambulance were on the scene. The wildlife preservationist also joined them and a group was sent out to search for other survivors, since they assumed the child had been aboard a wrecked ship or other sea vessel damaged during last night's storm. Feeling a strong attachment to the baby, Barbara insisted on traveling to the hospital with the child.

As the sun began to rise and chase the darkness away, Barbara sat in the back of the ambulance watching as the medics did another search of the baby for injuries. For the balance of the day, Barbara stayed with the child. Although she worked at the hospital anyway, she had taken the day off. By nightfall, the doctors had determined the baby girl was about six months old, and was extremely healthy. To their surprise, she hadn't sustained any bruising nor did she have any lacerations. And in spite of the low 40-degree temperature early that morning, she hadn't suffered any adverse reactions to the cold.

However, the question remained of how she happened to be on the beach alone? The search continued two more days with no results. No wreckage was found, no nearby campsites, no other bodies; nothing was within 30 miles of where the baby was found to indicate an accident. Though by the second day Barbara had resumed her duties as head nurse of the oncology department, she spent every free moment in the nursery.

By the third day, Child Protective Services had been called in in case the child had been abandoned. As was their protocol, once the child was declared healthy, they would take her and place her into temporary foster care until they could locate her parents or a relative.

Barbara was approached by Mrs. Stein, the tall woman in charge of placement, who asked to speak with her privately. The two women went into a small room where Barbara closed the door and took a seat. She assumed the woman wanted more details about the condition and circumstances she had found the child in, so Barbara looked expectantly at her.

"Ms. Cotton, I want to begin by commending you on how you handled the situation that morning on the beach. Most people would have taken the baby to shelter first and called the authorities later. You were right to keep the scene in tact in case there was physical evidence we could use to find her family."

Barbara smiled and replied, "I guess I've seen enough episodes of Law and Order to know not to tamper with a potential crime scene."

"Well, score one for Team TV," she quipped back. The two women shared a smile and Mrs. Stein's tone became serious. "I also wanted you to know that we are doing everything in our power to find out who she is and where she comes from. So far, we have ruled out nearly every family in the state of Latin, Polynesian, East Indian and Asian ancestry with a baby girl under one year old."

Barbara had spent some time discussing the child's possible ancestry with the other nurses. The child's tan complexion, curly black hair and almond-shaped eyes made Barbara agree with Mrs. Stein's department beginning their search in that manner. "In the meantime however, I have been tasked with finding a suitable home until we do."

Barbara's heart tightened in her chest. She knew the baby couldn't stay in the hospital forever, but only now did she realize Mrs. Stein was there to take Carienne away. Carienne was the name Barbara began calling the baby the first day she found her, and the other nurse's picked it up as well. Barbara had explained to them that Carienne was the Egyptian word for water, and she thought the name and its meaning both beautiful and relevant.

Mrs. Stein was just about to say something more when Barbara bolted up in her chair and blurted out, "Let me take her!" Unsure where that outburst had come from, she knew instantly that she wanted to care for the beautiful baby girl. If not forever, at least until they sorted out what had become of her parents.

Before Mrs. Stein could turn her down, Barbara went into a hasty explanation of why she would be the best candidate for temporary custody. "I know I'm not a registered foster care provider, but I can pass any of the background checks; I have a house with plenty of space for her to have a room; I don't have any children of my own to divide my time between; and..." Mrs. Stein raised her hand to cut her off before she was finished.

"Ms. Cotton, I know all of that already. Your record is impeccable, you're a highly respected nurse, you own a home and from what I hear, the baby you've already named won't let anyone else near her except you."

Barbara sat back and closed her mouth. Mrs. Stein continued. "I know this is highly unorthodox, but when I asked to speak with you, it was to ask if you would consider taking her. At this time, foster families with the capacity to take infants in the area is slim, and we believe keeping her close to the area of discovery will help us find who she belongs to."

Many different questions were swirling around Barbara's head; had she lost her mind? How could she work and care for a baby? But between those thoughts were others such as, which room should she convert into a nursery? Which stores have the prettiest baby clothes?

Her reverie was broken as Mrs. Stein became serious once more. "There's one thing I have to warn you about in this situation; it will only be temporary. I know that an attachment is already forming between you and the child, but I must caution you to be careful. If her parents are found and this was a mistake, or the child has been reported missing, she will be reunited with her family. And quite frankly Ms. Cotton, keeping families together is always our primary goal." She said that part softly, but Barbara understood her meaning fully; if the child's parents were located, Carienne would be taken from her. Mrs. Stein asked if she still wanted to take the baby, and Barbara nodded that she did.

"Good!" the woman exclaimed. "There is a lot of paperwork to go through and sign, but I've spoken with my supervisors and they agree with the solution. Your background check was already approved since it was done by the hospital and backed by the state medical board. The same applies for your fingerprints." As she opened her briefcase and extracted a large sheaf of papers, she continued. "After I got the approval from my supervisor, I spoke with the hospital administrators. They have agreed to let you take two weeks of your vacation time now so you can get yourself situated."

Hearing that made Barbara smile. She had well over two months of vacation saved up, but hadn't planned on taking any trips. Getting time off usually required submitting the request months in advance and hoping nothing came up that would change your plans.

For the next hour, she and Mrs. Stein went through all of the legal documentation that would name her as the child's temporary guardian and instate her as foster care provider for the state of South Carolina. By mid-afternoon, Barbara Cotton was the proud foster mother of a healthy, beautiful, six-month old baby girl.

The next several years passed by in a blur. No one had ever come forward to claim the child and after three years, Barbara was allowed to fully adopt Carienne. Although Barbara still wondered who the child's parents were and what the circumstances were which led to her abandonment, she often found herself praying for the mystery parents and thanking God for the blessing of having the child in her life.

By the time Carienne was six, Barbara had begun to sense that something was different about her daughter. One afternoon when she and Carienne were frolicking on the beach, Carienne ran into the ocean and slipped beneath the waves before Barbara could catch her. The child stayed underwater for several minutes. Barbara, who had run after the girl, frantically called for the life guards. The guards, along with two young men on surfboards searched the area for the girl. Barbara, who had been made to return to the beach, stood there crying and praying; feeling powerless to do more. Nearly 20 minutes later, Carienne emerged in the ocean, far from the shore. She was so far out, that one of the guards had to get on a jet-ski to reach her. She was laughing and playing and swimming; totally unharmed.

A few minutes later, Carienne was brought ashore by a very puzzled looking life guard. "Ma'am," he told Barbara, "I don't know how she got that far out. Not even the most experienced swimmers go out that far without gear," he stated.

Barbara was hugging her child close but managed to thank the man an tell him that God had protected the girl. It wasn't clear whether the man bought that explanation or not, but he nodded and left. While Barbara had not said so to the man, she had seen Carienne go under the water and knew she hadn't come back up for several minutes.

Though she forbade Carienne from ever going into the water without her, a few years later Barbara woke up in the middle of the night when she heard something at the door. She quietly grabbed her Louisville Slugger baseball bat and discovered the front door was unlocked. With her heart in her throat, she quickly went to check on Carienne, only to find the child missing. Running outside, she caught a glimpse of a small body rushing into the ocean. She screamed out to her, but the waves swallowed the small form.

Panic consumed Barbara as she rushed out to the ocean and jumped in, desperate to find the girl. Ignoring the almost unbearable cold and pushing past the fatigue she felt in her limbs, she worked against the pull of the water. Shortly thereafter, the powerful current grabbed her and she went under. And though she was a very good swimmer, the midnight tide was too strong. She fought to get to the surface for what seemed like an hour, but soon fatigue and the inevitable stripped her of her strength and she began to sink further.

As she thought of her last prayer and begged God to take care of her daughter, she felt two small hands wrap around her waist and pull her to the surface. Once on dry land, Barbara lay across the sand coughing and spitting up water. Once she'd caught her breath and thanked God for saving her, she sat up trying to understand what had happened. Carienne was sitting next to her looking just as confused. The girl asked her, "Why didn't you just breathe, Mama?" At that moment Barbara knew that Carienne was no ordinary child.

Chapter Two: The Trek

Guatemala, February 10th, 25 Years ago

Anuka cried out in the dark and sat straight up on the bed of animal furs she shared with her husband Mmoju. She calmed down a bit when she felt his strong arms wrap around her and hold tightly. She felt badly for having awakened him, but the vision she just had warranted her alarm. All around them the night was quiet, dark and still, but the remembrances of what she had seen were still clear to Anuka's wide open eyes.

Turning to Mmoju, she whispered "We have to leave here. There are men coming soon. Bad men who will kill us all!" Mmoju held his wife closer and promised her he would let no harm come to her or their unborn child. Upon hearing his words, Anuka ran her hand over her stomach. Her condition was just becoming visible, but she knew the life growing inside her was precious.

That morning, the sun rose bright and warm, but the day held little beauty for Anuka. Upon her insistence, everyone had gathered inside their meeting house. She could tell by the looks on some of their faces that not all of her kinsmen wanted to be there. However, though she was barely 22 years of age, Anuka's strong gift as a seer and her position as Mmoju's wife made her an elder; a position respected by all. The board of elders consisted of 12 people, both male and female. Though all of the elders shared the same level of respect and authority, Mmoju was looked upon as the head of the board because of his strength, courage and wisdom.

Once everyone was settled, Mmoju's mother, Nadah, led the group in prayer and the meeting began. Anuka was taller than all of the other women, and held herself with the bearing of a queen. As she looked out over the hundreds of faces waiting to hear what she had to say, gut-wrenching flashes of her previous vision rendered her momentarily unable to begin. In them she saw the bruised and beaten bodies of her people, corpses strewn all over the ground, and the soldiers who were shooting them from atop horses.

Finally regaining her composure, she told them what she had seen. "For years we have been left alone in this area. We have been able to enjoy our solitude and freedom from the wickedness and vice of the outside world. But now the time has come for us to leave and seek new shelter." Upon hearing this, shouts of disbelief and frustrated groans filled the air.

Holding up her hand to silence the group, Anuka continued. "I wish it were not so, but I have seen them. They will come and tell us to move, saying that we have no legal rights to this land. They will tell us it is the property of the government and that they have chosen to plant coffee beans through here for their international export. They will say that we are interlopers who don't belong here, and that if we refuse to leave we will be arrested and jailed." More hissing and cries of 'NO!' followed that comment, but Anuka continued. "But they lie! They have no interest in jailing us. They will have their soldiers come with their guns and bombs to kill us all!"

Anuka sank down into her seat as everyone shouted their disbelief and concerns. In an attempt to restore order, Jaffe, another one of the elders, stood. "Quiet everyone! I know the news we have heard from Anuka is devastating, but we must not panic. It is true that we have lived here for over 150 years and all of us were born here, but our people have moved before. The important thing is that we give thanks to God for sending us a warning before destruction befell us. Just as He did for our brothers and sisters in Israel, He will lead us to a new land. Praise be to God in the highest!" Many of the men and women in attendance were clapping and praising God when Mmoju stood.

"Praise be the Lord, my rock! Who trains my hands for war, my fingers for battle. He is my loving God and my fortress, my stronghold and my deliverer, my shield in Whom I take refuge, Who subdues people under me." A hush had fallen over the gathering when Mmoju began speaking.

They all recognized his words as a psalm of David, one of God's most loved children. "Yes, He has given us a warning that the enemy is coming. But He did not tell us to run. We know that God is our mighty rock and our strong fortress. If He is with us, who in the world can stand against us?" His brief speech was met with thunderous applause. It seemed to Anuka that everyone there agreed with Mmoju and would stay and fight despite the warning she had given them. Even Jaffe, who had originally supported leaving, was now clapping wildly with the others. Only Mmoju's mother and few others shared Anuka's concern.

The remainder of the day and well into the night was spent discussing defensive and offensive tactics to thwart the soldiers they knew were coming. When Mmoju finally returned to their home, he had expected Anuka to be asleep so he was a bit surprised to find her sitting up in the shadow shrouded room. Silently, he crossed the room and sat next to the woman he loved more than life. Anuka knew that the dye had been set and there was little use in trying to talk her husband or the others out of fighting. No words were spoken because they both understood the position of the other. Instead, they sat together with Anuka pressed firmly against his side until morning.

Early the next morning, two dozen men dressed in the standard uniforms of the military arrived. And as Anuka had predicted, they instructed her people to leave the area. "You are trespassing on government property. This warning is a courtesy for you to leave now. Anyone who remains here in two days' time will be arrested and imprisoned." With that said, the soldiers turned and left.

Upon their departure, Anuka tried again to tell them of her vision, and again her warning fell on deaf ears. Mmoju took his distraught wife back to their house. "You should rest, Anuka. Being upset is not good for you or our child," he said gently.

Anuka looked up at Mmoju and replied quietly, "neither is being killed." Mmoju slightly winced from the censure in her words, but maintained his position. He tried to explain to her that while he and the others knew her visions to be accurate; he didn't believe their people were meant to cower and flee. He took her hand and told her, "God has protected us for centuries. He has given us the strength to defend ourselves and promises us that He will be with us in battle. Don't you see that if we run we will be telling the Almighty that we don't believe He is strong enough to protect us against the enemy?"

Anuka shook her head sadly. Running a gentle hand over his cheek and cupping his jaw, she countered softly, "And warning comes before destruction, my love."

Mmoju sighed heavily. He had come to a decision. "At first light tomorrow, I want you to leave. Head north to America and when all of this is over I will come for you. Even though I am confident we will prevail, I don't want you in harm's way during the battle."

Anuka shook her head no. "I won't leave you, Mmoju. My place is here with you and our people. I am an elder and the

15

people look to us for guidance." He loved her for her bravery and loyalty to their people, but he could not allow her to stay.

"I would like nothing more than to have you fighting at my side." In addition to being a seer, Anuka was faster and stronger than most of the men in their tribe, and both of those attributes could be helpful in a fight. "But you must leave, Anuka. If not for yourself, then for our child."

Anuka knew he was right. The night that Mmoju had given her the child now growing inside her womb, she'd had a vision that the girl would be used mightily by God. Though the details were unclear, she knew that her daughter was special, and that she had to protect her at all costs. With that, she agreed to leave her husband and her people, all the while knowing she might never see any of them again.

The next morning, Anuka fiercely hugged her husband good-bye. She didn't want to admit to herself that she knew she would never see his warm smile again. She would never be held against his broad chest or hear his deep, rumbling laughter. Finally breaking their embrace before she lost her courage to leave, she turned and walked away without looking back. She had not taken more than a few steps when Blanco and Cachee fell in beside her. It did not surprise her that the cream-white, male jaguar and the tan-and-black spotted female leopard were with her.

When Anuka was about 12, she'd happened upon the distinctive male cub whose mother had been recently killed by illegal fur poachers. She had named him Blanco because of his all-white fur, and had promised to protect him from hunters. The two had become inseparable. She was a bit shocked to see Cachee, however. The female leopard had never taken to Anuka well, but since she was the mate of Blanco, the big she-cat had tolerated Anuka's presence.

The trio traveled together in silence through the jungle. Anuka carried with her a large, woven bag containing a change of clothes, two blankets and food items consisting of various dried fruits, vegetables and nuts. She also had a goat-skin canteen filled with fresh water and a large, very sharp machete. At the end of each day, Anuka would gather wood and build a small fire and settle in for the night. The cats would hunt for their food and return to sleep next to her, offering both their protection and their warmth.

For the next several weeks Anuka and her companions traveled through jungle and heavily wooded areas. They tried to steer clear of populated areas to avoid detection, but on occasion had to run through open clearings and the outskirts of towns. In the beginning of their journey Anuka could keep pace with the cats while running, but as the weeks turned into months and her condition became more apparent, she tired more easily. By the time they reached Central Mexico, she was entering her eighth month of pregnancy. Her condition, along with the heavy rains of the season had slowed them down considerably, but she continued on despite her fatigue.

Staying out of sight became harder as they neared Northern Mexico, and Anuka feared that the presence of the cats would do them all more harm than good. Knowing that she had only a short distance left to travel, she stroked them both affectionately and told them to go back home. During the course of their travel, Cachee had become attached to Anuka, and both had to be told several times to leave before they finally complied.

Alone now, Anuka set her mind to getting across the border. As usual, there were several other people trying to sneak across the border into the States via Texas. Many of the men and women tried to dissuade her from attempting to cross in her condition, but she would not be deterred. Under the cover of darkness, Anuka and a group of men, women and children from Mexico to Oaxaca snuck across the Rio Grande into the States.

Many of the women with small children had claimed to have no interest in staying in America, but wanted to beg charity from the patrons of local businesses a short distance from the border. Others had claimed to have relatives waiting for them to help them find jobs and housing. Anuka had no idea what she planned to do once she was there, but had little time to figure it out. Shortly after the group made it across, the border patrol arrived and chaos ensued with people trying to outrun the law enforcers. Among the ones trying to run deeper into the state was Anuka.

She had made it nearly a mile into the border-town when the first contraction stopped her short and doubled her over in pain. Her cries of distress alerted the patrolman who was chasing them, and within seconds he was by her side. Anuka cared little about the patrolman because another contraction caused her to drop to the ground. Recognizing her condition and the situation, the patrolman called for assistance. Three more officers arrived to witness Anuka's water breaking. Having little other choice, they loaded her into one of their vehicles and rushed her to the nearest healthcare facility; a small, Catholic sponsored clinic on the US side of the border.

Her contractions were coming faster and faster and she knew the time to give birth was upon her. She was barely aware of the several women wearing the habits associated with their position as nuns, who were rushing around her. After she was laid on a pallet in a corner, a young woman took her hand. The woman was young and pretty. She introduced herself as Sister Magali, and promised Anuka that everything would be alright.

For a moment, Anuka forgot about her pain because the face of the young nun was familiar to her. She had seen her in her visions whenever she'd dreamed of her unborn daughter. Since those visions and dreams were always so hazy, she could never be sure of the details or how the pieces fit together, but she did feel at peace with the woman's presence.

Still holding tightly to her hand, Sister Magali instructed Anuka to push. For the next several minutes, Anuka pushed and strained to bring forth the child. Finally, she heard the distinctive wail of the baby. She smiled, thanked God, then all turned to darkness for Anuka.

While the women worked to clean up the newborn babe, Sister Magali felt the hand she was holding go limp. Looking down into the woman's face, she saw a look of peace and knew that the woman had died. Saying a short prayer for the unknown woman's soul, Sister Magali alerted the others to what had happened. The squalling baby was cleaned up and handed to Sister Magali while Anuka's body was carried out for burial in a potter's field.

Sister Magali peered down at the big, beautiful baby girl and smiled. The child was as dark as midnight and as beautiful as an angel. She then said another prayer for the child's health, safety and soul. Being from the Dominican Republic herself, she was accustomed to the varying shades of Hispanic people, but never before had she encountered one so dark. The fact that the mother had been speaking in Spanish let her know they were from a Latin-American country, but she didn't know where. Sister Magali named the child Anjelita Azul. In Spanish it meant little blue angel, and she felt the name described the babe perfectly.

Over the next several weeks, the nuns, along with some of the Latino Rights activists lobbied to have Anjelita declared a

19

US citizen. Since she had been born on US soil, this was easy to do. In most cases where a Latino child was orphaned there were families willing to adopt. However, no one wanted to claim the jet-black Anjelita as their own. Secretly, this suited Sister Magali just fine. She had become attached to the baby and wanted to take her to the orphanage she had been assigned to in Southern California. It was a highly irregular thing to ask, but God was merciful and Sister Magali was able to take Anjelita with her. Though she could not keep the child herself, in this way she would be able to watch over her and know that she was growing and thriving.

Chapter Three: The Order of All Things

Present Day

Dakkar had been on the run for nearly two months, and was no closer to finding his way home than he had been when he'd started. In fact, he'd mused, he was much closer to being recaptured than he was to getting back to his people. For over eight years, the now 21-year-old Senegalese man had been detained in a facility in the Philippines. He'd endured a battery of tests, poking, prodding and a number of experiments designed to test his abilities; many of which had caused him excruciating pain. Throughout his ordeal, his belief that the Almighty would see him safely home and back to his kinsmen was all that kept him alive.

A few months ago, while lying on the steel-framed cot in his below-ground bunker, he'd learned that he could manipulate matter. Careful to keep what he was doing from the eyes of the cameras, he practiced opening and closing holes in the steel frame, the walls and even the floor. Once he was confident that he could bore through the walls of his cell, he'd made his plans to escape. Unfortunately, at the time he'd had no idea what lay beyond the cell walls or how he would make it back to his home, but he knew for certain that if he didn't try to escape he would die.

With that in mind, he'd waited until late that evening to execute his partial plan. Knowing that guards were watching him constantly via the cameras in his bunker, he moved quickly. Using his back as a shield from the cameras, he stood there and opened a hole the width of his back and deep enough for him to crawl inside. Though he was burrowing through as quickly as he could, the wall was extremely thick and it had taken him nearly 30 minutes to get through it. Fortunately, his positioning blocked the view of the soldiers he knew were watching. Turning quickly, he crawled inside the hole and closed the outer opening.

From his weeks of practice, he knew that closing a hole was much easier than opening one. He thanked God for that because as soon as he'd entered the hole, he'd heard the sound of sirens blaring to alert the other guards of his escape.

Careful to leave small holes in the stone for ventilation, he moved as fast as he could through the wall. As soon as he bore through the last inch of the concrete, the ice-cold waters of the North Pacific Ocean rushed him. Switching his focus from boring through material to the process of extracting oxygen from the water, he was able to breathe with relative ease. This was a skill he'd learned as a child swimming in the Gambia River. His first inclination was to make his way to the surface and fly away, but he'd decided that it would be too risky.

Though his plan was to stay well beneath the surface and swim towards a shore, he realized he had no idea where he was or which way he should travel. Also, he soon realized that the exertion of swimming while extracting oxygen would be too much for him. A few moments later Dakkar tentatively stuck his head through the water. That proved to be a mistake.

He'd barely had time to map his position when the lights of a boat caught him. He could hear them telling him to swim towards the boat, but that was the last thing he'd planned on doing. Diving back below the surface he tried to swim, but was finding it just as difficult as before. Making up his mind to break the surface once more and fly, he moved upwards again. However, before he reached the surface he realized that he was no longer swimming, but had begun to fly while still underwater. Elated by the discovery that he could move through the water as easily as he could in the air, he slid down several feet and sliced through the chilly waters.

Two weeks ago he'd entered the United States through California, but quickly learned his troubles were not over. Everywhere he looked he'd seen pictures of himself; on billboards, on the sides of buses, on magazine covers and newspapers, as well as on the huge screens in the city's downtown areas. All of them showed his likeness, and all displayed the word TERRORIST in bold font.

Having no money to buy clothes or change his appearance, he knew he was an easy target for anyone wanting to collect the sizeable reward being offered for his capture. Keeping as close to the coastline as possible, Dakkar picked his way east from southern California through Texas. He had been crossing into Arkansas when he'd had to run from a group of gun-wielding young White men in pick-up trucks. They had almost cornered him when another similar group rode up and began to argue about who would claim the money for his capture. Having no interests in the outcome of their squabble, Dakkar used their distraction to take flight and get away.

That had been a week ago, and since then he had been chased by dogs and more groups of people. He'd had to stay on ground from eastern Texas to Florida because of the alligators and water moccasins that infested the swampy waters leading out to the coast. Now, as he dragged himself into the hollow of a huge tree, he tried desperately to think of some way out of his current situation.

Two hours earlier, as he was being chased, he'd had no alternative but to fly. As he took flight, he'd been shot in his side. Fortunately, he had been far enough out of range for it not to have killed him, but he was wounded and was in pain. He'd had to tie his dirty, tattered shirt around his side and chest to slow the bleeding, though it did nothing for the pain.

He knew he should keep moving, but with the blood he'd lost and his utter fatigue, he couldn't move another inch if he tried. Dakkar leaned his head back onto the tree and did the only thing he knew to do; pray. He must have fallen asleep he realized, because a short while later he was being jostled awake. He jumped and prepared himself to fight, but the searing pain in his side stole his breath and he fell back against the tree. The man who had awakened him was smiling down at him. "Don't be afraid. We're here to help you."

Dakkar tried once more to sit up, but noticed a pretty, young woman kneeling at his side removing the shirt from around him. "Who," he struggled to speak in spite of the pain, "are you?" In the place of an answer, he felt cool water spilling down his side where he'd been shot. As the water pooled around the open flesh, he felt the bullet being pulled out. The pain made him scream out and try again to get up and away from the girl, but a tall, muscular White man held him in place. The young woman continued to pour water onto his wound for another few seconds. Finally, she looked up at Dakkar and smiled triumphantly. "Done!" she exclaimed.

Dakkar looked down at the place where he had been shot. To his amazement, the flesh was once again together and only a jagged, raw line remained. Somehow this strange girl had extracted the bulled and mended his flesh in a matter of minutes. Now doubly confused, he asked again. "Who are you?"

The brown-skinned man who had first jostled him awake answered simply, "Friends." He'd spoken the word in Dakkar's native language, but before he could say more, the group was attacked by four men who had been tracking Dakkar.

To the young man's further surprise, both of the men quickly went into action with a series of kicks and punches that left the attackers sprawled on the ground. Just as quickly, the two began tying the men up while the girl rushed to take their weapons and communication devices. With the immediate threat abated, Dakkar was helped to his feet and they took off as quickly as his injury would allow.

Once they had covered a fair distance, Dakkar stopped and demanded answers. Again, the brown-skinned man answered. "There is no need to be afraid, Dakkar. We are friends, and we have come to take you to Sanctuary. There, you will receive the answers you seek. I am Jahmil, he is Kafeel and the young woman is called Myla. We mean you no harm, but you must trust us." Though Dakkar asked for more information, he received none. Jahmil and the others continued to walk on, so a frustrated Dakkar followed.

He rationalized that if they had meant to capture him or hurt him, they could have done so easily when he was wounded. Yet, somehow the girl he now knew to be named Myla had healed him using only an ordinary looking bottle of water. And the way the two men fought and tied up four men with guns using only their hands and feet was astonishing. Dakkar's mind was a jumble of questions but he had no way of getting any answers, which made him very uneasy.

Late that evening, the group set up camp for the night. While the others rested, Dakkar decided to slip away from this decidedly strange group and make his own way. He was grateful for their assistance back there, but since he didn't know who they really were, where they planned to take him or why, he felt it was best to strike out on his own.

Chapter Four: Air and Water

Dakkar traveled in a northern direction all night and flew up into a tree to sleep during the day. In order to avoid leaving any tracks, he flew a few inches above ground each night, covering several miles. By the fourth day he was relatively sure he wasn't being followed, but he kept sharp for any signs of trouble. He wasn't sure why he was going in that particular direction, but with each passing mile he felt as if he was being drawn closer to something.

By his eighth day of travel, he'd reached South Carolina. Though his wound had been healed somewhat, it still hurt and kept him from moving as swiftly as he'd wanted to. He also tired more easily than he should have, and that bothered him as well. He had moved in a northeastern direction and followed the calmer coastline of the Atlantic Ocean. Shortly before dawn, Dakkar found a cove along a deserted beach and decided he would sleep there. Less than an hour had passed when Dakkar woke up to the sound of someone singing. Cautiously peering around the opening of the cove, he saw a lone Black woman walking along the beach singing. Deciding she was no threat to him, he slipped further back into the cave and slept.

When he awakened and stepped out onto the beach, the moon was high in the sky. Angry with himself for having slept so long and for losing valuable travel time, but too hungry to start out right then, he decided to go out into the water to catch a fish for a meal. Seeing no one on the beach in either direction, Dakkar jumped into the water. Once he had acclimated to the frosty temperature of the water several feet below the surface, he waited for his meal to arrive. A few minutes later he saw a fat sea perch swimming by. Smiling to himself, he reached out with lightning speed to catch it. However, the sudden movements ripped open the wound in his side and caused him so much pain he could do little more than concentrate on breathing.

So intense was his pain that he hadn't seen the young girl floating beside him who had been watching him for several minutes. The girl reached him and took him by his hand to lead him back to the shore. Once there, she assessed his wound and healed him. This time, Dakkar noticed that there was no more pain or soreness, and not even a scar remained.

Once she was finished, she took a moment to stare at Dakkar. "Who are you? And how can you be under water like that?" In all of her nearly 16 years, Carienne had never known anyone who could breathe underwater like she could. For the next few minutes, Dakkar told her who he was and she did the same. Though they wanted to continue their conversation, Dakkar was very hungry so the two of them headed back into the water to catch fish. This time, Dakkar was able to catch two fish without hurting himself. Back up on the beach, near the cove where he'd slept the entire day, Dakkar made a small fire and cooked his fish while they talked. The conversation went slowly because though he could understand English well; his ability to speak it was limited.

Shortly after he had finished his meal, Carienne was about to ask him another question when three men slipped up on them. Carienne screamed and turned to run when one of the men grabbed her. She struggled against the man wearing a soldier's uniform, but he was much bigger and stronger. Dakkar could not take off in flight and leave his new friend, so he prepared to fight them. He was able to land a few good punches before he was struck in the back of the head with the butt of a rifle.

As he slumped to his knees he heard one of the solders giving the order to release the girl. "We have what we came for." As two of the soldiers grabbed his arms and drug him to his feet, he saw Kafeel and Jahmil jumping down from the top of the cove and landing on the two soldier's backs. With dizzying speed, they disarmed the men in the same way they had done before. But this time, Myla joined the fight and had ambushed the third soldier who had been holding Carienne in check. Again, they tied the men up and dragged them into the cove.

Chapter Five: Myla Speaks

K afeel and Jahmil made short work of restraining the agents with the last of the rope they had. They employed a series of knots that they were sure would take the agents a full day to work loose. Still holding the back of his head where he had been struck, a groggy Dakkar staggered o his feet.

"How did you find me?" he asked in his native tongue. He knew that at least Jahmil, who seemed to be the leader, spoke his language. To that Jamil just smiled, but did not reply. Ignoring his irritation at the non-answer he'd just received, he shook his head and added, "Well thanks for the rescue. Again."

Dakkar was about to introduce the group to Carienne, who was still a bit shaken up by the rush of events. However, a smiling Myla approached the young woman, and said simply, "Sister." Carienne's head whipped around to face the young woman who appeared to be only slightly older than herself. Peering closely at the girl, Carienne was confused at why she had addressed her as sister. She pondered whether they could, in fact be somehow related. Carienne took in the girl's long, jet-black hair, almond shaped eyes and slender build. She admitted that while they shared those attributes, nothing else was the same.

Carienne's golden-tan color was vastly different from the deep, reddish-brown of the girl called Myla. Myla's straight, keen nose was a contrast to her own wider, flatter nostrils. Also, she noted, Myla's eyes did not have the narrow slant hers had. And though they shared the same hair color, Carienne's raven tresses were very curly. So the one-word puzzle remained; why had Myla called her sister?

Sensing that she had Carienne's full attention, Myla stepped over to Dakkar. Lifting the plastic bottle of water she held over his head, Myla poured. The small gash on the back of his head caused by the earlier blow mended itself as the water flowed over it. Carienne was shocked. "You healed him!" she exclaimed.

Smiling, Myla turned back to Carienne. "Yes sister, by the grace of God." Still smiling, Myla continued. "You and I share the gift of healing. We are both sisters of God's Spirit in the Great Waters. We are especially blessed by this because water is the first place He moved His Spirit through. "

Carienne's mind raced to make sense of what Myla was saying. She remembered from Sunday school that God created the Earth and everything in it, but she would have to ask her mother about God's Spirit and It's connection to water. She'd momentarily forgotten the others with them, but was reminded when Jahmil cut into the conversation and stopped her from asking one of the hundred questions she had.

"We have to go. It's not safe to stay out here in the open," he warned. Looking at the young woman with interest, he added, "And you must come with us."

Carienne agreed that staying out on the beach might cause more trouble for her new friends, but she had no intentions on going anywhere with them. She had seen enough TV shows to know that girls should never leave with strangers, no matter how nice they seemed. By then the hour was late and she knew her mother would be home soon, so she bid them a hasty good night, turned, and ran up the beach towards home.

Dakkar was not happy with what happened. He'd wanted to spend more time talking to the girl, but Jahmil had caused her to run away. "It wasn't necessary to scare her like that," he said, the irritation in his voice plain. "She has nothing to do with any of this."

Jahmil understood the young man's frustration and answered quietly, "Yes, she does. Now that she's been seen with you it will only be a matter of time before someone finds out what she can do. Then she will be captured and suffer the same things you did, by the same people who held you."

That got Dakkar's attention. Though he'd only known the girl a short while, he felt somehow connected to her, and was therefore loathe to think that she might be imprisoned because of him. Resigning himself to the truth in Jahmil's words, Dakkar asked, "So what do we do now? She's gone. Besides, I don't blame her for not wanting to run away with a group of people she doesn't even know." Dakkar wanted to admit that not even he was sure about the safety of traveling with them, but decided to keep that to himself.

The next morning, Carienne woke up and began getting ready for school. She was tired because she had not slept much last night. Her mind kept replaying the events. For the first time in her life, she'd met someone who could breathe under water and she wanted to know more about him. The language barrier had prevented them from talking as freely as she would have liked, and the conversation had been cut short by those scary men with guns. She'd wondered why they wanted him and what they planned to do with him, but had no answers to those questions either. Her mind then settled on the three people who had come and rescued her new friend, and more specifically on the young woman named Myla. How had she known about her? And why had she called her sister? Again, Carienne knew she had no answers, so decided to act as though nothing happened last night at all.

31

After finding a suitable place to make camp for the night, Kafeel and Myla turned in to rest. Jahmil was on the first watch to allow the others time to sleep. Dakkar, who was fully healed and well-rested, stayed up with Jahmil. He thought it was time for the mysterious man to give him answers. Seated high on a tree branch so he could watch for an attack from any direction, Jahmil was not surprised to see Dakkar flying up to meet him.

Dakkar landed on the sturdy branch next to Jahmil and the two sat in silence for a few minutes. Dakkar half expected Jahmil to admonish him about the dangers of flying, but the man said nothing. After a few more minutes, Dakkar turned his head to the odd man and asked the first in the series of questions he had. "Who are you people? And where is this 'Sanctuary' you keep telling me you're taking me to? And who is this 'keeper'?"

Jahmil sat so long without answering that Dakkar wondered if he planned to speak at all. He was working hard to keep his anger at the man's refusal to answer in check, when Jahmil finally faced him. "As I told you before, my name is Jahmil and I am the seeker. Myla is the healer and Kafeel is the protector. We are part of an Order that is ordained by the Almighty God. My job is to bring you, and now Carienne, to Sanctuary. There, you will meet the Keeper, and all of your questions will be answered. I can tell you no more than that."

Dakkar tried to make sense of the answer he'd been given, but the attempt only brought on more questions. Questions that he knew Jahmil would not answer. The man must have sensed his frustration because he added, "I know this is hard for you to understand now, but if you will just trust us, you will know everything. It is not my place to explain things to you, nor is it time. Carienne is a part of this, and you can rest knowing that like you, she will not be harmed by us. But if she doesn't come with us, she will be in grave danger."

Dakkar sat for a few minutes more waiting to see if Jahmil would say more. When he didn't, Dakkar jumped down from the tree and floated to the ground below. Lying close to the sleeping Kafeel and Myla, he continued to think about what little he'd learned. He was torn because part of him wanted to leave this group again and take his chances on getting back to Senegal. But a stronger part knew that he could not allow Carienne to be harmed. Despite the fact that he had slept most of the day, he soon drifted off to sleep. His last thoughts were of how he could get Carienne to safety, and then leave the group.

Chapter Six: A Time to Run

"See ya' later," Carienne called out to her friends as she left them for the ½ mile walk home from the bus stop. She knew they were disappointed because they'd wanted her to record their jam session and post it online. The music group *Night-Light* had been formed by five of her friends, and they performed Christian rock and rap songs. She had learned at an early age that she could not sing like her mother Barbara, but she did have a knack for videography. For the past two years, she had been in charge of filming and editing the group's performances. Now that her mother was working second shift at the hospital, she usually had most of the evening to edit, hang with her friends, do her homework and swim. But today she was tired and just wanted to get some sleep.

All day she had been unable to focus on much of anything because she kept thinking about the events of last night. As she walked towards her house, she could see Dakkar waiting for her. She didn't know whether to be glad that he was alright, or frightened for what might happen if they were attacked again.

Smiling her way, Dakkar approached her. Dakkar knew that his 5'7" height did not qualify him as tall, but he was amazed at how he towered over the young girl by at least six inches. Last night she'd told him that she was almost 16, but to him she appeared no older than 12 or 13. As he came abreast of her on the road, he noticed that she seemed uneasy. He didn't blame her; after last night's ambush and series of events, he understood.

"Hello," he said to her softly.

She replied in kind, and then added, "I'm glad you're alright. I was a bit worried about you after I went home." Dakkar smiled. Her concern touched him.

In his halting English, he sought to explain as much as he could about what was happening. For the first time since he'd met them, he wished Jahmil was there to help interpret for him. As they walked, he told her about his captivity for eight long years. He didn't go into detail about all of the things they had done to him, but he shared enough so she would understand the depths of the danger she would be in if his pursuers were to find her. He then told her all he knew about Myla and the others.

He wasn't completely sure she'd understood everything, but she seemed to grasp the overall meaning. He was in the process of telling her his plan to get her out of harm's way when she screamed and doubled over. Alarmed, Dakkar placed his arm around her back and asked if she was okay.

"No!" She screamed as she straightened up and took off at a run towards her house. Not knowing what was going on, Dakkar followed. As soon as they rushed inside, Dakkar's eyes widened at the sight of a brown-skinned woman lying on the living room floor in a puddle of blood. It was clear that the woman had been severely beaten and then shot.

The young girl looked at Dakkar with tears in her eyes. "Help me, please!"

As if on cue, Jahmil, Kafeel and Myla appeared at the door. Kafeel was able to lift the small woman up with little difficulty. "Get her to the water," Myla urged. Within a few short minutes, the group had the barely breathing woman in the cool water. Carienne and Myla began to work on her. Carienne, though terrified for her mother's life, worked on

35

stopping the internal bleeding. Myla was tending to the swelling, bruising and lacerations.

While Kafeel held Barbara and the women worked, Jahmil had Dakkar to follow him back inside the house. As they entered the neat home of the two ladies, Jahmil instructed Dakkar to grab pants, shirts and undergarments for Carienne. He busied himself doing the same for the girl's mother. Dakkar wanted to protest going through their personal items, but figured arguing would only waste time.

Jahmil and Dakkar returned to the beach just in time to see a revived Barbara sitting in the sand. It was clear that she was weak, and would undoubtedly be sore for a while, but she looked infinitely better to everyone. As she caught her breath she looked around at the group and asked, "Who are you?"

For the next few minutes, they introduced themselves to Barbara and asked her for an account of what happened. Though the anger and frustration could be seen on her face, she told them about the events of the afternoon.

"I was getting ready for work when some men came to the house, saying that they were with the government. I had no idea what they wanted, but when they started asking me questions about my daughter and the circumstances of my adopting her, I felt a sense of dread. I thought they had somehow found out about the things she could do in water and wanted to take her away." She paused for a few minutes and smiled at Carienne. "But I refused to tell them anything. Then they began asking me questions about a young man she had been seen with recently and again I told them nothing. In truth, there was nothing I could tell them because I didn't know she had met a boy." Again she looked at Carienne, but the look was pointed.

"After about the fourth time I told them I didn't know anything, one of the men hit me so hard I fell out of the chair I was sitting in." Barbara's tone became hard as she continued. "They kept yelling at me to tell them the truth. Where was the boy? Where was my daughter? What did I know? And each time I said I didn't know anything, they would hit me. Again and again. I just lay there finally, and stopped saying anything to them. I just prayed. They finally stopped asking me questions and I heard the man who was the leader say that it was useless, and for the others to tie up the loose ends. That's when I was shot. I don't know how much time passed after that, but I could feel myself being picked up and then Carienne and the rest of you were around me on the beach."

Jahmil did not like hearing about the suffering the woman had endured and would have liked to console her in some way, but he knew they had to get off the beach and out of the open. He reached down and helped Barbara to her feet and told them they had to get moving. As they headed towards the house, they heard the distinctive roar of a helicopter and knew they had been spotted.

"Run!" Myla screamed. The group moved up the beach as fast as they could on the sand, but Barbara was slower because of the soreness in her body. Once again, Kafeel picked up the small woman and they dashed to the house. Once there, Jahmil asked for the keys to Barbara's van. As he slid into the driver's seat, the rest of the group piled into the back. Throwing the gear into reverse, Jahmil pulled out of the driveway, turned the vehicle towards the road and sped towards the bridge. His plan was to cross into the mainland and try to lose the helicopter among the trees along the side roads.

He had just made a quick turn onto a two-lane stretch of road when Kafeel, who was sitting in the cargo hold of the van announced, "We've got more company!" As the others turned to look out of the van's back window and Jahmil glanced into the rear-view mirror, they saw two, late-model, dark blue sedans speeding up the road towards them. Though Jahmil had successfully out-maneuvered the helicopter, Barbara's 10-year-old van was no match for the approaching sedans.

Soon the cars were less than a mile behind them, and Barbara was terrified. She closed her eyes tightly and began to pray silently. Kafeel told Jahmil to keep moving as fast he could, and that he would try to buy them some time. Before anyone could comprehend what the large White man had said, he'd unlocked the van's back doors and jumped out.

Barbara and Carienne stared speechlessly as they watched him land on the ground and roll to the side of the road. Kafeel had just righted himself in the ditch as the first car sped by. With marksman precision, he aimed first at the front, passenger-side tire, and then the rear. Both times he hit his mark and the speeding sedan careened out of control. As the driver of the lead car tried to slow down and right themselves, they went into a spin in the center of the road. The second car, which had been following closely, could not avoid running into the out-of-control car. Upon impact, the second car flipped high into the air and landed on its hood a few feet in front of the first. Again, unable to stop, the first car slammed into the second sedan and exploded.

In the ditch, less than a quarter mile back, Kafeel covered his head as bits of twisted metal, fiberglass and steel rained down on the road from the wreckage. When he was sure that everything had settled, he tried to stand up. He grimaced in pain as he realized he'd broken his leg, but ignored it and climbed back up onto the road.

A short distance ahead Jahmil, who had been watching the scene unfold from the mirror, spun the van around and raced back to pick up their friend. He smiled and thanked God for His help. The others were also cheering their excitement as Kafeel was pulled back into the van. "Wow!" exclaimed Carienne. "That was amazing!"

Kafeel smiled his thanks, but soon it became clear by the beads of perspiration across his forehead that he had been injured. Myla, who was seated in the back of the van, immediately went to his side. Seeing that she might be of some assistance as well, Carienne climbed over the back seat and the two began to heal the man's broken leg, as well as the many scrapes and bruises he had.

While the girls worked, Jahmil told them that they needed to get another vehicle. Barbara thought for a few minutes and told the driver to head into town and to the hospital where she worked. "I think I know of a car we can use," she stated. Once they arrived at the main entrance to the hospital, Barbara got out of the van as quickly as her sore limbs would allow. "Be right back," she promised.

Once inside, she ignored the looks of surprise on the faces of some of her co-workers as they saw her torn and blood-stained clothes. She made her way to the oncology department and was thankful to find her best friend, Tara Coles, at the nurse's station. Tara glanced up as Barbara approached and smiled. "I thought you were playing hook..." her sentence trailed off as she took in her friend's appearance. "My God, Barb! What happened to you?" The 38-year-old woman rushed to Barbara's side. "Sit down. Where are you hurt?" The woman was about to alert one of the male orderlies when Barbara stopped her.

"I'm fine. Really I am." She knew her friend was genuinely concerned, but she didn't have time to explain. "I need your truck."

Tara was confused, but hurriedly went and got the keys from her purse behind the desk. "Sure, but what's going on?" It was obvious that she would have to tell the woman something because she could see her friend was near panicking.

"Tara, I'm fine. But I need to move in a hurry. Carienne is in danger." She waved off the rest of the rapid-fire questions the woman was asking. "I can't explain it all now, but I promise you I will call as soon as I can. And please, don't tell anyone anything. If asked, you haven't seen me." As she took the keys from her friend, she knew how worried the heavy-set blonde woman was. Giving her a fierce hug of thanks and good-bye, Barbara turned and departed the same way she had come.

Barbara hadn't exited the building before Tara picked up the phone and called her husband Joe. Joseph Coles was a sheriff, and Tara knew that if Barbara and her daughter were in trouble, her husband would move heaven and earth to help them. Not only was Barbara her best friend, but she and her husband were god-parents to Carienne and they both loved the young girl deeply.

Once outside, Barbara waved Jahmil to the place Tara had indicated she'd parked. Clicking off the alarm, they all piled into the brand-new, cream-colored Cadillac Escalade. Barbara felt a slight tinge of guilt for needing to take the SUV because she knew Tara loved it. Her husband had bought if for her birthday two months ago, and she knew the likelihood of her returning it was slim. With Jahmil at the wheel again and Kafeel in the front passenger seat, they headed off once more. They made a quick stop to fill up the enormous tank with gas, grab some food and bottled water, and headed towards the highway.

Jahmil told them that he wanted to head north-east so he could get them back to Sanctuary, but Dakkar interjected. "No. I think we should head North-west." Barbara admitted to not knowing which way they should go, but asked the usually quiet young man why he wanted to go in the opposite direction.

Before he could answer, Carienne said that she felt the same way Dakkar did. "We need to go that way," she added. No one had any objections, so Jahmil headed them to North Highway 17.

Chapter Seven: A Test of Faith

One Month Earlier

Sister Magali was walking on clouds when she left Father Michaels' office. She was just informed that she had been selected to go to Rome for a special project which she had been recommended for by the Cardinal. According to Father Michaels, her years of service, hard work and dedication to the less fortunate and orphans had not gone unnoticed. She was set to leave in two weeks and would spend 10 days working on the project. In truth, Father Michaels didn't seem to know anything about the project she'd be working on, but that mattered little to Sister Magali; she was just overjoyed at the opportunity to visit the Holy City.

After a long and blessedly uneventful flight into Italy, Sister Magali arrived at the Vatican. From the moment she'd been picked up from the airport, her travel fatigue left her and she sat staring out of the window of the car at everything. She had a million questions she wanted to ask about everything, but decided not to overwhelm the young man who had been sent to pick her up. She sat back grinning like a child on Christmas morning taking in the sights, sounds and smells of the city.

She'd expected to be housed somewhere in the Italian city of Rome and was ecstatic to learn that she would be staying in the Vatican Palace. Like most Catholic nuns, she knew that the 110 acres of land that held the Vatican was a sovereign state under the rule of the Pope, and that the majority of the roughly 900 residents were clergymen and members of the Swiss Guard. Her joy at residing in one of the palace's 1,000 rooms knew no bounds.

Upon being escorted to a room that was so beautiful it stole her breath away, she was left to settle in and rest from her journey. Being too excited to sleep, she walked around the spacious interior and was further awed by its size and beauty. The anteroom was large and featured floor-to- ceiling windows with a fantastic view of St. Peter's Basilica. She watched as tourists poured in and out of the ancient structure and hoped she would have a chance to visit the city's famed attractions as well.

Turning from the window, she took in the lavish furnishings in the room. The big, white couch and matching chairs sported embroidered pillows in royal purple and gold. The plush, matching white carpet was inlaid with a purple diamond bordered in gold. Everywhere she looked she saw green, leafy plants and crystal vases filled with lilies and purple irises that gave off a beautiful scent.

The bedroom was fit for queen, Sister Magali thought, as she took in the embroidered spread atop the huge, four-poster bed. The fine-gauge netting shrouding the bed was so lovely, she didn't believe she would be able to do more than just look at it. However, after she was treated to the fine meal brought up to her by the young female attendant, the fatigue of her journey caught up with her and she finally resigned herself to a hot bath and sleep.

The next morning, after she'd dressed and eaten breakfast, the attendant returned and told her that she would be meeting Cardinal Reginald after morning mass. During her brief meeting with the Cardinal, she was told that for the next few days she was to relax and enjoy the city. He had arranged for her to have tours of the Sistine Chapel, St. Peter's Basilica, several of the museums and the gardens. In spite of the royal treatment she was receiving, she wanted to know about the project she had been asked to work on. To her inquiry, the cardinal smiled and told her that she would be given all of the details soon. "For now, you are a guest. And as a guest, I want you to relax and enjoy yourself," he said. With that, she was left in the hands of a young man named Silas, who would act as her guide and interpreter when needed during her stay.

Sister Magali found herself moved to tears more than once as she took in the sheer beauty of her surroundings. Having grown up poor outside of the city of Santo Domingo in the Dominican Republic, she was the fourth child and third daughter of a Bachata musician and a Haitian sugar plantation laborer. She remembered how as a child she would sneak down to the Colonial Zone and stare in awe at the oldest monastery in the Americas.

Though she never had the money to actually go into any of the old structures, it was then that she'd decided to become a nun. To her way of thinking, any religion that was capable of creating so much beauty was one she wanted to be a part of. At the time, she had expected her parents to have been upset that was leaving their religion of Santeria; especially since she had already gone through the week-long rituals that established her as a priestess. To her surprise, no one seemed shocked or upset by her decision. Her padrino (godfather) was also the Babaaláwo (Father who knows secrets) and told her that she was on the right path. He told her that as long as she stayed true to herself and followed the teachings of her people, the ancestors and the Orichás would take her far in life.

And now she stood staring up at the famous ceiling of the Cappella Magna with tears streaming freely down her cheeks. Art and beauty had always been her secret passion and to now stand and see with her own eyes what she had only seen in pictures, nearly stole her breath away. It also humbled her in many ways. She spent a few more minutes marveling at her surroundings and saying a few short, silent prayers to the Orichás and the saints.

As he'd promised, Cardinal Reginald had allowed her to see much of the city during the week she'd been there. So when he announced that the next day she should be ready at noon, she was excited and anxious all over again. She was finally going to know what service she could provide that would serve the Vatican.

The noon hour saw a very nervous Sister Magali being escorted through the palace and down to the halls beneath the grand building. She had heard of the fabled below-ground rooms before, but never dreamed she would ever be walking through them as she was now. She was finally led into a large room that was sparsely furnished. Inside, there was an altar on one side of the room, a table and a few chairs on the other side. In the center of the altar was a basin filled with water and several white linen cloths that concealed something. She'd assumed it was the trappings of communion.

She was asked to have a seat at the lone table and her escort departed quietly. Alone now, she sat nervously wondering what all of this was about. Initially, she'd assumed she would be asked to do something with a group of orphans. In the past 25 years her work had consisted primarily of working with the children who were either abandoned or had parents who were unable to provide for them. She was aware that there were droves of refugees flooding the American borders from Latin America, Haiti, Bosnia and other countries, so while she sat waiting, she imagined being given a post that would have her working with the children who'd been orphaned once their families reached the States.

Her musing was cut short by the sounds of the door opening and the rustle of fabric as three men entered the room.

She knew Cardinal Reginald, but did not know the other man wearing the signature robes of a cardinal, or the strikingly handsome man in the tailored navy-blue suit who was with them.

She immediately stood and rendered the appropriate greeting to both of the cardinals. The short, heavy-set, stern-looking cardinal was introduced as Cardinal Peters. The handsome man with them was named Mr. Cilfure. After the appropriate introductions had concluded, she was asked to have a seat. Sister Magali realized that her hands were shaking badly; a symptom of her extreme nervousness. Hoping the men wouldn't notice, she clamped them together and placed them on her lap.

Cardinal Reginald began by thanking her for coming all this way and asked if she had enjoyed her time in the Vatican. She sensed that even though they were making small talk, there was seriousness in the atmosphere. She replied as pleasantly as she could, but the thoughts of why she had really been summoned were playing along the fringes of her mind. She didn't have to wait long.

"Yes, well we are certainly glad that you have enjoyed your time here," began Cardinal Peters, after clearing his throat. "But I'm sure you are curious as to why we summoned you." Before she could reply in the affirmative, he continued. "Evil is all around us, Sister. Even as we speak, there are forces of darkness looming nearby to undermine the good works we are trying to do." His gravelly voice had taken on a quiet, almost reverent tone. The fervor in which he spoke caused her to dart her eyes around as if she could catch a glimpse of the evil he was speaking of in that very room.

Shaking off that idea, Sister Magali agreed with the Cardinal's statement by nodding her understanding. Since she had not been asked a direct question, she thought it best not to speak. After a brief pause, Cardinal Peters further explained. "From the beginning of time, the Dark One has forged many alliances with people who were willing to carry out his evil plans." Pausing again, he studied Sister Magali's face intently. "How familiar are you with Pope Constantine, Sister?" he then asked.

She was taken off guard by the question and hesitated a moment before she answered. "He was the first Christian emperor of the Byzantine Empire. He sought to end the persecution of the Christians during that time. So great was his zeal for our Lord, that he gathered up the books of the bible and had them canonized into one text; our Holy Bible." While she hoped her answer was sufficient, she was more pleased with the fact that she'd been able to answer at all. The men's silent scrutiny made her so nervous that she was afraid she would trip all over her words. When Cardinal Reginald replied that her answer was correct, she let out the pent-up breath she hadn't known she'd been holding until then.

"While you are correct, Sister, there is more to the story," Cardinal Reginald offered. "But before we can tell you more, you must understand that you have been chosen for a task of the utmost importance to the cause of Christianity. What you will be shown, told and asked to do will affect the lives of all mankind. However, you must prove that you are dedicated to our cause and that you will not waver when the times comes for you to fulfill your destiny."

Sister Magali was overcome with emotion. On the one hand, she was honored and excited to be part of something so important. On the other hand, she was terrified at what that task might actually be. For a few moments she sat quietly, letting what she had been told sink in. She also remembered what the Babaaláwo told her before she left for the convent. "You are destined for something great, young one. There will come a time when you will be asked to make a great sacrifice and to perform a task that will change the world. In that moment, call on the spirits of your people and the Orichás to guide you."

Her hand subconsciously ran over the elekes that she always wore beneath her habit unless she was on her monthly cycle. Taking strength from the prophecy about her future, she looked each of the men in the eye and told them that she was committed to doing whatever would aid their cause. Pleased by her answer and the resolve they saw in her eyes, they stood and led her over to the alter she'd seen when she'd arrived earlier. She was instructed to wash her hands in the basin of water provided. While she did, the Cardinals chanted in Latin. It struck her that while she did not understand most of what they were saying, the few words she did recognize were the same as the ones she and her people would say during their ceremonies.

For the first time since she'd arrived, she saw the two men standing in the shadows holding ceremonial drums. Their faces were covered by fierce-looking masks and their bodies seemed to be completely unclothed save for the drums they held shielding their genitalia. Their skin was covered in painted symbols but she could not tell exactly what they were because of the darkness where they stood.

Once she had washed her hands, Cardinal Reginald dried them with a white, linen towel. He quietly moved the other towels covering objects on the table. Her eyes strayed to the items and she gasped softly as she saw a beautiful antique dagger. The handle was gold and gleaming. There were four grooves on it so that the wielder could grip it easily. Beyond the five-inch handle was a short hilt that had intricately designed symbols carved into it. On the left was a pyramid surrounded by fleur-de-lis. On the right was a goat's head with squiggly lines that looked like heat-waves around it in a semi-circle. In the center of the hilt was a beautifully rendered eye. So piercing was the eye that Sister Magali stared in awe at it, almost transfixed.

The spell was broken as Mr. Cilfure, who had been silent up to that point, picked up the blade on the linen towel. Swinging her attention from the blade to the man holding it, she found herself struck again by his beauty. She found that she couldn't describe exactly what it was about him that was so attractive; she just knew that he was the most gorgeous person she had ever seen. "Take this knife and draw it across the flesh of your left hand. Allow the blood to run down into the silver bowl on the alter. Make this sacrifice to prove your worthiness and commitment to your Lord. For he knows that blood covers a multitude of sins."

If Sister Magali thought the man was beautiful to look at, hearing his voice was a treat to her other senses. The voice speaking to her was so smooth and calming, it sounded like music. Standing so close to him, she could smell the inviting warmth of his breath, which to her smelled of everything familiar. The rhythmic cadence of the drummer's beat seemed to be in time with the beating of her own heart. Moving as if in a trance, she reached out and took hold of the beautiful weapon. Without a second thought, she used the six-inch blade to cut open her palm.

While the dagger looked to be centuries old, its blade was true. The incision she made was fairly deep and the gash was as straight as if it had been made by a surgeon's scalpel. Dark red blood poured from her hand from just below her index finger to the lower right-side of her palm. Fascinated, she watched on with the others as the wound dripped its crimson flow into the silver bowl. Only after the bottom of the small bowl was covered in her blood did Cardinal Reginald rinse the wound. Using surgical tape, he closed the gash and bound her hand with the third linen towel.

Without another word, she was led from the room and down to a floor even deeper beneath the Vatican. They made several turns and after a while, Sister Magali wasn't sure exactly where she was. Finally, they reached a heavy wooden door at the end of a long hall. The door was beautifully made and highly polished. The beauty of the craftsmanship struck her as she took in the many signs and symbols. She was unable to look at the symbols for long because Cardinal Peters had opened the door and was ushering her inside, but she did see a duplicate of the beautiful eye from the dagger in the door's center.

Along the walls of the room were several shelves upon which rested what appeared to be oblong packages. She wasn't close enough to get a good look, but she sensed that whatever was in the packages was very old. She was led to a table and asked to have a seat. As they settled into the chairs around the large, round table, she noticed there was a package in the center that resembled the ones along the walls. It was wrapped in oilcloth and Cardinal Peters removed the wrapping slowly and with reverence.

As he did, Cardinal Peters began to speak. "Sister, what you are about to see has only been shown to a handful of people in the last 14 centuries. Our founders thought it best that people be shielded from this knowledge in order to prevent panic." By then, Cardinal Peters had opened the package to reveal a scroll that was undoubtedly centuries old. For several long minutes, they sat and just looked at it. Though she was unable to read what it said, she was humbled by the feel of its importance.

"This scroll contains information about a prophecy that was not included in the canonized Bible," Cardinal Reginald was saying. "It is common knowledge that Holy Pope Constantine wanted to travel to the Holy Lands and be baptized in the waters of the Jordan River. Also known is the fact that he died before he was able to make the trip. However, what is not known is why he was unable to make the pilgrimage." He sat back in his chair for a moment as if thinking about how to proceed. Sister Magali used the break in his story to glance again at the scroll in front of her. The only thing she recognized was the official seal of Holy Pope Constantine.

"When Constantine became the ruler of the Byzantine Empire, he was opposed by many of the Roman forces because of his belief in Christianity. After the death of Jesus, many of His followers were hunted down and killed. But in spite of that fact, more and more people began to accept the teachings of Jesus and converted to Christianity. This enraged the Romans who were pagans. As both emperor and pope, Constantine worked to bring peace to the land and end the persecution of the Christians, and his attempts were becoming successful, though some bible historians and theologians have criticized some of his methods."

Sister Magali cocked her head to one side in confusion. She had never heard that there was controversy surrounding their first pope. She wanted to question the Cardinal about it, but didn't want to appear rude or ignorant, so she just listened. Cardinal Reginald must have seen her confusion because he elaborated more.

"Before Constantine became the ruler of the Byzantine Empire and instituted Christianity as the official state religion, the Romans worshiped several gods. One of their most popular deities was Sol Invictus; the unconquered sun. Not only was this god's likeness featured on Roman coin, but he was considered to be a companion to the emperor. Though Constantine was a devout Christian, he adopted the use of the sun-god in many ways. The arch he built at the coliseum features a statue of Sol Invictus which, if viewed from above, clearly marks the deity as a dominant force. He also decreed on March 7, 321 that Sunday would become a day of rest in honor of the sun-god, effectively moving the Sabbath from Saturday to Sunday. It is also known that December 25th is the traditional celebration day of Sol Invictus, and many early Christians resented Constantine's claim that the Christ was born on that date when it was clear the Savior was born between September and October. Keep in mind that in addition to being a Christian, Constantine was also a politician. In his attempts to promote Christianity, he could not ignore the Romans or their gods. So as a way of compromise, he allowed the Romans to keep their holidays, but changed the themes to coincide with Christian observances."

Cardinal Reginald had learned many years ago about the reasons Christians gave Sunday to the Lord when the Jews had continued to hold Saturday as the Sabbath. To his way of thinking, it mattered little which day a man chose to praise the Lord; as long as he did. Looking over at the nun seated across from him, he noted that she seemed to accept what he'd told her thus far. Pleased by her understanding, he moved on to the next part of the story.

"As I said, Holy Pope Constantine worked hard to maintain peace while promoting Christianity, and his choices; though controversial in some cases, were yielding his desired results. Unfortunately, not everyone was happy about his success. In a last, desperate attempt to suppress Christianity, the Romans aligned themselves with other pagans to defeat the

Christians. They, along with the African Donatists' *traditores* made sacrifices to the Dark One, then called Baal. These traditores were Christians who, under the persecution of Diocletian, had publicly renounced their faith and had turned over their holy texts and sacraments. Once the persecution ended, they were not allowed to resume their practice of Christianity and joined forces with the Roman pagans. In exchange for their loyalty and obedience to him, the Dark One promised that one day three children would be born under his sign. They would recognize them by the gifts he would give them; power over air, earth and water. He promised that the three of them together would usher in a time of darkness where he would reign supreme and that they would be at his side. The three children would grow up to lead mankind away from Jesus and His teachings forever. But God rose up Constantine and showed him the plot that was under way. He was able to seek out and find the scrolls that the Africans and Romans had written, detailing their nefarious scheme."

Sister Magali shuddered involuntarily as she listened to Cardinal Reginald explain what was on the scroll. The very thought that there would be people whose only purpose was to turn everyone away from God seemed so evil that she could barely comprehend such a thing. Finally finding her voice she asked, "Is that why Holy Pope Constantine never went to the Jordan River?"

"Yes. So great was his commitment to finding the scrolls and trying to put a stop to the evil plan, that he died shortly after he found them. But not before he established a core of bishops and righteous men who were the predecessors of the Knights Templar to protect the secret and watch for the arrival of these demons," Cardinal Peters answered. "And that is why we need your help."

Sister Magali wasn't sure how she could be of assistance against such wickedness, but she was willing to do whatever she could to assist. "How can I help?" she asked eagerly.

The two cardinals glanced at each other briefly, and then Reginald began to speak again. "Over the years our group has watched and waited for these demons to appear. On several occasions we have believed we'd located one of them and hastened to destroy them. But the Dark One is relentless. When one is destroyed, he raises up another. But greater is He who is in us than he who is in the world. We will never stop tracking these monsters and destroying them. And now, another has been found that must meet the same fate as the others."

Cardinal Reginald spoke with such conviction and certainty that Sister Magali didn't question the truth in his words. As Cardinal Peters picked up the telling and she swung her attention to him, but what she heard next rocked her to her very core.

"The reason we have called you in and shared this knowledge with you is because these demons are very crafty. They are powerful, strong and possess supernatural powers. I must tell you that in the past, we have lost a number of our members before we were able to kill the beasts. But in this case, we are confident that you alone will be successful." The room was quiet and tense as Sister Magali searched her mind and their eyes in an attempt to understand how she could help.

"We are certain that one of the demons is disguised as a female. A parentless child who has no allegiances to others. She goes by the name you gave her, Sister; Anjelita Azul," Cardinal Reginald stated softly.

Sister Magali's stomach roiled and her head began spinning. "NO!" she cried out. "It can't be! I was there when she was born. I have helped raised her. She is a fine girl who loves the Lord. She was raised Catholic, for heaven's sake!" She was so overwhelmed by disbelief that she was shaking. She tried to calm herself by taking in deep breaths or air. *They must be mistaken!* Her mind screamed.

Mr. Cilfure stood then and walked over to where she sat. Crouching down in front of her, he took her hands in his. "I know how difficult all of this is for you to believe, but I assure you that it is true," he said softly. Again, the beauty of his voice and his nearness fired her senses and she began to relax.

"Ask yourself this; what do you know about the girl's parentage?" She had no answer for that question, so he asked another. "Growing up, did she have many friends?"

She didn't have to think long about the answer to that; the answer was no. The other children stayed away from her mostly. Anjelita was always quiet, but even as a child she had a presence. She attributed the other children's distance to the fact that Anjelita was taller than they were and had a maturity that was a stark contrast to the mischievous natures of the other children. To answer Mr. Cilfure's question, she shook her head and said no.

Nodding his understanding and acknowledging how difficult this was for the brown-skinned nun, he continued just as softly. "Tell me, did she seem to possess power or knowledge far beyond the other children?"

Again, Sister Magali didn't need to ponder long. At a very early age Anjelita had a way with animals that was uncanny. She recalled how, when Anjelita was six years old, one of the orphanage's benefactors had arranged for the children to be taken camping. During the four-day trip the children were exposed to nature, hiking, fishing and taught about the flora and fauna in a wooded area in Southern California. On the third night out, she heard Anjelita get up from her sleeping bag and slip outside the tent. At first, she thought the girl was simply answering the call of nature, but when she didn't return after nearly 15 minutes, she'd gotten up to go find her.

After nearly 30 minutes of searching she'd began to panic and was about to head back to their camp to enlist the other adult's help in searching for the missing child. In the darkness she heard the familiar giggle of a child and picked her way through the woods toward the sound. There, sitting on the ground laughing and romping was Anjelita and a small pack of wild dogs. To her, they looked more like wolves, but she couldn't be sure. As she approached, two of the animals growled at her and surely would have attacked, but Anjelita spoke to them and they stopped. She'd been shaken by the incident, but had never told anyone.

Sister Magali also knew that Anjelita was smarter and stronger than the others. So much so, that she'd breezed through secondary school by the time she was 15, and were it not for her status as an orphan, would have undoubtedly been able to finish much earlier. Her academic prowess earned her a full scholarship to the University of Colorado where she'd studied veterinarian medicine. And when Robert Benson, a portly 12-year-old had fallen from a tree in the local park and broken his leg, a then 13-year-old Anjelita picked up the 160 pound boy and carried him the two blocks back to the orphanage. At the time, everyone, including Sister Magali, attributed the show of strength to adrenaline. But now she knew differently.

She shook her head once again; still trying to find some other explanation. "I know how painful this must be, Sister," Mr. Cilfure continued. "But think about it for just a moment. Her unnatural strength, her disassociation with other people and the fact that she communicates with beasts all points to the fact that she herself is a beast! Even her skin is as black as the depths of hell! She has the guile and cunning of a serpent. Even the children knew to steer clear of her."

She sat there for a silent moment as tears ran unchecked down her cheeks. She knew what he was saying was true. How could it not be? Soon, the sadness of the revelation was replaced by anger. The child she had cared for was Satan-spawn and must be stopped! She knew then why they had chosen her; she could get close enough to the vile creature and destroy her before she could carry out her plan. Looking into the beautiful blue eyes of Mr. Cilfure she vowed solemnly, "I will kill this treacherous beast in the name of God!"

Chapter Eight: Betrayal

Anjelita woke up in the middle of the night in a cold sweat, screaming. She'd had the dream again; a horrible nightmare that caused her to awaken terrified. *It was always the same*; she thought as she slipped from her bed and opened the window to let in the cool late-night breeze. Ever since she was a child she'd been plagued with nocturnal horrors. In them were visions of glowing eyes, sharp claws and huge fangs. Lately it seemed that every time she closed her eyes the animal would be there; waiting.

Drawing in breaths of the cool air, she willed herself to calm, but the images continued to flood her mind. In each of her dreams she was in a hallway with several doors. The beast was after her and she was running. In her attempts to escape, she'd tried all of the doors, but they were locked. In most of her dreams, just as the animal was about to catch her she would awaken.

She'd been having variations of that same dream since she was a child. She could remember waking up screaming. Sister Magali would come to the room she shared with three other girls after getting the other children resettled from being awakened. She would sit on the edge of the small bed with Anjelita's head in her lap and pray with her until she calmed down. Anjelita smiled at the memory of how the Dominican nun would coo to her in Spanish and in English until she drifted back to sleep.

By the time she was 10, the nightmares were so bad, that she sought help from Father Michaels, the orphanage priest. Father Michaels told her that the dreams were the Lord's way of telling her that she was not following Him as she should. The beast in the dreams was a portrayal of the enemy who had been sent to kill her. The Lord helped her escape so that she could dedicate herself to Him and to do His work. Father Michaels went on to say that only God knows the heart of man and that hers had been found wanting. He explained that her lackluster dedication to God was causing these dreams. For the next 30 days, Anjelita fasted and prayed that the Lord would deliver her from evil. For several months at a time Anjelita would not be visited by the nightmares, and when she was, she would immediately spend several weeks in prayer. This pattern seemed to help her through the years that followed, but lately the visions were coming almost every night; and tonight the dream was worse.

In the past, the dreams were mostly visions of glowing eyes and the feeling that she was in danger. She would run through the hallways seeking refuge from the beast but there never was any clear path to salvation. Tonight's dream was different. As with the others, she was running down the hallway, but as she tried to get into one of the rooms, the door swung open. Glancing over her shoulder to gauge the progress of the beast, she saw a man standing down the hall. He was very attractive and he smiled at her. He motioned for her to come with him, but she didn't. Instead, she rushed into what appeared to be a classroom. As quickly as she could, she slid a desk in front of the door to give her extra protection. As she listened to hear if the beast was still outside the door she could feel her heart racing. It seemed that several moments passed and all was silent. There was no scratching or pounding from the monster outside the door. Relief washed over her and she sank down into a chair. On the wall to her right was a large mirror and when she turned to glance at her reflection, she screamed. That was when she woke up.

The next morning Anjelita started her day with fervent prayer. She was tired and still very afraid of the nightmare she'd had. As she headed to the animal hospital, her mind kept replaying the dream. She tried to shake off the images and the fear, but was unsuccessful. She considered turning back and going home for the day, but she knew the animals in her care needed her. As she arrived at the small hospital, the phone was ringing and on the line was the one person who could make her forget her troubles; Sister Magali. The two friends chatted for a few minutes with Sister telling Anjelita that she was in Colorado and would be stopping in to see her before heading back to the orphanage. Anjelita was very happy to hear that news.

After talking to Sister Magali, Anjelita felt better and began her day. By noon, her stomach reminded her that she had been too upset to eat breakfast, so she stopped working to head to her office to eat lunch. As she did, she noticed a group of people walking up to the clinic. They had no pets with them so she had no idea what they wanted. They came in and introduced themselves as Jahmil, Kafeel, Carienne, Barbara, Dakkar and Myla. They were of various ages and ethnicities. Curious as to why the group had sought her out and claimed the need to speak with her urgently, she invited them into her office.

Jahmil spoke first. "Ms. Azul we have come a long way to see you. We know that you are in danger and it is imperative that you come with us immediately." Anjelita looked around at the group. Normally, she didn't fear strangers because she was confident that if she had to, she could protect herself. But there was something off about this group. Nothing about them made her feel she was in danger from them. In fact, she thought; if it became necessary, she was sure she could easily overthrow the three women and most likely the slim-built Black man and the short brown-skinned man. The only one who could possible subdue her was the giant, well-muscled White man with them.

No, she realized, she was not afraid of these strangers but she wanted them gone. She told them they needed to leave. Jahmil tried to remain calm as he urged her to come with them. "Please. We know that you are very different from other people. You can do things no one else can. You have power and it frightens you. But you must not be afraid. We can take you to someone who can help you hone your gifts. Please." Hearing the man tell her what only she knew about herself began to scare her. She didn't know who they were or what they wanted from her, but she refused to be seduced by the enemy. She was hungry, tired and in no mood for whatever games they were playing at.

"Get out! All of you!" She shouted. She picked up a letter opener from atop her desk and held it out in front of her. In reality, she knew that the dulled edge of a four-inch, tin letter opener posed no real threat, but it was all she had at the time. To her relief, however, the group did not press her further. They turned and headed back the way they came. Before they left, Jahmil turned to Anjelita and told her; "You may not believe us now, but the time is at hand that almost everything you believed to be true will ring hollow. Until we meet again." He politely inclined his head toward her, turned and left.

Anjelita was visibly shaken after her encounter with the strangers. As she ate the turkey and Swiss cheese sandwich she had brought for lunch, she was still trying to rid herself of the feeling she had that something was indeed about to happen. She tried to shake off those feelings by telling herself that she was just tired from not getting much sleep in the past few weeks. But questions about what the man said still echoed through her mind. *'You are not like other people. You have power.'* How had he known? Who was he? And what did he mean that soon almost everything I believe would ring hollow? She asked herself these questions so many times that when she looked up it was nearly half-past three in the afternoon. Saying a quick prayer and reciting the Lord's Prayer to herself, she opened her eyes to find Sister Magali standing in the doorway.

"Sister!" Anjelita exclaimed as she rushed to embrace her friend. "How are you? How was the Vatican? Did you meet the Pope?" she asked the questions in a blur as she made the sign of the cross over her chest and forehead. Sister Magali smiled at the exuberance of Anjelita's questions, and for a brief moment saw the young woman as the sweet child she remembered.

"No, I didn't get to meet the pope, but I did have a wonderful time. She answered the questions in an attempt to keep from raising the young woman's suspicions while she gathered the courage to do what needed to be done. In her nervousness, she rattled on about the things she'd seen and the places she'd visited while at the Vatican. The two talked for a few minutes but Anjelita felt something wasn't right with her friend.

"Sister, what's wrong? Are you ill?" The woman looked pale and seemed distant.

"No, I'm fine," she answered. "It's just that while I was in the Holy City I was charged with a task that will affect all of mankind." Anjelita was interested and asked if Sister Magali could share her task with her. At that, Sister Magali stood and told her that yes, she could. In a flash, Magali whipped out the same dagger that she had used during her sacrifice and lunged toward Anjelita screaming; "You can die foul beast!" Anjelita screamed and jumped out of way of the blade just in time. But Magali would not be deterred. She jumped across the desk and swung the knife at Anjelita again. Terrified and confused, Anjelita tried to move out of the way again, but everything went black.

A while later Anjelita found herself lying across the floor of her office. As she fought to sit up and shake off the haze surrounding her mind, she saw Sister Magali lying in a pool of her own blood; still clutching the knife. As Anjelita stared at her friend in horror, she saw that the woman's neck had been torn out and her chest clawed open. Flashes of memories of what happened flooded her brain. She was the beast who had savagely attacked her oldest and dearest friend! The realization of this made her lurch forward and empty her stomach of its contents. She felt sick and weak. She began crying and praying all at once.

So engrossed was she in her prayers that she did not see the group had returned. They were standing in the doorway looking at the carnage. The sound of Jahmil's voice made her snap her head up and look at them. "We have to go Anjelita. Now!" Startled, she jumped up and told them to go away. The moment she stood up however, she immediately fell down again; she was that weak.

"Please, you don't understand. You have to leave me right now. I'm not safe to be around." She was half pleading and half crying at the same time. Carienne walked around the desk to her and knelt in front of her.

"It's alright. You'll be okay. But you need to come with us now; there isn't much time." Anjelita only half heard what the young girl was saying. "You're bleeding." Carienne stated softly. "Let me help you." Anjelita looked down at herself and saw blood gushing from a long, deep, ugly gash on her side.

"Sit still. I can help you." Within a few seconds, Carienne touched the site of the wound and the flesh began to mend itself. "It will still be sore for a few days and you've lost a good deal of blood, but you'll be fine." Anjelita started first at the place where the wound had been and then down into the kind brown eyes of the young woman.

"Who are you?" she asked. Before Carienne could respond, Jahmil answered for her.

"We are friends. You are not the only person who has gifts, but all will be revealed in time. Right now we must go!" Although she wasn't sure of anything at the time, Anjelita knew the strangers were correct. It would only be a matter of time until someone found the body of Sister Magali or someone else would show up trying to kill her. Maybe these strangers could help her find a way to kill the beast that she becomes. So many questions flooded her mind, but she left her office with the help of the tall White man called Kafeel.

As she was helped into the back of a luxury SUV, she looked back at the animal clinic once more. She knew she would never see this place again. Nor would she have the love, humor and support of Sister Magali. *Sister Magali.* Why had the one person she trusted in the world tried to kill her? She closed her eyes tightly to block out the hurt and pain of the betrayal. But even with her eyes shut, the tears spilled down her onyx cheeks in a steady stream. After a long while of silence, Anjelita drifted off into a deep sleep that was unencumbered by nightmares. In her subconscious, she knew she had nothing to fear from the vision because she was the beast. That final thought gave her as much peace as it terrified her.

Chapter Nine: Mind Control

Anjelita awakened as the morning sun casted its beams through the back window of the SUV. She had been asleep since the afternoon before and noticed that someone had placed a light blanket over her. As her eyes focused she looked into the cinnamon-brown face of the smiling older woman named Barbara who was sitting next to her.

"Good morning sweetheart. You slept peacefully all night. I trust you're rested now?" She asked. Anjelita sat up and stretched as best she could in the cargo area of the vehicle.

"I did, thank you. Where are we?" Anjelita looked outside the window to see unfamiliar landscape. She and Barbara were talking quietly to not wake up Carienne, Myla and Dakkar who were in the backseat. She also saw that Kafeel was driving and Jahmil was asleep in the passenger seat. Barbara informed her that they were just crossing the state border into Kansas. Barbara told Kafeel that they needed to stop for a minute to use the bathroom and get food. Fifteen minutes later they were pulling up to a trucker's rest stop.

The group spent the next 30 minutes washing up as best they could in the bathrooms and ordering food to go from the in-store diner. Kafeel rushed into the store and told them they had to leave immediately. As was his habit whenever they stopped, he would climb atop a building and survey the area for approaching danger. He saw three sedans of the same color, make and model as the ones driven by the men who were chasing them in Florida.

Unfortunately, Carienne was in the back of the store helping Anjelita get a new set of clothes because her old ones were tattered and blood-soaked. Kafeel herded the others to the truck while Jahmil rushed to them in hopes of getting them out of the back door before they could be seen. Anjelita had donned the new top with plans on paying for it when Jahmil intercepted them and rushed them to the back of the store. One of the store clerks saw the trio rushing the back door and alerted the security guard. By then, the six agents were inside the store and coming towards them. Jahmil tried to offer the clerk money, but he kept insisting that the authorities be called.

One of the men flashed a badge to the clerk and told him that he would take it from there. Satisfied, the clerk returned to the front of the store leaving the three with the six federal agents. "Look, we don't have any interest in you. We just want to know where the boy is. We believe he is a dangerous criminal and we want to question him. That's all." The one who seemed to be in charge asked the questions.

Jahmil answered, "We don't know what you're talking about."

"We can do this easily, or we can do it the hard way. But either way; you will tell us what we want to know." One of the other men made a move to grab Carienne. Anjelita quickly jumped in front of the young girl and knocked the man down. Within a split second, four of the remaining five men had drawn their guns.

Carienne shouted, "Stop this!" Everyone, including Jahmil and Anjelita looked at her. Carienne focused her attention on the men with the guns and told them in a very calm voice, "Put those away. You don't want to hurt us. You know that you have the wrong people. In fact, you saw the boy you're looking for nearly 100 miles back the opposite way. Please just turn around, tell the clerk you let us off with a warning, and get back into your cars and leave."

The men blinked a few times then lowered their guns. "Sorry folks, we were looking for someone else. Sorry about the trouble." They turned and walked back through the store, stopping briefly to tell the clerk that they let the girls off with a warning. Anjelita and Jahmil were too stunned to say much of anything as they followed Carienne out of the store. Kafeel was perched on the rooftop waiting to jump down on the agents to free his friends, but saw the men leaving alone. Dakkar, Myla and Barbara were around back with the car. When Kafeel saw the three of them exit the front door with the clerk in tow warning them to never come back, he quickly scrambled back down to the ground.

They hurriedly jumped into the truck and headed back to the highway. Once everyone had caught their breath, Kafeel, who had resumed driving, asked what happened.

This time Anjelita piped in before Jahmil could answer. "It was incredible!" She went into a rapid telling of the events which concluded with how Carienne did some kind of hypnosis on the agents and made them leave. Barbara, who was sitting next to Carienne holding her daughter in her arms, leaned back and looked first at Anjelita and then to her child.

"Hypnosis? What do you mean?" Barbara asked in confusion.

Myla failed to suppress the giggle she let out. Everyone turned to the cargo area where she was seated next to Anjelita. "Sorry," she said sheepishly. "It's just that this is better than I thought." Dakkar looked at the young girl and asked her to explain. Glancing at Anjelita briefly she told them, "I laughed because you said Carienne hypnotized them. She did no such thing."

As Myla glanced around at the confused faces of her new friends she continued. "Carienne understands water better than anyone. She has many of the same powers as the ocean. Most people know that water has the power to heal and the power to destroy, but since the human body consists of 70% water, manipulating it in a person's body is also possible. What Carienne did was shift the water balance in those men's brains and then told them what she wanted them to believe. With their minds off-balance, they readily accepted whatever she told them."

Carienne, who had been very silent up to that point, was startled back into the conversation when Barbara asked her how she knew she could do that. The girl avoided her mother's stare and squirmed in her seat a bit.

"Carienne Cotton, you'd better answer me right now! Have you ever done this before?" Carienne had never lied to her mother outright. She had on occasion not told the full story of something when asked, but she had never lied and didn't plan to start now.

"Um, yes. A few times I suppose," came her weak answer. Upon Barbara's insistence, Carienne confessed to having manipulated her mother into agreeing to buy her a car on her birthday next month. Barbara was furious and told the girl she was grounded, although in their present situation it was not a punishment that could be carried out.

After a few minutes of Barbara lecturing her daughter on the importance of honesty, her anger at them being found again surfaced. "How do they keep finding us?" She asked. The fear and frustration in her voice was clear. The group had been careful not to use credit cards and had thrown out their cell phones. Kafeel told them that they needed a different vehicle. Barbara's friend had given up her truck, but he knew there was a GPS on board and believed that was how they were being tracked. With the help of Carienne's suggestive abilities, the group got a new ride from a dealership in Kansas City using the false ID's and insurance cards of Jahmil.

Chapter Ten: The Gathering Storm

Mr. Cilfure sat cross-legged in a chair across from Major General John Riley. The man was visibly shaken. "I'm sorry Mr. Cilfure," he began. "I don't know how this happened. Just as you instructed, the subject had been sequestered in the underground facility with no windows and limited human contact. For the past eight years we have studied the subject extensively and have not been able to locate which part of the brain allows him to fly. But we never had any indication that he had other abilities." Riley went on to explain how it was not his fault the boy escaped their custody.

Mr. Cilfure sat and listened to the military man with no expression on his handsome face. He finally told Riley that obviously he and his people had overlooked something. "There is no way that the boy could just wake up and walk through a wall without knowing if he could. There has to be footage of him attempting this beforehand," he stated calmly.

Riley assured him that there wasn't. "But we did implant the tracking device on him and have nearly caught him a few times."

Cilfure stood up so quickly, Riley jumped in his seat. "Nearly isn't good enough. How is it that you have managed to let an unarmed boy who is lost in a foreign country get away from you so many times?"

Riley hung his head and stated quietly, "He had help."

Cilfure glared at Riley and demanded, "From whom?"

"I-I'm not sure. We haven't been able to get an ID on the people." Riley could see that his financier was angry, but he didn't want to take the sole blame for the boy's escape and his men not being able to catch him, so he quickly told him all he knew.

"We did lose him for a couple of weeks when he first escaped. When we were finally able to track him he'd made it to the US. Shortly after that, we closed in on him and one of my men shot him. It didn't kill him, but it brought him down. As they were about to capture him, two men ambushed four of my best guys. They disarmed them and left them tied up. It took us a couple days to regroup and get a fix on his whereabouts. This time, a dozen of my men were sent. They spotted him on a beach down in South Carolina with a young, local girl." Riley attempted to lighten his benefactor's mood by adding, "He must still think he's only 13 because the girl he was with couldn't have been more than 12."

Seeing that his attempt at humor had failed, Riley cleared his throat and went on. "After scouting the area, the men reported that the two men who'd helped him were not around so they went in to get him. They assumed that since he was injured he wouldn't put up much of a fight, but the way he was able to move indicated that he had somehow been healed or that his tolerance for pain is off-the-charts high. My men reported that out of nowhere those same two men appeared and subdued my agents in much the same way as the first time. They got away again, but the tracking device showed he was still in the area. We figured that this meant the girl was someone important to him, and we needed to know why. It took most of the next day to find out who the girl was. Apparently she is just a local high-school girl about 15 or 16 years old. She must have just met him on the beach near her home and was talking to him when my men arrived, but just to be sure, we went to talk to the girl's mother. She refused to tell us anything, even after being;" he paused briefly, "persuaded."

Not sure if Mr. Cilfure was accepting his explanation or not, he plowed on. "The more we tried to make her talk, the more she'd just sit and pray. We knew she was hiding something, but to protect that little adopted daughter of hers, she'd rather die. So we obliged her. After we left, we continued to track him and that led us back to the girl's house. I hopped in the chopper and caught him, along with the two men and three women get into the mother's van and speed off. The trees kept us from getting a shot at them, but we had two cars in pursuit. I don't know how he did it, but one of the men jumped from the back of the van and shot out the tires on the cars."

Riley paused a moment to gauge Mr. Cilfure's reaction to his story. His expression was stony, but he asked the Air Force pilot pointedly, "Tell me what you know about the girl."

Jumping at the chance to further shift the blame from himself, Riley answered. "Not a lot. Just that she is a local girl. She was adopted by the Black woman we talked about."

Mr. Cilfure raised an eyebrow. "Is the girl Black as well?" He asked.

No. I don't think so anyway." Riley opened his desk drawer and pulled out the pictures his men had taken of the girl and her mother during their surveillance. Mr. Cilfure looked into the face of a young girl. Though the accompanying information claimed her to be nearly 16, she looked more like she was 12. She was a petite girl with shoulder-length jet-black hair with skin the color of honey. At first glance, she appeared to be Latina, but the high, flat cheekbones and almond-shaped eyes indicated she might have been of Asian ancestry. He scanned the rest of the information and learned that the girl had been found by the woman who adopted her. She'd been abandoned on the very beach where Riley said his men had caught up to the boy.

Dammit! He thought. *Two of them are together and The Order has gotten to them first. Sister Magali had better not fail.* He handed the photo back to Riley and headed to the door. "Handle this Riley. Immediately. I want them found and killed."

Before he could walk out, Riley stopped him. "Wait! There's more." He knew that Mr. Cilfure still held him responsible, so he wanted to make sure the man knew everything.

"Make it quick. I have important things to do."

"Yes, of course. Well, like I said, that was the third time we caught up to him. My men tracked them down to a truck stop in Kansas. I still don't have a clear understanding of what exactly happened that they escaped, but they had another person with them."

Cilfure spun and stared at Riley. "Who?"

"Um, a woman. Young. She's tall, very dark and she's with them now but we don't know who she is or why she's with them."

Cilfure turned to the door to leave. He glanced back at Riley and smiled. The middle-aged man's eyes widened as he clutched his left arm and fell to the floor. "You are no longer of any use to me. See you later Riley," the man said as he exited the well-furnished office. Mr. Cilfure knew now that all three of the Unifiers were together. He had to move quickly if he was going to stop them, so he headed back to Rome. He'd need all the help he could get.

Chapter Eleven: Mind Matters

A day and a half later, the group was about to cross into New York. They had made it across the country and Jahmil and Kafeel told them that they had a ride waiting to take them the next part of their journey. As they approached the border however, a road block was set up about a mile ahead of them and dozens of armed policemen were up ahead. Kafeel tried to back the Range Rover up but a half-dozen more police cars blocked the road.

"Turn off your engine and get out of the vehicle slowly," came the command of one of the officers.

"What are we going to do?" Carienne cried. Barbara took her daughters hand and began praying.

"It's me they want. I'll turn myself in in exchange for them letting you all go," Dakkar said in his broken English. Jahmil and Kafeel told him no; they had other plans.

"Ladies, you all stay in the truck. We'll distract them. Barbara, ease over into the driver's seat and when the shooting starts, drive like you have never driven before. Get you, Dakkar and the girls out of here. Myla knows the way to our transport. We'll meet you there later."

Anjelita piped in. "I'm coming with you guys. If there's to be a fight; count me in." One look into the dark woman's eyes and Kafeel knew better than to argue.

Dakkar also stated he was coming as well. "This is my fight, and I can't ask you to fight for me." Kafeel told him that he was too valuable to lose in a gun-fight and it would be best if he stayed with the women. The young man would not hear it. He shook his head vehemently.

"No. I fight too," he stated. Jahmil knew they didn't have the time to dissuade him, so he acquiesced.

Slowly, the doors opened and Kafeel, Jahmil, Dakkar and Anjelita emerged. Weapons drawn, the officers moved towards them cautiously. As they approached, Kafeel jumped in the air and kicked the first officer in the head with such force the man flew back at least 10 feet.

The astonished officers took a moment to grasp what had just happened and began shooting. With lightning speed, Kafeel grabbed the 12-gauge shotgun from the patrolman to his right and answered the shots being fired.

At the same time, Jahmil crouched to the ground and did a sweeping kick that knocked another officer off his feet. He too grabbed the policeman's weapon and added bullets to the fray. Dakkar flew to where two officers were rushing up and snatched their guns from them in mid-air. So stunned were some of the other officers that they missed their chance to fire on Dakkar before he landed behind one of their own men. Using the officer as a human shield, he continued to dispatch three of the officers.

Anjelita allowed three of the agents to seize her and push her roughly toward the half-dozen officers who were crouched behind an armored transport vehicle. Once there, an officer struck her face so hard she nearly fell to the ground. They reached for her with the intent on roughing her up a bit before putting cuffs on her and throwing her into a squad car. Seconds later, the screams of the officers could be heard over the din of gunfire and the sound of Barbara speeding down the road. Two of the men who had been with Anjelita were shot by members of their own crew because they could not see what was attacking them in the dark. But as each officer felt sharp fangs pierce their legs, thighs and one of their faces, they knew it was too late. Excruciating pain became their world before they each fell to the ground and slipped out of consciousness.

Kafeel and Jahmil were holding their own against the incoming shots. With Dakkar's help of taking weapons from the fallen officers, the two had enough ammunition to keep the officers pinned down behind their service vehicles.

Barbara was trying to maneuver around the cars blocking the road and had just made it through when a helicopter loomed in front of her. Knowing that the women were in trouble, Dakkar soared through the air towards the mechanical bird. His plan had been to get into the cockpit of the chopper and stop the pilot's attack on his female friends.

He was moving fast, but could not reach the chopper before bullets began raining down in front of the truck. Anger and fear gripped Dakkar and as his hand stretched in the direction of the helicopter, it careened back and down. He was astonished as he realized he'd willed the copter back.

Unfortunately however, the pilot was very experienced and the bird recovered quickly and came back towards him. He understood in that instance that the force of his thoughts could affect the helicopter. As it was bearing down on him and the women, he concentrated and flung the chopper forcefully into the four squad cars lining the right side of the road, sending the officers who were crouched down behind scrambling to avoid the collision. Dakkar turned in the air to wave Barbara on. In that moment, he did not see the officer who had trained his gun on him. Dakkar felt a sharp pain in the left side of his neck and fell the 20 feet towards the ground. Myla's warning scream had come too late, but Barbara stopped the truck just in time for Dakkar to fall onto the hood.

By then, the majority of the agents were either dead, wounded or had deserted their posts. The few bullets that continued to ring out from their side were so wildly off-target that Kafeel and Jahmil knew they could move from their safety place behind two of the cars on the left side of the road.

Upon seeing Dakkar fall onto the truck, the men ran down the roadside to help Carienne and Myla get him into the SUV. As they ran, they saw a large black jungle cat pass them. It moved so swiftly that it reached the women before Jahmil and Kafeel did. Transforming back to her regular form, Anjelita gently lifted Dakkar and put him in the back of the truck as an impressed Kafeel and Jahmil looked on. By then Kafeel and Jahmil had caught up and the group hopped into the truck and sped off. They decided to take back roads in hopes of avoiding any further roadblocks.

Carienne and Myla moved over the still body of their friend. Carienne saw the bullet wound at the base of Dakkar's skull and gasped. Using the overhead interior light to see by, she and Myla worked in tandem on healing him. Using a bottle of water, Carienne rinsed the blood away and extracted the bullet slowly. She peered into the wound to make sure there was no dirt or bullet fragments in the opening when she saw something tiny and metal in the gash. Not sure what is was, she slowly extracted it. Satisfied that the wound was clean, she began mending the flesh. Myla had seen to his broken bones and after several tense minutes, Dakkar's once-labored breathing became even.

"He's lost a lot of blood, Sister," Myla told Carienne. "He'll need to rest a while, but he'll be fine soon."

Nodding her understanding, the young girl crawled into the back seat next to her mother. She silently wiped at the tears that were streaming down her face. For the first time since meeting Dakkar and the others, she felt the truth of her age and the seriousness of the situation. Never in her life had she dreamed she could do the things she had. The violence, blood and gore she had witnessed made her feel weak. A few weeks ago, she could barely stand hearing her mother tell her about some of the wounds she'd had to dress, but here she was mending gashes, extracting bullets and resetting bones. Until now, she hadn't thought much about it because it just needed to be done and her first concern had been the welfare of her friends and mother. But now, as she cuddled next to Barbara, who had been softly singing the Lord's Prayer the whole time she worked on Dakkar, she silently wondered how much she would be changed at the end of this adventure.

Carienne was just about to drift off to sleep when she remembered the small metal object. Sitting up again, she asked Jahmil if he know what it was. She handed it to him and he looked at it closely before showing it to Kafeel, who'd taken over driving.

"Yes. It's a tracking device. They must have implanted it on Dakkar when they were holding him hostage. This is how they have known where we were all this time." Without another word, Jahmil lowered the window to throw it out.

"Wait." Anjelita said. Earlier she'd admitted to being to wound up to sleep, so she had been listening to the short exchange. "I have another idea," she smiled. Transforming herself into bird, she took the device in her beak and flew out of the window. About 30 minutes later she returned. "I fed it to a pigeon. That way, they will spend at least a day or two tracking it. They'll probably think that it's Dakkar flying around." She laughed at her cleverness. An impressed Kafeel met her eyes in the rear-view mirror and smiled.

Taking the back-roads did slow them down some, but it allowed them to reach the easternmost part of state without further incident two days later. Dakkar was almost back to himself, though he was still a bit weak. Later that morning Barbara marveled at the amount of food Dakkar could eat.

Late yesterday evening, they had stopped to get gas and Barbara went alone to the chicken restaurant next to the station. She ordered three, 15-piece boxes with biscuits, large containers of mashed potatoes, green beans and corn. She even threw in a dozen and a half of the fried apple pies they advertised at two for a dollar. Grateful that they had been able to get food, gas, wash up, use the facilities and stretch their limbs without incident, Barbara hurried back to the van they'd switched to after the roadblock fight, juggling the several large bags of hot food.

As she watched him consume his sixth piece of chicken, she thought that though he might still have been recovering, his appetite had not diminished. She had expected a man of Kafeel's size to eat so much, but was shocked to learn that neither he, Jahmil nor Myla ate meat. In answer to her question of where he put all the food, Dakkar simply smiled at the woman, who in many ways reminded him of his aunt Cassa.

Thoughts of his aunt brought back memories of his family and friends back in Senegal and he wondered if he would ever see them again. He ignored the soft look in Barbara's eyes at his sudden shift in mood and concentrated instead on finishing his food. Once he was done eating, he lay back down in the back of the van and closed his eyes. He hoped the others would think he was just tired, but in reality, his thoughts were on his home. For years he'd fought off the urge to think about his people. Thoughts of whether his father and uncle believed he was dead and how his cousins had fared over the years always threatened to make him sad. In his refusal to show weakness to his captors, he'd refused to think on those he'd left behind. But now, as he lay there surrounded by his new friends, all of his worries flooded his mind and tears streamed down his face.

Early the next morning, the group ditched the van and made their way down to the docks and boarded a relatively small ocean liner. "The Almighty has shown us favor once again," said Jahmil.

"He led Carienne to discover the tracker. If He hadn't, we would be sitting ducks in the Atlantic Ocean," Kafeel added solemnly.

"Yes. Everything happens for a reason. Even the tragedy of Dakkar getting shot turned out to be a blessing." Barbara agreed. As the group, along with the two-man crew of the *Barak* set sail, Barbara turned her eyes to the dawn sky and let the tears of joy stream unchecked down her brown cheeks as she praised God for their deliverance.

Chapter Twelve: Finding Sanctuary

After spending nearly eight days aboard the sea-vessel, Carienne was tired of travelling. Although she admitted having enjoyed that part of the trip, she missed her friends and her home. The small, impromptu celebration commemorating her 16th year of life served as a bittersweet reminder of how much her life had changed in the past few weeks.

To keep her melancholy mood at bay, she'd spent her time on board talking to Dakkar and Myla, playing solitaire and teaching Kafeel to play checkers. For someone who had never played before, he not only caught on quickly, but by day three he was beating Carienne, the reigning checker champion from Cape Romain to Charleston, regularly.

Upon seeing her grim face as he looked on, Jahmil explained that since the game was based on battle strategy, she needed to get used to Kafeel winning. She'd shot Jahmil a quelling look to which he'd smiled. She returned her attention back to the board and saw that Kafeel had more kings on his side than the bible.

They'd reached land five days ago, and once they had arrived in Iraq, she thought their trip had ended. Before they left the ship, all of the women were given a set of clothing. Anjelita held her blue and white garment up and asked, "What is this?" There was a long-sleeved, white cotton crew shirt and an ankle-length blue skirt. The matching over-blouse was designed to slip over the neck and hang loosely to the wearers hips. While those items were recognizable, she had no idea what to do with the large piece of blue fabric.

"It's called a hijab," Myla answered. "Here in Iraq it is unacceptable for a woman to be seen in public with her hair showing. And a proper woman of class further displays her modesty by covering her face."

"We are strangers in this area and will probably be noticed, so the covering also serves as added protection. The fewer people who can identify you, the better," Jahmil added.

For the next 20 minutes, Myla helped the other women to dress and properly set their veils and hijabs. Barbara didn't mind her simple garment of pink and yellow. She thought she looked exotic in the outfit. She laughed aloud as she said "Ladies, these hijabs are a blessing because after several weeks of running and travelling, my hair is a through-piece; ya' hur me!" She stated using a mix of slang and country grammar while snapping her finger in an upward motion for emphasis. Carienne winced at what she considered to be her mother trying to sound hip and cool. Anjelita smiled and agreed because she knew that her medium-length afro was undoubtedly a sight.

Jahmil instructed them to stay close and move quickly. "The last thing we need is someone inviting us to their home for supper."

"Why would someone do that?" Barbara asked. "No one here knows us, do they?" She glanced around quickly at the many faces of the men and women along the docks.

"It is the custom. Westerners generally don't know this, but the Iraqi's are very welcoming and hospitable people. When they meet someone who is a visitor, they invite them to their homes to share a meal. They treat the guests like royalty. And since it is an insult to refuse the invitation, we would have to go; and we don't have the time to spare," Kafeel explained as he led them through the docks and past several stands of people hawking wares.

For a brief moment, Barbara wished she could browse through the crowded marketplace. She could feel that in those simple wooden stalls was a wealth of treasures. Shaking off that longing, she reminded herself that she was not on vacation, and that a shopping spree was out of the question. Besides, she mused; she had no money. She'd left everything back home including her purse.

Carienne, on the other hand, was hoping they would not stay in the area long. Unlike her mother, her gaze fell on the poor, malnourished, dirty children that seemed to be everywhere. The bombed out buildings and the boarded up windows were all a reminder of the war that was still raging in this country. Young men stood in the doorways of run-down buildings, smoking cigarettes and looking defeated. She could smell the food being prepared by old women on fires outside. She could also smell the sweat of too many bodies on a warm day. But beyond all of what she saw, she could feel the hopelessness and despair of the people. The sickness and disease brought on by abject poverty was almost too much for her.

Her steps faltered a few times and the ever-observant Dakkar noticed. "Are you alright?" he asked. His concern touched her. She nodded that she was fine and concentrated on keeping up with the group. She was admittedly afraid of being in such a war-torn environment, but tried to act brave. She was sure her mother knew how she felt, but she didn't want to appear weak and frightened to the others. Not after all they had been through together.

A few minutes later, a man stepped from around a building and approached them. The women were alarmed at first, but when Jahmil shook the man's hand and kissed both his right and left cheeks, they relaxed. The man led them around the building to a large Jeep. It wasn't new by a long-shot, but Jahmil thanked the man and they piled in.

"Where are we going?" asked an irritated Anjelita, after they had been driving all night. Being so tall and cramped up in the backseat of the vehicle with Myla and Dakkar had her stiff and sore, and she was cranky.

"Where none can follow. Don't worry; you'll be safe," answered Jahmil.

Kafeel smiled back at her from the driver's seat. "We're almost there," he added.

Carienne didn't think that was much of an answer, but chose to keep that thought to herself. Instead of worrying about possible dangers, she focused on keeping her veils in place. She wasn't used to having her head, face and body so fully covered, but understood it was the custom in this area.

After another three hours of travelling along a long, dusty road in the Jeep Jahmil's contact provided, they approached a high stone wall that was run down and covered in graffiti. As they neared the wall, Dakkar, Carienne, Barbara and Anjelita craned their necks to see a gate or an opening because it didn't seem as if Kafeel was slowing down. Myla and Jahmil didn't seem concerned as Kafeel drove up to a portion of the wall, and to the sheer amazement of his passengers; through it.

"Oh my God!" exclaimed Anjelita. "How did you do that? We just drove through a solid wall!" Her questions and confusion were reflected on the faces of Carienne, Barbara and Dakkar.

Jahmil shared a speaking glance with Myla and Kafeel before he answered. "All will be revealed soon. You are safe here." He knew they were getting tired of his vague answers,

84

but it was not his place to explain things to them. He would leave that to the Keeper. "I promise you, you will soon have more answers than you have questions for."

The silence that followed that statement was tense. It was Barbara who finally broke the silence to ask "Where are we? This place is beautiful." The rest of her party looked out of the Jeep's windows to see the most lush, green fields any of them had ever seen. The air was heavily scented by an array of the most colorful flowers imaginable. Their senses were almost overwhelmed by the breathtaking beauty of the area. There were unidentifiable birds of every color singing almost in unison. The sounds were so pure and moving, that within minutes the entire group had tears in their eyes.

"Mama, what is this place?" asked Carienne. "I've never felt so...." She couldn't find the words to express what she was feeling. Even Kafeel wore a rare smile that was full of contentment.

"Home," was the one-word answer Myla offered.

Chapter Thirteen: The Keeper of Order

Looking around the beautiful grounds, the newcomers stared in awe at the lush greenery and the riot of colors provided by the flowers. They took in the huge trees and marveled at the wondrous fruit hanging from their limbs. They saw several small, neat houses spread across the area and a large vegetable garden. "They must spend a fortune on landscapers," Barbara intoned. Nothing in the vast area was out of place.

As they disembarked from the Jeep, several people came out of the houses to greet them. Myla jumped down and ran pell-mell towards a giantess of a woman. "Mama Bear!" the young woman exclaimed excitedly as she wrapped her arms around the woman's waist.

Smiling affectionately at the group, she called out, "Welcome. I'm glad you all have arrived safely." She spent a moment hugging Kafeel and Jahmil before turning her attention back to Dakkar and the others who, up to that point, was content watching the happy reunion. "My name is Bridget, but many have called me Mama Bear," she said with a warm smile.

Barbara thought the nickname fit her well. The woman stood well over six feet tall and was large. She wasn't fat, Barbara mused, just big. Dressed in a simple, but pretty tunic-style dress, the exposed arms and calves were femininely muscular. Her skin was the color of copper and her shoulder-length hair was a mass of pure silver, silky curls. She thought that strange because the woman's face still bore the unlined beauty of youth.

"Come, let's eat and talk," Bridget invited.

For the first time, they noticed the other people standing nearby. They all smiled in greeting as they loaded a long table with a bounty of food. After they sat on the benches at the table and Bridget offered up a prayer for the meal, everyone began filling their plates. There was squash, wild rice, still-warm bread, ears of sweet corn that had been roasted in their husks, beans flavored with onions and peppers, honeyed carrots and yams and a variety of fruit ranging from bananas to watermelon.

The brief moments of silence ended as Bridget made the introductions. "Jahmil, Myla and Kafeel you already know," she began, addressing the group. She then introduced the six other people sitting with them. Barbara knew it would take her some time to remember all their names and to pronounce them properly, but she and the others smiled and greeted each of them.

To the amazement of Barbara and the others, Bridget began to introduce them. "This is Barbara Cotton, adoptive mother of Carienne. I am very pleased to have you here and hope you will consent to honoring us with a song later," she stated. Barbara was floored. *How had she known all of that?* She wondered.

"The tall beauty seated beside her is Anjelita Azul. Anjelita comes from a long line of people who commune with the animals, and she herself can transform into any one of them she chooses. She is also blessed with extraordinary speed, intelligence and the gift of sight."

Before Anjelita could form one of the many questions flooding her mind, Bridget continued. "The young man seated with us is Dakkar I'gba. He is a decedent of people who can fly. He can also manipulate all matter and move objects with just a thought," she smiled. He shared the same look of confusion and wonder as Barbara and Anjelita. He had told no one his family name; not even his captors, so how had she known?

"And last, but certainly not least, is our sister from the sea; Carienne. She comes from the people who live in the water. She is an empath, a healer and she can manipulate water at will. The three of them are the Unifiers, and I give thanks to God Almighty for finally making your acquaintance. We have waited for you a long time." She smiled softly at the look on their faces and added, "After our meal, I will explain more." With that, they continued eating.

They finished the meal shortly after and Bridget asked them to follow her. She led them over to a huge tree next to a meandering river. Once they were all seated on the grass around her, she began. "I know that you all have quite a few questions, and I will try to answer them as best I can. But first, I'll tell you more about myself and my companions." Bridget sat silently for a few moments as if contemplating where to begin.

"The first thing you all must understand is that God is the beginning of everything I am about to tell you. You already know that in the beginning He created the earth and all of its inhabitants?" They each nodded that they were familiar with the story of Creation.

"What most people don't know is that before He created this planet, He created a similar world. He named the planet Ehyeh Asher Ehyeh, which means 'I Am.' The people were fashioned from the stars, and like the people of Earth, were sentient beings. They were made to praise the Almighty, a task which they enjoyed tremendously."

The group listened intently as Bridget continued. "The people of the planet could see into the heavens, and marveled as God created the earth. When He made man in His own image, the people of Ehyeh Asher Ehyeh rejoiced. Because God loved man so much, the people of the elder planet did as well. When man disobeyed God and fell from His Grace, the people mourned and were distraught. Being cut off from God's presence was a fate too horrible for them to image. So, with His blessings, several of the people from the elder planet came to Earth to tell man that God still loved them, and that He stood ready to forgive them and to reconnect with them. Man was given tools to help him while he toiled in the fields; gifts to let them know they were not alone."

Bridget paused briefly before telling them the next part of her story. "Unfortunately, Satan was there and saw the gifts that were brought. He convinced the people that it was their own intelligence that had created the tools, and it became clear that the influence of the enemy was too strong for the people of the elder planet, so they left in anguish."

"That's really sad," Carienne stated softly. "But if the people were there giving them the gifts and telling them the truth, why didn't the people believe them?" The earnestly asked question touched Bridget.

"They didn't believe because they didn't want too. If the people would have accepted the gifts as being from God, then they would have had to acknowledge Him. And to do so would mean they would have had to turn away from their wickedness; something they did not want to do." Upon receiving the answer to her query, the young girl shook her head sadly, but was silent.

"After a while, the wickedness of man was running rampant and God was angry with them. The king of Ehyeh Asher Ehyeh had a daughter. She had been one of the people who had come to Earth. She fell on her face before the Lord and begged Him not to destroy the people. She asked that she be allowed to return because, in her naiveté, she believed she could help them. Through His righteous anger, He found pleasure in the girl's request. He told her that He'd already decided to give man another chance. He was sending His son to be the living sacrifice for their sins, and all who followed Him would be restored. He told her that although the gift of eternal life was for everyone, very few people would believe it. He then told the young woman that at the appointed time, He would designate three young people to speak His truth to all of mankind. Their arrival will be in the last days, and will herald an end to the reign of the enemy. She was told that they would have certain gifts to be used to prove who they are. And until the time of their arrival, the king's daughter would indeed return to Earth and gather nine special children to assist her in locating the Unifiers and making them ready for their task." She looked around at the tense faces and added, "I am the woman from Ehyeh Asher Ehyeh, and you three are the Unifiers."

Quiet settled around them for several long moments. Each person was trying to make sense of what the big woman had said. Finally, Dakkar spoke. "No. It's not true! I just want to go home to my people and tend our land. I am not what you say!" Even in his broken English, his meaning was clear. It was also the unspoken sentiment of the others.

Chapter Fourteen: The People Could Fly

"I have shared a great deal with you this night. Perhaps we should rest and continue tomorrow. It may be best if you can take time to think about what I've told you before I go on," Bridget said softly.

"I think it will take more than time to fully process what you have told us," Barbara stated wisely.

Bridget nodded in acknowledgement of Barbara's assessment. "Yes, well, a new day can bring a fresh perspective. Come, let me show you where you will sleep," she added. They each stood and followed Bridget towards the large house near the tables where they had shared their meal. Each of them were quiet and seemed deep in thought.

Once inside the candle-lit house, Barbara and Carienne were shown to a small, neat room with a large pallet on the floor. The lone, east-facing window was open and gave a clear view of the early night sky. From the beautifully carved wooden chest along one of the walls Bridget extracted two, long, cotton gowns and handed one to each of the women.

"These may be a bit too big for you, but you should find them comfortable. You can place your clothes across the chair there," she said, motioning towards the desk and chair near the window, which were the only other pieces of furniture in the room. Both women thanked her, and Bridget bade them good-night and exited.

Anjelita was led to a similarly furnished room in another, smaller house. The dark-skinned woman named Imani would be housing her during her stay. Once she was given a night gown, she too was left to settle in.

Dakkar had not been led into the house with the women. Instead, Kafeel took him to his house, a short distance from where the women were taken. Kafeel sensed Dakkar's mood and didn't say much more than good-night. Left alone in the darkened room, Dakkar made himself comfortable on the feather-filled pallet and nestled in. Though he was admittedly tired, his mind was still racing. People from distant planets, prophecies from the Almighty, he and his friends being called Unifiers; it was all too much for him to take. After a long while of tossing and turning, Dakkar finally drifted off to sleep, praying that what the woman had told them was all a joke.

The next morning Dakkar and the others joined Bridget at their meeting place by the tree after a big breakfast of cooked oats flavored with honey, fruit and bread. Though what they had learned the night before still weighed heavily on their minds, they found that they had rested peacefully and as a result, were in better spirits.

Bridget wasted little time picking up the story. "Dakkar," she began, "how much do you know about the history of your people?"

Taken slightly off guard by the question, he answered, "I know the stories about our people that reach back before the Europeans came." He wasn't sure if that was what she wanted to know, but when she nodded and smiled, he assumed it was.

She then addressed the others. "Dakkar is a descendant of the Mtumbe people. They were a relatively small clan who'd lived in the southwestern region of Senegal for a millennium before the Jolof Kingdom was established in the 13th century. During that time the area was populated by the ancestors of the Fula and Wolof peoples. Though it seemed that there was peace among the three groups, the Fula and Wolof hated the Mtumbe."

Unable to hold her question, Carienne asked, "Why? Were they mean or bad people?"

"No," Bridget answered. "In fact, they were very good people. They stayed to themselves and farmed their small plots of land. The reason the others didn't like them was because the Mtumbe didn't trade with them. It was no secret that the crops they yielded were the best in the area. They could see that the land and the animals of the Mtumbe flourished, and they wanted what the Mtumbe had. Another reason they disliked them was because they didn't intermarry with the other tribes. This infuriated the Fula and Wolof because they thought the Mtumbe people considered themselves to be better than they were. But the main reason was because the Mtumbe could do things others could not; they could fly. Even though they were rarely seen doing it, it was this ability that made them nearly impervious to attack from any group."

For the next half hour, Bridget told them more about the Mtumbe people. She explained how, between 1300 and 1900, Europeans had invaded the area. Due to the in-fighting between the chiefdoms, they were able to enslave nearly 1/3 of the population in that time. After establishing a small slave port, the Europeans were told about the Mtumbe people.

According to Bridget, no matter how much the various groups disliked each other, the one group they hated in unison were the Mtumbe. Believing that the Europeans could defeat the Mtumbe with their guns, they told the Europeans all they knew about the people. The Europeans laughed at their claims of the people being able to fly, but went to capture them anyway. When they arrived at the village and opened fire, the people took off in flight, amazing the European slavers. By morning, the Europeans had killed nearly ½ of the Mtumbe people, but the others were able to escape to the island of Pico Basille.

Bridget concluded the telling by explaining how the Mtumbe people stayed in the mountainous region of the island for many years until the Portuguese came and overran the area, enslaving the natives in the process. "Again, the people took flight and disappeared. No one knew where they settled after that, but in the years that followed, the stories of the people who could fly were reduced to African myths and fairy tales."

Once she was done telling the history of Dakkar's people, she added, "It is important to understand the history of your people. It will help you to understand who you are and the type of people you come from. God, in His infinite wisdom, had ordained you for this purpose at the beginning of time." Looking at Dakkar directly, she added, "Even the tragedies that have befallen you were necessary to bring you to this place at this time."

Chapter Fifteen: The Air Down There

The entire group listened as Bridget told them about the people of the Mtumbe tribe and about the parentage of Anjelita. Dakkar already knew most of the history of his people because his parents and the Old Ones had taught him and the other children their history. He had been a child when he was captured; barely 13 years old. He had been warned about flying, but felt that it was such a strong part of him he couldn't resist. For years he lay in that bunker night after night, after having had all manner of tests run on him, crying. He'd wished he'd listened. As he grew older however, he spent his time praying and asking the Great Spirit to deliver him from his captors. To keep from losing his mind altogether, he found peace in his situation by talking to God. Praying was the one thing they could not stop him from doing, observe or measure, so he did it as often as he could for all those years.

Anjelita however, sat quietly as tears streamed down her face. She had known that her mother was an immigrant who had crossed the US border illegally and died after giving birth to her, but she never knew anything about her father or the rest of her people, let alone why a woman so heavy with child would make such a trip alone. In her heart she knew that there had to be more to her mother's story because if she were indeed Mexican or South American, why was she so tall and dark?

Bridget could see the pain on the young woman's face and turned to her. "Anjelita, I know you have a lot more questions about your people and how and why this happened. And truthfully, I don't have all of the answers. But I do know that the news of your birth filled your family's hearts with joy. Your mother was a seer. Like you. The only difference is that she was raised in a place that embraced her gift and encouraged it while you were surrounded by people who feared your gifts. And though I can't tell you exactly why you went through the things you did, I do know that the Almighty had a divine plan for you and that being here and now and having faced all of the trials you've endured was not in vain." Anjelita wiped at the tears rolling down her cheeks.

Bridget squeezed the girl's hand lightly and looked into the teary eyes of the others. "I can't stress enough that each and every one of you were hand-picked and pre-selected to do God's work in this appointed time. There are no 'lucky breaks' or coincidences with the Father. Barbara, God knew you would be on the beach that morning, singing and praying out to the heavens. He knew the heartbreak you felt when you learned you could never have children. Believe me, the people from my planet love the Almighty so much that we too love what He loves. And He weeps when His children are hurting. That's part of the reason I begged Him to let me help in some small way. So please understand that it was meant for you to find Carienne. You have shared more than a mother's love with her Barbara; you have taught her to be a young woman of faith and to commune with the Father."

Bridget then turned her soft gaze on Carienne. "And you; beautiful daughter of the sea. You are loved and missed by your parents very much. Not a day passes that they don't say a prayer for your safety."

Carienne's eye's widened. "I have other parents?" She'd always known she was adopted but had figured that her family had died at sea and she alone somehow survived. She had often included a thank-you to God for rescuing her from whatever tragedy befell her parents whenever she prayed. Her mother never let her believe that she'd been unwanted or abandoned.

"Yes, you do," Bridget answered softly. "Your people live mostly in the islands off the Philippines. Your parents are from a place called Micronesia. Much like the Mtumbe people and Anjelita's people, they keep mostly to themselves. Like you, they can breathe under water and can stay under for hours at a time. The past fifty years have been very hard for them though. As the world continues to change and more technology is developed, they are having a more difficult time finding 'safe waters' if you understand my meaning."

The look on the young girl's face indicated that she did not, so Bridget continued. "In past centuries your people had all of the waters of the world to explore. When they established their homes in small enclaves in coastal areas, they had little to worry about. The only thing they had to fear was being spotted by some fisherman out to sea. In the few times that they were seen, it was mostly because they dared to help someone who'd fallen overboard. Of course the stories about men and women who lived in the sea were contorted into fables about merfolk with tails and scales like fish. Once, in ancient Rome, a ship hit some rocks off the shores of Greece and many of the men were throw off the vessel. A group of your people rushed to help them. Once they had seen them safely to the shore, they returned to the sea and disappeared under the waters, never to be seen again. Many of the theorists at that time believed that they were some sort of sub-human species who lived in an underwater city they called Atlantis. But the stories were so exaggerated that they were never taken seriously or widely accepted. Lately, marine technology greatly hampers their ability to move around the waters totally undetected. In fact, that was why a group of your people were out to sea the night you washed up on Barbara's beach, practically at her front door. They were in search of a new home. You were with them Carienne; just a baby at the time. But a terrible storm rose out of nowhere. So strong were the winds and currents that you were ripped from your mother's arms. Your people were powerless to do anything but escape deeper into the waters until the storm passed. For years they searched for you but as you know; never found you."

Carienne didn't know what to say or what to think. She was afraid that if she said she wanted to find them that Barbara would be hurt. Knowing the child of her heart so well, Barbara wrapped her arms around her. "We'll find them, baby." Carienne felt relief wash over her as she held onto the woman who had been the only mother she'd ever known. The group sat in silence for a very long time. Finally, the young Asian girl known as "Princess" came out to where they sat and announced that it was time to eat.

Chapter Sixteen: Breaking Bread

O ver a huge feast of more of the freshest vegetables any of them had ever seen, conversation began again slowly. Anjelita was the first to comment. "Everything is delicious, but why no meat?" She looked around and immediately felt sorry for the comment. The last thing she'd wanted to do was insult or offend their host. "I'm sorry. I-I mean..." she stammered again trying to think of how to correct her mistake.

Bridget smiled genuinely. "No need to apologize; that was a fair question. We don't eat meat here. Eating meat would mean having to kill one of His creatures. And while I don't think there is anything wrong with killing for food, He has provided us with a bounty that doesn't require us to kill to live or eat." Everyone accepted that as a good answer.

Still a bit embarrassed by her social blunder, Anjelita asked what she hoped was a neutral question. "Who cooks all of this food?"

She was answered by the fairly tall man with long, black hair known as Laqat. His light-brown face was handsome and he appeared to be about 28 years of age. Smiling, he answered, "Imani does most of it. She has a real gift for cooking." Anjelita didn't miss the soft look he gave the dark woman, or the shy smile she returned his way. As if catching himself, he added, "Princess and Ezer help her."

Bridget, wearing a knowing smile, changed the subject by discussing the various roles of her companions. "Jahmil is the seeker. Historically, it has been the job of the seeker to 'seek out' the next member of the Order, but we are blessed to be in the time when the seeker's true job is fulfilled. Their main function is to find the Unifiers and bring them here."

Pausing to eat a bit more of her lunch, Bridget went on. "Laqat is the provider. He and the others who have shared that role are adept at getting whatever is needed at a certain time." Turning her attention to Princess, she stated "Princess is a seer; like you Anjelita. Her gift is not as strong as yours is, but God gives her visions of things to come, things which have passed and things that are occurring now when it suits His purpose." Smiling affectionately at the young girl, she added, "We call her Princess because when Jahmil found her and brought her here, she was wearing a princess pajama set." They all chuckled at that explanation.

"Kafeel is the protector, and since he was with you on your journey here, I'm sure you all know some of his strengths. Myla, like Carienne, is a healer. She understands the power of water and has the gift of using it. Tefilah has the gift of intercession through prayer."

The group had met the elderly woman only once since their arrival. They now understood that she tended to spend the majority of her time praying. They glanced at the middle-aged fraternal twins with them who rarely said much. Bridget introduced them as Shama and Ezer.

"The last seeker we had before Jahmil brought the twins to us," Bridget told them. "Theirs was truly a remarkable tale, because the seer had told us about them before they were actually born." Seeing the astonished looks, she went on.

"The seeker was sent into the area now called Alaska. At the time, there was a lot of fighting for rights to the natural resources in the area. Laws were being passed that made it illegal for the natives to hunt and fish for the game that had sustained their people for centuries. Diseases brought by the European settlers had decimated their population, and those who'd survived were having their ways of living taken from them. In many ways, the Eskimos, as they are sometimes called, fared little better than their Native American cousins." She shook her head sadly.

"By the time the twins were being born, the people of the Iñupiat and Aleut tribes had to move around in search of an area that could sustain them. During their travels, tragedy stuck as a group of Europeans attempted to rob them. The men of their tribe fought back, only to be killed. The Russian settlers seized the able-bodies women and some of the older children and took them away, leaving the twins' mother alone among the dead. She had gone into labor, but the Russians didn't care; they left her there to go through her ordeal alone. She'd just used the last of her strength to push out the second baby; Shama, when the seeker arrived. The healer couldn't do much for the mother who died shortly afterwards."

Though the tale was sad, Bridget perked up as she smiled at the two affectionately. "I'd never had newborn babies here before, but God instructed me to feed them fresh goat's milk until they grew stronger. The boy was named Ezer because he has the gift of helping. His sister was named Shama because she is obedient."

As the meal came to a close, Barbara asked Bridget a question. "You know; 20 years ago I would never have believed that there were people who could fly or turn into animals or even live under water. And although I knew Carienne was special, I never imagined that such things were even possible. What I don't understand is how and why they can do these things? I mean, it's not every day that you meet someone who can fly," she smiled at Dakkar. The group turned expectant eyes towards their hostess in anticipation of her answer.

Bridget told them they should clear the table and then she would explain further. Imani, another member of the Order piped in. "Don't worry about it Mama Bear. Princess and I will take care of it. You can go on with our guests."

The medium-built, brown-skinned woman who appeared to be in her early to mid-twenties smiled and began clearing away the last vestiges of the meal. The group also noticed that though she held her head high, she had a severe limp. As the woman departed with the first of the dishes, Barbara asked Bridget about Imani.

"I love her name. It means 'faith'," Barbara stated.

"Yes," Bridget answered. "She is very special to us for many reasons." As the group resettled at the base of the enormous tree, Bridget held off answering Barbara's initial question, and instead told them more about Imani.

"Imani is the only member of the Order who was not brought to us as a small child. Typically, all members are found when they are less than five years old, but Imani was a young woman almost full-grown when Jahmil found her." Bridget's eyes looked up towards the heavens and she was silent for a few moments.

"In 1994 Imani was 15. Her family was very prominent and wealthy Hutu's. At the time, there was a lot of fighting in Rwanda between her people and the Tutsi's for political power. The Hutu's leader was assassinated and this set off 100 days of pure evil. Hundreds of thousands of Tutsi's were slaughtered; many at the hands of Imani's father."

Smiling softly, she continued. "But God always has a plan. When she was small, Christian missionaries had gone to Rwanda and set up a school. Her father believed that having her attend would gain the support of the Westerners. What he didn't know was that she gave her life to Christ in earnest."

Her manner became solemn once more. "During those terrible, hate-filled days, that child was terrified, but she stood for what was right. For many days and nights she fasted and prayed that God would help both the Hutus and the Tutsis. But deep inside, she knew that there was a time for prayer and a time for action. So, she sneaked off and helped several Tutsi children escape into Uganda. However, she was found out and labeled a traitor. One of the men who captured her knew who she was and took her to her father. He spat on her and said she was dead to him. He told the Hutu soldiers to take her and do what they wanted with her; she was not his daughter. That poor girl was raped and beaten by several men that night. In fact, they were about to kill her when Jahmil arrived. He didn't know at the time that she was the one he'd come for, but he intervened because as he approached the men doing their foul deeds, all he could hear was her faint prayer for God to forgive them. Long story short, Jahmil brought her here and the healer before Myla did as much for her as she could. As I'm sure you've noticed, she still walks with a limp. But God is merciful and hears the cries of His children. Imani has the blessed gift of great faith."

Chapter Seventeen: In the Beginning

E veryone in their group felt their heart-strings tighten at hearing of the horrors that befell the sweet woman who had prepared their meals. After a few silent moments, Bridget smiled warmly. "Now, to answer your question Barbara; 'How can these special people do what they do?'" At this question, everyone turned their attention back to Bridget. Of all the questions they each had, this one was common to all of them.

"Well, let's start at the beginning. In the beginning God created the world and everything in it. Everybody who ever went to a church service or Sunday school has heard this. People also tend to understand that on the sixth day, God created man in His own image. The trouble is; people don't often really understand or embrace what that actually means. When the Almighty gathered together dust from the earth and fashioned it into man, that was not enough for Him. He breathed life into him. He *breathed* it into man. Up to that point, He had merely spoken things into existence. But with man, He got His celestial hands dirty. He was a hands-on God then, and He is still that today. With man, God breathed life into him; got right up in his face and blew into man His very essence. And I know firsthand that God is so powerful that just His breath alone infused every cell in man's body, making him an image of God's love in its purest form."

She spoke with such reverence and awe that Barbara and the others could feel His presence. Looking into the faces of her guests, she went on just as fervently. "And with that breath came the potential to do all things in His name. With God, nothing is impossible. But in His divine wisdom He chose to give man free will. And so it was that the enemy tempted man and he fell. As punishment, God casted them out of the Garden of Eden, and since then the children of man has had to fight the enemy."

She was quiet for so long, they were not sure she would finish. It was clear that the thought of man's failure saddened her immensely, but she finally went on. "After Cain had slain his own brother Abel, he was forced to leave his family and wander in a strange land to the east. Though he was shamed and an outcast himself, he taught his children about God. Some of them listened and took to heart the teachings of their father and learned from his mistakes, like his son Enoch. Others did not. Over time, the ones who listened began to forge strong relationships with the Almighty and were restored."

Smiling excitedly now, she added, "Oh, what a day of rejoicing that was! All over the heavens and our planet were the cheers and praises that some of man's children had been reclaimed. One of the things I love about Him is that He can restore and redeem anything and anyone. So strong was their connection to Him that they were able to do many things that were seemingly impossible; fly, survive under water, and even shape-shift."

Unable to remain sitting, she stood. "I sometimes shake my head at the people who deny God's existence in favor of science. God IS science! Everything He created He did with love and mathematics and science. The reason Dakkar can fly and Carienne can breathe under water is because of science. In its most basic form, all you're doing is rearranging molecules. The same is true for you, Anjelita. You only rearrange the cells of your body into another form."

Bridget was so passionate about what she was saying that she had to catch herself from moving too fast. "I'm sorry. I'm getting ahead of myself." Re-taking her seat, she concluded the answer to Barbara's question.

"Anyway, over time people grew further and further away from the truth of God's love and in so doing, lost their deep connection to Him. Man became so consumed with material wealth and power and trying to have dominion over the earth, that they forgot that God had already given them this beautiful world already. So, to protect themselves from the growing influence of sin, some of the people sanctified themselves by separating from evil-doers. Those who preferred the open skies took flight and settled around Africa. I told you about them earlier. Others who favored the vast sea mostly settled in the coastal waters of Asia. And your people, Anjelita, wanted to be near their animal brothers and chose the jungles of South America."

Dakkar stood and stretched. "This is absolutely amazing. So are you saying that the three of us are descendants of a murderer?" He had always believed that his people were unique and favored by the Creator with these special gifts. He told Bridget and the others just that.

"You are all the descendants of a man who made a terrible mistake. But God forgives all. When Cain cried out in fear that being away from his family would make him an easy target for murder, God heard him. He placed a mark on Cain to protect him. And when Cain begged for forgiveness and turned his heart to Him, God forgave him."

Carienne, who had been silent most of the afternoon, said "I remember the story about him. I know that God can forgive you, but if he was forgiven how come he never got to come back home; him or Adam and Eve."

Bridget smiled at the young girl and told her the truth. "Forgiveness doesn't mean that you don't have to face the consequences of your actions. It just means that He will forgive us when we make mistakes, and He will help us endure the consequences of our actions. It is then up to us to learn from those mistakes; put them behind us and strive to do better. Judging him is not for us to do. He lived several millennia ago, but the lessons of truth and love he instilled in his children still lives on." Glancing around at the tired faces of the guests she added, "That's enough for today. I know you all must be tired still from the journey, so spend the rest of the afternoon relaxing. You need to get your rest because we have work to do tomorrow."

Chapter Eighteen: As the Flowers Bloom

A s usual, Barbara was up shortly before dawn. Though she didn't get much sleep the night before, she felt well rested. She got up from her comfortable pallet, dressed quickly and quietly so as not to disturb her still-slumbering child, and headed outside. She truly missed the familiar sound of the waves lapping against the shore of the beach, but this place was so lush and beautiful that she realized she didn't mind the change of scenery.

By the pre-dawn light she looked around at all of the trees and listened to the unfamiliar calls of the wild birds. She gazed up as a large, distinctive bird circled overhead. The snow-white breast was a contrast to the indigo feathers on its back. She had always considered herself a fairly decent ornithologist, but couldn't figure out what type of bird it was. She stood and watched it until it flew out of sight.

The air was fragrant with the flowers growing all around. She breathed deeply and felt a deep sense of inner peace. She had spent most of the night thinking about all of what Bridget had shared with her, but admitted to herself that she was a bit overwhelmed. As she strolled through trees the likes of which she had never seen before, she saw Bridget walking westward. Wanting to speak to the woman in private, Barbara picked up her pace to follow. Bridget disappeared through a stand of trees and Barbara was about to call out to her to wait when Jahmil stepped from behind another tree and startled her.

"I'm sorry if I scared you. Good morning."

Barbara was a bit startled at first, but seeing that it was Jahmil she slowed her pace and spoke to him. "It's alright. I just didn't see you there is all. I was about to try to catch up with Bridget. I wanted to speak with her before everyone got up."

Jahmil favored her with a rare smile, but told her that she could not follow Bridget there beyond the trees. Confusion flashed across the woman's face. Instead of explaining further he asked her if she would like a cup of coffee.

Hesitating for a moment, she looked towards the area where Bridget had disappeared and wondered why she was not allowed to follow her? Shaking herself free of the early morning conundrum, she focused her attention on the handsome man who was waiting patiently for her answer.

"Yes," she answered quickly. "A cup of coffee would be nice." Barbara realized there was something in the way he looked at her that made her uncharacteristically shy. She found herself unable to hold his soft gaze for long, and set her attention elsewhere. She noticed for the first time the small, neat house a short distance away. They covered the distance in silence and once inside, he motioned for her to take a seat on the large pillows on the floor beside a short-legged wooden table that gleamed with care.

She glanced around the sun-filled interior and smiled. Along one wall was a bookshelf lined with   books. From her seat, she recognized the volumes of Shakespeare, Keats, Phyllis Wheatley, and several other well-known works of literature. She also noticed the various translations of the Bible, the Quran, the Torah, and what she assumed were the doctrines of other world religions. She was impressed, and told him so when he returned and handed her a steaming mug of the best smelling and best tasting coffee she had ever had.

As he settled onto a pillow opposite her at the table, he thanked her for the compliment. "There are many different views in the world about Our Father. As a seeker, it is important for me know the various customs and religions so when I am in different countries, I don't offend anyone or draw unnecessary attention to myself."

Barbara had never thought about the reality of what Jahmil did in his role as a seeker. Since they'd met, she'd sensed a quiet wisdom in him, but only now was she beginning to see that it was rooted in years of study. "I suppose that makes sense, but does it ever get confusing trying to figure out which religion is right?"

For the first time since she had known him, Jahmil did not hesitate to answer. "No. Religion and doctrine are in many ways man-made. In the best of circumstances they are man's attempts to understand God and His plan for our lives. But throughout the years some have been instituted as a means to oppress people. However, the truth of God's love, grace and mercy will not be denied."

Jahmil glanced at the books in his shelf. "In those books are the writings and teachings of God's prophets. There is beauty and some truth in all of them, but there are still too many false prophets who claim to be the Messiah or who say they have been given a divine word. Anything or anyone who does not recognize God as the Creator of all and His son Jesus as the Savior will be lost, no matter how closely they follow their religion. So no, I don't get confused about God's truth when I read other religious books."

Barbara nodded and sipped her coffee as she thought about what he had told her. Silence resettled for a moment before Barbara remembered what she wanted to ask him. "Why couldn't I try to catch up with Bridget this morning? I really wanted to speak with her," she added by way of explanation.

True to his usual self, instead of answering her question, he posed one of his own. "Do you know where we are Barbara?"

Taken aback by the question, she looked at Jahmil over her coffee cup. "Yes. I think so," she answered tentatively. "We're somewhere in the middle of Iraq I believe."

Jahmil nodded his head. "You are correct. Technically." He smiled into his cup of java at the puzzled look on Barbara's face. Seeing that he was enjoying keeping her in suspense, she cocked her head to the side and raised an eyebrow in anticipation of what would come next. "Are you familiar with the story of Creation?" he asked.

She nodded. "Of course." If she'd forgotten the story in the past, last night's lesson was a refresher course.

"Well, welcome to Eden, Barbara."

Shock and awe was all over her face. "You mean we are in Eden? As in Adam and Eve and the trees of life and knowledge?" The implication almost made her spill her coffee. Placing the cup onto the table with shaking hands, she stared at her host in wonder.

Jahmil couldn't contain his mirth any longer and began laughing. Once he'd finally regained his composure he answered. "Almost. We are actually just east of Eden." Though he still enjoyed the look of wonder on her face, he continued solemnly.

"When Adam and Eve were banished from the garden, God decreed that neither he nor his children would ever be allowed to return. The actual garden is somewhere beyond that stand of trees you saw Bridget walking through. Since she is not from this planet, she can enter at will. But in His great mercy,

He has allowed her to establish this sanctuary nearby. Here, we can live in peace and harmony with nature and commune with God with no interruptions."

Barbara was so excited about being so near Eden that she nearly knocked over her cup as she reached for it. "But how do you keep people out? I mean, there is that huge wall, but if you all have been here for centuries, how have you kept this place hidden?"

Jahmil was thoroughly enjoying her company and her eager questions. "The wall you see doesn't actually exist for us. When we came in the other morning and drove through it; there was no magic or mysticism involved. God is the Master Protector and He placed that wall around us. Anyone else driving through only sees a stone wall; a dead end. And since this place is far from anywhere, people rarely come out here. The ground around it is so dense that no farmers ever wanted it, and the mountains being so close makes travel up this way difficult."

Barbara sat quietly for a few minutes and thought about what she'd just been told by Jahmil. Her mind was racing to process all of the information she had received over the past 48 hours, and as usual, she couldn't quite believe all she was seeing. As was her custom, she closed her eyes and began praying to herself. She prayed for guidance and understanding. She also prayed for the strength to accomplish whatever the Lord had guided her to this place to do. She was so caught up in her meditations that she'd forgotten where she was. When she opened her eyes, Jahmil was sitting across from her watching quietly.

"I'm sorry," she said. "I guess I am just overwhelmed by all that has happened."

Jahmil nodded understandingly. "Never be sorry for your prayers," he told her softly. "Sometimes our prayers are all that truly matters. They help us deal with things and God gives us understanding in His time." She found the truth in his words comforting. Barbara looked at the man she knew only as Jahmil and realized she knew very little about him. She was just about to ask him more about himself when he asked her a question.

"If you don't mind my asking, how is it that such a young, beautiful, vibrant flower in God's garden as you are, has been left untouched?"

Barbara was taken off guard by the question. He'd actually referred to her as young and beautiful. At nearly 58 years of age, she considered herself well beyond the age of being flattered; especially by a mysterious man who appeared to be much younger than herself. Choosing her words carefully, she smiled a bit shyly and answered him truthfully.

"I was married once, many years ago. But I found out that I couldn't have children and that put a strain on my marriage that finally broke it. But, that was a long time ago and God knew best. He blessed me with a wonderful daughter to love in spite of the fact that I couldn't conceive." She had long-since given up her anger at not being able to have a child. She recalled briefly how in the years following her divorce she'd been angry with God. She'd blamed Him for making her body imperfect. She had been an only child and all through her childhood she'd planned to grow up, get married and have a lot of babies. But as she'd told Jahmil; God knew best.

"Oh, I don't know," Jahmil responded. "Everything happens in God's own time. You're a healthy woman so if you were to marry at some point I don't see why the Lord wouldn't bless you with a child if that is His will."

He said that part with a sly smile that gave Barbara pause. Realizing that she wasn't sure what this man was thinking, she decided to set him straight. Her years of walking the beach, swimming with Carienne, yoga classes with Tara and her simple carbohydrate-free diet had kept her medium-slim frame firm, flexible and in shape. She knew that she could easily pass for a woman in her mid-forties, and figured that Jahmil must think that as well.

"I appreciate the compliment Jahmil, but I'm not Sarah," she laughed, referring to Abraham's wife who had conceived in her 90's. "I will be 58 in March," she added, thinking that would deter him from any further musings on her ability to have children.

Jahmil stood and brought the coffee pot to where they sat and refreshed her cup and his. As he did, he looked her in the eyes and asked, "And your point is? Like I said before, you are a beautiful young woman." The way he emphasized the word "young" made Barbara flutter a bit in spite of herself.

Regaining her composure she replied back, "Be that as it may, I'm far too old for a young man who may still want children."

Jahmil retook his seat and smiled again over his cup. A few minutes later his manner turned serious as he looked at her. "My life has been spent here in Sanctuary. It has been a wonderful life thus far and I'm blessed to be a part of this work. And until recently, I never gave much thought to marrying or having children. I'd always assumed it was a small price to pay for the blessed life I have. But I have a confession to make." He paused a moment to gauge her reaction.

At that, Barbara sat totally still, trying to will herself to breathe normally. She was nervous under his silent scrutiny, and the kind, knowing brown eyes he had fixed on hers was unsettling. It was a pleasant sensation, but one that was either unfamiliar or long-forgotten. As he continued, she silently let out the breath she'd been holding.

"Several years ago I had a dream that one day I would marry and have children. Of course I dismissed that thought because of the work here. But since meeting you, I'm now convinced that is was God showing me that there was something more I would have than just the work."

His sincerity touched Barbara in places in her heart that she had long since closed off. For the first time in nearly 20 years, she admitted that she missed the companionship of a special man in her life. She had focused her attentions on God, Carienne and her job. For years she had told herself she had no time and no desire for a husband. But now, those boasts rang hollow.

Looking up at Jahmil, she couldn't deny that she was attracted to him, but the difference in their age was vast. No matter how nice she thought he was, nothing could ever come of an attraction between them. So, with that in mind, she told him quietly, "I do pray that you will find that right woman. But like I said; I'm pushing 60 soon and you are young enough to almost be my son." She showed him a bitter-sweet smile.

To that, Jahmil told her, "No, you're not. If anything, you're almost too young for me." Barbara cocked her head to the side and looked at him. "I'll celebrate my 70th birthday in November if the Lord permits."

Again, Barbara was floored. He had to be joking! He didn't look a day over 45! She knew she had taken pretty good care of herself and looked a decade younger than she was, but if Jahmil was telling her the truth about his age, that would be incredible.

Jahmil chuckled again in response to her expressions which ranged from shock, to disbelief to wonder. To further shock her he added, "And Princess is 20."

"What!?" Barbara exclaimed. "But she looks... I mean, I thought..."

"I know. You thought she was about 12." Taking pity on Barbara in her flabbergasted state, he explained. "Unlike Bridget, we are not immortal beings, but God gives us unusually long lives and we don't age in the same way that most people do. It is not uncommon for one of us to live 300 years. You've met Tefilah; she is about 260 years old."

Barbara had met the quiet, older woman when they arrived. She also knew that according to Bridget, her role in the Order was to pray. She'd initially thought the Canadian-born French woman to be in her 70s, and had to shake her head at this newest revelation.

She was just about to ask him more about himself when they heard Bridget calling to them through the open door of Jahmil's house. Setting their cups aside, they went out and joined her.

"Good morning," she said cheerily. "This is a beautiful day that the Lord has made!"

Barbara smiled and added, "And I will rejoice and be glad in it." It occurred to her then that in spite of all the shocking news she had learned, her spirit was rejoicing. She was still unsure about what God had in store for their journey or how Jahmil might fit into her life, but she was content being in this beautiful place.

Bridget's smile widened upon hearing Barbara's completion of the passage. "Do you understand what that passage means, Barbara?" she asked softly.

Barbara looked at the tall woman and answered, "Yes. I believe I do." Glancing quickly at Jahmil, she continued. "The first part; 'This is the day that the Lord has made' is a testament to the greatness of God. It acknowledges His majesty and splendor and the fact that He alone has created everything. To me, it means that no matter what happens in the course of the day, He is in control of it all because He made it. That knowledge is the reason for the second part. 'I will rejoice and be glad in it.' When we truly understand that He has made everything and that everything He made was good, I can't help but to rejoice that He has seen fit to allow me to enjoy the bounty of what He has made."

Turning her attention to Jahmil, she added "Since tomorrow is not promised to anyone, all we have is this day; this moment in this time. We only have this day to live, to love, to cry, to rejoice; and I *will* rejoice and be glad in this day. This beautiful, glorious day that He has made so that we can seize it and stand in awe and bear witness to what He has done."

Barbara wiped away the joyful tears spilling down her face as she finished her answer. She realized that she had poured her heart out to not only God, but to Jahmil as well. She believed with every fiber of her being that each day was a special gift from God and that the opportunities He gave her to laugh, smile, sing, praise him and even to love should be seized and appreciated. However, she hadn't meant to lay bare her soul in front of their hostess, and was a bit embarrassed that she had done so.

The trio headed back to the main house in silence. Barbara's words were still reverberating through each of them and no other words were needed. As they came closer to the main house, Bridget looked over at Jahmil and said, "God has favored you greatly, son. She was well worth the wait."

Barbara stopped dead in her tracks. Had Jahmil confided in Bridget about his feeling for her? Or had the woman sensed the truth in what she'd said earlier? She felt embarrassed and a bit excited at the same time. "What do you mean?" Barbara asked Bridget as she tried to catch up to the tall woman.

Bridget was taking long strides and didn't answer her with anything more than a knowing smile. "Come, let's get those lazy youngsters up and eat breakfast. We have a lot to do today." With that, she went towards the large house she shared with Myla and Princess.

Chapter Nineteen: Nomenclature

Carienne woke up early and looked around for her mother. After a few minutes she gave up the search and went to wash up and dress. When she was finished, she heard soft singing coming from the large kitchen and decided to find out who it was. The melodic soprano voice was sweet and full of feeling. Inside she found Imani preparing to cook breakfast.

Carienne immediately remembered the tragic story of how she'd gotten the limp. She was so engrossed in her thoughts that when Imani spoke to her, she realized she'd been staring. Chagrinned, the young woman stated, "I'm sorry. And good morning to you.

Imani smiled at the girl. "No problem. I'd imagine you're a bit curious about my limp?" Carienne's face turned hot with embarrassment.

"Yes. I mean no," she tried to catch herself before she said something rude. "I mean, Miss Bridget told us about what happened to you, and I'm real sorry."

Imani smiled at the girl again. "It's alright."

Carienne was silent for a moment as she continued to watch Imani slicing through several large pieces of fruit. Finally, she confessed with admiration plain in her voice, "I wish I was as brave as you are, Ms. Imani. When we heard about what you did for those children I was really impressed. I don't think I could ever be that brave."

"I'm not sure it was bravery; I was scared the whole time. But I knew something had to be done and everybody had gone crazy. I'd never seen such hate and violence." She was quiet for a long while as she remembered that time in her life.

119

"But it was what God wanted me to do and I don't regret any of it. Not even the limp," she said with a grin.

Carienne perked up with excitement. "Myla says that my gift of healing is stronger than hers. I'd be happy to see if I can help you." She was so enthusiastic about her idea that Imani felt compelled to hug the young girl. Placing the knife on the long table she was working at, she pulled her into a strong embrace.

When she let the girl go, she had tears standing in her bright, dark eyes. "Thank you so much for wanting to help me. The strength of God's love and compassion flows mightily in you, young Unifier. But actually, I don't mind it. It doesn't hurt me at all. As long as I can walk with God, I don't care if I limp beside Him. Besides, this is a constant reminder to pray before I run into a situation."

Carienne wasn't totally sure why the woman didn't want her help, but she did understand that if the woman was declining her offer, she must have good reason. "Okay," she said reluctantly. "But if you change your mind, let me know." She turned to walk out of the kitchen but Imani stopped her.

"And where do you think you're going? You're here in the kitchen with me, so wash your hands and help me get breakfast ready," she winked. Carienne grinned and did as she was asked.

Directly following breakfast, Bridget gathered the members of the Order with rest of the group and they all knelt in prayer led by Tefilah. After a short, but fervent prayer, the group dispersed into pairs and small groups. Carienne was taken by Myla to the edge of Sanctuary where a beautiful, clear body of water flowed.

"This is part of the Euphrates River," Myla explained. "There are four rivers that flow from the Garden of Eden including this one."

"*The* Garden of Eden?" Carienne asked, confused. "From the Bible?"

Smiling, Myla nodded her head. "Yes. Sanctuary is located just outside of Eden." She spent a few minutes explaining how God had given Bridget and the members of the Order the use of the land that had been blocked off from other people since the fall of man. It was clear to Myla that her friend had many more questions, but they had work to do. With that in mind, she began tutoring Carienne on the extent of her gifts concerning water.

Kafeel took Anjelita into a clearing to begin training her. Her strength and agility impressed him as he taught her both defensive and offensive maneuvers. He pushed her further throughout the day to help her master control of her gifts of strength and speed. He taught her a series of holds and disarming techniques which she caught onto and mastered easily.

As they worked through the morning, she asked him more about his role in the Order as protector. Lunging towards her, he made a move to bring her down. With dazzling speed, she spun around and hooked right arm through his left arm. Positioned on his side, she used the sweeping kick he taught her to the back of his knees, while using her body weight to bring him flat on his back.

Smiling at how well she'd executed the move, he answered her query. "Like you, I have been given physical strength and speed as well as a keen knowledge of tactical maneuvers and battle strategies. I have studied Dambe, Lutte and Nuba, the African martial art styles, in addition to Karate, Jujitsu and Tae Kwon Do from the East. I have practiced archery, fencing, the Japanese sword-fighting style known as kendo, and marksmanship with guns. Whenever a member of the Order travels outside of Sanctuary, a protector always accompanies them. With God's help, I am able to get them back home safely. In short; I fight. I try to find ways to avoid confrontations, but if it can't be avoided, I look for ways to exploit the opponent's weaknesses."

Kafeel was dusting himself off from the last time she'd laid him flat and smiled. "Of course, I am not as strong or apparently as fast as you are!" Sharing a smile, he lunged towards her screaming, "Again!"

Dakkar was led to another area of the clearing by Laqat. There was a long table set to the side with several objects atop it. There were wooden bowls of various sizes, large rocks, fruit and cups filled with water.

"You have several great gifts, Dakkar, but the ability to move objects may prove to be one of your greatest strengths once you learn to control it properly," Laqat said. Without saying another word, Laqat picked up a nice-sized rock and threw it at Dakkar's head.

Startled, Dakkar swiftly sent the lump of hardened earth in the other direction. He started to ask Laqat why he'd thrown a rock at him, when he saw another coming his way. Dakkar had decided the man had gone crazy, but was too busy focusing on sending the rocks elsewhere to comment on it.

After a few more minutes of dodging rocks, Dakkar had had enough. Using his abilities to lift Laqat from his feet, Dakkar turned the man upside down in mid-air. "Why did you do that?" Dakkar demanded as he walked towards the suspended man.

Initially he'd been angry, but upon seeing the impressed smile on Laqat's face, decided he was more confused at the attack than upset. After Dakkar dropped him back to the soft ground with a faint thud, he reached out his hand to help him up.

"I needed to see you in action," Laqat offered in explanation, as he rubbed the shoulder he'd fallen on. Seeing this, Dakkar apologized for dropping him. He hadn't meant to let him go so abruptly, but he'd lost his focus.

"In battle, you can move objects easily as a defensive maneuver. That's good, but now let me see you lift that apple," he challenged, pointing to the fruit on the table.

Dakkar was still smarting a bit from having rocks thrown at his head, but understood the man's reasoning. Turning his attention to the table he concentrated on the bright, red apple. It took him a while, but he finally managed to lift it a few inches from the tabletop. His triumphant smile faded instantly when he turned to Laqat's stony face.

"That is what I thought," he said. "You move things out of emotion and self-preservation. You need to concentrate and move them without your emotions being involved."

Dakkar grew frustrated over the course of the morning as he tried to lift the objects. At best, he was only able to move small things a short distance. "I don't understand!" His anger over not being able to complete the small tasks was clear. "I try to concentrate like you say, but nothing happens," the young man lamented.

Sensing that his friend needed a break, Laqat had him sit down a while to relax and calm down. After a few silent moments, Laqat turned to Dakkar and asked, "How do you fly?"

Still in his mood, Dakkar shrugged and answered, "I just can. I don't really have to think about it."

"Exactly!" Laqat replied.

The odd response made Dakkar turn to his new friend with a puzzled look. In response, Laqat tried to explain. "When you fly, you don't have to think about it; you just do it. You trust yourself and your ability." Laqat could tell Dakkar still didn't understand so he went on.

"When God created the world, everything was made up of matter. In its most basic form, all matter can be reduced to energy, and therefore manipulated. God also gave man dominion over all the things on the earth. In His Word, He says that a man who is connected to Him can divide waters and move mountains. Everything that has matter will obey a man who is connected to the Father; the Supreme Creator of all things."

Dakkar nodded his understanding of that, but was still unsure what it had to do with him flying. To that question, Laqat answered, "Everything. When you fly, whether you are thinking about it or not, you are making the air molecules support your weight and propel you through the air. But it all begins with a thought. You think about what you want to do and where you want to go, and take flight, right?"

Again Dakkar nodded. "Yes. That is true; I only have to think about it and will myself to move through the air." He thought about how he'd discovered he could move through water during his escape from captivity. It hadn't taken any deep concentration; he just thought of what he'd wanted to do and willed himself forward.

Grinning like an excited boy, Dakkar jumped up and stood in front of the table. He took a deep, relaxing breath and thought about what he wanted. One of the wooden bowls began to spin on its side. As it moved faster, a rock lifted and began smashing the fruit. The glasses of water joined the animated scene by hovering several feet above the table and dumping out its contents, only to drop back to the table and catch it before it wet the table.

Laqat cheered Dakkar on as he watched the play. However, Dakkar turned a mischievous eye on Laqat and sent him running around the glade to escape the smashed pieces of fruit being hurled at him. After a few more moments, the two men laughed until they had tears in their eyes. Laqat was a sticky mess after having pieces of watermelon, peaches, mangoes, bananas and apples flung at him from head to toe. Picking pieces of pineapple from his hair, Laqat smiled and told Dakkar to keep practicing while he went to wash up.

Back at the main house, Barbara, Bridget and Imani sat at the table talking and preparing lunch. Barbara watched as Imani cut up the okra, tomatoes, peppers and onions she would use for the mid-day meal. Atop her own lap sat a bowl of fresh sweet peas that she was supposed to be shelling. Her thoughts were filled with Jahmil, the things she'd learned, Jahmil, the wonderful people she'd met, Jahmil, the peaceful surroundings, and again, Jahmil.

She wondered what he was doing since she hadn't seen him since this morning. There were so many things she wanted to talk to him about; wanted to know about him. Thoughts of their early-morning conversation brought a smile to her lips.

"Barbara," Bridget said, bringing her out of her reverie. "Those peas won't shell themselves."

When Barbara looked up into the grinning faces of her companions, she felt a bit embarrassed. She sincerely hoped mind-reading wasn't among the list of the Bridget's talents.

Turning her attention to the still-giggling Imani, Bridget added, "Love is definitely in the air it seems, don't you agree Imani?"

Trying to hide her smile, she nodded and pretended to concentrate on cutting the piece of corn in her hand off the cob. The subject of her own attraction to Laqat was not one she was ready to broach with her mentor. She glanced up at Barbara whose smile was waiting for her. When the woman threw her a quick wink, they both laughed again.

After a few more minutes of soft smiles and giggling, Bridget's tone became a bit serious. "Barbara, do you know why you are here?"

Barbara studied the smooth face of the woman everyone called Mama Bear and tried to glean some understanding of the question. Of all the many questions she'd had, the reason for her being there hadn't been one of them. "I assumed because I'm Carienne's mother and I needed to come to bring her." That was the only answer she could give. Until then, it had not dawned on her that God might have some other purpose for her being with them.

"Yes, that is definitely part of it. In many ways, Carienne is still a very young woman and taking her from the only family she has ever known would have been unwise. But there are other reasons you were included," Bridget told her.

"This morning when I was talking with the Father, He revealed to me that you are to travel with us when the time comes to leave Sanctuary. He told me that you are a woman of great faith with an indomitable spirit, and your gifts of courage and strength will be needed."

Barbara found herself speechless once again. She knew that eventually they would have to leave this beautiful place, but she'd thought only Carienne, Dakkar and Anjelita would be going on the quest. She'd assumed she would be returning home or possibly staying on at Sanctuary until they returned.

"We'll let the Unifiers spend the rest of this week training with Kafeel and the others, but next week you will join them."

"You mean I have to learn to fight?" Barbara asked with wide eyes. She, Ezer and Princess had taken refreshments out to the others earlier and she'd witnessed some of the moves Anjelita and Kafeel were practicing.

"Yes, but not with the intensity of Kafeel and the others. You will be taught to use weapons and to defend yourself if the need arises. It will be very physical, but God said you can do it," she stated with a confident smile.

"Well, if He says I can, then I will," she smiled, shaking her head at how things were unfolding.

"You have a beautiful attitude," she praised the woman. "That is why He has given you a new name," she added seriously.

"A new name?" Barbara asked. She thought if she received one more piece of news her head would burst.

"Yes. This morning He told me that from now on, you shall be called *Tehilla*."

"Tehilla," Barbara repeated, trying to get the feel of the name.

"Yes. Tehilla means to give praise through song. You lift your voice in praise to Him from your heart and that pleases Him. So, after we have our evening meal, you will be baptized in the Euphrates River and your new name will be made known to the others."

Even after the events of the past few weeks and the things she'd learned up to that point, none of it had moved her the way this did. The God of all creation had taken the time to bestow on her a gift that was almost as precious to her as His Son's sacrifice on Calvary. There were no words to describe the unbridled joy she felt. Crying, she reached to the heavens and let out a shout of praise and thanksgiving that could be heard across all of Sanctuary.

Chapter Twenty: Preparations

In the following weeks, Carienne, Dakkar and Anjelita continued their training, and to their delight, Tehilla joined them. Carienne was especially proud of how hard her mother worked to learn what they were being taught. She was also pleased by the new name her mother had been given, and once she'd learned its meaning; thought it very fitting.

Their training regimen rotated them between the members of the Order as they were taught more. From Princess, they each learned to see the things that were true, good, pure and of God. They were also trained to recognize the enemy. Princess who, though appeared to be only 12 years old, taught them that the key to seeing was to ignore what their eyes alone saw. "We walk by faith and not by sight," she explained. "Your connection to the Most High will allow you to see things as He sees them. When He shows you these things you will have a deeper understand of what His plan for you is, and you will be able to recognize evil in any form it takes. Only with His sight can you rightly divide the word of truth and not be deceived by the enemy. "

"Discernment," Tehilla said.

"That's exactly right. One of the most powerful tools of the enemy is to shroud lies with truth. Since he can't create anything, he uses what God has made and perverts it to fit his own purposes. He makes things 'look like' they are safe and good, but in reality, he has laid a trap inside," she explained with a look of pure disgust on her angelic face.

"Do not fall prey to what you see with your eyes alone. The eyes are part of our fleshly bodies and the flesh desires things that are not of God. See with the eyes of His Spirit which dwells in each of you. Only then can you tell God's truth from the lies of the enemy."

They were all very impressed by how well she trained them. Her manner was very business-like, which was a contrast to the always-smiling, giggling young girl they thought her to be. Tehilla knew Princess was actually 20 years old, but her serious tone and wisdom was decades beyond her years.

The time they spent with Jahmil was learning the importance of seeking God. "Mankind seeks out fame, glory, worldly wisdom and power, but the only thing worth having is the favor of the Lord. If it is power you want, true power only comes from having a strong connection to God. Strong, unbreakable power that is free of pride or corruption. The powers to heal, fly and even change form are just small things to Him. While each of you are blessed by having an un-severed connection to God and His power through your lineage, He wants all of his children to be reconciled with Him so that they too can enjoy the gifts He has to give them. But they have to open their hearts and seek Him first."

"Seek ye first the kingdom of God and all these things will be added unto you," Anjelita added. Having been raised in a Catholic orphanage, she considered herself fairly well-versed in the Scriptures.

Jahmil smiled and nodded as he praised her for her comment. He silently thanked God for allowing each of the Unifiers to have been taught the Word from a young age. Even young Carienne understood and accepted the teaching of Christ, so he didn't have to spend a lot of time teaching them the key elements. Instead, he could focus on helping them to implement what they already knew and how to apply it to themselves; a task that would be critical to their success. He knew that if any one of them gave themselves over to hubris, pride or worldly desires, the work they had been sent to do would be greatly impacted.

The first thing that Kafeel taught them was a Psalm of David. "Blessed be the Lord my strength, which teaches my hands to war and my fingers to fight." He explained that they would fight many battles in the days to come and being prepared was essential to their survival. "And while there are many types of ways to fight against evil, there will be some physical fights as well. Throughout time righteous men and women of God have waged war against the powers of the enemy. He is our rock and our fortress. In His name alone will we prevail. I can teach you how to fight, but only He can tell us when to fight."

Under the instruction of Laqat, a Native American man who appeared to be in his late 20's, they learned to appreciate the bounty that God had given them. "God is a provider, and will give His children everything they need at the exact time they need it." Laqat further explained that there is a time to gather things and a time to trust that God will provide what is needed, no matter what it is. His exuberant manner and excitement over the goodness of God as a provider was infectious, and soon they were all too busy giving thanks to go into more of Laqat's lesson.

Myla spent time teaching them of the importance of water. "Water is a natural conductor of the Lord. Water constitutes the majority of our bodies for a reason. As a conductor, water transmits the vibration of the word of God to us. It can heal our bodies and uplift our spirits. However, if not cared for properly, it can destroy. In the days of Noah, God sent a powerful flood to rid the earth of wickedness. It is no coincidence that He chose water."

131

They all knew the story of how God chose Noah, a known drunk, to build an ark that would house a pair of every animal on the planet, as well as keep his family safe when He sent the torrential rains that lasted for 40 days and 40 nights.

"We know that God does not have coincidences, but why choose water?" Dakkar asked. He was getting over his apprehension of speaking in English. No one had made fun of him when he didn't know what a word meant, and they all seemed to understand him just fine.

"That is a very good question, Dakkar. Though it can destroy, water can also restore and renew," she answered. "Powerful winds can destroy by blowing things around, but it can't restore anything. Fire can consume everything, but once it dies out, what has burned can't be renewed. Only water can do both. No matter how bad a flood may be, once the waters recede, things can be dried out and made useful again in most cases." She paused briefly to see if that answered his questions. When he answered that it had, she went on to teach them some of the other properties of water, and how they could use it.

Though they did not spend a lot of time with Imani, she explained to them that above all the things they were learning, was the importance of true faith. She told them from her own experiences that the enemy would try to make them doubt themselves and doubt the instructions that God had given them. "When all else seems to fail us, an unwavering faith that God is in control and will see us through any hardship we may face will prove to be our greatest weapon against the enemy. The Dark One will try to break our resolve and make us doubt who we are and what we are supposed to be doing, but he cannot take your life. He can only try to break your will, and the only safeguard against him in this is total trust and belief in the Almighty."

Shama and Ezer joined forces to teach them their lessons. "Obedience is better than sacrifice," Shama told them. "In the days of old, people would bring an animal sacrifice and kill it to atone for their sins. The blood of the animal was given to wipe clean the sins of the person making the sacrifice. However, thanks to the ultimate sacrifice of our Lord and Savior Jesus Christ, we no longer have to spill blood for our sins. Jesus made the final sacrifice for us all, no matter who we are or what sins we have committed. As followers of the teachings of Christ, we are no longer bound by the old laws that demanded sacrifices because we are saved by His grace. Now, we are charged with being obedient to Him."

"So that's why we call Jesus the 'Lamb of God!'" Anjelita exclaimed. For years she had head that reference to the Son of God, but never knew what it actually meant.

"Absolutely!" Shama replied. "Jesus was the sacrificial lamb. After His resurrection, He left us the Holy Spirit to help us and guide us in what is right. The challenge for most people is in obeying what they are supposed to do. It's easy to obey God when what He wants us to do is in line with what we want. But when a task seems to be hard, dangerous, unpopular, or simply distasteful to us, we try to find ways to avoid being obedient. Sometimes making a sacrifice seems easier; do what you want to do then kill an animal and be forgiven. Or, do what you want to do and ask Jesus to go to the Father on our behalf to grant us forgiveness. While God will forgive us, we often have to deal with the consequences of our disobedience, and in the end we still have to do what He told us to do. So again; obedience is better than sacrifice."

The quieter twin, Ezer, spent his time with the group discussing his role and how important helping is. "Many people have great talents that they bring to the Lord. Some are powerful speakers, engaging teachers, gifted singers and musicians, as well as many other talents. While those talents are necessary and they do please the Father, everyone always wants those gifts; to be out front in leadership roles. But there are helping gifts that are just as important to the building of God's kingdom as the leadership roles. When Jesus fed the five-thousand, someone had to wash the dishes!" he chuckled.

His tone became more serious as he continued. "Being in service to others is a duty and a responsibility that we should accept gladly. If we are to emulate Jesus Christ then we are to serve our fellow man. People often think that serving others is a lowly position, but Christ teaches us that being humble enough to serve others with a glad heart is to serve Him. As you go wherever He leads you, remember that Jesus, the very Son of God; came to serve man and that as His followers, we can do no less. Take every opportunity to help someone, no matter who they are. And when asked why you did it, tell them the Lord loves them and that you are being obedient to His desire to see them prosper."

In closing their lesson, Shama piggy-backed off her brother's comment by adding, "Again I say; obedience is better than sacrifice!"

Chapter Twenty-One: Faith and Work

A s they were mastering their lessons and honing their gifts, they saw less and less of Bridget. She had begun spending the majority of her time in the Garden communing with God. She didn't tell them what they talked about and no one had the courage to ask. Weeks turned into months as they worked to strengthen both their gifts and their connection with God.

Anjelita realized that for the first time in her life, she was totally at peace. She had not been plagued by the nightmares since the night before Sister Magali had tried to kill her. She still felt sadness at the loss of her friend as well as confusion over the woman's motives, but in spite of those feelings, she relished her newfound inner peace.

During dinner one evening, Anjelita asked Bridget a question that had been on her mind. "Bridget," she began, "I'm wondering how it is that I never felt this close to God before? I grew up in a Catholic orphanage and always believed in the power of prayer and thought I had a good relationship with Him. How could I have been so wrong all that time?"

Bridget heard the sincerity in the young woman's voice. She sat quietly for a moment, praying for God to give her the correct words to answer the woman's question.

Before she answered however, Tehilla added to the question by making a comment. "I know what you mean. I'm a Christian. I was raised to believe in the Holy Trinity and have tried to live my life according to His Word as I understood it. But since we have been here, I can't help but wonder if what I was taught was correct. I notice that most of names of the people here are Hebrew. So I just wonder, what is the correct religion; Judaism? Christianity? Which one?"

Bridget knew this question would come up and knew that it was time to explain more. "Anjelita, I know that you feel betrayed by the Catholic Church. After all, it was your closest friend and surrogate mother, Sister Magali, who was sent to kill you. But understand that each person must build a relationship with Him for themselves. As long as they are following His commandments, have faith in Him, and find salvation through His Son, they are on the right path. This includes people who follow Christ through the Catholic faith. Over the years, the Catholic Church has received some pretty bad publicity and, sadly, some of it was warranted. But know that there are many people who have been led to the Son and His Father through the many good works of the Church, and we shouldn't throw the baby out with the bathwater because of a few people who misused their authority."

Turning to Tehilla, she continued. "The reason we speak and pray in Hebrew is not because we are saying that the Jews are 100% right. It's just that Hebrew, and more specifically, Aramaic, is the language of the Covenant. Sadly, the enemy has worked to infiltrate religion in order to carry out his dastardly plans. He has perverted the true Word of God and twisted it to be used to oppress man instead of leading them to God. In so many ways, some churches have led people further away from God rather than to Him. But know this; God's way is not hidden, nor will His Word return void. There is only one truth and that truth comes from God. Each of the world's Holy Books contains much of the same information. Unfortunately, the enemy has tried to pervert its meaning. If we look to the writings of old, we understand our history and God's law which has not changed. It can't change because He is the same yesterday, today and tomorrow. When God sent His Son to die for the sins of man, some people accepted those teachings and others did not. Many of those who accepted Christ as the Messiah were so intent on looking at His teachings, that they forgot the original

136

laws. That's sad because Christ clearly stated He didn't come to change the law; only to fulfill it. So right and wrong religion is not the question we should be asking; but what must I do to become saved? And the answer to that question is clear; believe in your heart and confess with your mouth that Jesus is the Son of God, because none cometh unto the Father but through the Son. And we fortunate few are blessed to be a part of His plan to help man reconnect with Him." Bridget smiled softly at the members of the group and stood.

Before she left them, she added, "God has told me that the time is growing close to begin our journey. It will not be easy, but He promises us victory." Bridget strolled off to the sounds of Tehilla's beautiful voice being lifted in a hymn of praise that was carried across the evening on a breath of God.

Chapter Twenty-Two: What's in a Name?

The remaining days bled together as everyone worked tirelessly to train their bodies for battle and their minds and hearts to hear God. Nearly eight months had passed since they'd arrived at Sanctuary, and in that time, all three of the Unifiers had not only renewed their commitment to God, but had been baptized by Bridget. At the end of the eighth month, Bridget called everyone together and told them that the time to begin the journey was very close. They were told to rest up for a few days because they would be leaving on Sunday morning.

Laqat and Ezer had spent several days making each of them full-bodied suits made from wool that Bridget had brought back from the sheep in the Garden. "God continues to favor us," she told them. "This is no ordinary wool. It is nearly impervious to any weapon created by man."

At that statement, the women shouted their joy. "It is good that He gave us this protection. I'm still not very confident in my fighting abilities," Tehilla laughed. The last few months had really toughened her up, but she wasn't sure she would be much help fighting.

Bridget turned a serious eye towards the woman and said quietly, "For we wrestle not against flesh and blood, but against principalities, against powers, against the rulers of the darkness of this world, against spiritual wickedness in high places. The suits will help protect you from physical harm, but the enemy will attack you in ways that will make you doubt what you know to be true. He is cunning and his trickery knows no bounds. We'd all do well to remember who and what we're dealing with."

The group was sobered after hearing Bridget's wise words. Dakkar, who was often quiet and kept his own counsel, asked Bridget a question that had been on everyone's mind. "What are we supposed to do? And who exactly are we fighting? You make it sound like we are about to go up against Satan himself." Again, Bridget had the group sit down. What she was about to tell them now she hadn't even shared with the members of the Order.

"Your question is a good one Dakkar," she began. "And to answer it fully, I have to go back to the beginning." Everyone settled around her in a loose half-circle beneath what they affectionately called, "the talking tree."

She leaned back against the huge tree and began. "As I told you all before, I am from Ehyeh Asher Ehyeh; a planet far from here. The name of my planet means simply 'I AM' because when the Almighty created it, He named it such. Much like the people of this planet, God created us to take care of our world. But the one thing He did not do was breathe life into us. He fashioned us from the stars and spoke us into existence. He gave us free will, and for millennia, that will has been only to serve and please Him. We could see into Heaven and all that He created in the universe and what we saw baffled us. In heaven, there was one angel who was created more beautiful than any other. He was in many ways, the most favored of God. But when the Almighty created this world and breathed life into man, the angel became jealous of the love God bestowed upon man. In his own hubris, he fought God for the throne of heaven and was cast down with a third of the angels who'd foolishly followed him. It was in that very Garden that he deceived man and caused him to disobey God," she said, motioning towards the Garden.

"I'm sure you all know the story of how that turned out. Man was exiled from the garden and made to earn a living by the sweat of his brow, Eve was to be tormented through the birthing process and the serpent was cursed to slither on its belly."

As they all listened to Bridget, they nodded their heads that they did know the story of the fall of man. "What you may not fully know is that in addition to these angels who fell, there were other angels who were called Watchers. Their job was to do just that; watch over man. Even though they were being punished, God still showed them mercy and loved them infinitely. But some 200 of these Watchers began to lust after the daughters of man and made a vow to each other that they would go down to Earth and take women as their wives. The children they had with these women were giants and are known as Nephilim."

With the exception of Tehilla and the members of the Order, no one had ever heard of Nephilim. They sat and listened as Bridget explained further about how the Nephilim were huge giants who began to devour man when the people could no longer keep them fed and satisfied. "These savages ran amok and did all manner of wicked deeds. In addition to what the Nephilim were doing, the fallen Watchers began to teach the people the 'secrets of Heaven.' They taught men about Astrology, metallurgy and weapon-making. They taught the women how to make cosmetics to become more alluring so as to attract men. At their hands man learned about the constellations and the rotations of the moon and sun. Man was also taught to chant and to work charms.

"The wickedness of man was being increased by the mixing of their blood with the Nephilim. In order to minimize this growing threat, God sent a mighty flood to wash the earth clean. I'm sure you all are familiar with the story of Noah. But not all of the Nephilim were destroyed and their evil, promoted by Satan himself, grew once more. They made another appearance in the bible when David was a boy. One of the giants was terrorizing the children of God and David, a young boy at the time, killed him with a slingshot. The Watchers, led by an angel named Azazel, were cast into the bowels of the earth; bound and in total darkness where they will remain until the Day of Judgment. Over the centuries, some of those remaining Nephilim mixed with some of the people. In their descendants lies the genetic blueprint that the enemy thinks will help him in achieving his ultimate goal."

Before any of them could ask the question of what that goal was, Bridget headed them off. "Satan once challenged God for the throne of Heaven because he wants to not only rule the world, but to *be* God. It's pure nonsense of course, but his plan is to 'create man in his own image.' Much of the cloning research and attempts to make people is simply his way of trying to attain that goal. But make no mistake; this is not his first attempt."

Looking around at the astonished faces of the group she shook her head sadly. "The Word tells us that there is nothing new under the sun. The evil one has been attempting to create his own type of people for millennia. In the past, some of the hybrids and abominations from his attempts were known to man, but were reduced to fairy tales."

Bridget paused for a moment before explaining what she meant. "When the Watchers descended from their place in the heavens and joined with the daughters of man, the people believed that they were gods. Their vast knowledge, power and strength were used to deceive the people into worshipping them. Many of the Greek, Roman, Celtic and Norse gods some of you may have learned about were in fact these fallen angels.

"Really" Anjelita asked. "I remember reading stories about how the 'gods' would come down from heaven and take mortal women as wives. If you can call them wives, that is. If memory serves correctly, some of the women already had husbands but these celestial beings were too powerful to be opposed and they took the women anyway."

Bridget nodded that what Anjelita remembered about mythology was correct. "Keep in mind that when they came down among the people, there were many who saw them. What might you have thought if you'd seen beautiful and awesome beings coming down from the sky?" The question had been rhetorical, so when no one answered, she continued.

Ever since Adam disobeyed God in the Garden by eating the fruit from the Tree of Knowledge, man has been busy seeking new ways to promote himself as he tries to become like God according to the promise told to Adam by the serpent. Man tries to gain as much knowledge as he can about his environment so that he can try to disprove the very existence of the Almighty and to exercise power over others. So, when these 'gods' came possessing power and knowledge that surpassed everything they had previously known, the people accepted them and agreed to worship them in exchange for that knowledge and power."

"Miss Bridget," Carienne began. "I get how the people could have believed that the fallen angels were gods, but what I don't understand is what the people thought they were going to get in return for worshipping these angels? I mean, didn't you and Anjelita say that they were mean to the people and abused the women?"

"I know you've heard the saying 'knowledge is power,' right?" When Carienne and the others nodded that they had, she went on. "Well it is true. When you know things that others do not, you can use that power to either help them or destroy them. If one group was taught the celestial patterns and the constellations, think what impact that would have on travel and navigation. No more wandering around hoping to reach a destination; you can now plot your course by the unchanging sky. Add to that the knowledge of boat building and weapon making, and you have the first conquerors going out to subdue others."

Pausing to take a sip of her water and to gauge how they were reacting to the information, she thought about how to tell them the next part of the story. "We all know that Satan is the master deceiver, so he always tempts others with something they want in order to ensnare them and get them to do his bidding. In the case of the Watchers, he made them desire the daughters of Adam so much that they were willing to disobey God to have them. Once they left Heaven, Satan made them believe they had gotten what they wanted, but in truth, he'd just used them to turn the people further from God. And for their part, the people believed they were getting supreme knowledge and had the protection of the gods. In truth, all they had were the tools of destruction. The so-called knowledge and power they wielded was rooted in sorcery and witchcraft."

"So they were practicing black magic?" Anjelita asked. When she was a teen-ager, she had become very interested in learning more about her ability to see things that would happen, and had begun to study everything she could find on the phenomenon. However, most of the things she'd come across fell into the category of dark or black magic and she had stayed away from it. She shared that with Bridget and the others in hopes they could shed light on her gifts.

"There is no such thing as black or white magic. All of it is sorcery and all of it is connected to the enemy. He lures people into his web by enticing them with the ability to do things that would guarantee them a particular outcome, but make no mistake; it is all demonic. People who claim to tell the future by communicating with the dead are practitioners of necromancy. In truth, they are not communicating with the dead; they are communing with demons. People have become fascinated with the idea of being able to cast spells to protect themselves or to bring them wealth, power and fame. They flock to entertainments that feature various elements of witchcraft, sorcery, necromancy, chanting, conjuring spirits; and that's just in the children's section. But in the end, they have only succeeded in opening their minds and bodies up for possession by these evil spirits."

Looking directly at Anjelita, she told her softly, "When you see things that have happened or will happen, you are not conjuring up any spirits. You do not summon anything at will to advise you. What you have is a great gift from Yahweh, and it is pure."

Hoping that would ease Anjelita's mind, she went back to discussing the Watchers. "Under the guidance of Satan, they did many perverse things against nature. Using their God-given knowledge of genetics and other scientific laws, they crossbred various animals such as eagles and lions; goats, lions and serpents; as well as mixing humans with various animals."

Tehilla shook her head in disbelief. "Are you saying that creatures such as the chimera, centaurs and griffins actually existed?" She remembered the many tales of Greek mythology she'd learned during her studies in college.

"I'm afraid so. Of course, some of the creatures were seriously exaggerated, but yes; many of them did exist and they were an abomination, having been made in wretched uncleanliness. The enemy, in his quest to make what he considers the perfect man, can't create anything so he tries to pervert what God has made. Remember, everything that God made was good. So, Lucifer wanted to find the best mixture of strong animals and people to create these abominations. Fortunately, the most exaggerated tales concerned human hybrids because so few animals are close enough to man for one to impregnate the other; but not from lack of trying," she shook her head in disgust.

"In fact, a few did exist such as the minotaur, which was actually a cross between the bull and a Nephilim. Also, many of the children of the Nephilim were war-mongers who had been taught the art of demonic possession and became so dreaded that the local people called them berserkers, according to Norse mythology."

"So they weren't just in Rome and Greece then?" Dakkar asked. He'd grown up isolated with his clan in Senegal and did not know about the stories or myths they were referring to.

"Absolutely not. The Watchers descended from heaven into various places. We tend to know a bit more about the stories associated with the Greeks and Romans, however these fallen angels had a presence all over the world. Odin, known as one of the gods from Norse mythology was said to have come to earth with his sons Thor, the god of the sky and Frikko, the god of peace and pleasure. Though Odin was referred to as the 'All-father' and was known for his war-like nature, it was the son Thor who was often revered as the mightiest. As always, Satan perverts the truth to suit his purposes. He casts Odin as an evil, war-like tyrant while Thor; who happens to share Lucifer's position as prince of the air, is the good guy. And of course Frikko is loved because he represents every sinful lust and desire."

"In South America," Bridget explained, "the god known as Quetzalcoatl was worshipped. This 'god' was depicted as being a 'feathery serpent' and was the god over the air and wisdom, among other things. Again, the parallels between Satan and the 'god' being worshipped are nearly identical. Quetzalcoatl was also a very bloodthirsty deity and required the deaths of many people to keep him satisfied. If any of you have read the folklore of the Native peoples in North America, you will find many tales about spirits; spirits of the waters, the sky and of the earth. Some of the elements of their accounts have been changed over the centuries, but the truths of these spirits' existence remain."

Laqat, who had been five years old when he had been found by the seeker spoke up. "I remember a bit about my people and how they would pray to the spirits for rain and for the crops. I hadn't thought about that in years, and the memory is hazy at best, but it seems like there was a party or something to honor the spirits." He was silent for a moment as he tried to dig into his mind further to recall more about the events of his early childhood. Unable to remember more, he asked a question. "I thought that the fallen angels were actual beings. Were they actually spirits?"

"No. The fallen Watchers were live beings; that's how they were able to mate with the mortal women. Remember when Lucifer and 1/3 of the angels attempted to challenge God for the throne of Heaven?" When everyone nodded that they did, she explained further.

"Well, those original fallen angels became demons. Using their powers to take on other forms and shapes, they convinced people they were spirits and they should be worshipped. They made people believe they had control over the earth and the elements and somehow held the fate of people in their hands. There were many such festivals in honor of the spirits in hopes of gaining their favor for their crops and during their hunts. Of course, there always had to be a sacrifice made to seal the pact; and that meant the killing of a young woman or a brave warrior in most cases."

Bridget shook her head again, thinking about the many other stories from around the world where people had had encounters with demons in various forms. She told them of the Japanese tale of the Yuki Onna, a female snow demon that killed people. "Many other stories were told of female demons such as Lilith, who, like the Aztec god Quetzalcoatl, is depicted as flying serpent. She is a creature of the night and is said to be a man-hater who kills babies and children."

"You also need to know that in many cases, the people actually knew the beings were demons. In India, the Buddhists have a group of primeval gods known as Asura, and they are often referred to as being a group of demons. They were taught to meditate and chant while aligning their bodies in a sitting position that would make their legs form a triangle. Their hands are placed atop their knees and the sign of Baal is given with their fingers. But they are not the only ones to conjure up spirits and consort with demons. The Egyptian's belief in the sun-god, Ra and how he came down from the heavens to rule and enlighten them are nearly identical to the accounts of other people in the world concerning their gods."

Bridget shocked them by telling them that the accounts of demons and workers of dark magic was not limited to mythology, but also had a presence in Biblical history. "The Bible; both the Old and New Testaments, is littered with stories of magicians, demon possession, soothsayers, diviners, necromancers and all types of spell-casters. When Moses went to the pharaoh to demand the release of God's people and he showed them signs by the power of the Almighty, he was laughed at because there were magicians and practitioners of the dark arts in the ruler's company. In fact, most of the so-called great civilizations had kings and queens who allied themselves with sorcerers and witches. Camelot had Merlin, Ireland's King Conchobhar had the Druid Cathbadh, and the Greeks had Laocoon, Tiresias and the Oracle of Delphi."

She knew she had been speaking on the subject a while, but felt it was imperative that they fully understood all that was going on. "We have learned many scriptures from God's holy Word, but all too often we don't fully understand what it means. We know that our fight is rarely a flesh-and-blood battle and that the real struggle is spiritual, but most people fail to realize just what that means. Satan knows he can't just stand up and say, 'Hey everybody; I'm Lucifer and I want all of you to follow me to the depths of Hell!' No; his ways are highly visible, yet covert at the same time. I call it the smoke-and-mirrors tactic. He puts up the big banners with flashing lights to take people's focus off God. Then he introduces them to things that seem harmless or even beneficial when in fact, he's opening them up to demonic influences. And one of his most destructive and craftiest weapons has been to make people believe that neither he nor God exists."

"Even across other areas on the continent of Africa where most of the people are monotheistic, they have stories about beings who'd descended from the heavens and told them that God was not concerned with them and that He was dissatisfied with what He created. The people's beliefs began to change as they accepted the idea of a disinterested god and that they should put their faith and trust in the ancestors and other 'spirits' who would guide them; often through the practice of divination. Much the same is true of Asia. But of all his tricks, the worse tactic he uses is man's own desire to see himself as God rather than as an image of Him. It is in that place of pride and arrogance that man tries to grasp any concept that allows him to place his will above the will of Jehovah; and believe me when I say that Lucifer is not short on ideas to supply man with. Satan has no respect of person and seeks to disconnect all of man from God and His love, so the list of examples covers the entire world and all the people in it."

They sat in silence for a moment as they took in what they were being told. Picking up the explanation of the hybrid abominations, Bridget went on to discuss the different types of crossbreeds and what they were capable of. "The Watchers unleashed creatures that were so vile and bloodthirsty that the people became more and more afraid of the 'gods.' When God had the Watchers bound and cast down into the Earth, the absence of the cruel, demanding deities would have been celebrated were it not for their off-spring who were proving themselves to be just as bad, if not worse, than their parents. For years the giants tormented the people by abusing them, destroying their homes, livestock and fields for sport, as well as killing them and raping their women at will. However, the presence of the ferocious crossbreeds was competition that the Nephilim did not want, so they killed many of the beasts. These battles and feats became the legendary tales of the half-human offspring of the 'gods' featuring their strength and benevolent natures. Unfortunately however, these stories have often left out their brutality as well as their blood-thirsty nature. The benign stories of Perseus and Hercules as heroes and mighty men have further seduced people into believing that these aberrations are to be accepted and celebrated. So widespread are the stories of kind, super-beings, that if the enemy were to become successful, these demons will be accepted, feted and praised. Even now, most of the world follows the ideals of

Roman society as set down by their 'gods,' especially in the Western part of the world."

Carienne, who had been studying ancient Roman civilization before having to leave home, nodded her understanding of what Bridget was talking about. "I know that most of the American or Western philosophies about government and law were modeled after the rulers of Ancient Rome. Is that part of a trick as well?" At this point the young woman wouldn't put it past the enemy to plant deception in the very fabric of the country.

"You catch on quickly, young one," Bridget answered. "The idea of democracy, as we understand it is a seemingly fair and just system; each person having a say in how they are governed. If it were able to be executed as fairly it would be wonderful indeed. Unfortunately, laws are written by men and men are driven by the desires of the flesh and their sinful, deceitful hearts. In your country Carienne, America proudly declares it's democracy. In so doing, the laws attempt to protect the rights of everyone with respect to all religious beliefs. This 'impartiality' in the law removes God's law from being the standard by which all other laws are based. By ignoring God's Word and His divine law, the law of the land is man-made and therefore fallible and corruptible."

Bridget paused in the telling momentarily. She knew what she was telling them was a lot to take in at one time. But they needed to know the full story of what and whom they were up against, and time was not a luxury they had. Dakkar shook his head slowly. "So we are going to fight against Satan." He said it as a statement and not a question.

"Well, yes and no," she began again. "In an indirect way we are fighting against the enemy, but he won't likely come at us directly. He will send his agents to try and destroy us. You have to understand that his direct involvement could usher in a battle that he knows he can't win. Our task is very simple," she chuckled as she said that part. "We will tell people the truth of God's love for us and His desire that we surrender ourselves to His will willingly."

Tehilla picked up on Bridget's humorless tone. "I take it that you believe we will fail, or that our task isn't really just that simple?"

To this she responded, "I know we will be successful in getting the word out and showing people the truth. I was being a bit facetious because the sad part is that people won't want to hear what we have to say. But the Glory of God will be shown and told. There will be some people who will believe and use this chance to reconnect with the Almighty. But be prepared for the many others who will not. After all, He sent His Son and they refused to accept Him," she answered somberly.

She'd also deliberately avoided mentioning that if the enemy became desperate enough to stop them, he would come out of hiding and face them himself. That was not a possibility she felt comfortable sharing with them at this point. If that became an issue, they would pray about it and proceed in God's will at that time.

The group sat awhile in the early evening quiet, each one harboring their own thoughts. Finally, Carienne raised her hand as if she were in school. At that sign Bridget smiled warmly. "You don't have to raise your hand," she said with a small giggle.

Carienne dipped her head to hide her own chagrined smile. "Okay, Ms. Bridget. But I was wondering about something," she began slowly. "I remember you saying that all of the members of the Order are chosen as very small children.

All except Ms. Imani, that is. How do you know which kid is the right one, and why do you only take small kids?"

Bridget smiled again at the young woman's questions. "Well, those are very good question as well. But why don't we let Jahmil and Princess answer those for you?"

The group turned to the two in expectation of the answer. Princess started first. "Whenever it is nearing time for one of us to go on to be with God, the seer will have a vision of a child. We generally know where they are in the world and if they are boys or girls. The seer then reports this back to Mama Bear and the other members. At that point the seeker, the protector and the healer sets off to find them. When they do, they bring them back here to Sanctuary."

Carienne nodded her understanding of that part of the story and said, "That sounds pretty easy."

Princess smiled at the girl and replied, "Not exactly. You see, in most cases I can describe the child and pinpoint an area where the child is. But because there are often times several children in that location who match the description, it gets a bit tricky for the seeker," she laughed.

At that point, Jahmil took up the explaining. "*Very* tricky sometimes," he chuckled. His tone became a bit more serious as he looked at Carienne and began telling her more about the role of the seekers. "When a new member is chosen by God, we are sent to find them when they are still very young. There are two reasons for this. First, young children have not become jaded and disillusioned to the truth of God. They are still innocent and have no fear, no guile and no reason not to trust God. The bible often speaks of 'having faith like a little child'. The second reason has to do with the pineal gland. This is an area in the brain that is only about the size of a grain of rice. It is dead center at the top of the head. Perhaps you have heard of the 'third eye' or 'God's throne' in man'?"

He took their collective nods as his cue to go on. "Well, that tiny part of the brain, when open and unobstructed, acts as a conduit to the spiritual world. For lack of an easier explanation, it works like an antenna. The thoughts we have and our emotions, desires and prayers are strongest when that area is open. Unfortunately, as most people grow older, deposits settle there and form a callous over that gland, therefore making it more difficult to 'tune in' to God. Carienne, you, Dakkar and Anjelita are descendants of people whose pineal glands are genetically unobstructed, which allows you and your people to do things others cannot. All babies are born with their connection to God open. That's why we get them as small children."

Jahmil paused for a moment and took a sip of the water next to him. "Now as for how we know which child is the right one; that's the fun part," he said with a sarcastic grin. "When were are in the correct area and have narrowed down our lists of possibilities, we seek out the children individually. This is usually done by what law enforcement calls 'breaking and entering.' The seeker then gently turns the child to their right side and whisper the role they are to take in the Order."

Before he could go on, an excited Carienne asked, "You just whisper it? Like saying 'seeker'. Or 'healer'?"

Tehilla reached over and squeezed Carienne's hand gently to calm her. "Let him finishing explaining," she softly admonished her child.

Jahmil caught Tehilla's eye and said softly, "It's quite alright. I like the fact that she is so interested." His gaze stayed on Tehilla so long that Bridget cleared her throat to get him to remember he was supposed to explaining the process further.

Slightly embarrassed, he went on. "Um, yes. Sort of. We don't just say their role like that. We speak respectfully in the ancient tongue."

He knew the girl didn't understand, so he turned to Laqat who was seated beside him. He had the man pull his long plait to the left so everyone could see the right side of his neck. In a hushed and reverent tone, Jahmil whispered, "Jehovah Jireh."

A small star glowed brightly on the man's neck behind his ear. Jahmil turned to Myla and she cocked her head to the left, exposing her neck as well. He then whispered, "Jehovah Rophe," and the same thing happened. Without being asked, Princess leaned over towards Jahmil and let her head fall forward. "El-Roi."

Carienne thought this was the most amazing thing she had ever seen. Since they had been in Sanctuary she had learned many of the words and terms in Hebrew. She understood that Jehovah Rophe meant "The Lord Heals" and that Jehovah Jireh meant "The Lord Provides." She had not heard "El-Roi" before and asked what that meant.

Tehilla wrapped an arm around the girl and said, "It means 'The strong one who sees.'" Carienne looked up at her mother in awe; she was impressed. Tehilla smiled and added softly, "Genesis 16, verse 13."

Jahmil beamed with joy as Tehilla answered Carienne's question. Satisfied with the answers she had been given, she and the rest of the group members began to slowly get up and head off to enjoy the rest of their evening.

As had become her habit, Carienne followed Imani back into the house to assist Ezer and Shama with the after-dinner cleaning. Myla and Princess wanted to go for a swim and took off towards the river. Dakkar, Anjelita and Kafeel headed back to the clearing to practice a bit more before it became too dark. Laqat headed to his small house to make a few last-minute adjustments to the suits he'd made, and Bridget preferred to spend the last of the day in the Garden communing with God.

This left Jahmil and Tehilla alone under the huge tree. Both wanted to talk more about whatever it was growing between them, but neither brought it up. They sat in companionable silence for a while. Jahmil looked at her and asked softly, "will you sing something?" A little while later, the sun made its final decent over the western horizon to the sound of Tehilla's voice being lifted in song once more.

Chapter Twenty-Three: Travel by Starlight

With the exception of Tafilah, Princess, Imani and the remaining two members of the Order, the group prepared to leave Sanctuary. Bridget spent the majority of the preceding day in the Garden and when she rejoined them, she looked fit for battle. She was dressed in a pure white dress that hung to the tops of her feet. Her bronze-colored arms were bare and the lean, powerful muscles were oiled and gleaming. Gone were her soft curls. Her silver hair was parted down the middle and braided back, giving an unobstructed view of the clear beauty of her face. But what drew everyone's attention was the wide crimson belt she wore around her waist that carried a long, unsheathed sword.

The weapon was unlike anything they had ever seen. The blade went from her hip down past her knee. It appeared to be silver, but no one could be sure with the way it glittered in the sunlight iridescently. Awed by the mighty looking weapon, Anjelita stated, "Everybody needs to stand away from Ms. Bridget. That sword looks like it can cut through anything!"

"She can," Bridget replied calmly. "But you will never have to worry; Chaverah won't hurt you." To prove her point, Bridget pulled the weapon out and swung it mightily towards the young woman. Striking the girl's upper arm, she drew back the blade and replaced it in her belt. They all stared wide-eyed at Anjelita's unmarked arm. With that understood, the tall woman walked away from the puzzled looks on Anjelita and Tehilla's faces.

Both ladies turned their gazes on Kafeel in hopes that he could shed more light on what Bridget meant. To their pointed looks, he shrugged. "All I know is that 'Chaverah' means friend.

As you all can see, if she says it won't hurt you, then I wouldn't worry about it."

Myla, who had been watching the exchange with amusement added, "I have learned that if Mama Bear says a mosquito can pull a plow or a duck can pull a truck, don't ask questions; just hook 'em up!" she laughed.

That Sunday morning at dawn, they stood near the river with their hands joined being led in prayer by Tefilah. In addition to asking for His mercy, guidance and safe return, she implored the Almighty to reveal His plan to them so that they might obey. At the end of the entreaty, the old woman dipped her hands in oil and anointed each of them on their heads, hands and feet.

Afterwards, Laqat drove around from the back of his house in a long, sleek, silver vehicle. Like Bridget's sword, it looked like nothing any of them had ever seen. Princess smiled widely. "Wow Laqat, it looks exactly like I envisioned it!" Laqat returned the young girl's smile.

"You have done well, Laqat," Bridget said. The group walked around the conveyance that was similar to a small bus. The front was lower to the ground and the hood was rounded. There were few windows and the body was smooth and extremely shiny. However, the most astonishing part to the onlookers was there were no tires; the vehicle hovered above ground about two feet.

"What is this?" Tehilla asked in awe.

Bridget looked at the still smiling Laqat to have him explain. "It's our mode of transportation. I named her the *Starlight*. Princess had a vision of it the night you all arrived. She shared the vision with Mama Bear and I and I got busy working on it, with Ezer's help." It was clear that Laqat was very excited and very proud of the machine.

"The body is made with material from Bridget's craft when she came to our planet," he further explained.

Bridget nodded and added, "Yes, and that craft was made from a fallen star in my galaxy. It's light-weight and virtually indestructible."

Dakkar, who like most young men loved cars of any kind, asked the next question. "How did you build it if the metal and materials are indestructible? I mean, how could you weld it or cut the pieces?"

That question really excited Laqat. "It's not metal at all. Like Mama Bear said before, 'it is a star'. Stars are living substances that can take a variety of shapes. I had only to talk to it and tell it what I needed it to do." Seeing the confusion on everyone's faces, Laqat explained further. "As you all well know, even the stars obey the will of God. He gave Princess the vision and me the instructions on what to do. But I can give you a better run-down on the road. It's time to go."

The group piled into the vehicle which turned out to be quite spacious. Laqat started off driving, but Jahmil, Kafeel, Dakkar and Tehilla watched as he set the vehicle in motion. "One of the things to know about this bus is that it is solar powered. It can store energy for weeks if necessary, so we need not fear dark or overcast days." Laqat continued showing them that the gears were all identical to a regular automatic car. He went on to tell them that the windshield was not only bullet-proof, but it was a one-way glass. "That way we can see out but no one can see in." He then set the navigational system westward and they headed back towards the States.

As they approached the Mediterranean Sea, Laqat smiled at his friends and said, "You guys are going to love this!" If they had been amazed at the incredible speeds they were traveling at across Iraq, they were rendered speechless when Laqat pushed a button and they traveled over the water. Bridget chuckled at their amazed reaction.

"We can travel as easily over water as we can on land. We can also move under water or take to the sky, but I prefer not to do that. In the past, whenever I have gone out for a flight in Mama Bear's craft, someone catches a glimpse of me and it takes people years to stop talking about the 'unidentified flying object.'" The group sat back and made themselves comfortable as Laqat guided them across the Mediterranean Sea and into the North Atlantic Ocean.

Dakkar, who was a bit edgy about being caught again asked, "Won't we be spotted out here going across open water?" He knew about the type of equipment that ships had to detect anything in the water.

To that question Laqat replied, "Don't worry. We have the equipment to locate any vessel out here so we can stay out sight if anyone is using binoculars. And as for them detecting us with their equipment; they can't. We are virtually invisible to their sonar and AIS, or Automatic Identification Systems because the craft isn't made of anything readily identifiable. And at the speeds we travel, a chance manual sighting is extremely unlikely. The same is true for electronic aerial surveillance."

Impressed again, Dakkar and the others settled in for the day-long trip across the ocean. Shortly before dawn, Bridget awakened the group. "Look ahead. We are about to enter Honduras."

Chapter Twenty-Four: Welcome Home

A yawning Myla stretched and peered out of the wind-shied of the Starlight. "Why are we in Honduras? I thought we were heading to the U.S. Or are we making a stop to look up some of Laqat's family members?" she giggled sleepily at her own joke. She and most of the others knew that nearly 50 years ago, the then five-year-old Laqat was chosen to become the provider.

The man who appeared to be no more than 30 looked back at the girl and smiled. "Even if I knew who they were, they would never believe who I am," he retorted.

In answer to Myla's question, Bridget told them that they needed to begin searching out allies. Her serious tone was one that discouraged further questions, so no one asked any.

Once they were in Honduras and on land, Bridget had Laqat find a suitable hiding place for the Starlight in the unpopulated areas near the border of Guatemala. "We need to travel the rest of the way on foot," she instructed. After attending to their individual needs in the well-appointed Starlight, they had a quick breakfast and said a prayer for safe passage.

The group walked for four days through the uninhabited jungles of Guatemala. Using her sword as a machete, Bridget easily sliced through the thick foliage and overgrowth of the area. The huge, leafy trees blocked out the sun and made the early November day chillier. They had covered over 150 miles, and though they were all pretty tired, they were happy that for once they were not being chased.

The group had purposefully skirted around the cities and heavily populated areas to avoid run-ins with anyone who might try to cause them problems. No one was sure exactly where they were headed or what they might find when they arrived, but all of them were keenly aware of the potential dangers.

As they rested on the evening of the fifth day, Anjelita sat straight up. Her movement alerted the rest of the group, but before they could ask her what was wrong, two fierce-looking wildcats came out of the darkness. Kafeel grabbed his gun and aimed, intending to fire a round to scare them off.

Bridget, who was seated nearest to Kafeel, stayed his hand and looked at first to the animals, then at Anjelita who was slowly rising.

Just as slowly as she had risen, she walked toward them, making low growling sounds. It was obvious to the group that the pair of felines seemed shocked. Within a few tense minutes, the large jungle cats approached her and after sniffing around her for a moment longer, allowed themselves to be petted and stroked. She told them to go and meet the rest of her friends, and the cats began slowly circling the other members of the group.

This terrified the women, but they sat still while the cats familiarized themselves with each of them. Once they were done, they bounded back over to Anjelita and began mewling and jostling for the woman's affections as if they were nothing more than a pair of housecats. It was clear that she was immersed in a conversation with them, and at the end she stood and addressed the group.

"They tell me that there are others who are like me not far from here! They want us to follow them." Anjelita was uncharacteristically excited at the prospect of meeting someone else who was like herself. She didn't know what "like her" actually meant, but the idea of it filled her with hope. Bridget agreed that at first light they would follow the huge spotted cats. They settled back down to rest for the night while the cats went to hunt for their supper.

Just before dawn, Tehilla woke up and headed into the brush to attend her morning needs. Once done, she stood and looked around, admiring the wild beauty of her surroundings. It wasn't like Sanctuary, but it had a beauty that was indescribably. She spent a few long moments taking in the scenery and marveling at God's creation. Overcome by His presence, she began singing in a soft voice and was soon so caught up in her praise, that she hadn't noticed she wasn't alone.

As she finished the first verse of the song, she opened her eyes and saw the two cats sitting less than five feet from her. Fear gripped her for a moment, but when she stopped singing, they looked up at her with a human-like expectancy for her to continue. So she did. By the time she finished the song, the sun was rising and the cats were standing beside her, nuzzling her legs.

She felt Jahmil behind her and turned. "Good morning. It looks like you have an admiring audience," he smiled.

Before she could respond, Anjelita stepped up to them. "Yes. They love music, but we need to get moving. Bridget sent me to get you." Anjelita then crouched down and stroked the cats and told them it was time to go.

They ate a hasty breakfast of fruit and nuts while they walked. They had to nearly run to keep up with Anjelita and the cats, but before the morning was over they had reached a small clearing in what seemed like the thickest part of the jungle.

The cats ran up to a young girl of about 16 years. She turned to them and greeted them fondly, but stopped short when she saw Anjelita. Staggering into the clearing came the rest of the group, breathing hard in some cases; panting in others.

Alarmed, the girl turned and ran towards a small house screaming, "Abuela! Abuela!"

A small, spry, old woman moved quickly from the back of the house to see what the child was screaming about. Grabbing the old woman by the hand and talking so fast it was doubtful the woman could understand a word, she brought her to where Anjelita stood. The woman took one look at Anjelita and instructed the girl to get her father quickly.

The old woman finally shifted her sharp gaze from Anjelita to the rest of the group. "I am Nadah, but everyone here calls me Abuela." Having grown up in a Catholic orphanage in the American Southwest, Anjelita spoke Spanish fluently. She began introducing the woman to the rest of the group and learned that Bridget, Laqat and Jahmil also understood the language as well. Carienne confessed that she had taken Spanish in school for nearly three years, but had difficulty keeping up with all that was being said.

The woman was cordial, but not overly friendly. It was clear that she did not know what to make of these foreigners. "How do you come to be here?" she asked.

Glancing momentarily at Bridget, Anjelita told her simply; "they brought us," referring to the cats who were lying at her feet. The woman continued to look at Anjelita, but finally turned towards the house and said, "Come."

They were led around to the back of the small house and shown to a large table with bench-style seats that reminded them of where they'd taken their meals in Sanctuary. She disappeared into the house for such a long time that the group wondered if she had forgotten about them. When she did return, she was carrying a large tray.

There were two huge steaming bowls of food. The first had a variety of cooked greens in it. The second bowl contained what looked like mashed potatoes, but the color was orange. On the side of the bowls were flat pieces of bread.

Before they could ask what the dishes were, another girl stepped out of the house with a large bucket of water. The girl was introduced by Abuela simply as Lanaia. The girl appeared to be in her later teens, and no one missed the fact that she bore a strong resemblance to Anjelita. She was not as tall, nor did she have Anjelita's coloring; but the shape of the eyes, nose and mouth were nearly identical. But, since their hostess didn't mention it, they decided to play along and see what was going on before asking questions.

Abuela sensed the strangers had questions, but instead of opening a discussion, she told them to use the bucket of water to wash their hands and begin eating. "We eat first. Then we will talk when Mmoju arrives." No one knew who she was referring to, but rather than risk offending their hostess, they did as they were told.

As they were eating the food that was quickly identified as pounded yam, wild greens and bread made of corn flour, the younger girl Abuela had sent off earlier returned with a tall, handsome, dark-skinned man who appeared to be in his early to mid-fifties. While the group finished their meal in silence, the man and Abuela stepped inside the house to talk privately.

165

When they returned he introduced himself as Mmoju. Before he addressed the rest of the group further, he asked Anjelita to come with him. Glancing at Bridget before she stood, she acknowledged the nearly imperceptible nod to mean she should follow the man. She didn't really want to be separated from her friends, but was confident that she could take care of herself if he tried to harm her; though she felt that he wouldn't.

Abuela then instructed the younger girl, whom she introduced as Daieh, to get some food and go into the house. She then told the group to follow her. Lanaia picked up the remaining food and the polished wooden plates they had eaten from and headed into the house as well.

Abuela led them through a stand of trees to a long, low wooden structure. Surrounding the building were sculptures of various animals. The old woman ushered them inside and they saw several benches lined in the middle of the room. At the far end were several candles sitting atop a gleaming wooden alter. In front of it lay a beautiful colored woven carpet and the group knew they were inside of a church.

"We don't have much space around here, but you can rest safely here." Abuela moved to the back of the building and produced several large pillows and handmade blankets from a cupboard built into the far wall. She set about making them pallets near the back. "Rest now. Mmoju will come for you when it is time." The woman said no more and exited the building.

Tehilla broke the silence following the woman's departure by asking, "Should we be afraid?"

Bridget smiled at the woman and answered. "Save your fear for the Lord, daughter. But rest assured that we are in no danger here." With that, Bridget settled herself down on one of the pallets and laid down to rest. Having no other choice, the others did the same.

Chapter Twenty-Five: In My Father's House

Mmoju considered himself to be the happiest man in the world as he led Anjelita to the clearing near his house. As an elder, he had a small place to himself, unlike the common houses shared by the single men. Before tragedy stuck their village, there were at least a dozen such places for the unmarried men. When his small house was being erected, he had protested that because his wife did not live with him, he could reside in the common house as well. Now he saw that having a private place to bring his daughter to was a blessing.

Anjelita was excited and nervous all at once. She was actually with her father! As a child living in an orphanage, she had often wondered about her parents. She knew that her mother had died during childbirth, but she'd always wondered about her father. She had spent countless hours wondering if she had been unwanted by him, or had her mother's cross-country trek been the result of him turning out his pregnant woman? Of course she'd had no answers, so like most resilient children in her situation, she had imagined that he never knew about her at all. She dreamed that maybe he had known and had spent the past quarter-century searching the world for her. But now she didn't have to wonder; he was right beside her and she knew the truth.

"You look just like her," Mmoju said, breaking the silence that settled around them as they sat near his house.

"Really? I've always wondered what she was like. How she looked. What she did," Anjelita replied.

Mmoju smiled softly. "She was a beautiful woman, inside and out and she cared about others genuinely. Our people have stayed separated from the rest of the world for several millennia because we are committed to following our Heavenly Father and the teachings of His Son. In so doing, we strive to treat others with love and respect. But, since people have their different personalities they sometimes obey the commandment because it is right; and not because it is in their hearts to do so."

As Anjelita listened, she was a bit shocked at this insight. When she'd learned about how her people had separated themselves from others to maintain their connection to God, she had never considered that any of them would not hold His love in their hearts to the fullest degree possible. Not wanting to miss anything Mmoju was saying, she made a mental note to ask him more about that later.

"But my Anuka was not like that," he was saying. The love and affection in his eyes and tone were clear. "She truly loved everyone with an open honesty that made some people consider her to be a bit naïve. Of course, no one would ever be loco enough to challenge her in any way," he added, chuckling.

Seeing the confused look on his daughter's face, he explained. "In addition to being the most beautiful and loving woman around, she was also the strongest." He had to suppress his laugh when he saw how Anjelita's eye's widened is surprise.

"What do you mean?"

"I mean that almost no one could best her in any physical challenge. Every year in the spring we have contests. Actually, they are more like exhibitions. Every unmarried person between the ages of 16 and 24 participates. There are challenges of speed, strength, agility and intellect. Of the first three, no one else could beat her; except me of course," he said that with a sly smile.

Anjelita grinned as well. She was intrigued by the games and asked him to tell her more.

"There were foot races along the river. Judges were seated at the far end and the first person to make the 20-mile run would be given a large, 50 pound stone. Each person to arrive after the first would be given a stone in decreasing size. Depending on the number of participants, the stones could decrease by two to five pounds."

"But that doesn't make sense. Why penalize the first person? Isn't the point to be the fastest?" she asked.

"Not really. Of course speed is a part of the challenge, but endurance is just as important. Any one of us can run 20 miles easily; even Abuela can do that and she is almost 80. But to run carrying an additional 50 pounds the 20 miles back is harder; especially since you have to watch for other runners who may have fallen."

"Wait, so if you're in the lead and someone falls, you have to stop and help them?" That seemed like the oddest thing, given they were in a race.

"Yes. Winning means nothing is your kinsmen are all dead," he said that part with a sadness in his eyes that gave Anjelita pause. Catching himself lest he succumb to memories that had no place in this happy reunion, he went on.

"If someone has fallen, stopped or can't continue; you stop and offer them assistance. Once they reach the judges at the 20-mile mark, the stone they are given is in a large sack. Also in the sack is water and bandages in case of emergency. When you stop to help someone, they then offer you their stone."

Anjelita stared at him. "You stop to help them and they give you more weight to carry?"

"Correct. It is called a burden of love. Once you have their stone and know that they will be alright, you resume the race." Smiling at her confusion, he told her "When you reach the end; which is where the race begins, it is not always the person who arrived first who wins. The person who returns with the most stones is declared the winner."

Anjelita didn't know what to make of that, so she said nothing as he concluded his explanation. "The race represents life, and the stones are the burdens of sin we all carry. Stopping to pick up the burdens of others reminds us of Christ's sacrifice. As He made that journey to Calvary, He alone shouldered the burden of our sins. Because of Him, we don't have to. For us, the heavy stones are a light thing; after all, no one was whipping us up the hills and we would not have to die at the end of the journey. It also reminds us that in life, helping others carry their burdens makes the trip worth taking."

Shaking her head at the uniqueness of the race, she didn't have the heart to ask about the other challenges. So instead, she asked him about his claim of being the only person to beat her mother.

At that, Mmoju smiled widely. "Like I told you before; your mother was both swift and loving. It was that second trait that put her in the lead. That year, over 25 people were in the race with half being between 16 and 18. Being that they were still pretty young, they had not learned to pace themselves and had little endurance. By the time they reached the five-mile mark heading back with their stones, they were exhausted. Anuka had already stopped and assisted three of the young women and had picked up an additional 124 pounds."

Mmoju paused briefly and smiled at the memory. "That was in addition to her own 48-pound stone; since she was second only to me. I had stopped a couple times to assist others and was rewarded with 120 pounds of stones to add to my own 50. By the time we were about seven miles from the finish line, I noticed Anuka didn't look too good. The strain on her was clear, so I offered to lighten her load. She told me no; she was fine and that she could make it. Lord, that woman could be stubborn when she wanted to be."

Anjelita smiled at the description that had been applied to her many times growing up.

"She was slowing down, but still running as we came upon the last five miles. For a moment, I thought she would tough it out and make it in, but all of a sudden, she stopped short and fell to her knees. I rushed over to her and gave her some water, but after a couple more minutes I knew she couldn't take another step. So I scooped her up; rocks and all, and finished the race with her in my arms."

"So you won the race and got the girl, huh?"

"Sure did," he stated proudly. "500 pounds of solid rock and woman," he chuckled. "Before the race, she and I had bested all challengers in wrestling and had faced each other. I won that challenge too; barely. But her being a seer made defeating her in any intellectual challenges impossible, so she had won that and the agility challenge. Since we were tied in all the events, I challenged her to be my wife," the inner glow he exuded spoke volumes to the love he still had for her mother.

"Wow!" Anjelita gushed. "That is so romantic!" They shared twin smiles for a few moments while silence resettled. She had a million questions she wanted to ask him, but focused on one. "You said my mother was a seer?"

Mmoju turned to face her. "Yes. And a very powerful one. The gift of sight was stronger in her than in any of the others who share that gift."

"So there are other people who can see things here as well?"

"Yes. It is a fairly common gift among our people, as are strength and speed." He was pleased that Anjelita was so interested in learning about their people.

"And shape-shifting," she added. Since their arrival she had been anxious to meet others who could do the things she could. She'd already learned that her speed, strength and ability to see things that would happen was not unique to her and she was relieved and elated. When she looked over at Mmoju, he seemed shocked.

Wary, she asked, "Did I say something wrong, Father?" She was just getting used to having a father of her own and hoped she'd not offended him with her questions.

"No," he answered hastily. "No you didn't." He peered at her for a few long moments before asking, "Anjelita, can you change your form?"

His serious tone made her nervous. "Um, yes." In her attempt to explain that she hadn't meant any disrespect, she quickly added, "I thought everyone here could do that." Uncharacteristic tears were welling up in her eyes.

Mmoju reached over and hugged her to him tightly. He knew she thought she had upset him and he wanted to make sure she knew she hadn't. When he finally turned her loose, he gently wiped away the tears that had fallen down her cheeks. "You did nothing wrong. I was just surprised to hear that you have that gift."

"So, no one else can change?" She didn't know why, but the thought of no one else being able to do what she could saddened her. Since their arrival, she had imagined a whole tribe of people who looked like her and shared her abilities.

"Not in a long while." He thought of how best to explain things to her. "Remember I told you that some of our people are different?" When she nodded, he continued. "Well, over the years our clan has become weaker. The elders and I have noticed the changes; especially in some of the young ones. Many have begun to question why we live as we do. And while they still enjoy the benefits of our connection to God, they have been exposed to some of the influences from the outside world. So while we are still much more connected to Him than many in the outside world, some of the gifts are no longer with us. Anuka had been the last seer born to our people in nearly 30 years, and there has not been a shape-shifter in over 100 years," he told her.

Smiling, he added, "Until now. You are both a seer and a shape-shifter; two very powerful gifts,"

Anjelita was buoyed by the encouragement. When he asked her to show him her gift, she didn't hesitate. Standing a ways from him in the clearing, she changed into a bear, a giraffe, a bird and finally a jaguar. She returned to her original form as Mmoju smiled and told her what she could was most excellent. "I see that you can take any form, and that is wonderful!"

His tone became a bit more serious. "Just make sure you don't take the form of a serpent," he warned.

Anjelita stilled. "Why not," she asked. She was afraid to tell him that she had already taken the form of a Blue Krait during the fight with the policemen back in the States.

"No one ever has, is all. The serpent was the animal the enemy used to deceive Eve in the garden. It believed itself to be more cunning and intelligent than the other animals. So its own hubris and pride made it easily used by the enemy. That's why we don't take that form." Mmoju noticed a slight shift in the young woman's mood, but decided not to question her about it.

Instead, he looked over the clearing and saw that the sun was starting to go down. "Come," he told her. "We'd better head back to the others before they send Juba and Jalle after us," he laughed. Smiling once more, Anjelita followed him back the way they had come.

Early that evening, the group was awakened by a smiling Anjelita. "Get up everybody. We have to talk." Individually the members of their party sat up and stretched. They looked up to see a very excited Anjelita, along with Mmoju, Lanaia, Daieh, Abuela and a few other people they had not seen before.

A smiling Mmoju greeted them again and asked them to come and sit on the benches. The five men and women who were with Mmoju sat on one of the long benches facing them. Their ages varied some, but it was clear they were all 40 and over; and in the case of one of the men; *way* over. Each of them were dressed in long, flowing robes in bright, vibrant colors. Some were deep red with patterns of gold and black, while others were purple, green or orange with similar patterns embroidered along the sleeves and collars.

The women took seats on the bench facing their hosts while Kafeel, Jahmil, Laqat and Dakkar made themselves comfortable on the hard-packed earth beside them. Lanaia and Daieh took seats behind the women.

Turning to the group of elders as he stood, Mmoju asked them for permission to speak. One of the men handed Mmoju an elaborately carved staff and granted his request. With that, Mmoju thanked them and began the meeting by welcoming the visitors. He then introduced the people with him as the council of elders. Abuela, they already knew, but she was introduced as Nadah. Seated with her were three other women and two men. Tenee, Loah, Malan, Jafee and Kono were their names respectively. All of them had dark skin and nodded a welcome to the visitors. After the greetings, Mmoju got right down to business.

"I am very glad to meet each of you, and thank you for bringing Anjelita home to us." Jahmil was quietly translating the conversation to the rest of the group. Upon hearing Mmoju's comment, Carienne and some of the others glanced quickly from their friend to these people.

He continued. "Many years ago, my wife Anuka and I were expecting our first child. Anuka was a powerful seer and forewarned us that many men were coming to the place we'd called home for many centuries." Where at first he had been smiling, his expression and tone saddened. "Even though she was never wrong, I decided to stay and fight for our land. I was young and full of pride. I believed that I could lead my people to victory against these men." He hung his head in shame.

"I was wrong and that pride cost us all greatly." He was quiet for several minutes. The elders also hung their heads and one of the women dashed away tears. Mmoju raised his head and went on. "Before the men came, I sent Anuka away so she and our unborn child would be safe. We fought the soldiers for several days, and with the help of our jaguar brothers and many of the other animals, we were able to hold our ground for a while. But in the end, only a small group of us remained. We proved to be no match for their numbers and guns, so we had to run or face being rounded up and imprisoned or executed."

Again, the man paused in the telling of his story. The emotions of sadness and shame displayed on his face were unmistakable to all who were there. "I had been injured during the fight, but I struck out anyway to find my wife. After only two days, I was so weak that I nearly died. That's when the jaguars found me. They ran and got Abuela, Jafee and Kono who brought me to the camp they had set up. By the time I was well enough to travel, Abuela told me that Anuka no longer walked the earth." The man turned from the group and wiped away the tears that had been standing in his eyes during the telling.

In a quiet, but clear voice, Abuela added to the story. "I am a seer, but my gift is not as strong as Anuka's was. I could see her far away in a foreign land. She was in childbirth; that part I was sure of. But I couldn't see the delivery because my vision faded when she died. I could almost feel her spirit leaving her body." The old woman paused momentarily, and then continued.

"I believed she was in the United States, but I had no idea where. It is a big place and with Anuka passing into the Spirit world, I had no connection to go on. I didn't know if you were a boy or girl, or even if you had lived, although I have prayed for you and your safe return to us daily." She gave a small smile to Anjelita.

"So when you walked up, I knew in my heart who you were. The child of Mmoju and Anuka returned to us. Besides, you look like her, and you have your father's eyes."

The group talked a bit longer when Lanaia stood and asked to be excused. The young woman claimed to be tired and ready to go home. Mmoju looked disappointed. "I thought you would be happy to learn that you have an older sister and that she is back home where she belongs."

177

To this Lanaia smiled. "Yes Father, I am happy to know her. But it has been a long day. Besides, I think Mama wanted me to help her prepare for tomorrow." Mmoju could tell by his daughter's nervousness that there was more to her departure than just her claims of fatigue, but he didn't feel this was the time or the place to interrogate her further, so he nodded his consent for her to leave.

"Are you coming Daieh?" she asked her younger sibling.

The teenager shook her head no. "I will stay here with Father and Abuela." The mask Lanaia wore to keep her emotions in check slipped momentarily and her anger at Daieh's refusal to leave with her was plain. Without another word, she turned on her heel and left the building.

Mmoju turned to the group and apologized for his daughter's behavior, but rather than dwell on the young woman's mood, he went on with the story. "After the fight and learning that my wife was dead, I had to choose another wife. Unfortunately, we had lost so many of our people that I had to marry a woman from a nearby village. She is not of our clan, but I believed at the time that she would embrace our ways. After Daieh was born I realized that she had no such intentions. She was raised to pray to the Virgin Mary and a host of other saints represented by idols. Lanaia follows the ways of her mother's people. She goes to their schools, watches television and prefers all of the comforts of the world to the simple life we lead here. Only Daieh stays with us and learns the ways of our people. I have lost much, but I am glad that God has blessed me with a daughter who loves truth." He smiled with pride at Daieh.

"And now He has sent my firstborn home to me. He is worthy of the highest praise!"

After Lanaia's abrupt departure, everyone noticed that some of the tension drained from the room. Carienne had been able to feel the young woman's anger and frustration, but had no idea why the girl had felt that way. In the silence that followed Lanaia's leaving and Mmoju's story, Bridget spoke up. "We are very grateful for your hospitality, but there is some business we must discuss. We came here to get your support. "

"Yes. I knew there was a reason that you all have traveled all this way, and it was more than just reuniting Anjelita with us." Abuela stated.

Kono spoke up then. He had been staring intently at Bridget since they arrived. "Before you tell us what you need from us, tell us who you really are. I can sense something is different about you."

Bridget smiled at the older man. "Yes, you are right." She then spent the next hour telling their group who she was and where she came from. She patiently answered their many questions, and in the end, earned their approval, trust and respect. Jafee and Malan shocked the group by telling them what they knew of her people.

"For thousands of years our people have said that when man was young and the world was turning away from God, our people separated from the evil-doers and made a home among the animals. They said that when He looked down from the heavens He vowed to destroy man. He sent a great flood to cleanse the earth, but He would spare a pair of animals."

Loah and Tenee joined the telling of the story at that point. "We were told to travel to where a man named Noah lived. Back then, many of our people could transform into animals, and so they did. Once the waters rescinded, our people left the boat and journeyed back to their homes. They were told to remain in animal form until they had had one male and one female of the species they had taken the form of. The people of our clan had taken the forms of jungle cats, which is why we are so close to the large felines and call them our brothers and sisters. After that, they were allowed to resume their original form. Shortly after the Great Flood, the children of Noah began to turn away from God again. We cried out to the Lord and begged Him not to destroy the world again. Then we are told of something amazing happening. A woman from another world came and told us that God had a plan for us all. She spoke special words to some of our children and a star glowed on two of their necks! She took them with her, but said that when God was ready, she would return."

Tehilla, Dakkar and the others stared at Bridget as if they had never seen her before. They all knew that the big woman was immortal and that she had been on Earth for centuries, but none of them had any idea she had been here Pre-Deluge. Also previously unknown was that she had visited Anjelita's ancestors.

"Wow!" Tehilla exclaimed in a reverent, hushed tone. "Here we all are in the 21st century after Christ lived, talking and gathering support for events that He knew would take place since the beginning of Creation."

Looking up at the rest of the people in the church, she added, "It's very humbling and somewhat overwhelming. To think that all my life I have been going through my days totally unaware what He had planned for me. I always knew there was no such thing as coincidence, but this detailed planning..." her voice trailed off as she came into the understanding of the awesomeness of God and His divine foresight.

Jahmil reached over and gave Tehilla's hand an affectionate squeeze. He and the others knew how she felt because they too, were humbled by the power and greatness of the Lord. All over the small church, His power was being acknowledged. Some had raised their hands and were quietly praising Him, while others had their heads bowed and were praying.

After some time had passed, Bridget focused her attention on Loah and the elders. "Yes. This is true. I am glad that your people have continued to share that part of the story through these many years."

Kafeel and the others were still amazed at learning she had been there with the ancestors of these people before, and could not help looking at their friend with surprise. To their astonished looks, she chuckled. "I had to gather the first members of the Order myself. The first protector and seer came from this clan."

As was his way, before speaking, Dakkar stood up. Shaking his head he laughingly told them, "My family has told me a similar story as well. We were told to transform into various birds. I never knew that the woman they said came from the stars was you, Ms. Bridget. I guess I always thought those were just stories because no one from my clan can change their forms."

Bridget assured him that they were not just stories, and were an account of events that happened more than 4,000 years ago. They spent the remainder of the evening and well into the night discussing the reason for their arrival and what they wanted from Mmoju and his people.

Chapter Twenty-Six: Redemption

Major General John Alexander Riley lay on the floor of his posh office suite gasping for breath. What he had just seen was so horrific that his mind could barely process it, and his body had gone into cardiac arrest because of it. He had just looked pure evil in the eye.

As he lay in the dimly lit room his mind replayed various events in his life. He thought of all the things he had wanted to do, but now would never have the chance. He stared at the plush, hunter green carpet he was laying on. He remembered choosing it because it reminded him of the forests he had flown over so many times in the past. The interior decorator had protested his desire for the green carpet and the sky-blue walls. She'd tried to explain that the colors did not match or complement each other. But once the room was finished, he'd liked the feel of it and it felt comfortable to him.

He fought to remain conscious, but knew his end was near. His last coherent thoughts settled on something his mother had taught him. In a weak, nearly inaudible voice he began reciting the Lord's Prayer. "Our Father, Who art in heaven. Hallowed be Thy name..."

Riley had never put much stock in prayers and found it oddly comforting that in his last moments of life, he would find himself doing so. Though his mother and grandmother had both been women of faith, the only time he'd ever prayed was the day his only child died. He remembered standing in the hospital room as the doctor explained to a then 28-year-old-Riley that his son had an inoperable brain tumor. He'd spent most of the night in the hospital chapel staring at the statue of Jesus standing with open arms, praying that his precious three-year-old son not be taken from him. When a nurse came and found him in the wee hours of the morning and told him his son was dead, he'd turned his back on that statue and never prayed again.

"Give us this day..." he continued. His recitation was cut short by the sight of a pair of worn work boots. He willed his head to turn so he could see better, and what he saw was a man in a janitor's uniform standing over him. Riley thought he was hallucinating, and blinked a few times until the man's face came into focus.

The man smiled down at Riley and told him "That's what He is doing now; if you let Him."

Riley was weak, but managed to turn his body a bit to see the man more clearly. "What did you say?" He wasn't sure he'd understood what the man had said, but he thought his time would be better spent getting to a hospital. "Call for an ambulance," he urged the man.

Without leaving Riley's side the man repeated his earlier statement. "That is what He is trying to do. You asked God to give you this day, and He has."

Riley figured the man must be crazy. "No. I need a doctor! Please!"

The man shook his head. "No John. What you need is to know the truth. And the truth is that God loves you and He is here for you. Only He can heal what is wrong with you."

Riley turned his face from the man. "God? God doesn't love me. Mister, you don't know all of the things I have done. I was working with the devil! It's too late for me. So either call for a doctor or let me die in peace!" The tears were rolling down his face, but he was too weak to wipe them away. He asked himself why God was doing this to him? Why now? Where was

God when his son lay there dying? Where was God when his wife had called him crazy and left him? And where was God when that demon Cilfure offered him the chance to reclaim his life, only to have him nearly take it from him? The last thing he wanted or needed was some preaching janitor in his final moments. Riley finally turned back to the man. "Are you going to send for an ambulance or not?"

Still smiling, the man answered Riley simply. "No. You don't need a doctor; I already told you that. You are already healed. God is not ready for you to come to Him yet."

Riley was angry at this point. He'd never been a patient man and was used to having his orders carried out so, without thinking, he jumped up and shouted at the man. "Can't you see I'm laying here almost dead? And all you can do is sit there with that stupid grin talking about God!" Riley stopped his rant short. He realized he was not still lying on the floor. He was standing up and he was not in pain. "Wh-What's going on?" In spite of his regained strength, he felt strange.

The man, who had been hunkered down beside Riley, slowly rose to his feet. For the first time Riley really looked at the man. He was fairly tall; roughly six feet. His skin was golden and his hair was black and wavy. He appeared to be muscular judging by the solid-looking bulges under his uniform shirt.

"John, you are not about to die; not now anyway. God is the only healer you need. But He wants to heal more than just your body tonight. He wants to heal your spirit and your mind. He has a great plan for you, but you have to be willing to let Him in. Will you let Him in John?"

There was sincerity in the man's eyes and a truth in his voice so powerful, it made Riley sink down into a chair and put his head in his hands. "How can I? God doesn't want me; not after all I've done." His voice was shaking and tears were welling up in his eyes. "Don't you see that? I'm too old to be of any use to God now. I've been a fool for so long, and I've done too many things." He wept silently for a few moments.

The janitor knelt down in front of him. "No John, you're wrong. God knows what you have done, but He stands ready to forgive you. He loves you so much that He is giving you this chance right now. He will wipe your slate clean if you just let Him. And don't worry about how old you are; God has all the time in the world. He created time and will give you as much as you need to serve your true purpose. The question is; will you let Him in? Will you follow Him?"

John Alexander Riley fell to his knees on the plush, hunter green carpet of his office and cried out to the Lord. He said yes to God, and yes to do His will. More tears spilled from his eyes, but this time, they were tears of utter joy. By the time Riley looked up, the sun was streaming through the window of his office and he was alone. He looked around for the janitor, but the man was gone. As he stood up, he saw a badge on the floor. It was one that the contractors who worked in the building used, and he figured it came from the janitor last night. He picked it up and on it was the smiling face of the man who was there last night, and the name said simply; "Gabriel."

Chapter Twenty-Seven: Game Change

As Cilfure left the building that housed Riley's office, he was furious. For years he had hunted down and killed every one of the people who might have posed a threat to his plans. Through the years he had come across various children who he believed was one of the Unifiers and had taken great joy in having each one killed. He had especially enjoyed the pain it caused the families of his victims. Some had been from prominent families like the Lindbergh's and the Goebbels', while others had been dirt poor. He recalled fondly how he'd been unsure as to which of the Goebbels' children had powers so he'd instructed his long-time disciples, Joseph and Magda Goebbels to kill all six of their children and then to kill themselves.

Throughout the centuries, the gender, race, nationalities or political standing of the children meant nothing. To him, they were all useless sacks of meat that deserved whatever tragedies befell them.

Ever since God created man, he had hated them and did everything he could to destroy them. While he didn't have the power to kill them outright, he mused, he made sure they did it to themselves. Those "faithful few" whom he had not been able to get, he watched for and waited; always alert for an opportunity to sway them. But now, with the confirmed arrival of the Unifiers, he knew his time was running short.

When Riley captured the boy from Senegal, he should have had him killed immediately. At the time, he did not know that the boy was to be one of the Unifiers. He had known about the boy's people for millennia, but had not considered him a threat. He'd had his spies tell him everything they knew about the boy, but aside from the fact that he shared the gifts of his people, he had considered him only marginally useful to his plans.

So instead of killing him, he had decided to extract some of Dakkar's DNA to help him create the perfect man; a man in his own image. The work he was having done in cloning was nearly perfected. Soon, he would be able to mesh the DNA of the remaining Nephilim with the boy's DNA and create a whole nation of warriors like the world had never seen.

Though the years of mixing with humans had rendered them indistinguishable from man, the Nephilim still carried with them the guile and ruthlessness of their fore parents. They shared the same bloodlines as Hitler, Stalin, Genghis Khan, Mussolini, Napoleon and hundreds of other warriors, assassins and mercenaries. With no lingering connection to God, this new breed would be totally without conscious and obedient only to him and their own lust for blood, violence and destruction. The power they would wield in his name would make their predecessors look like choir boys. With them, he could enslave all of mankind, outlaw all forms of religion that did not have him at the center, and eradicate the Christians once and for all.

Thoughts of how his warriors would usher in an era of his complete reign had tempered his anger somewhat. As it stood, he needed more of the boy's DNA as well as the other two Unifiers to complete his plan, but Riley was a fool! He'd let the boy escape and now he was with the other two Unifiers becoming stronger.

To make matters worse, the three of them were with the Star Woman and her merry band of helpers. He'd known about her coming and speaking with the groups of people who were still connected to God, but had only recently discovered that she had returned. For years he'd searched for her and her people, but could never find where they were hiding. Stopping them would prove difficult, but he still had a few good tricks up his sleeves.

His first move was to call a meeting of his faithful followers. These included many of the world leaders and spanned religion, science, politics and entertainment. The group he'd assembled that afternoon in Rome had country presidents seated next to pop music icons. There were business scions rubbing shoulders with religious figures.

He stood in front of the gathering of 100 men and women and smiled. "My friends. The time has come to fulfill our destiny; to become rulers of this world. Not just in our own backyards, but we will have dominion over the whole earth!" The practiced conviction in his voice was met with thunderous applause.

"There is only one threat to our success, and we will crush it. There is a group of three people who are intent on destroying our way of life. I have intercepted their plans to bring down our world economies. They plan to use technology to rob us all and control us. Are we going to allow them to do this?" The room shuddered with the resounding NO's that the attendees shouted out in unison.

"Good. Then we must be prepared to stop them at all cost!" Again the room erupted into cheers as the members of the group pledged their allegiance. He spent the rest of the evening explaining to them what they each had to do.

Chapter Twenty-Eight: Sibling Rivalry

Lanaia rushed back to the village as fast as her legs could carry her. When she reached the well-appointed house she shared with her mother and her uncle Alejandro, she was nearly out of breath. "Mama!" she called. "Come quickly. I have news!"

The attractive, 40-year-old Latina emerged from the kitchen, drying her hands on her apron. "What is it? I am up to my elbows in ceviche, and you were supposed to be here hours ago to help me! It's bad enough that your sister insists on staying with those savages, but you know better!" Esperanza's rant was cut short by Lanaia.

"Mama, listen to me! They're here!"

Esperanza stood stock still. She didn't have to ask who the girl was referring to; she'd always known. "Are you sure? I mean, how do you know?" She wanted all of the details because she had to be sure. Even though her name meant "hope," she didn't dare hope that her time of torture was coming to an end.

Nearly 22 years ago, a group of people were discovered living in a remote area of her country. She had been taught that these people were highly dangerous and that they worshiped animals. Their skin was jet-black; a sign of their allegiance to the enemy. She remembered her single-parent father, who was a soldier, telling her and her younger brother Alejandro of how they even slept with some of the animals.

She had been raised to believe in God and spent many hours lighting candles and praying to the saints and the Virgin Mary for her father's safe return the spring he left with the other soldiers to confront them. But not even the saints could protect him from their evil. Her father had been killed during the fight between their government and those savages.

When the officials brought back the bodies of the men who had died in battle, she had to go make positive identification and to ready him for burial. She was prepared to find her father's body riddled with bullet holes or punctured by a blade. But to find that he had been savaged by a wild beast made her stomach roil. The claw marks on his face and chest coupled with the unmistakable fang-marks let her know her beloved father had died a horrific and gruesome death.

As a soldier, her father did not earn a lot of money, but was able to provide food and shelter for her and her and Alejandro, who at the time was only ten. She'd just turned 18, and had few marketable skills. Even with no dowry, she was pretty enough to find a man to marry, but very few were willing to take her and her brother. She refused to sell her body, but things were becoming desperate. She blamed the savages for the problems she was having and hated them for what they had done to her family.

On the day the landlord came to the house demanding that she either pay the rent or get out, a man came to see her. He gave her an envelope choked full of cash and told her that he needed her to do something very special. She was assured that it would not be anything that would bring damnation to her immortal soul, but it would help her country. When he told her she was to marry the leader of those people, she tried to refuse, but her family was poor and the money being offered would help them.

The man explained that her only job would be to marry the man, and keep an eye on him and their people. They were searching for someone with special powers, and when they arrived she was to notify him. He confirmed that though they were savages, and their customs were foreign and bestial, the man would not harm her in any way. She was to act like a willing bride and go to him whenever he asked.

Knowing that her family's future depended on her decision, she agreed. She married the man they called Mmoju and had two daughters. She tried fiercely to keep them from spending much time with his people, but her youngest child refused to live in the house with her. Even as a toddler, every time she brought the girl home, she would wail and scream all night. Finally, she gave up and allowed Daieh to stay there with her father and his mother. But now her favorite child, Lanaia, was standing before her telling her that someone had arrived.

"Yes, I'm sure. She is Mmoju's eldest daughter. The one he had with his first wife, Anuka. She came this morning with a group of people and Mmoju took her off to talk to her and learn what she could do. I followed them for a while and saw her change from being a woman into a lion! It's true, Mama! After I saw that, I rushed back to Abuela's house so I wouldn't be missed. They held a council meeting with the strangers and the elders."

Esperanza felt faint. According to Lanaia, the daughter of Mmoju was a shape-shifter. During the early years of her marriage to Mmoju, he had tried to get her to accept their ways. They told her about their special bonds with nature and animals. She was told that in the past, some of their people could take the forms of the animals, though no-one had had that ability in nearly 100 years. She had witnessed first-hand the feats of strength, speed and agility of his people, and that had been enough to convince her of their allegiance ti the enemy.

Mmoju's mother, Nadah, could also predict the future. On several occasions the old woman had told her things that would happen, and she'd never been wrong. Admittedly,

Esperanza was always afraid of the strange old woman, and believed more than ever that they were in league with the devil himself. How else could she explain the things she'd seen?

She clutched the golden crucifix that hung around her neck. "What did they say in this meeting?" She wanted to know everything she could before she alerted her contacts.

"Nothing much. They just introduced themselves and then Mmoju starting crying about his dead wife Anuka. I couldn't stomach it anymore and left. I wanted to get home to tell you as soon as I could."

Lanaia's mouth was turned up in a snarl. She hated Mmoju as much as her mother did. All her life she was told that she should feel a connection to the animals around them, and especially to the jaguars. She was afraid of those huge cats and hated everything else about her father's people. Then when Daieh was born, she seemed to be everything that he wanted; she loved the jaguars, always wanted to pray with the clan, and talked non-stop about the goodness of the Almighty. Daieh was Mmoju's favorite and everyone knew it. That was why she never called him Father unless she was within his earshot.

"You have done well, my child," Esperanza stated as she rushed to her bedroom to retrieve the special phone she was given by the man who'd come to visit her. She had spoken to him a few times since she had married Mmoju, but this time, she had real news to report.

The man answered the phone and Esperanza wasted no time in telling him all she knew. In truth, the man scared her, even though she remembered him as being extremely handsome. When she'd finished telling him everything, he gave her clear directions on what she was to do next. He told her that he was arranging for a very special ingredient to be delivered to her tonight. From there, she had her instructions. Esperanza's hands were shaking so badly when she hung up the phone that she nearly dropped it.

Chapter Twenty-nine: The Walls Have Ears

As the meeting came to an end, the elders and Mmoju headed back to their homes, leaving Anjelita and the others to turn in for the night at the church. They had decided they would call together the entire clan to discuss what Bridget had asked of them.

Daieh had planned to go back home with Abuela, but the feeling that something was going on with Lanaia kept nagging at her. She decided to walk the twenty-two miles back to the village to speak with her older sister and find out why she was so angry. They had just learned they had an older sister and Daieh thought it was great. She had not had the opportunity to talk to Anjelita yet, but the enthusiastic smiles she'd sent to Daieh were encouraging. *And,* she thought, *she is a shape-shifter!* She couldn't wait to see her new-found sibling change her form.

Abuela didn't object to her heading home at such a late hour because Juba would be with her. Juba was the sleek, black jaguar who was born the same day as she was, and was affectionately known as her twin. Unlike Lanaia, her color was a deep brown; not nearly as dark as her father and the others, but she did not share the light-gold skin-tone of her sister.

While she walked, she continued to ponder on what was wrong with Lanaia. Knowing her older sibling as she did, she first thought the girl's mood stemmed from not being the oldest any more. They had always known about their father's first wife and the unborn child, but neither of them ever thought they'd meet her. However, Daieh sensed there was more to it than that. It was true that Lanaia had always been spoiled by their mother and was somewhat self-absorbed, but to actually be rude to their father; and in front of the elders and visitors, no

194

less, was unacceptable. She loved her sister dearly, but sometimes she wanted to take a whip to the girl.

As she approached the small house, she could see all of the lights on, but this didn't surprise her. Her mother was a caterer and often prepared food into the late hours of the night for parties on the next day. But what did raise her pique was the man who was leaving the house from the back door.

All her life she knew that her mother only tolerated her father, but she had never even suspected that the woman might be unfaithful. Esperanza was a devout Christian woman who would faint at the thought of being involved with something so sordid.

Ruling out the idea that the man might be a lover for the time being, she moved closer trying to get a good look at him. He was fairly tall and wearing a suit that looked expensive. She couldn't see his face because he was wearing a hat, which he tipped politely to Esperanza before he turned and headed the opposite direction. There was nothing in her mother's manner that said she was familiar with him. In fact, Daieh thought she seemed a bit nervous as she turned and closed the door following his departure.

She knew he wasn't a relative and was now sure he wasn't her mother's paramour, so who was he? And why was he visiting past midnight and using the back door? Daieh was puzzled by what she had seen, but instead of calling out to her mother to have her hold the door, something told her to approach the house quietly. She could feel Juba's muscles tightening and knew something was amiss.

Not sure what she was about to find, she eased up to the back door of the house which led into the kitchen. The kitchen window above the sink was open, and she heard Lanaia asking their mother what was in the package that had just been delivered. Daieh could hear fear and worry in her mother's voice as she answered.

Daieh eased closer to the window and crouched down to better hear what her mother would say without alerting them to her presence.

"It's poison." Esperanza answered flatly. "Mr. Cilfure, the man I told you about, is stuck in Rome right now, but he wants them captured either dead or alive. The easiest and most painless way is for me to cook this poison into the tamales for tomorrow. When they eat them, they will be knocked unconscious. The militia will be on their way to round all of them up and take them away. Quite frankly, I'd prefer them dead," Esperanza said bitterly as she turned to Lanaia and continued. "There is no other way. Mmoju and his band of savages must pay for what they have done to our family."

Daieh was frozen in shock with her back pressed flat against the house. She didn't dare breathe for fear of being detected. She wanted to take off running back to the safety of Abuela's house and cry out her anger. She wanted to run inside the house and confront her mother, and she wanted to know all of the details of their plan. It was the latter desire which won out.

Although Lanaia didn't voice an objection to the plans, she did have one question. "But what about Daieh? She will be there, and you know how much she loves your tamales. What about her?"

Daieh was still holding her breath. She couldn't believe what she was hearing. It took Esperanza a long time to answer, but when she did, I broke the teen-ager's heart.

"Daieh has chosen them over us. She can share their fate."

Daieh wanted to throw up. How could her own mother and sister plan to do something so terrible? She'd always known that Esperanza didn't love Mmoju, but she had no idea the woman harbored such hate for him. Also known was the fact she loved Lanaia more; a fact that had never really bothered her because she had Abuela, Mmoju and her kinsmen's love and support. And though she knew she was not her mother's favorite, she never thought for an instant that the woman hated her.

After what seemed like an eternity of silence, the light in the kitchen went out and she could hear the soft footfalls fading as Esperanza and Lanaia went into another part of the house. She willed herself to calm, stood, and ran back to warn her family as fast as she could with tears running down her face and Juba keeping pace beside her.

During the 40-minute run back, the sadness and frustration she'd initial felt had been replaced by anger. Daieh bypassed the house she shared with Abuela and headed straight to the meeting house. It was Anjelita and the others who were being targeted, so she thought it best to warn them first.

When she reached he door of the meeting place, Anjelita was standing outside crying. Daieh approached her eldest sibling with concern. But instead of asking why she was outside well after midnight weeping, Daieh felt the need to share her terrible tale first.

"Sister, I have news. You are in danger here."

Anjelita turned to the young woman and wiped the tears from her eyes. "I know. I saw it in a vision."

By then, Bridget had come outside and they could see the small, spry Abuela crossing into the courtyard. As soon as she came up to them she asked solemnly, "you saw it, too?"

Anjelita nodded sadly.

"And I overheard it, Abuela. How could they do it? How can my own mother and sister be so evil?" she sobbed into the shoulder of Abuela who had no ready answer for her.

Bridget told them that there was no point in worrying about it now. They needed to get some sleep because they were likely to have a long day ahead of them. Nodding acknowledgement to the wisdom in the Star Woman's words, Abuela kept her arm around Daieh and led her back to her house.

Daieh lay on her pallet next to Abuela wide awake. The old woman's light snores were as familiar to her as her own heartbeat and usually just as comforting. But not tonight; though she tried, she could not find the peace to sleep. The words her mother had said kept repeating themselves over and over in her mind; *"Daieh has chosen them over us. She can share their fate."*

She was still awake when she heard someone come into the house. She sat up and was very still. "Daieh! Wake up!" It was Lanaia, whispering fiercely as she approached Daieh's pallet.

Not wanting to awaken Abuela, she got up from her pallet and stormed outside with Lanaia in tow. Hurt and fury were coursing through her young body. "What do you want!?"

She was not ready to confront her sister about her plans yet by revealing what she knew.

"I came to get you. Come with me now. Please Daieh!" She looked into her older sister's eyes and saw unveiled fear and desperation. The emotions she recognized in her sister gave her pause and softened her momentarily, but she was still angry.

"Why? What's going on?" She wondered if Lanaia would tell her the truth.

"I can't explain right now, but trust me. I need you to come with me. I don't want you here tomorrow!" Lanaia grabbed the girl's arm and tried to drag her towards the road.

Lanaia was older, but Daieh was taller and stronger. She jerked her arm back. "No! Not until you tell me what's going to happen tomorrow."

Lanaia faced Daieh and tried once more. "Please. Can't you just listen to me for once?"

Daieh crossed her arms over her chest. "Not until you tell me what this is about!" Though she already knew, she needed to hear Lanaia say it.

Lanaia shook her head and pulled a pistol out of the pocket of the jacket she was wearing. Daieh recognized it as the weapon that Uncle Alejandro always left with their mother when he was away on business, like now. "I'm sorry Daieh, but this is for your own good. You have to come with me now. We've lost time as it is."

Lanaia used the gun to point the direction she wanted Daieh to go in. Daieh was furious, but knew that if Lanaia was desperate enough to pull out a pistol, there was no telling if she'd actually use it. And since Daieh didn't want to challenge just how crazy her sister had gone, she did as she'd been commanded.

They hadn't taken more than four steps when Juba sprang out bit Lanaia on the arm. The young woman screamed in pain and dropped the firearm. The cat was about to attack her again when Daieh shouted, "No Juba!" The cat didn't attack the young woman, but kept growling and pacing back and forth.

In the bright moonlight, the bite on Lanaia's arm looked deep, but Daieh knew that had Juba wanted to, he could have taken the girl's whole arm off. Backing away from the jaguar, Lanaia stared at her sister.

"Fine then. Stay here!" She turned and ran back towards the village.

Daieh called for her to come back, but she didn't. Part of her wanted to run her down, but another part said to let her go. It broke her heart, but she just stood in the road and watched until her sister disappeared from sight. When she finally turned to go back to Abuela's house she saw Mmoju standing there with Juba's sister Jalle. She ran to him and wrapped her arms around his waist.

"Mama told me about Esperanza's plan. I'm so sorry." He held her for a long time while she cried.

"But how could she do it, Baba? She's my sister!" The girl wailed.

"I know it hurts, querida. But please understand that Lanaia was just trying to protect you by getting you away from here. For all her faults Daieh, your sister loves you very much." His words may have been true, but they did little to mend her broken heart.

The next morning before dawn, Mmoju had gathered the remainder of his people. In all, there were about 50 men, women and children. After a very brief introduction of Anjelita, Bridget and the others, Bridget addressed the group. "We are in great danger. There are forces of evil that, even now, are plotting against us. You must join us to abate this threat. I don't have time to go into all of the details now, but we need people who will fight with us. I can't promise that all of you will return to your families, but if we don't fight, there will be no families to return to."

Mmoju appreciated the woman's straight talk, and how she didn't sugar-coat the gravity of the situation. He then told the group that he planned to fight and asked if there were any others who would join him.

A middle-aged man who was leaning on a cane spoke up. "The last time we followed you into battle, it cost us our homes and the lives of most of our people. Why should we follow you now, Mmoju?"

Mmoju faced the group once more. He'd been expecting this type of opposition. "Yes, the last time I insisted we fight we lost. We lost nearly everything because I didn't listen when Anuka warned us. But I am listening now. And this time, I am fighting for what the Almighty wants, and not for my own pride. Search your hearts and find the truth." He'd spoken in a clear, quiet voice that was filled with humility. He knew what he was asking of them was a hard thing to do, but his short, heart-felt plea was all he had to give.

For a few tense moments, people conversed with each other and prayed. Finally, a young man of about 20 stepped up to Mmoju. "May I have permission to speak?"

Mmoju handed the young man the talking stick.

"I have heard the stories about a time that would come. A time when one of us will be able to change our form to that of any beast from the earth. It will signal a time when we must join others, leave our homes and everything that we know to fight an enemy worse than anything we could imagine."

He turned to Abuela and the elders. "Is this not what you taught us, Wise Ones?" Almost in unison, the elders nodded their heads that they had.

"Then I, Binah, will fight in the army that the Great Almighty is amassing!" He raised the staff high in the air and thunderous applause broke out.

Within minutes, 13 men and women from Anjelita's tribe had pledged to follow Bridget and Mmoju. Among them was Daieh. The rest of the people were either too old or too young to go into whatever battles lay ahead, so Mmoju had the elders lead their people to someplace safe and out of the reach of Esperanza and whoever she was working for.

Chapter Thirty: And the Wicked Shall Fall on their Own Swords

B y the time the sun had fully risen, Bridget's expanded party was headed back to the Starlight. The group made surprisingly good time as they traveled back through the jungle, led by Juba and Jalle. Throughout the morning, the pair would take off and stalk the area, seemingly searching for any potential dangers. A few minutes later, they would return, satisfied that the path was clear.

During their first trek into the jungle, they'd encountered several of the area's native wildlife. They had seen beautiful quetzal birds, a few toucans, and saw a small group of spider monkeys swinging in the trees. But this time, there was nothing. No birds were calling out warnings to alert other animals to the presence of the visitors; and no other sounds could be heard except the steady footfalls of the travelers.

By early afternoon, they stopped for rest and to eat some of the food Laqat had gathered while the meeting was taking place. When the jaguars slipped off, Anjelita explained they were going to hunt down a meal for themselves.

Carienne slid next to Bridget and whispered, "I can feel something; like we're not alone." The young woman had always been able to sense the moods and feelings of others, but it had been limited to people who were closest to her. However, since meeting up with Dakkar and Anjelita, the feelings were much stronger and panned out to total strangers. While in Sanctuary, Bridget had explained what an empath was and how to decipher the various feelings, their origins and how to control it and keep from letting it overwhelm her.

"Being an empath is a true gift," Bridget had told her. "But you must be able to control it. You are connected to the emotions of other people in much the same way you are connected to the water. Keep in mind that the human body is comprised mostly of water, so however their internal tides are moving, you can sense it. This will help you discern the true nature and intentions of people you meet."

Bridget smiled at the young woman and answered quietly, "I know." Wrapping a comforting arm around the girl, she added, "Don't be afraid."

Nearly an hour had passed and they were about to resume their trek when they heard a scream. From the trees behind them ran a terrified Lanaia with both Juba and Jalle snarling behind her.

Daieh ran to where the girl had tripped and fallen in her attempts to get away from the circling cats and had them stand down. As the shaking and still frightened young woman stood, Daieh saw she was covered in blood; her arms, the front of her dress, and even the side of her face had blood dried on it.

Though she hadn't wanted the wildcats to make a meal of her sister, she was furious. "What are you doing here?" the younger sister demanded. "Have you come to spy on us so you can tell your mother where we are? Or did you come in hopes of killing us all while we slept?" No one missed the anger in the girl's tone, or the way she had emphasized "your mother" when speaking of Esperanza.

Lanaia shrank back from the scolding tone in her sister's voice. "No," She answered weakly.

Daieh gave her no quarter. "Liar! Why should I believe anything you say? We all know of your treachery!" Daieh was so angry she was tempted to hit her sister. But she feared if she did, she wouldn't be able to stop and cause the woman serious harm.

"No!" This time, Lanaia screamed her answer. "No!"

Mmoju went to his daughters and pulled Lanaia into his arms. "It's alright," he whispered to his middle child. "Daieh, calm down," he then said to his youngest. He helped Lanaia to the felled tree trunk the group had gathered around. "Now, tell us why you've been following us all day." His tone was gentle, but firm.

Lanaia looked around at the faces that ranged from angry and suspicious to curious. "I-I had nowhere else to go," she stammered.

Mmoju glanced back at the others briefly, then asked. "What do you mean; 'you had nowhere to go'?"

Lanaia started crying again, but she continued in a rush. "When I got back home, Mama was in the kitchen and furious. She saw that I had been bitten by one of the cats and laughed at me. She said they should have killed me for disobeying her and that I put our family in jeopardy. I tried to tell her that I just went to get Daieh and she called me a liar. She said I went to warn you, Father. That's when she came at me and began hitting me." Lanaia sat for a few silent moments thinking about what had happened. The tears continued to roll down her face, but an encouraging squeeze from Mmoju made her continue.

"I was scared, so I grabbed a knife from the counter. I thought she would just back up and I could talk to her. But she ran towards me and grabbed the arm where I had the bite, and it hurt so badly that I tripped backwards. She tried to get the knife from me saying that she'd take care of me and then she'd deal with Daieh and the rest of the savages. She was crazed, and I knew she would hurt you," she looked at Daieh pleadingly.

Daieh just stood there, saying nothing, so Lanaia continued. "When I tripped, she was still holding on to me and we both fell to the floor, wrestling for the knife. She was taunting me; saying I was weak and she should have known I would try to ruin things for her. I was able to wrench my hand free of her grasp and I... the knife..."

The young woman started crying hysterically then. Her hand flew up and slashed the air at something only she could see. She kept screaming over and over, "I can't let you hurt Daieh! Not Daieh!" Finally spent, the woman slumped off the log and cried uncontrollably.

Mmoju went to the girl again and held her against his chest and let her cry a while longer. When she finally stopped, she looked up at her father and whispered, "I'm so sorry. So sorry," as more tears spilled down her light-brown face.

Jahmil shook his head sadly at the tale. "But the sword of the wicked shall enter their own hearts and their bows shall be broken," he stated quietly.

Tehilla, who was standing beside him, gently took his hand and added, "Psalm 37:15." The two shared a small smile, and then refocused their attention on Lanaia.

Myla and Carienne went to the girl and helped her up. "We'll get her cleaned up and see about her wounds."

Lanaia looked back over her shoulder and met Daieh's unreadable eyes. The knowledge of how she'd hurt her sister almost threatened to make her crying begin anew, so she turned and let herself be led away by Myla and Carienne.

Nearly 30 minutes later, a much cleaner Lanaia was fed and as ready to travel as could be. Dressed in a pair of Carienne's sweat-pants and one of Myla's shirts, the newly healed woman silently fell in with the rest of the group and continued their journey.

As they walked, Daieh found that she was no longer angry with her sister, but she was still sad and hurt. She had never been close to her mother, but would never have wished the woman such an awful death; not even in light of her own murderous plans. In truth, she didn't really know how to feel. Emotions of sadness warred with feelings of anger, hurt and betrayal. At the same time, she felt some peace in knowing that Lanaia had never intended to harm her, and that she had risked her own life and safety to spare hers. Still, the knowledge of what Lanaia had been willing to do to their father and kinsmen evoked feelings for which she had no name.

The group set up camp just as night fell. They designated pairs of people to keep watch, though, thanks to Juba and Jalle, they were not worried about animal predators. After the pair would hunt and satisfy their own needs, they would come back and rest with the others. Juba stayed close to Daieh, but Jalle had attached herself to the still-wary Tehilla.

By the fourth day, the group had reached the Starlight and Tehilla asked how everyone was going to fit inside the craft. To that Laqat smiled and answered, "Fear not fair lady; we will all fit just fine."

As they climbed aboard, they realized he was right. There was enough room for everyone. The group spent a few minutes stroking the large cats and thanking them for all their help, as they would not be traveling with them. Even Tehilla gave an affectionate pat to the neck of Jalle. They settled in while Kafeel, who had been anxious to command the conveyance, took his seat and headed them towards the Pacific Ocean.

Chapter Thirty-One: Doppelgangers and Sea Monsters

The Starlight had been hidden outside of a city called Gracias a Dios which means Thank God, and the group began the next phase of their trip by doing just that. Kafeel led them over the southern edge of Mexico and out into the North Pacific Ocean. Though they were able to travel at a much faster speed, they chose to go slowly and keep out of sight of city-dwellers. Once over the Ocean, they picked up speed as they headed toward the islands of Polynesia.

They arrived on a deserted beach on one of the inhabited islands and the group got out of the Starlight while Laqat and Kafeel went to find a place to secure it.

"What now?" Dakkar asked.

Bridget looked around the deserted beach before answering. "We head north," she said. "There are some people here we need to find."

A slight chill ran up Tehilla's spine as she too looked around the beach. "Are we looking for Carienne's parents?" She already knew the answer, but needed to hear it in order to prepare her heart. Ever since she had adopted Carienne, the fear that one day someone would come to claim her child had plagued her. She had rehearsed what she would say to them, and imagined how she would feel meeting them, but never in her musing had she thought she would actually be seeking them out. The idea of meeting them on her doorstep gave her a slight advantage, but now she might be facing them on their turf, as it were; and the idea terrified her.

"In a way, yes. If not her own family, then some of her people." Bridget didn't want to say anymore because she didn't want to get Carienne's hopes up if they couldn't find her parents, nor did she want to add to the anxiety she knew was building up in Tehilla.

The group spent two days searching the beaches hoping to find others like Carienne. That evening, Anjelita asked Bridget what they would do if they couldn't find anyone else like Carienne. "It's not like we can tell them apart from all these other folks, and we can't just start asking them if they can breathe under water," she quipped.

Though she had been addressing Bridget, it was Dakkar who spoke up first. "I have an idea. Let's try a different tact in the morning." They all turned to Dakkar to hear what his plan was.

"Carienne, you and I will swim out. Either we will find them, or they will be curious enough if they see us to come to us."

Bridget grinned; she liked the idea. "And how do you know they will be curious enough to come if they do see you?" she asked with a knowing smile.

Dakkar didn't hesitate to answer. "When I escaped from that place I was being held in, I had to swim to keep from being shot down flying. I met three people who were very curious about me. I couldn't understand what they were saying, but the helicopters that were tracking me were easily understood by them. They took my arm and led me deep under the water. But instead of guiding me east, which was the direction I was heading, they doubled back with me and brought me to an inland cove somewhere around here; or at least I think it was near here. They fed me and kept asking me questions, but I had no idea what they were saying until they finally brought a woman who spoke English. I told her where I was trying to go and she said they would help me. She also made me promise that if I was captured again I would not tell them about her and her people." Dakkar smiled at the end of his tale and added, "And that's why I think if they see us they will want to know more about us." With a plan formulated, the group settled down to sleep under the stars on the beach.

By mid-afternoon, it was just as Dakkar had predicted; four people had met up with them in the ocean. Together, they swam back to shore to talk. Bridget and the others were pleased to meet the 40-ish man, a woman of about 30 and a pair of identical twin boys who appeared to be roughly 12. The woman spoke some English but all of them were fairly fluent in Spanish, so that was the language they conversed in.

"I am known as Mahi, like the fish," she joked. "And this is my uncle Nopere and my cousins Dolph and Philippe. We don't usually get visitors from other pods out here, so we were surprised to see them," she motioned toward Dakkar and Carienne.

Bridget and the others voiced their pleasure at meeting the foursome as well, and then explained that they had been looking for her and her people. She assured them that they meant them no harm, but needed to speak with whoever was in charge. During the introductions, Nopere kept looking at Carienne, but he said nothing.

"We do not live on this island," Mahi told them. "But we can take you to Micronesia. That's where we live now."

Since the majority of the group could not swim there, they all headed back to the Starlight and traveled that way. Mahi and the twins were very impressed with the Starlight. "Wow! Look at this!" exclaimed one of the boys. The unreadable mask over Nopere's face slipped momentarily as he smiled affectionately at his nephews. Their enthusiasm was infectious and not even his wariness of the strangers could keep his grin hidden.

Once everyone was aboard and comfortable, Laqat and Kafeel briefly discussed the best way to travel. "The vast number of sea vessels in the area will make traveling above water risky. Even with our equipment, we won't be able to avoid all of the fishermen and cruise liners," Laqat was explaining.

"The same would be true of flying," Kafeel added. "So what do you suggest?" the big man asked.

Smiling widely, Laqat waggled his brows mischievously. "Oh, I have an idea up my sleeve. Move over," he instructed Kafeel.

Kafeel felt a bit disappointed at having to relinquish the controls initially, but as he watched Laqat pushing a series of buttons and guiding the vehicle underwater, his mood shifted to awe. "Now that is nice," he whispered.

Laqat grinned at his friend and the others who were watching. Within a few minutes, they were well over 100 feet below the surface and were gliding through the dark waters with ease.

The group soon learned that the talkative twin was Dolph, and his questions about everything from the Starlight to why Dakkar and Carienne had been looking for them, never stopped. The adults found his exuberance a bit overwhelming and his energy exhausting, but everyone was glad for his chatter; it kept them from their own thoughts.

Carienne could feel her mother's mood and knew where it stemmed from, but there wasn't a lot she could say to help.

She too was harboring mixed feelings about meeting others like herself; even if they did not find her parents. In an attempt to calm the young boy down, she jumped towards the window and exclaimed, "Did you see that?"

The two curious boys moved to where she was and peered out. "I don't see anything. What was it?" the curious Dolph asked.

Smiling to herself at how easily she had been able to gain their attention, she looked around at the adults and whispered to the boys, "I think it was the Cetus."

"What's that?" the quieter Philippe asked. Looking around again as if what she was about to tell them couldn't be overheard by the adults, she had them sit down next her and began to explain. Before she met Dakkar and left her home and school, she had been studying Ancient Roman civilization and the Greek myths. One of the ancient tales about a huge sea monster had captured her imagination, and she believed it would do the same for theirs.

For the next hour, she regaled the boys with stories of the dashing hero Perseus and how he, with the help of Pegasus, outsmarted the Fates and defeated both Medusa and the Cetus. The trio was so engrossed in the telling and listening of the story that they had not noticed that many of the others had moved closer to hear her rendition.

As she finished the story, Kafeel chuckled and shook his head. "If this Perseus killed the Cetus, then that couldn't have been the monster you saw out of the window earlier. Perhaps what you saw might have been the Leviathan."

Kafeel had realized that everyone aboard were from areas that held strong story-telling traditions. So when Carienne had finished her story, he'd decided to keep their attention by telling another tale. He sent a quick wink to Carienne, and plunged into the Old Testament account of the sea creature Leviathan.

Being that he specialized in war history, any story that had fighting or a formidable foe in it had fascinated him; and the Leviathan was one of the fiercest creatures in the Bible. As he went into an animated description of the creature and how fire shoots from its mouth and smoke pours from its nostrils, Tehilla shook her head in wonder. Looking over at Jahmil and Anjelita seated across from her, she confessed, "I will probably never read Job 41 again."

Chapter Thirty-Two: Custody Battle

W hen they arrived, Nopere and Mahi led them to a set a coves on a deserted part of the beach. Nopere took Dolph and Philippe to get their parents and the others. In their absence, she gave them a brief history of when they'd come to the island. "Until the summer of 1998, our pod lived between two of the Caribbean islands off the coast of Florida. The beaches were beautiful and deserted; unspoiled by people. The fruit trees were bountiful and there were plenty of fish to keep us all well fed. We loved it there," she said the last part wistfully.

Carienne wanted to know everything about Mahi and her people, so asked, "Then why did you leave?"

Mahi wore a bittersweet smile as she answered the girl's question. "We had lived there uninterrupted for decades but left for two reasons. Occasionally a group of young people from one of the nearby islands would come to camp or have parties, but they never stayed more than a couple of days. When they did come, we would stay out of sight and out of the water. But over time, more people began coming to the island with equipment to dig up artifacts. They were trying to prove that the island was the first landfall of Columbus."

"I thought Columbus first came to San Salvador," Anjelita added, puzzled.

"Yes, well, some people don't believe that, so they came and set up their equipment to prove their theory," Mahi answered. "But that was only a part of it. That summer, the hurricane season was the fiercest we'd ever seen. The winds and heavy rains were causing a lot of destruction. So, with the growing presence of cruise ships and fishing boats equipped with sonar, and the encroaching explorers, the elders decided

215

we needed to move on. Of course, I was a small child at the time, but I remember how sad everyone was to have to leave."

"That was in 1998, you say?" Tehilla asked. "I remember the storms that year. That was the summer I found Carienne," she added. The idea that she may soon learn the fate of Carienne's family and the circumstances that led to her being abandoned rocked the short woman back on her heels. If the other members of the group fully understood the implications of the statement she'd just made, they didn't let on.

Instead, they turned their attention to the group of about 20 people who were coming out to meet them. Among them were two of the people who had helped Dakkar over a year ago and recognition lit his face with a smile. He greeted them warmly and tried to introduce his friends. They quickly converted to Spanish, with Mahi translating for her people and Jahmil translating for his. Bridget wasted no time explaining who they were and why they had come. They had many questions, but over the course of the evening, all were answered; except one.

A woman of about 40 wanted to know how they could be under water like her people. She'd introduced herself as Yanni. Bridget explained that Dakkar and Anjelita could do many things and had only recently learned to move about in water as they did on land. "Carienne, however, has always been able to move through the water in this way." Bridget spoke the next part softly. "She was found as a baby, washed up on land in America."

The man who was seated beside Yanni jumped to his feet. His name was Carlos, and he stared straight at Carienne. "When were you found?" His voice was a hoarse whisper. He stood with his hands clamped so tightly together, that his knuckles shone white in the firelight.

Nervous, Carienne stood up slowly and looked into the faces of Carlos and Yanni. "Um, about 16 years ago, sir." Her voice was shaking.

He felt his mouth go dry so he licked his lips and he moved towards her. "Was there a storm around the time you were found?"

By then, Carienne was so overwhelmed by the idea that these might be her parents that she couldn't speak.

"Yes, there was. A horrible storm blew over the ocean that night. I found her on the beach the next morning, alone." Tehilla's voice was shaking as well, but she had been preparing for this moment since she'd found the girl. During Bridget's discussion with the island people, Tehilla had not been able to take her eyes off the woman called Yanni. The shape of her eyes and smile were mirror images of Carienne's. And as she studied Carlos, she saw the resemblance to her daughter in his curly black hair and the set of his jaw.

Yanni finally found her voice. "Do you have a birthmark on your shoulder of a strawberry?" she asked. Still unable to speak, Carienne looked at the woman and nodded. She tugged at the neckline of her loose-fitting top to reveal it. The fire-light flickered across the bared upper arm showing the red, raised birthmark that did resemble a strawberry.

Carlos and Yanni rushed to the girl and hugged her fiercely. They cried and kept hugging her. When they finally let her go, Yanni waved the twins over. "These are your brothers," she said as the two boys embraced their newfound sister.

Nopere appeared at Carlos' side and was introduced as Yanni's brother, making him Carienne's uncle. The man who had been silently observing her since they'd met earlier finally

217

spoke up. "When I saw you today with your friends, I knew in my heart who you were. You look exactly as your mother did when she was a girl. But I didn't dare let my hopes get too high. But now you are home with us. Thanks be to God Who heard our prayer!" He said emotionally as he hugged his niece tightly.

The rest of the group looked on the reunion happily, but Tehilla admittedly did not know how to feel. She was happy because her daughter was happy, but she was afraid at the same time. Jahmil slipped up beside her and took her hand, giving it a supportive squeeze. She gave a soft smile to the man who, in the relatively short time they had known each other, always seemed to know exactly what she needed.

After all of the hugging finally stopped, Yanni explained what had happened that terrible night. "We had been living on a small island in the Bahamas," she began. "But the fishermen began getting boats with equipment to help them locate fish. We knew we had to leave because soon they would detect us. There was no warning that a storm was brewing; especially one of that strength. The rains were coming down so hard that we dove deeper trying to escape it." The emotion and sorrow in her voice were almost palpable.

Carlos wrapped an arm around Yanni and picked up the tale. "The currents were so strong that we could barely move. We couldn't go deeper and the surface was worse. I saw Yanni flailing around and you weren't in her arms anymore." He hung his head and dashed away the tears. "After the storm we spent weeks looking for you, but we had to make it here or we'd have all perished. For years, we took groups of people out that way trying to find you, but we didn't know where to look. In our hearts we knew you were okay because we'd prayed it to be so." He sent Tehilla a grateful smile, which she acknowledged with a nod.

By then it was very late and everyone needed to rest. "Mama," Carienne addressed Tehilla, "I think I want to stay and talk to Yanni and Carlos a while longer." She refused to meet Tehilla's eyes; afraid of seeing the pain she sensed was in them.

"Alright," Tehilla answered softly. She dearly wanted to hug the child; to be sure that she had not lost her place in the girl's heart, but knew that was foolish. Instead, she plastered on a smile and added, "Just don't stay up too long."

Carienne promised that she wouldn't. She too wanted to run into the familiar embrace of the woman who had been her mother for 16 years, but Yanni's light, possessive hand on her shoulder stayed her. Nodding a good-night to the three of them, Tehilla and Jahmil headed back to the Starlight to sleep.

The next morning Bridget told Mahi and the others the rest of the reason they had come. As she had done with Mmoju and his people, she explained that danger was on the horizon and the time had come to fight.

Mahi told them that they knew this day was coming and told of the ancient stories about the one who came from the stars many years ago. Again, with the exception of the elders, children and a few of the women, eight of them had chosen to fight.

Pleased that they too had kept the stories of the prophecy alive and that as many who could be spared were joining them, Bridget told them it was time to go. "We've already lost time, so you need to prepare to leave as quickly as you can," she explained.

Yanni jumped up, "Wait! You can't mean that you're taking Carienne!" Though it was not the name she had given her child, she thought the Egyptian word for water was a name that fit well. She had only just been reunited with her child and they were telling her they were taking her off on a crusade.

Bridget had anticipated the woman's reaction." I'm sorry, Yanni, but yes, she is coming with us. She has a key part in all of this." She knew how difficult this was on the woman, but tried to explain that they had no choice.

In spite of Bridget's efforts to soothe her, the woman would not be swayed. "No! I forbid it! She is my child and I say no! Tell them Carlos!" She turned to her husband for support, but didn't wait for his reply. "Tell them they can't take our baby from us again. I won't let you take her!"

Tehilla could see the anguish in the woman's face, as could everyone else. She tried to console her as well. "Please. I know this is hard for you, but you must understand; we need her."

Yanni would not relent. "What do you know? You took her in and we're very glad that you did, but she is OUR child and I say NO! You're not her mother; I am!"

Over the past few months, Jahmil had been teaching her Spanish, so she didn't need an interpreter to understand what Yanni was saying, and upon hearing it, Tehilla felt slapped. In truth, Yanni was correct; she was the girl's mother. But it had been she who had cared for her and loved her all these years. It was she who had taken her to school the first day, had attended her recitals and plays, had taken her to church and had her baptized. She was the one who stood smiling and crying when, at age 13, Carienne accepted Christ as her Savior. It was she, Barbara Jean "Tehilla" Cotton who had loved and nurtured the child and had nearly lost her own life more than once trying to protect her. But it seemed none of that made any difference now, Yanni was the girl's mother and had just as much right; if not more, in deciding the child's future.

Carienne could feel all of their emotions washing over her and it made her sick. Clutching her head she screamed, "Stop this! All of you!"

Silence fell over the group as Carienne stood between them, breathing heavily. "Listen to me, please." She turned first to Tehilla. "Mom, you know I love you. You took me in and cared for me when you had no reason to. I love you and nothing will ever change that."

She then turned to Yanni and Carlos. "You are my parents. You brought me into the world and I love you. I always have. But Barbara "Tehilla" Cotton is my mother. *She* took me to my first day of school. *She* sang me to sleep every night. *She* taught me to ride a bike, how to read and cook pancakes. *She* taught me how to pray. And believe it or not, *she* taught me that it was okay to leave room in my heart for the parents she said one day I would find."

The group was quiet as the young woman continued. "She gave up her life to take me in and she risked her life for me when she thought I was in trouble. I want to spend more time to get to know you both better, but I have a purpose. And that purpose is with my mother, *Tehilla*."

The young woman could see the hurt in Yanni's eyes, so she wrapped her arms around the woman who had brought her into the world and whom tragedy had taken her from. "Please Mama Yanni, don't fight against us. Fight with us. We need you."

The woman held on to her child a few minutes longer. As she released her, she looked into eyes that were an exact replica of her own. "No, you all don't need me."

Carienne looked at the woman and said quietly, "Maybe they don't, but I do. I need you both. Will you please come with us?"

Yanni looked back at Carlos who nodded slightly. "Actually, I had planned to come along anyway, I just hadn't thought of how to tell Yanni yet," he smiled.

Once again, their group expanded as they headed back to the Starlight, and once again, everyone fit. Dakkar looked over Jahmil's shoulder as he prepared to pilot to craft. "Let me guess; Senegal?" he joked. Bridget smiled affirmation and gave Jahmil the orders.

Anjelita looked up at Dakkar from her seat behind Jahmil and said semi-jokingly, "I hope your family reunion isn't like ours."

Dakkar responded with a bittersweet smile. In truth, he didn't know what kind of reception he would have. After nine years of being gone, would they be happy to see him? Would they be angry that he'd disobeyed his elders and went flying? He had no more answers to these questions now than he did when he'd first been captured and began posing them to himself. As he turned his head back toward the window, he prayed he could turn his mind away from pondering whatever lay ahead.

Chapter Thirty-Three: And in Other News...

John Riley walked into his penthouse suite and headed to his bedroom. He had just returned from his volunteer work at one of the local charities. Nearly a year had passed since he'd had his near-death experience. Since then, he had retired and spent the majority of his time helping the less fortunate and praying for God to show him what to do next. As was his habit after a long day, he flipped on the television and stretched out across his bed to watch the news. One of his favorite newscasters, an attractive blonde named Candace Jordan, graced his wide screen.

"Tonight we have a very special newscast. In the studio with me are bank presidents Len Crowder and Donald Pikes, economists Clara Steele and Reginald Parker, theologians Rabbi Eugene Liebowitz and Dr. R.M. Like. Also joining us via live feed from her university lab is biologist Dr. Jenifer Meadows and her colleague Dr. Frank Perkins. Thank you all for joining us this evening."

Riley immediately sat up on his bed because he recognized Dr. Meadows. She had been one of the physicians who did a battery of tests on the young man he had captured in Senegal. During those years, whenever he'd encountered the 50-year-old woman, she'd struck him as being driven, committed and seemingly without compassion.

On more than a few occasions he'd had to leave the building to escape the tortured screams of the young man as Dr. Meadows "worked" on him. She'd explained to him that she was testing his thresholds for pain, because it seemed that his was higher than any other living person. She wanted to know what part of his brain he was accessing to block the neuro-transmissions which trigger the sensation of pain. At the time, he'd just nodded and told her to carry on while he ignored the sick feeling he had in his stomach.

The group on his television screen offered up the requisite "It's nice to be here," comments and Candace went straight to her questions. "Mr. Crowder I'll start with you and Mr. Pikes. You have both just come forward to announce some pretty radical policy changes in your banks. Tell us more about what those changes are please."

Mr. Pikes, president of the largest bank in America spoke first. "Yes Ms. Jordan, we have." He turned slightly and faced the camera. His winning smile and sincere, easy-going manner gave the impression that he was not a financial leader or someone to doubt or fear; he was a friend who simply wanted to share his ideas.

"As many Americans know, cybercrime and identity theft are on the rise. Cornerstone financial institutions, lending companies and insurance companies are going belly-up from the sheer volume of fraudulent claims they have to process. Good, honest American people are being robbed of their life savings and having their credit destroyed by these terrorists. I call them terrorists because that's what they are," he stated emphatically. He spent another moment recounting a few of the largest and most well-known computer-based financial crimes of the past decade.

"But I am happy to announce that those types of crimes will soon be a thing of the past. We have adopted a new process that is quick, easy and fool-proof." As he spoke, he held up the index finger of his right hand. "With this."

Candace leaned forward and the cameraman zoomed in on the man's very ordinary looking digit. By way of explanation he continued. "In my finger is an electronic chip the size of half a grain of rice. On it is my personal health and financial information."

Following his statement, several of the panel members began voicing their opinions. Candace raised a hand and brought order to the group. "So you're telling me that you have a tiny microchip in your finger that contains all of your information?" she asked.

"Yes. If I were to pass out, the medical team would be able to know if I have had any recent surgeries or medical conditions that would impact how they treat me. Also, if I wanted to purchase a car or a new hat, all I would need to do is scan my finger and the funds would be transferred immediately and accurately. This eliminates the opportunity for hackers to retrieve the credit card and billing information that is collected by various systems during the time of purchase."

Before any of the others could respond, Mr. Crowder jumped in and added more details. "I know this sounds very much like an episode of Star Trek, but I assure you it is being done for the safety and security of the American people. When I had mine put in, it took less than five minutes. It was painless and it will be free. Over the next six months, we are urging all patrons of our banks to have it done because shortly afterwards, we are doing away with checks, credit and debit cards, and eventually cash."

Candace turned to the economists next. "Ms. Steele, I know you have much to add to this new development." The cameras focused on an ultra-thin, red-haired woman who appeared to be in her mid-30s. She looked uncomfortable in the expensive-looking suit she was wearing, making it clear that she was probably more accustomed to jeans and tee-shirts. The fact that someone had gone to great lengths to hide the green and purple streaks in her hair by fashioning it into a sophisticated French roll, was not lost on Riley.

Pushing the designer frames of her spectacles up onto the bridge of her pierced nose and nervously brushing aside her bangs, she answered. "Yes of course. For nearly a decade, financial institutions have been on board with developing this type of technology. As an economist, I have to agree that this policy will revolutionize and revitalize our weakened economy. For one, the US dollar has been losing ground steadily in the world markets because of counterfeiting, cybercrime and irresponsible government spending. Billions of dollars are lost each year to criminal activity. This includes everything from drug sales and prostitution to black market economies and bootleg movie distribution. Millions more are lost each month from social programs like food stamp benefits which are there to help the needy, but it cost the tax payers when those same benefits are being sold to buy liquor, cigarettes and drugs. It also bears noting that after the financial collapse of Greece two years ago, much of Europe and China are adopting similar policies."

Dr. Meadows piped in at that point. "Can I just add one quick comment?"

Candace nodded her permission. "I have been working closely with the development of this project since 1998, and I can assure people that not only is it completely safe, but it has been used successfully for the past eight years. Many people with elderly loved ones have chosen the chip in case of emergency. Several of the state prisons have included convicts taking the chip as a condition of parole in violent offenders; especially sexually based offenses. Mothers and fathers of newborns have opted to have the chip placed in their infants to protect them from abduction. In fact, since this practice began,

14 children who were abducted with the chip were located immediately and returned to their families unharmed. The practical applications are boundless in ensuring the physical and financial safety of our citizens," she explained.

Unlike his colleague Ms. Steele, Mr. Parker was very polished in his dress, speech and manner. The economist, who claimed he worked primarily with small businesses and grass-roots organizations disagreed with her assessment. He declared that a money-less system would destroy the cottage industry. He pointed out that nearly 20% of the country's economy was based on small, cash-based businesses from school and church-sponsored fund-raisers, to grass cutters, snow shovelers, child care providers and hair-braiders. He warned that by eliminating this vital piece of our economy, the entire system would topple. "And of course, poor people who live in both rural and urban areas will be disproportionately affected," he stated emphatically.

Ms. Steele rolled her eyes towards the ceiling. "Don't try to make this about race, Reg," she told him.

Looking directly into the camera, the hard purpose in Mr. Parker's slate blue eyes was unmistakable. "It's not about race. It's about the haves and the have-nots. A struggling single mother may not have the money to pay a mechanic at a shop $500 to fix her car; but she can afford to buy the $75 part and pay the man up the street $50 dollars to fix it. And while the 'shade-tree mechanic' may not be able to send his wife to a fancy salon to get her hair done, he can send her around the corner to the woman who does hair in her basement and only charges $25 for a perm. Across the country men and women have been making an honest living working in cash-based industries." Up to that point he had remained rather calm, but it was clear that the muscularly built White man with the graying hair was becoming agitated.

"Yes, cash based businesses that are often illegal and untaxed. It's those 'businesses' that undermine the legitimate operations in communities across the country. Once we go to a cash-less society, real businesses will be able to flourish and stimulate the economy by offering those so-called honest people jobs; that is, *if* they really want to work," Ms. Steele replied, with a triumphant smirk.

Reginald Parker admitted that he had never liked Clara Steele. Her family's vast fortune had clouded her vision to the truth of what was going on in the country. She truly believed that her grunge, new-age, vegan lifestyle made her an expert on grass-roots culture. The last time they had talked, they'd ended up arguing the fact that a totally organic, vegan diet was too expensive for the average American to maintain. She'd vehemently disagreed and blamed their poor food choices for the drain on the medical system.

He was about to give her a stinging retort, but before he could set her straight, Candace interjected. "Now, now boys and girls; let's all play nicely," she said as she turned the attention to the other guests.

Dr. Perkins was happy to move the discussion away from economics and into his area, which was medicine. He discussed how they had been running clinical trials for nearly 15 years with volunteers from all over the world. What he admitted to next made a chill run down Riley's spine. "We have been collaborating with the French government and have a lab set up in Senegal. We have been successful in meeting all of the rigid requirements of the Food and Drug Administration and can happily report that the volunteers have suffered no adverse reactions to the implant."

Candace announced a brief intermission, but promised to return with more on the subject. Riley began pacing his room. He knew first-hand that the so-called V-chip did much more than they were saying. He had overheard Meadows and her team of scientist discussing how the chip could transfer DNA information back to their super-computers which would be invaluable to their understanding and development of cloning technology. At the time, the conversation seemed to revolve around collecting the data to develop cures for a variety of ailments, but now he wasn't so sure.

The fact that the chip would make the wearer easy to locate in any part of world via satellite links was touted as a benefit to everyone from worried parents and caretakers to the police. It was that fact alone that convinced him not to take the implant, even though highly ranking military officers were considering adopting the practice for all military personnel. Being a baby-boomer who had come of age in the turbulent late 60's and early 70's, he was wary of any technology which threatened his freedom. In many ways it had been his idealistic, whole-hearted love of freedom that had prompted him to enlist in the first place.

As promised, Candace reappeared on his screen and briefly recapped what had happened thus far on her newscast. She turned to Rabbi Liebowitz and said, "Okay, now we want to hear from our prominent guests in the world of theology. Some would argue that this chip is evil and the work of the devil. What do you say to that, Rabbi?"

Rabbi Liebowitz nodded his head. "Yes, there are some people who would say that this is something bad. We of the Jewish faith, the predecessors to Christianity, do not believe that this chip is anything more than what it is; a piece of technology that will provide a greater good to the community.

And while I don't want to get into a theological debate with my esteemed colleague Dr. Like, I have to point out that with the arrival of the Messiah, all worldly things will be laid aside. We are not afraid of new things. I am reminded how the people in Father Abraham's times must have reacted when he shared the news of the One God. Or how the people must have looked when Moses returned from Mount Sinai with the tablets of law. God has been pushing man towards a better understanding of Him and His world since the beginning of time. So do I fear this newest thing? No, I do not."

Candace looked over at Dr. Like who was shaking his head vehemently. "What say you Dr. Like?" she asked. Dr. Like was an enigmatic speaker and bible scholar. Riley had watched his telecasts often and found the tall, attractive, middle-aged African-American theologian to be knowledgeable and witty.

"First of all, let me say that the question is not whether we should fear the chip," he began. "In Christ, we need not fear anything. However, we must be wise and observant. According to the Apostle John in the Book of Revelations, people will accept the mark of the beast willingly. On the outset, most people will say that they would never knowingly enter into a relationship with the Antichrist. But you must understand that the willingness to accept the mark comes from the inability to buy or sell goods without it. People will accept it because they refuse to humble themselves before the Lord and trust Him to provide their needs. Their love of mammon, or money, will drive them to take the mark."

Turning to Mr. Crowder and Mr. Pikes, he added, "It's like you said; people want to protect their money from criminals. Their money means so much to them that they will forfeit their eternal souls for it. No one should fear the mark. It is already written what will be, so trying to stop it is useless. But be aware of what it is and what it really means." The camera zoomed in on a very nervous-looking Crowder and Pikes.

For the second hour of the program, the group continued to debate the economic, political and moral issues surrounding this new policy. By the time the program ended with Perkins claiming that they had the full support of the FDIC (Federal Deposit Insurance Corporation), the FDA and the IMF (International Monetary Fund), Riley felt sick. With the things he'd seen and done over the last decade, he knew that Dr. Like was right on the money; this was about much more than financial security. And with that demon Cilfure involved, he was positive it was a part of the end-times prophecy.

With that knowledge, he flipped off the set, knelt beside the bed and prayed for a long time. When he rose from his knees, he picked up his phone and booked a flight to Senegal.

Chapter Thirty-Four: The Prodigal Son Returns

By early morning, the group had reached the shores of Senegal. As they approached, Daieh asked where they were exactly. Dakkar answered her. "We are entering the country through Dakar, and then we will travel towards the Gambia River."

"Are you making that up?" the young woman asked him after hearing the name of the city.

"No. It's located on the Capvert Peninsula and is the oldest city in the Old World. My mother named me Dakkar for this place. She said it was to remind us of the evil in the hearts of men." Daieh and the others looked confused and Carienne wanted to know what he meant.

"Many years ago, this was a small slave port. Although most of the Africans were moved from the northern ports in St. Louis and south at the Gambia River, our people have a connection to this one. Our elders say that it was this port that some of our ancestors were taken to after being captured. Our people staged a rescue by flying in and catching the Europeans off guard. They wore white robes and shot at them from the air with arrows that had been set afire. They thought it was the wrath of God raining down on them and ran," he explained.

Daieh still wasn't sure he wasn't just making up the story, but decided to let it go.

Jahmil guided the Starlight over land to just north of the Gambia River where Dakkar said his people lived. Again they concealed the craft and headed out on foot. As they approached the area Dakkar was leading them to, he stopped short. "Something is wrong," he stated.

He moved slowly forward, scanning the area. "My cousin's house was right over there. And beyond it was my uncle's home. They're gone. All the houses are gone." He was trying not to panic, and blamed the emptiness of the area on his faulty memory. He told himself that maybe he was mistaken. They moved closer to the land where the homes had been and they saw the charred remains of the houses.

Fear gripped him. *Where was everyone? What happened here?* Questions began swirling around his mind so fast he couldn't keep them straight.

Out of the corner of his eye, he caught movement in the nearby trees. Without thinking, he flew to where he saw it and perched on a low-hanging branch. He hopped down in front of a young man about his own age. His eyes widened with recognition. "Tookey, is that you?"

The young man backed up and peered at him.

"It's me; Dakkar!" In his relief and joy, he moved forward to embrace him, but the man jumped back and extended his machete.

"What are you doing, Tookey? It's me, your cousin, Dakkar. I know you remember me."

The man's hand didn't waiver. "I know who you are. You are the one who brought destruction to our people!"

Dakkar was shocked and confused. "What are you talking about?"

Before the man could answer, Anjelita had slipped up behind him and restrained him. His arms were forced into a downward position with hers looped underneath them and her hands were linked behind his head. Kafeel had taught them that

233

move and in spite of himself, Dakkar was impressed by how well she'd executed it. He caught himself and told the tall woman to let him go, that he was his cousin.

Anjelita let him go, but took his machete just the same. By then, the rest of the group had arrived. Dakkar asked Tookey again what was going on. Defeated, Tookey looked around nervously. "Okay, but not here. Come this way."

The shorter man swiftly led the group west. They'd traveled for nearly an hour when they reached a small campsite. As Tookey and the others entered the site, tense-looking people came out of their make-shift homes to see who these strangers were. Dakkar recognized a few of the faces and rushed towards them. He'd expected them to be shocked to see him, but he had not expected their cold and hostile reception.

Only one of the men, his uncle Badee, embraced him tightly. "I am glad to see that you were not killed Dakkar." When he released him, he looked down into the eyes of his brother's son and said emotionally, "But you cannot stay here. Take your friends and go away." With that said, he turned and started walking away.

Dakkar had never raised his voice to his uncle before, but he was furious and hurt. "I'm not going anywhere until somebody tells me what is going on! Why do you turn away from me? What offense have I committed?" Dakkar was on the verge of tears, but he was too angry to shed them.

Badee slowed his steps, sighed heavily and said, "Alright."

Eyeing Dakkar's companions, he motioned them to sit on the ground. Seeing the serious set of his nephews face, he noticed the young man didn't bother with introductions, so he sat as well and told them what he knew.

"The day you left to visit your mother's family changed all of our lives. When you never arrived there, we all went looking for you. We learned that White men had been in the area and they were asking about men who could fly. After you went missing, they left as well so we knew then what had become of you. But that was not the end of it. Over the next few years swarms of the White soldiers came here. They were searching for more flying people. They were looking for the family of a boy named Dakkar. We were terrified, so stayed close to our homes. No one was allowed to fly for any reason and under any circumstances." The memories were apparently very painful for Badee, but he went on anyway after raising a curious brow at Jahmil, who was quietly interpreting the conversation for the others.

"That seemed to work for a while and the Whites left. But last year they came back. They went through the open lands rounding up everyone whose families had lived in the rural areas for more than 30 years. We just made it out of our village ahead of them. In their anger at missing us, they burned our homes, killed our livestock and destroyed our crops. We've learned that they are taking people to a laboratory in Central Senegal near the city of Payar. It is said that they are conducting experiments on them. We don't know what kind of experiments, but we do know that no one ever comes back."

It broke Dakkar's heart to hear of the fate of his people. "I was captured uncle, but I promise you, I never told them anything about you or where you were."

Badee shook his head sadly. "I'm sure you didn't. If you had, they would have come directly to us and captured us as well. But by capturing you, they knew that we existed. For

235

centuries we have kept our presence unknown from them. Any stories about flying people were only myths and fairy tales. But when you were spotted flying and then captured; we could have no peace."

Dakkar looked around at the dozen or so faces of his kinsmen. Though he was almost afraid to ask, he wanted to know. "Where is everyone else?"

Badee would not look at him. "Dead," he said softly. "The soldiers have caught up with us twice. And both times the numbers who escaped them grew smaller. My eldest son, Nesom. Your father and at least two dozen others; including my Cassa." Badee turned his face from Dakkar and wiped away the tears.

Dakkar was choked up as well. Cassa was Badee's wife and Tookey's mother. When his own mother died when he was just six years old, Cassa took to him like a son. His father, Kalal, was their chief and was always very busy. In many ways, Badee and Cassa were his parents and Tookey, Nesom and their sister Lark were his siblings.

A petite, dark-skinned young woman came running across the field to where they were gathered. "Baba!" the young girl called out. "There's heading this way!"

In that instant, Dakkar knew two things; first, that the girl was Lark; all grown up. And second; he wanted to destroy these monsters.

Badee turned to have his people begin grabbing what they could and heading out, but Dakkar stopped him. "No uncle. If you believe I started this, then trust me to finish it!"

The resolve in the young man's eyes was one he had never seen before in Dakkar. The carefree boy of thirteen

236

summers who had once taken advantage of a beautiful sky was gone. In his place was a young man who had the eyes of a man who had seen much, and the spirit of a man who had lost nearly everything.

As if he were in charge, Dakkar turned to his friends. "Anjelita, stalk and disarm. Myla, Tehilla, Lanaia; stay here."

He looked at Daieh and knew better than to try to get her to say behind. "Jahmil, take a group and enter from the left. Kafeel, you do the same on the right. Carienne, Binah, Daieh and Carlos with me." He glanced at Bridget and said, "Well Mama Bear; shall we dance?"

The woman pulled out Chaverah and answered, "We shall."

Badee and his people stared with their mouths open as Anjelita took off at a run and turned into a lioness in front of their very eyes. Dakkar swiftly took to the sky and the others watched in amazement as he threw open his arms and parted the trees, exposing the encroaching soldiers. As they fired their weapons at Dakkar, who was above them, they soon realized that their ammunition was being redirected toward themselves. Seeing that they could not stop the airborne attack, they tried to rush ahead but were met by a woman with a blade so true, that the slightest touch from it severed limbs.

Out of nowhere, they were attacked by a ravenous lion. As they tried to escape to their right, they were stopped by a band of men and women who neutralized and disarmed them so quickly, they could do nothing. The same happened when they tried to escape to the left. Within 10 minutes, the platoon of 50 plus soldiers were defeated, captured and bewildered.

As they marched the captives back towards the campsite, Bridget asked Dakkar what he had planned.

The young man didn't hesitate in answering. "Learn all we can from them, and then kill them."

Bridget turned to the young man and stopped him. "No," she stated quietly. She was well aware of how much pain he was in and how raw his emotions were.

Dakkar's jaw tightened. "Why shouldn't I? You heard what they did to my people. You saw what they were trying to do even now!" Anger was coursing through the young man, but Bridget was calm and spoke gently to him.

"Son, they are not just your people. They are God's people first and always. I know that you are hurt and angry, but killing these men will not bring any of your people back. And killing in cold blood is not what we do. Vengeance is mine, sayeth the Lord. You cannot take it on yourself to bring punishment to the wicked."

Dakkar was even more upset after hearing Bridget's words. He knew she was speaking the truth, but it was still hard for him to accept. They were nearly to the camp by then, but Dakkar could not face his people right then. "I need to be alone," he said as he turned and ran back the way they had come.

Chapter Thirty-Five: In the Beginning Was the Word

As Bridget and the others entered the camp, Badee stood in awe of her. "You are the one we were told about. The one who came from the stars many years ago when the world was still young," he gushed.

She answered simply, "Yes."

Badee continued. "Then if you have returned, it must be time for God to show His face again!" The people behind him buzzed with fear and excitement. All of them had been taught that in ancient times, when their people first came to this land a strange warrior woman came down from the stars to tell them that one day God would show the world His strength and might and end the suffering of man. During that time, their great scholars sat at the feet of the Star Woman and learned how God allowed them to do what others could not.

It was clear to Badee and his clan that the Star Woman did not want to spend time talking about ancient times and their history, so Badee asked what she planned to do with the soldiers.

"First, we try and find out what they know. Then we pray to the Almighty for guidance on how to defeat her plans."

With that, Bridget walked over to where the soldiers sat, tied hand to foot. Anjelita, still shaped as a lioness, strolled beside her. "Tell me why you hunt these people down," she asked.

The man who seemed to be in charge answered, "We will tell you nothing, witch!" And he spat at her. Anjelita growled and snapped at the man, who shrank back in fear. Though the young woman had no intentions on doing any of the men harm, she knew that her presence might frighten them into telling Bridget what they knew.

Sensing that she would get no answers from him, she walked down the line towards another man. "How about you? Will tell me what I want to know?" The man cowered, but didn't answer. Instead, he kept sneaking looks at a younger man positioned a few feet from where he sat.

Bridget turned to Carlos and Kafeel and pointed the younger man out. "Untie him and bring him forward," she instructed. Once they had, she could see that the man was little more than a boy; not even 20 years old. "Who are you? What are you called?" she asked the scared man.

He glanced at the man Bridget had just spoken to. "Um, my name is Haku," he stammered.

Standing in front of him, Bridget asked, "And why were you hunting down these people, Haku?"

The boy kept staring down at the ground and wouldn't answer. The man, who Bridget guessed was his father, spoke up. "He doesn't know anything! Leave him alone!"

Not taking her eyes off the boy in front of her she said, "Then you tell me what I want to know!" To help the man decide whether he should talk or not, Bridget pulled her sword from her belt. The man had witnessed what the woman and that sword were capable of and needed no further demonstrations.

The boy was trembling fiercely, but managed to answer. "We were told to round up all of the people in the outlands."

Bridget finally turned back to the older man. "Why?" She asked. With her blade so close to him, the man tried to scoot back.

"I don't know! We just have orders to capture them. Please, I don't know anything else."

Bridget wasn't quite satisfied. "Where were you taking them? Surely you must know that."

The leader of the group shouted at the man, "Say another word and I'll have your head, traitor!" If the man had been afraid of his superior, he was more afraid of the woman with the sword standing above him. "We were told to take them back to Payar."

"Thank you," Bridget said as she put Chaverah away and walked off.

Kafeel caught up to her and asked, "What are we to do with them?"

"We will feed them, tend to the wounded, and in the morning we will secure their ties and leave them here. It will take them at least 2-3 days to free themselves. Enough time for us to make it to Payar," she answered.

Dakkar headed to the place where he'd grown up; back to the place where his father had taken him on his first flight, and where he, Tookey and Nesom had played as children. He looked at the remains of the cook fire outside Badee's home where Cassa would prepare fufu from cassava and serve it with fish stew. He could almost hear the songs they sang and the conversations of his people on the wind. It had been such a happy place, but now it was all gone.

Many of the voices from his youth had been silenced. *All because he couldn't resist the urge to fly,* he admonished himself. He had been warned to walk the 40 miles to Mbour to visit his mother's kinsmen. Before then, he had traveled many times from his home in the west of Koalack to Mbour and knew that once he was a safe distance from town, he would be in deserted area for several miles. He did not heed the warning of his elders and thought he could safely fly 15-20 miles, saving him time while enjoying the day. The entire time he was imprisoned, he kept replaying how that one act of reckless disobedience had cost him so much. Now he could see that it cost a great deal more.

In his sorrow, Dakkar fell to his knees. He began to scream; to cry out to the heavens. "Why? Why has all this happened? I have accepted my being captured as punishment for my disobedience, so why punish the people I love? Why have they perished while I live?"

For the next hour, Dakkar cried and asked God why all of this was happening. "I'm no warrior! I'm no Unifier! I'm scared, and I'm tired. I miss my family and friends!" Dakkar pulled himself into a ball behind the ruins of his father's house and wept.

The sun was going down and he knew he needed to get back to the camp before they began to worry, but he couldn't seem to move. He lay there, listening to the sound of his own breathing, when he heard someone tell him to get up. He jumped up startled, and looked around for whoever had spoken.

"Dakkar," the voice said. He strained his eyes to see who was speaking.

"Who's there?" he demanded.

"You know My voice Dakkar. You heard Me while you were in that cell below ground. It was I who told you how to open holes in the steel frame of the bed you slept on. You heard Me tell you to follow your friends in the ocean when you were trying to escape. You heard My voice telling you to travel northeast to find Carienne and again when I led you to Anjelita."

Dakkar knelt down, but looked up towards the evening sky. "Yes Lord, I know Your voice. But why have You done this? Wasn't the eight years I spent imprisoned punishment enough?" He could barely see the fluffy, white clouds that were drifting lazily across the sky because his tears were flowing heavily.

"My son, you were not being punished; and neither were your kinsmen. I allowed all of the things you endured for a reason. I could not mold you and train you here at home. You were a boy of thirteen, but now you are a man. You have grown and matured in the face of all your trials. Trials that I brought you through. I made you for a special purpose, and I have given you everything you will need to fulfill that purpose."

Dakkar felt chastised and hung his head. "But I'm scared. What if I fail? I won't just be letting You down, but all of the people with me."

Again the Lord spoke. "I am with you Dakkar. Of whom should you be afraid? I created you perfectly for your purpose, and I can do anything but fail. And you can do anything through Me in My Son's Name because My Spirit resides in you."

Once the Lord had finished speaking to him, Dakkar noticed that the sun had gone down and night was settling in. Dakkar figured he should get back to the others, but instead of leaving, he rose to his feet and lit a fire. He then stripped out of his clothes and spent the next several hours dancing before the Lord and singing praises to the Most High.

Chapter Thirty-Six: Making Plans

D awn saw Badee and his people packing up their belongings in preparation to follow Bridget and the others. They had just sat down to eat breakfast when Dakkar strolled into the camp. He apologized for leaving so abruptly the day before and told them that he'd gone to talk to his father. No one was quite sure if he meant his earthly father's spirit or to the Almighty, but no one asked.

Over breakfast, Anjelita shared the vision she'd had the night before. "It wasn't totally clear," she began. "But I saw us telling people the truth about God's love and warning them that His Judgment is close at hand. I think that is our purpose; to tell people what is coming," she concluded.

Bridget nodded at the tall woman's interpretation. "Yes. That is definitely what He told me too. But as of yet, He has not revealed to me how He wants us to spread this message. I just keep praying and waiting for Him to reveal the next step in His plan." The group contemplated what Anjelita and Bridget said, but no one seemed to have any ideas on what direction to take.

"I think I have an idea," came a soft, quiet voice. It was Lanaia. Since she had joined their group, the young woman rarely said anything. When they weren't walking or in battle, she had been known to slip off and pray. They all noticed a change in the once prideful girl. Even Daieh realized that in her heart she had forgiven her sister, even though she had not said it to her yet.

Now, the group had turned their eyes on her and waited for what she had to say. She began nervously, but explained. "Well, I think we should use the media to let people know about God's plan."

Binah, who never strayed far from Lanaia smiled widely. "Yes! We will be able to reach millions of people that way."

Badee shook his head. "What is a media?" He and his people continued to reject the influences of the outside world, so he had no idea what the two young people were talking about.

In truth, Binah knew very little about it himself, but he remembered some of things Lanaia used to tell him about television and radio. Lanaia received supportive looks from Tehilla, Carienne and Anjelita, but it was the nod of approval from Daieh that made her continue.

"Well, I was just thinking that the best way to share information with a lot of people in a short time is to make videos and post them all over the internet. That way, you can tell people who you are and about the things you can do without exposing yourselves to the military and anybody else who might want to do you harm."

Bridget was intrigued by the idea and asked the girl, "And how do we do this video and internet?"

Lanaia told her. "All we have to do is get a laptop and video recorder, and then link into the internet. It's pretty easy and I can do it if you'd like." The girl knew she was no warrior and would be useless in a fight, but after all she had done to her father and sister, she felt this was the least she could do to earn her keep.

Carienne piped in, "It is pretty simple. I can help too. I used to make videos of my friends' band and post them on about six different sites. And you'd be surprised at how fast your fan base expands once people know it's out there."

With that kernel of a plan in place, they finished their meal and headed out.

Chapter Thirty-Seven: The Road to Payar

They'd decided that travelling on foot would be better than drawing attention to themselves in the Starlight. The plan was to travel primarily at night to reduce the chances of their large group being spotted by more soldiers or townspeople looking to make money by informing the authorities of their arrival.

They had no idea what might lay head, so after sharing their meal they prayed together. Yanni, Lanaia and the eight women, children and elders from Badee's tribe were escorted back to the Starlight. Many had seen cars and airplanes, but none had seen anything like the Starlight. Two of the older women were so wary of the craft that they didn't want to board.

"I assure you that this is the safest place for you," Bridget told them softly. "No one will be able to harm you, and there is food and places for you to rest."

"Please trust us. Do as she says; quickly." Lark added.

After Bridget told them that they would be safe there, and that she and the others would return for them soon, she and Badee made sure everyone was settled in. Laqat went to the controls and punched in a series of codes. No one knew what he was doing, but no one asked.

Bridget turned to the rest of her group and told them to suit up. She felt it was time to wear the special garments. While Dakkar, Carienne and the rest of the core group were putting on their suits, Bridget called for Daieh.

"Here, child. You will wear mine." She gave the young woman the suit of clothes that appeared to be too large for her. But having been raised not to question her elders, Daieh donned the suit. Once it was on her, she was amazed at how well it fit her. She thanked Bridget, but had no idea of the special properties of the garment.

Their party had been expanded once more and there was a total of 43 men and women determined to do whatever the Almighty had in store for them. They waited aboard the Starlight for night to fall and for Kafeel and Jahmil to return. The two had stayed in the camp to secure the soldiers with a series of knots that would take a minimum of two days to undo, and to bring the young soldier called Haku with them. He would know the way to the laboratory in Payar and save them valuable time.

When they returned, Bridget told Kafeel to untie the young soldier. The man was visible afraid, but she acted as if his fear was of no consequence to her. In spite of the fact that she'd wanted to assure the man he would not be harmed, she looked directly into his eyes and warned, "If you even think about running, alerting others to our presence or leading us the wrong way, Haku," she began, "think about something else." The seriousness of her words was not lost on the young man and he promised he wouldn't.

She pierced him with one last look, then turned to the others and said, "Let's move."

Under the cover of darkness, the group made their way east along the Gambia River. They'd traveled past the city of Nganda and by dawn had reached the outskirts of Koumpentoum, which lay north of the river. By then, Laqat had found them a good place to rest and explained that Koumpentoum is a relatively large village that serves as a central road town between the neighboring tribal people. He went on to tell them that there were less than 13,000 residents in the town. Bridget understood that to mean that they would definitely stand out. The last thing she wanted them to do was to call attention to themselves; especially since Payar was only about 30 miles away.

Deciding on only a few hours of rest, the group moved ahead in the late morning. They were all too anxious to sleep, even though they were rotating watch. By early afternoon, they found themselves roughly 10 miles from Payar, and surrounded by soldiers. Kafeel commended the soldiers on their stealthy approach because neither he nor Jahmil had heard a sound until they were descending on them. The soldiers knew they had the group outnumbered and that the 16th century weapons the small group carried were no match for the semi-automatic rifles they wielded.

The soldier who was in charge moved towards them to seize their weapons and the fight was on. Bridget ran through the first half-dozen men with her sword drawn. The other soldiers hesitated a moment as they were in awe of the big woman's speed and agility. They were also momentarily shocked as they watched several of their comrades fall in her wake.

They recovered quickly, but not quickly enough. Dakkar, Badee, Tookey, Lark and the men from his tribe immediately took to the skies. Badee had trained Dakkar and many of the other young people in the art of archery, and today would prove their skill. From the air they rained down arrow after arrow.

The soldiers began shooting up at them, but Dakkar deflected their bullets and sent them hurling back towards them. Within a few minutes, the air raid came to a halt as they ran out of arrows, but not before they had taken out or wounded over three dozen men. They returned to the ground to help with the fighting there.

Binah, Carlos, Kafeel and Anjelita, who'd decided to remain in human form, moved quickly to disarm as many of the soldiers as they could. A soldier ran up behind Carienne, who was bent over attending one in their group who had been shot. She didn't see the soldier until the blade of his knife slashed at her arm. She jumped back in fear, but realized the blade had not pierced her.

Using some of the fighting techniques she had learned from Kafeel, she was able to defend herself. The soldier figured he had missed her the first time and lunged towards her again. She quickly ducked to her right, spun around behind him and pushed him to the ground, using the momentum of his lunge to add to the power of her push. As soon as he hit the ground, Carienne was on him. He'd lost his rifle in the fall and she quickly retrieved it and knocked him unconscious with a blow to his head with the butt of the gun.

She turned just in time to see another soldier coming after her with his gun aimed at her. Before she could react, the man let out a strangled cry, and when he fell to the ground, Tehilla was standing behind him gripping a dagger that was dripping with blood.

Badee, Tookey and the others were fighting a small group of soldiers when Badee was shot in the leg. As he fell to the ground in pain, the soldier who had shot him raised his gun to finish the job when Lark rushed to her father to help him. She moved quickly, but not quickly enough. Just as he was firing a shot, the man's head was thrown back, sending the bullet off into the sky.

Lark could see a length of rope around his neck as he was being choked to death; his body wriggling as he clutched his neck trying to free himself from the rope. By then, Lark was at her father's side but her eyes were peeled for another attack, and to see who had killed the soldier.

After a few more jerks, the soldier's dead body slumped to the ground in a heap. Lark's eye's widened to see Haku stagger away from the man, breathing heavily. By then, Dakkar had reached Badee with Myla, who immediately began to help heal Badee's wound.

During the fight, the soldiers realized that their bullets were useless against the group, but they continued to try. The soldiers were sure that their sheer numbers would help them prevail, but as more of their numbers fell, they were at a loss. The members of Bridget's core group gave as much protection as possible to the men and women who did not have suits. The fighting lasted another few minutes, but the soldiers knew they were bested and retreated. Carienne and Myla rushed around to tend to the lacerations, bullet wounds and broken bones of their friends.

In the wake of the battle, they rejoiced that none of their members had been killed, but knew they had to move on quickly before the soldiers could return with more men. Tehilla was extremely quiet and everyone knew that the shock of having killed a man was weighing heavily on her. Jahmil went to her side to comfort her as best he could. He knew the pain she felt was warranted, but assured her it had been necessary.

Dakkar, who watched as Myla extracted the bullet from Badee's leg, looked up to see Haku standing to the side watching them. He walked over to the young soldier. "You had the chance to escape," Dakkar said to the man.

"Yes, I know," was all he replied with.

"But instead you stayed. And you helped us. Why?" By then, Bridget, Kafeel and Mmoju were standing behind him. The young man looked at the people who had taken him hostage.

After a few silent moments, Haku shrugged his shoulders. "I'm not exactly sure." He was quiet for another moment or two, but finally continued. "When you attacked us the other day, it was clear that you could have killed us all, but you didn't. I saw how you purposely knocked men down, took their weapons and in some cases wounded them. But you could have killed us all easily. Even when we were captured, you fed us and sent your healers to help us. Somehow I guess I figured that evil people don't really do that."

As he spoke, his gaze strayed to Lark more than once, and none of them missed it. Lark and many of the other women had had the task of tending to the soldiers and feeding them. Bridget looked at the young man and said "I asked you once why you were hunting down these people. Tell me everything you know now."

Haku looked up at the fierce woman. He admitted that he'd been terrified of her initially, but over the past few days he'd seen her to be kind, caring and compassionate. "I am from Matam. Two years ago, men came into our town and promised us fame, glory and riches if we would join their army. You must understand that most of the people were poor and were eager at a chance to earn money. Some of them volunteered to go, but many of us were simple farmers and had no desire to fight a war we knew nothing about. Six months later, the men came back. But this time they told us that if we didn't join them we would be considered traitors to their cause. They began terrorizing our people; threatening to kill our women and children, destroy our fields and burn our homes. So every man over 16 had to join them. We were given two weeks of training on firearms and told our job was to follow orders. Those orders were simple; round up the people living in the outlands and take them to Payar."

At this point, the young man faltered. "I have only been inside that place once. The building is large, but the underground areas are massive. I heard people screaming and crying and begging for their lives. It sickened me. I don't know what they were doing, but I tried to never have to go back down there again."

By then, Badee and the others were healed, though still a bit sore. They knew it was time to move on, so they did. Kafeel advised them that since the soldiers knew which direction they were heading, they would likely have an ambush waiting. He thought it would be best if they headed east, go around Toubere Bafal and enter from the east.

"It will add at least two days of travel, but it would minimize the chances of an ambush or another attack. Plus, it will give those wounded the time to heal properly." Bridget did not like the idea of such a lengthy delay, but she knew Kafeel was right and did not want to endanger her group unnecessarily.

As they resumed their travel, Haku strove to keep up with Dakkar who walked beside Bridget and Anjelita. He found it difficult, but tried nonetheless. When he was finally able to match the man's pace, he asked the question he'd been pondering since he'd met them. "Who are you people? I mean, I've never seen people do what you can. Flying and healing people with a touch. If I hadn't seen it with my own eyes I would never have believed it."

Dakkar glanced quickly at Bridget. He wasn't sure how much he was allowed to tell an outsider. Bridget nodded slightly and said softly, "Tell him Dakkar. It will be good practice," she smiled.

Dakkar was at a loss as to how to explain to someone what he was just beginning to understand. He began slowly at first, explaining to him how the Lord created man in His own image, but that man fell. In their fall they lost the abilities He had given them. "But there were groups of us who remained. We stayed to ourselves for millennia, rejecting the influences and vice of others. By keeping ourselves set apart, we have been able to maintain our connection to the Almighty and His gifts. But now, God is ready to pass judgment on man for his disobedience and refusal to accept Him and His love. Carienne, Anjelita and I are the Unifiers. We are meant to give man another chance to turn from their evil ways and reconnect with Him before it is too late."

After hearing this, Haku was speechless. He had been raised Catholic and believed in God. He even considered himself a Christian, but for the first time in his young life he sensed there was more to it than just believing in God. Haku stopped walking for a moment to think about what he'd just learned. Dakkar stopped as well. "What I still don't understand is why God needs you to tell people about Him. Most people already know and are Christians. Why do all this?" Not sure how to answer this question, Dakkar turned to Bridget once more.

"Haku, you must understand that it's not exactly about being a Christian in and of itself. I'd almost venture to say that Christians are part of the problem. God created man in His own image and gave him free will. He has waited patiently for men to use that gift to see the beauty and rightness of His love and that decision. But man has hid behind Christianity to justify all manners of wickedness; rape, murder, persecution, theft, slavery and nearly every other human atrocity you can imagine.

Right now, at least 30% of the world's population says they are Christians. But like the Pharisees and Sadducees, people view God in terms of a religious doctrine or political alliance instead of taking His teachings to heart and loving one another as Jesus commanded. What a world this would be if every person who claimed Christianity truly turned their hearts to God!" She exclaimed

Her smile faded as she continued. "He has grown tired of the rote prayers and self-serving ambitions of man. Of all the things we do during our time on Earth, only what we do for Him will last." Bridget smiled softly at the young man as he listened intently.

Finally, she broke the silence to say, "We have much to do young Haku. But know that we fight for good, and we only take a life if there is no other choice. If you can honor that, we will be honored to have you with us." Haku nodded his understanding and agreed to stand with them. The young man fell back as they continued walking. Bridget turned to Dakkar and whispered, "That is why God does not want us to kill His children needlessly. If we had done what you suggested in your anger, Haku would not have been here to help save your uncle's life." Dakkar nodded his understanding and silently gave thanks to God for Bridget's wise counsel.

The group reached the outskirts of Payar at dusk. They decided to try to enter the building under the cover of night. The building in question was a well-fortified lab where the people who lived in the outskirts of cities throughout Senegal were taken. No one knew what they might encounter once they entered, but they knew they had to go in. Ever the general, Bridget separated their group into four parts, carefully mixing the skills to give each group their best advantage. Though it was never said, they knew there was a possibility that not everyone would be returning.

Earlier that morning, Mr. Cilfure reached the lab in Payar, Senegal. His informants told him that the Unifiers were planning to attack the lab, and he couldn't be more pleased. Rather than spending time hunting them down, they were coming to him. He'd spent the morning preparing for his blow. He planned to not only put an end to their small group, but to capture the three of them. Once he had them, he could replicate their DNA and create a mighty army ready to do his bidding. His supporters were not only ready, they were eager to prove themselves to him. Although many of the scientists who were working for him were doing so without their knowledge, that deception pleased him even more. It never ceased to amaze him how the lure of money, fame and celebrity drove the so-called men and women of intellect to push further to pervert the laws of nature in the pursuit of scientific discovery.

Chapter Thirty-eight: Labyrinth

From outside, the lab looked to be only 4,000 square feet. It was about 25 feet high and was made of concrete. There was a row of barred windows surrounding the building at the top, but they were only about one foot long and less than that in height. They already knew that what was on top was just a front and that the actual labs and testing took place below ground. What they didn't know however, was how deep the structure went. Four armed guards walked the perimeter of the roof, while another half dozen men carrying automatic rifles secured the ground level.

Bridget waited until she was sure the other groups were in place before she, Anjelita, Jahmil, Binah and Nopere took the offensive. Moving with the stealth of assassins, they each quickly overtook their assigned targets before they could fire a shot or sound the alarms. The guards were dragged to the side of the building and tied up and gagged by the waiting Tehilla, Daieh and Kafeel.

Moving just as quietly, Lark, Tookey and Dakkar flew to the top of the building and let fly a volley of arrows laced with a powerful sleeping sedative concocted by Anjelita and Mmoju, striking the guards and rendering them instantly unconscious. After relieving the soldiers of their entrance badges, the three quickly descended to rejoin their groups.

Using the badges, they easily gained entrance through the side door of the facility. Once inside they overtook the four guards and Anjelita made her way to the front desk to disarm the alarm systems and unlock the doors for the others waiting outside.

Once inside, they began searching for the stairwells. Taking the elevators would be too risky, and Kafeel had just voiced his uneasiness about their getting inside so effortlessly. The others agreed. While their plan to get in was a good one, it had been *too* easy. Keeping their senses sharp, they split up into their groups again and went down several stairwells. As Haku had told them, there were several floors beneath ground level, but he didn't know what was housed on each floor.

"The one time I came in, it was to deliver a message to one of the scientists. A guard had me blind-folded and led me to an elevator. I can't tell you how many floors down we went, but when we stopped I was escorted to a stairwell and led even further down. The guard removed the blind-fold long enough for me to conduct my business, but before he put it back on me, I saw men in white coats dumping dead bodies into a pile along one of the walls," the fear in Haku's eyes was plain as he told them all he remembered.

A quick search of the first three floors turned up little; too little, in fact. There were no guards, no workers, no lab technicians; no one.

"I don't like this," Kafeel said.

They went down further checking the next six floors with the same results. When they had reached the 14th floor down, Carienne stopped short. A moment later, she doubled over with a whimper of pain. Bridget and the others had rejoined them on the preceding floor and rushed to the young woman's side.

"I feel something, "she panted out. Slowly standing again, she leaned against a wall for support. She had learned to control her empathetic gift, but this time there were too many people with too much pain. After taking in a series of calming

259

breaths she regained her composure and told her concerned friends, "I'm alright."

Still bracing herself against the wall, she added, "But there are people here; people who are suffering. I can feel them."

"Where are they?" asked Jahmil. "We've covered every floor in its entirety."

Carienne shrugged her slender shoulders. "I'm not sure, but they are close." Closing her eyes for a long moment, she worked to get a fix on their feelings. "Some are in pain physically, while others are terrified," she told them, shaking her head in sorrow.

Dakkar walked over to the solid steel wall. Within a few seconds he had opened a small hole. While the others watched silently, he bore in deeper. Once he had gotten through the steel, he found nothing but hard-packed earth. He went around the room and tried other walls with the same results. He'd hoped to find a secret panel or false wall that led elsewhere. Frustrated, he turned back to the group. "Nothing," he stated somberly.

While Dakkar was trying the walls, Anjelita went over to the computer consoles. Once she booted up the system, she entered a series of codes that would allow her access to the system's mainframe. The firewalls were well-constructed, but she knew computers like the back of her hand and within 15 minutes she had full access.

Pulling up the compound's security systems and disabling them, she turned her attention to the blueprints of the building she'd pulled up. Kafeel and Jahmil were both impressed by her work, but also surprised to see that the building was much more of a labyrinth than they'd originally thought. According to the blueprints, there were four floors beneath this one with access only through the floor near the southern wall of the room.

A brief search by Anjelita turned up the switch to open the hidden entrance. A dozen large tiles on the floor dropped about six inches then separated, revealing a wide set of stars leading below. Bridget, Anjelita, Kafeel, Jahmil and Laqat decided it would best if they went down first. With the rest of the group following behind them, they descended the stairs carefully and as quietly as they could. Once they reached the bottom, they had no time to view their surroundings because a dozen armed soldiers were rushing towards them.

Once again, the soldier's bullets were useless against the group who was returning their fire with marksman precision. It took only a short time to overthrow the guards. Lark, Binah, Nopere, Tookey and Haku busied themselves disarming and restraining the wounded soldiers, then followed quickly in the wake of the group.

If the soldiers had tried to alert their presence to anyone before they began their attack, it hadn't worked. Two soldiers were found at the bank of computers trying to sound the alarm, but Anjelita had disabled the systems in such a way that it would take all night to get them back online and operational. After neutralized them, Anjelita opened the next set of underground doors and they headed down.

This time, they hit pay-dirt. They'd entered into a main room, but could see the several glassed-in rooms lining the hall. One of the workers saw them coming down the stairs and ran, shouting a warning. Within seconds the hall filled with soldiers and the sounds of bullets firing and people screaming were deafening.

Anjelita preferred to fight as a large jungle cat, and the sight of her metamorphism scared many of the soldiers. Then, the sight of Badee, Lark, Tookey and Dakkar flying above them in the limited ceiling space, raining down arrows and bullets made several of them drop their weapons and run. Careful to stay behind Bridget and her team, Binah and the others added their bullets and arrows to the fight, taking out several of the soldiers with non-fatal hits to arms, legs, hands and shoulders.

Once the soldiers were under control, Carienne, Dakkar, Anjelita and Jahmil rushed the first set of doors. Guided by the growing connection to the people who were being kept there, they made it into one of the lab rooms. Inside were eight men and women strapped to gurneys with probes attached to their heads, chests and arms.

While the others worked quickly to unhook them from he machines, Carienne assessed them physically. Finding no physical maladies, she ushered them out of the lab and back to the rest of the group. One of the women was pointing frantically at the adjoining room of the lab she'd been in. Carienne couldn't understand the woman, but figured that she was alerting them to more people in need.

For the next half hour, they rushed through the lab's rooms and released the people in them. Most were physically alright, but they had been traumatized by the events. Others, unfortunately, were in need of more help that Carienne had time to give. She found lacerations and deep cuts along some of their arms and legs. Tissue and muscle had been carved out as if someone wanted samples of their flesh. Sadly, there were others who were found dead with holes having been bored through their skulls. The very thought of such evil sickened her, but she continued doing as much as she could to help them.

As she and the others brought the last of the living captives back to the main room where Bridget and the others were working with the people released earlier, the sight of about six or seven men and women in white coats trying to slip through a back-wall passage caught Bridget's attention. "Go get them! We need to ask them some questions," she shouted over the cacophony of noise.

Dakkar made it to the door just in time to keep it from closing. The white coats were scurrying down the hall like the lab rats they were, and Anjelita and her group were not far behind them. The scientists slipped around a corner and just as Dakkar and his group were about to follow, a huge metal wall slid down, blocking them.

Jamil was scanning the nearby wall for a control of some type to lift the wall. Finding none, the group turned to find an alternate route. Dakkar and the others knew that by the time he could open a hole large enough for them to get through, the scientists would be long gone. They'd rushed up the hall the way they had come only to have a second wall drop. They were now sealed in a 15 foot hallway with no doors, windows or visible means to get out.

Dakkar figured that since he had to open a hole anyway, it might as well be the one that followed the scientists. He had just begun to open a hole when the hall started filling with gas. Immediately the air became thinner and it was difficult to breath.

"Get down on the floor!" Anjelita told them. "The gas should be lighter than the air and will hopefully stay above us." She wasn't sure what type of gas it was, but hoped she was right about its properties. She also warned them not to move much so as not to stir up the gasses.

Dakkar worked frantically to open a hole deep enough to not only get them out, but to at least ventilate the hallway with fresh air. Although he was trying with all his might, his concentration was slipping due to the lack of air. Jahmil and the women were lying face down on floor. They were so still that Dakkar wasn't sure if they were even alive. His own breath was coming shorter and he too slid to the floor.

Dakkar fought to stay conscious, but just as he exhausted the last bit of oxygen, the wall the scientists had gone through opened and fresh air flooded the hallway. From the floor he could see a pair of well-polished boots. He fought to bring his eyes up to the person's face, and when he did, recognition and fear gripped him. "You!" he said right before he slipped out of consciousness.

Chapter Thirty-nine: Trust

A few minutes later, the group began to come around. As the fresh air filled their lungs and they regained consciousness. Still a bit lightheaded, Dakkar sat up and saw that his friends were struggling to stand up.

"Hurry up. We have to move. More soldiers will be here any moment!" The voice was one that Dakkar knew he would never forget. Riley. The man bent down to assist Carienne to her feet.

Dakkar, wobbly on his feet screamed at the man. "Don't touch her! Get away!"

Anjelita, who was already recovering, grabbed Riley and held him. She was surprised that the man hadn't tried to resist. "Who are you?" she asked.

Dakkar answered instead. "He's the man who captured me when I was a boy. He's the man who had me locked up all those years. He's the man who had all of those horrible tests done on me. That's who he is; a snake!" Though he was still suffering from a mild headache caused by the gas, his anger overrode all else.

Still being held in check by the large Black woman behind him, Riley looked Dakkar in the eyes. "You're right," he stated quietly. "I did do all of those things to you, and I'm sorry."

"You're sorry? You're sorry?" Dakkar spat. "You stole away my youth, destroyed my home and made me a prisoner for eight years and now you're sorry!?" He wasn't sure if his trembling was caused by the aftermath of the gas or his anger, but every fiber of his being wanted to kill Riley where he stood.

Still holding the younger man's eye's Riley said simply, "Yes, I am. But right now we have to move. If you want to kill me later I'll understand, but right now let me help you get out of here." Riley knew that Dakkar has absolutely no reason to trust him; not after all he'd put the young man through.

Dakkar was speechless and beyond angry. Jahmil looked at the middle-aged white man and asked him, "And how do we know you're not still working for the enemy and leading us into a trap?"

Riley thought that a fair question that deserved a fair answer. "Because if I was, I would've left you sealed in here another two minutes. You would have been completely unconscious and we wouldn't be having this conversation."

In spite of whatever problems he'd caused Dakkar, the man made sense. Also, there was sincerity in his apology to Dakkar that had touched him. Jahmil and the others knew they had no time to contemplate what to do next because they could hear the sound of several boots racing up the next hall.

Anjelita released Riley and the man swiped a badge in the corner of a wall to lower the steel wall that had imprisoned them earlier. He then swiped the badge in the center of the hallway wall to open another door which led to yet another set of rooms.

Riley rushed to the bank of computers and brought up the surveillance monitors for each of the floors. Anjelita silently admonished herself for not thinking to do that. They could see that the top four floors along with the ground level were swarming with soldiers. He punched in another set of codes and they could see the lower levels. They saw Bridget and the rest of their group attending to the 50 or so people who had been freed.

Riley was about to suggest they go back and join the rest of the group when Anjelita saw something on one of the monitors. "Wait a minute. I've seen him before. Who is he?" She pointed to a tall, handsome, well-dressed man holding court on the first floor of the building. She'd seen him in her nocturnal visions. Though in her dreams he had been a Black man, he was always handsome and well-dressed and regardless of his ethnicity, she knew it was the same man. She'd remembered the sound of his voice being soothing and beautiful. As she'd tried to escape the beast that was pursuing her, he'd been there offing her a way to escape. But in her dreams, she somehow never trusted him and always ran the other way.

Riley shook his head in disgust. "Pure evil. That is Mr. Cilfure; the man I *used* to work for. And believe me when I say, we want to stay as far away from him as possible." No one questioned his assessment.

Before they left the computer room, Riley entered another set of codes. As they rushed back to others, Jahmil asked what he'd done. "Hopefully bought us some time. I reset the passwords for all of the lower-level access points to slow them down in getting to us." Jahmil was admitted impressed, but noted Dakkar had said nothing.

A few minutes later they were back with the group. "What happened to you all? I was getting worried" Tehilla said, rushing to Carienne's side. They had been gone nearly two hours. After she assured them that she was alright, they introduced Riley to Bridget and the others.

Pulling Bridget off to the side, Jahmil told her of Riley's role in capturing Dakkar initially, and his help getting them out of the gas-filled hall. Bridget took in what they said, and turned to Riley.

"Welcome. And thank you for your help."

Dakkar was fit to be tied. Bridget smiled at the young man and placed a gentle hand on his shoulder. "Forgive him, young one. Just as God has forgiven us." With that, she walked away to let him calm down.

While the freed people were being attended by several members of the group, Bridget, the Unifiers, her team and Riley turned their discussion to how they were going to get out. "The upper doors are all sealed for now. And even if we opened them, the sheer number of soldiers would be too much," Anjelita stated.

Before any other ideas cropped up, Riley held up his badge. "We can get out with this. I know a back way through a series of tunnels that leads up and out. Of course, there are guards along the perimeter, so when we do reach the surface we may have to fight, but the majority of the soldiers are on the first floors." Having seen it themselves on the security monitors, Anjelita and Dakkar corroborated the man's report concerning the whereabouts of the soldiers.

Riley's plan sounded as good as any. A small number of soldiers they could handle, but not the entire army; and not while protecting the people they'd just freed.

As they made their way through the tunnels towards the surface, Haku asked a question. "Once we get up there, how are we going to get away unnoticed? I mean, the area is pretty open for nearly 10 miles in any direction."

His question was a good one, but instead of a direct answer, Laqat turned and smiled at the young man. "Already under control."

Chapter Forty: Fight and Flight

J ust as Riley predicted, there were guards when they came up. Fortunately, there were only a few on that side of the wall and they were busy laughing and smoking, as if they had abandoned some other post and slipped off to take a break. Bridget and Kafeel came up from the tunnel first and caught the half-dozen men by surprise. They were able to overtake them with relative ease, allowing the others time to surface.

Unfortunately, however, one of the soldiers was able to scream out for help as he fired his weapon at Kafeel. Momentarily forgetting that Kafeel could not be hurt by the bullets, Anjelita lunged at the man who'd fired and knocked him unconscious with one blow.

Within a few seconds more soldiers arrived. Soon shots were being fired and the fight was on. Unfortunately, the gunplay had alerted more soldiers and though they were able to hold their ground, the number of soldiers began to swell. Once again, Dakkar, Lark, Badee, Tookey and others from his tribe took to the skies and fought from the air. The volley of arrows they rained down upon the soldiers helped some, but the sheer volume of soldiers entering the area became overwhelming.

Dakkar told his people to return to the ground to assist the others. They were running low on arrows, and he was having more trouble dividing his talents between fighting and protecting his airborne comrades from the flying bullets; especially since they were being fired upon from several directions.

Once on the ground, Dakkar began pushing dozens of solders back using concentrated thoughts. Like the bowls and fruit he'd practiced on back in Sanctuary, he lifted screaming men off their feet and flung them towards the advancing troops, knocking them down and terrifying them in the process. It only took the soldiers a few minutes to untangle themselves from the small mass of bodies he'd created, and they were once again on the offensive. With the north-eastern side of the building to their backs and miles of open land to the front and side of them, Kafeel and the others knew they were effectively pinned down.

A short, muscular man in a uniform that seemed newer, cleaner and better than the others called for a retreat of his men. The soldiers didn't have to be told twice. Many of them had seen the strange and wondrous things those people could do and gladly stayed what they'd hoped was a safe distance back. They knew they had the advantage in terms of numbers and ammunition. They also knew that while there were nearly a hundred people in the opposing group, half of them were men, women and children who looked tired, sick and frightened.

The soldiers looked to their commander for instruction. The man remained silent for a while as he took in the situation. Like his men, he'd noticed the advantages his soldiers had and that half of the group's numbers were not fighters. But he had seen enough to know better than to underestimate the half who were fighting. He'd seen with his own eyes that they were powerful witches and sorcerers, and he knew he had to be cautious in how he planned to capture them.

Bridget and her group stood ready to resume fighting, but the soldiers had not advanced again since being called to retreat. Her eyes narrowed as she watched their leader quietly giving instructions and knew it wouldn't long before the fight would begin again. She was right.

After the commander had called for retreat, Daieh had Carlos and Jahmil follow her to the other side of the building out of sight. With Dakkar's help, the three were positioned on the roof behind two of the chimneys. Lark had told her about the huge brick chimneys when she and the other flyers took out the guards before gaining entrance to the building. She'd never seen one as large as these, but wanted to be situated behind them in case soldiers attacked from the rooftop.

The three had barely gotten into position when they heard the footfalls of a dozen soldiers trying to move quietly to their side of the building. Once the armed men had reached the center of the roof, Jahmil gave them their cue and Carlos and Daieh opened fire on the soldiers. Carlos, who didn't have the protection of a suit, stayed behind the smokestack and added his bullets from behind the safety of the bricks.

On the ground, the commander was obviously upset that his plan was being thwarted as he watched several of his men being shot down. In his rage, he screamed the command for his people to attack. He knew there would be more casualties than he'd wanted, but his future and a promotion was hanging in the balance. Even if he lost half his soldiers in the advance, he would succeed in taking down these foreign witches.

As soon as the soldiers began to run towards them, Carienne instructed Kafeel and Anjelita to bust the main water pipe for her. One they had, she directed the water's force towards the soldiers. The force of the blast knocked nearly two dozen soldiers back and tripped another half dozen as they tried to avoid stepping on their fallen allies. They screamed, cursed and tried to get away from the forceful stinging spray. The grass beneath them was now slick and wet and several places were pools of mud, making it difficult for them to maintain their footing.

Not sure how much water she had at her disposal, she planned to make the best use of what she did have. She swung the spray from side to side to keep the soldiers from gaining much ground. Catching on to what she was doing, Nopere, Mahi and others from her home assisted by keeping the rest of the spent water from soaking down into the earth so it could be used again. Though they didn't have nearly as much control over the water as Carienne had, their efforts were appreciated and she was able to keep her assault going.

Leaving Carlos and Jahmil on the rooftop to keep watch for more soldiers, Daieh rejoined Mmoju, Binah, Anjelita and her kinsmen on the ground below. As soldiers broke free of Carienne's defenses, she and the others used their speed and strength to fight any who got close.

Armed now with the automatic rifles they had taken from the fallen soldiers, Dakkar and his band retook the skies and sprayed bullets down on the soldiers. Still faced with the dual task of fighting and protecting his kinsmen, they only stayed airborne a few minutes at a time. The time they did spend in the air proved to be invaluable; from their vantage point they were able to take out over 100 soldiers at a time. Unlike the times they'd fought before, sparing lives was not an option.

Kafeel, Laqat and Myla were holding down the northern wall. Fortunately, the building had been situated close to a wadi. The ravine had steep banks that demanded respect. The distance between the building and the wadi was less than 50 feet, so their small band of three was effective in keeping that wall secure.

Bridget had positioned herself to the far left where Carienne's water weapon didn't reach. There was only a gap of about 20 feet between Carienne's defenses and the wadi, but the soldiers were trying to come through. Some of the soldiers had figured out this weakness and were trying to exploit it, only to find the large woman wielding Chaverah waiting for them. As soon as they approached, Bridget lunged towards them, slashing and hacking at them. In their terror, several men tried to turn and run, but in the chaos of some men trying to advance and others trying to retreat, many lost their footing and fell down the steep embankment.

The fight continued for a long while, but Bridget and the others knew they couldn't hold the soldiers back forever, but she was thankful that they had not lost any of their numbers thus far. She continued to trust God and thank Him for His strength as she sliced through the muscle, bone and sinew of the eight men who were advancing.

A few moments later, a command was given and the soldiers retreated once more. Not sure what was going on, Carienne returned the water to the pipes in case she'd need it again. Dakkar and his flyers returned to the ground beside Bridget.

As the soldiers moved back to the far western end of the glade, Tehilla and some of the other women gasped as they saw the carnage for the first time. Earlier they had been too busy fighting or holding their defensive positions to think about what war really looked like. All across the field were bodies, severed limbs and the tortured, pain-filled groans of those who were still alive. Well over a thousand men; most no older than Dakkar, lay dead. Dead for a cause they didn't understand and no one would benefit from.

273

Bridget stood viewing the scene as silent tears rolled down her unreadable face. She wept for these young men, but knew that what had happened was His will and it couldn't be changed. She also wept because she knew there would be much more bloodshed before their mission was complete; the enemy would see to it. None of them were left unmoved by what they saw, but as painful the scene was, they each silently gave thanks to God for their lives and the safety of their friends.

Chapter Forty-One: Anjelita's Choice

They were tense with anticipation of what was going to happen next. Again, their wait was a short one. The man Riley had identified as Mr. Cilfure stepped out from between the soldiers. "Stay still," Bridget warned. She knew who and what the fallen angel was and that as deadly as he was, he could not actually kill them; nor could they hurt him.

Smiling, he approached their group. Stopping about 20 feet from where they were, but close enough to see them clearly, he said "So, I finally get to meet the Unifiers. Dakkar and I have had the pleasure, but I am pleased to know you, young Carienne."

Carienne said nothing. Her head was pounding and she felt sick. She tightened her jaw and refused to let him see the pain she was in. But he wasn't fooled. "Ah yes. Not only can you heal others and control water, but you are an empath. Does my presence make you uncomfortable? Does it cause you pain?" His beautiful voice was mocking her.

"What you feel is power, child. Come with me and you will learn to control that wonderful gift. You will have the power to heal the masses. Think of how you and your family will live like royalty; because you will be."

Carienne looked the man straight in the eye. In spite of the body-wracking pain she was feeling, she told him, "I know who you are Lucifer. You promise everything and but have nothing to give."

The man smiled. "You say that now, but soon enough you will see the error in your thinking."

He turned to Anjelita. "And you, fair daughter of the dust. You have power that you don't even know about yet. Sure you are strong, swift, smart and can change your physical form, but there is so much more you can do. Surely you have seen this in your visions."

When she didn't respond, he continued. "Join me and rule by my side. Together you can have your revenge on the people whose petty greed caused your mother's death. Because of them you spent years in an orphanage being an outcast because of your gifts. All of the nights you cried yourself to sleep, lonely and believing something was wrong with you. Even now, you don't fully believe that your power and gifts are from the one they call the Almighty."

For a brief second the memories of her painful upbringing flooded her memory. She recalled how the other children had shunned her and how she'd heard Father Michaels telling Sister Magali that he believed she was possessed of evil spirits. Her mind briefly contemplated how her life might have been had her mother not died during childbirth after the long trek north. A trek she was forced to make because of greedy capitalists. She refused to look at him or even speak.

Cilfure shook his head sadly. "Well if you won't come willingly, maybe your mind will change once you see all of these people slaughtered. Maybe your mind will change with the knowledge that as we speak, my soldiers are awaiting my command in Guatemala, at your campsite in Senegal and on the beaches of Micronesia. Before you could even blink I could have everyone you love slaughtered. And not even the Star Woman can save them."

For the first time he addressed Bridget. "You're a long way from home Luz Estrella. And I am surprised to see you still

276

here. Where have you been hiding all this time?" His tone was light; almost friendly.

However, no one missed the seriousness of Cilfure's threats, least of all Bridget. She knew what type of evil this fallen angel was capable of, but she wouldn't waver. He'd called her by the name the early people used for her, 'Luz Estrella' which means Starlight in Spanish. But not even the term used affectionately by so many would sway her. She knew who and what he was. "You are a liar. You shroud your lies in truth and try to make people believe what you want them to. But I know the truth. Everything that happened was ordained by God, and everything these people have gone through has prepared them to do His work." Looking him straight in the eye she added, "You're wasting your time, Satan."

"Oh, am I? I will have what I want from the Unifiers, with or without their cooperation. Look around you. You're outnumbered and outgunned. We have fresh troops arriving constantly. Even with your gifts, you can't fight all of us."

Riley spoke up then. "I'd rather die for God than live under your control!" Cilfure turned his head and saw Riley.

"Oh really? That *can* be arranged, but didn't I kill you once before?" he taunted the man.

"You didn't give me life and you can't take my life," Riley said with conviction.

"Pity you've changed sides Riley. We had so much fun together. But that's alright, soon enough you'll beg to be back with me." With a final dismissive look, he turned his gaze back to Bridget to await her reply. When she still didn't respond, he turned his attention to the others.

"How about the rest of you?" He began addressing the people who had been freed and the kinsmen of the Unifiers. "Are you content with dying out here in the middle of nowhere for a cause and religion that you don't even believe in?" The gasps and sobs of some of the people tore at Bridget's heart, but she stood fast.

As he turned to head back towards the soldiers he told them, "Suit yourselves."

From somewhere behind her, she heard a woman call out, "What if we go back with you?" Bridget knew that these people had no idea what the fight between them and the enemy was about, or that to him their lives meant nothing. But she could understand that the fear of facing down the loaded guns pointed towards them outweighed all else for them.

Cilfure stopped and turned to them. In a grand gesture he opened his arms wide. "All who want to live; come to me now!" He and the soldiers were less than 50 feet away, so the sight and sound of nearly half the people they'd freed running towards their captors didn't surprise Bridget at all. The two dozen men and women running across the open field were half way to the soldiers when Cilfure's voice rang out in the silence of the night. "Kill them all and bring me the so-called Unifiers!"

Anjelita screamed out to Cilfure, "Wait!"

Bridget turned to the tall, dark-skinned woman and said vehemently, "No Anjelita!"

Holding up his hand to halt the soldier's fire, he turned to the young woman. For a long, tense moment she said nothing. Cilfure watched her intently; expectantly. Was this finally the moment he'd waited for? If she came to him willingly not only would he have more of the Unifiers DNA to continue his work, but he'd have a powerful ally; one who could help him defeat the plan of God after all. Without her, the rest of them didn't stand a chance.

"I will come with you," she said in a clear, strong voice. Once again, Bridget tried to dissuade her. Mmoju and Daieh, Carienne and Tehilla, as well as the others begged her to reconsider.

"No. My mind is made up!" she shouted at them. Facing Mmoju she wailed, "You should have come to find me! You should have listened to Anuka! But instead you let your pride and arrogance kill my mother! Do you have any idea what it was like growing up in a place where everyone hated you and feared you? Of course you don't! You were too busy trying to replace me with Daieh and Lanaia."

Mmoju tried to tell her it wasn't true, but she turned away from him. Facing Bridget, she continued. "And you. You speak of God being merciful. How could a god as powerful as you say allow all this disease, destruction, war and hatred to exist? I was blind, but now I see what *real* power looks like!"

"Enough!" Kafeel screamed. "Anjelita you don't really believe that and you know it. I know you; I know what a good heart you have. Just as you know that I love you. Stop this foolish talk now!" The big man was so upset he was shaking. None of them had ever seen him so distraught. They'd suspected that he'd harbored feelings for the woman, but to hear him publicly declare it was shocking.

Without turning around or looking back, she walked over to the soldiers. They were a bit wary of her, but they were relieved that one of their most formidable opponents would be fighting on their side.

Cilfure was elated! *Free will was joke*, he laughed to himself. "So," he asked her before he had his driver take him from the battlefield, "What should we do with them?" he pointed to the people who had started across the field a few moments ago.

Not bothering to look back, she walked deeper into the ranks of the solders and said, "Do what you want." Smiling, he gave the command to shoot them as he was being driven away. He was even more confident now that his plans were working. After Anjelita proved her worth to him by delivering the others, he would execute them all.

Bridget screamed her frustration at the sight of those men and women being gunned down like animals. She and her group were scrambling into defensible positions when they heard screams of agony coming from inside the soldier's ranks. Men were shouting and running and shooting; at what, Bridget and the others could not see.

A moment later they saw the horns of an African buffalo pierce a soldier and fling him high into the air. A second later, more screams followed as the sight of a boomslang viper snake struck several men. The soldiers tried to defend themselves by shooting at it, but in their fear they lost more bullets accidently shooting each other.

Being a veterinarian, Anjelita was well versed in the deadliest animals on the planet and she used that knowledge to her advantage. Changing forms every few seconds, the soldiers couldn't keep track of her and she was able to bite, sting and poison dozens of men each minute. As a saltwater alligator she tore limbs; as a carpet snake she bit arms and legs; as an elephant she trampled dozens; she jumped from one soldier's face to another as a poison dart frog. At one point while she was excreting the poison onto the face of a young man, one of his fellow soldiers tried to shoot her and blew the man's head off.

She was well aware that one of the soldiers might be able to kill her in animal form, but the chance to take out several hundred soldiers at once was a risk she was willing to take to save her friends. She also knew that she'd hurt them with the things she'd said, but she'd had to be convincing in order to be accepted behind enemy lines.

"Look!" Carienne cried. "Anjelita's taking them out!"

"She didn't betray us! Praise be to God in the Highest!" Bridget declared. In the 10 minutes that Anjelita had been with the soldiers, hundreds had already fallen. Smiling broadly, Daieh turned to Kafeel and the others. "Let's go help our sister!"

Though the soldiers' numbers reached nearly a thousand, Kafeel agreed that it was time to go on the offensive. With Dakkar leading the air raid, Bridget and the others on the ground pressing into their lines and Anjelita constantly changing forms and rendering them incapacitated, the soldiers knew they were defeated. Dropping their guns and running for their lives, they easily subdued the remaining soldiers who'd chosen to stay and fight.

But at the sight of a craft looming above them, they too dropped their weapons and ran. Looking up, Bridget and the others rejoiced at the sight of the Starlight as it came to rest right in front of them. The side door opened and Bridget herded the people onboard. Laqat jumped to the controls. Smiling at the surprise in the faces of his friends he stated, "Before we left I'd set the coordinates of the Starlight to hone in on us. When we were going through the tunnels I'd set the autopilot to come get us."

He held up his arm and pulled back the left sleeve to show two buttons on the underside. Smiling and shaking his head, Kafeel quipped, "So that's why we let you tag along!"

Lanaia showed a rare smile as she added, "And thanks for the automated message that played. When the ship started up and began moving we were pretty scared, but then that message came on and explained that you had sent for the craft." The fact that ship now held over 100 people was surprising to Carienne and she planned to ask about it later.

Once everyone was settled, Bridget gathered Anjelita in her arms and hugged her so tightly a woman with less strength might have been crushed. When she finally let her go, Mmoju and Daieh gave her a tight squeeze as well. They all let their hugs and the love in their eyes say what they were feeling.

All except Kafeel. "You scared me, woman. You could have been killed!" Though he was admonishing her for her daring play, the love and admiration he had for her was written all over his face. He too wanted to wrap his arms around her, but feared that if he did, he wouldn't let go.

Teasing him, she feigned annoyance and asked the onlookers, "Can you believe he actually tried to get me to believe he's in love with me?"

Grinning, Jahmil stated flatly, "He does. Boy's been sweet on you since the first time you knocked him down!" They spent a few more minutes teasing Kafeel and telling the ones who'd stayed aboard the Starlight the highlights of what transpired in their absence.

Mmoju was still worried about what Cilfure said about soldiers waiting to kill his family back home. When he brought up the subject, Bridget shook her head sadly. "I don't know if he's telling the truth or not. All we can do right now is pray for them."

Laqat, who had heard the question piped in. "Maybe not. I set up surveillance cameras everywhere we went." He gave the Starlight a command and a huge screen appeared where the windshield was. On one part of the screen they could see Abuela, Jafee and the others. They were just sitting down to the morning meal. Surrounding the area were Juba, Jalle and several other jaguars. They all appeared fine. Another part of the screen showed Yanni's family near the beach. They too seemed to be alright. Even though all of Dakkar's kin were with them, a quick scan of their former campsite showed no activity at all.

Cilfure was livid. The woman had deceived him. He'd been sure of her allegiance to him when she didn't try to bargain for the lives of her companions or plead mercy for the captives. He was so close to having the Unifiers, only to have lost them again. For him to realize his full plans, he needed their DNA.

When Dr. Meadows reported that she had trapped them in one of the hallways and had released a knock-out gas, he's been very excited. What he hadn't counted on was Riley's appearance. He realized he should have made sure the man was dead before he'd left the suite that night, but again he had underestimated his opponent. For centuries he had been so focused on convincing man that God either didn't exist or was unconcerned with them, that he'd almost forgotten how He would save His precious people. That was a mistake he swore to never make again.

He returned to the lab and picked up the phone. If he couldn't get them himself, he knew what to do. After placing a few calls, he learned that another part of his plan was going smoothly. At that, he smiled.

Chapter Forty-two: Plans Unravel

After dropping off the people they'd rescued from the labs in Payar, they warned them not to head back to their old homes. The soldiers were likely still in the area and would love to recapture them. After all they had seen, heard and been through, they didn't argue. Most had seen their villages raided and their homes destroyed and knew there was nothing to go back to anyway. Also, they could barely comprehend the events of the past day and knew no one would believe their tales of people who could fly, change their form and control water. No one would believe stories about a girl who could heal with a touch or that there were warriors so fierce that no bullet or blade could harm them. They knew this because they had seen these things for themselves and could scarcely believe it.

Once they were dropped off, the group decided to pick up the remaining people from Micronesia and head back to Guatemala. Because time was of the essence, they flew out. While en route, Anjelita asked Laqat if they had internet access. He chuckled and told her they did.

She called Carienne and Lanaia and told them they needed to get things set up to begin spreading their message. The three women wanted to search for the public websites that got the most traffic. "The best way to explain this," Lanaia began, "is to understand what the worldwide web is."

Bridget and the others wanted to know more about this social media campaign they were about to launch. "It is a computer-based system containing information. There are written documents, pictures, videos, music and a ton of other types of data. Companies, corporations and private citizens use the internet to learn about almost every topic known to man.

People also use it to share ideas, concepts, their own pictures and videos and information," Lanaia explained.

"Sounds complicated," Kafeel said.

"No, not really. In fact, it's pretty simple. All you have to do is write up whatever you want to say, or enter your video or pictures and push a button," Carienne told them. "Back home, some of my friends formed a Christian band called *Night Lights*, and I used to video them performing and upload it to the web." She knew that they didn't really understand it, but was pleased by their support. Turning to Anjelita, she said, "Let's just show them. Go online and look up my friends' band." She gave Anjelita the name of a popular site that she used to post the video clips.

Once she was on the web, she gasped at what she saw. Hurriedly moving aside and calling Bridget and the others over, they watched as portions of their last battle played across the screen. Newscasters worldwide were inundating the internet with footage and stories. Anjelita had Laqat turn the volume up so they could hear what was being said.

"Is Armageddon upon us; or have we been invaded by hostile alien forces?" One newswoman asked while airing footage of Badee, Tookey and Dakkar flying above the soldiers. She continued, "While the White House has not released an official statement, several military officials have claimed that the group of people flying overhead are part of a top-secret project. Claims have been made that the flying men and women shown here are wearing small jet packs. This reporter doesn't believe that because there are not jetpacks or any other apparatus visible. Also, how does the military explain this?" She switched to another bit of footage that clearly showed Dakkar deflecting the bullets of the soldiers.

"Perhaps the military expects us to believe that they are also testing some type of force field technology as well?"

Another link showed a similar newscast in French that contained footage from when they were inside the lab. On tape for the world to see was Anjelita changing form. Other sites featured Carienne's manipulation of water.

They watched for nearly an hour. It seemed that every news station in the world was showing the footage. And for every newscast, there were video blogs with people giving their opinion of what was going on.

There were scientists and sci-fi followers exclaiming that the technology to fly was available. There were metaphysicians and psychics discussing the reality of telekinesis. Conspiracy theorist claimed that it was a hoax to cause worldwide panic and drive up the prices of everything from food to oil. Theologians and religious leaders debated the possibility that Dakkar and the others were in fact angels who were preparing for the return of Christ.

Using footage of Bridget wielding Chaverah to illustrate his point, one theologian exclaimed, "You see the sword she wields? See how it slices through everything including the soldiers' guns? Surely it was not made on Earth! They are angels of the Lord Almighty, and they have come to prepare for the return of our Savior!"

"We're no angels," Tehilla stated, "but at least some of them get the general idea."

"Looks like our job just got 10 times harder," said Lanaia after watching so many broadcasts that her head hurt.

A thoughtful looking Bridget shook her head slowly. "Not necessarily. Lanaia, when you first mentioned using the media to spread the word I was a bit apprehensive. I wondered how many people would even see it and of those who did, how many would believe us. Now, with the whole world watching, we can use that to our advantage to let people know the truth."

Agreeing that the idea was a good one, they turned their attention back to what they would need, and how they planned to tell the story. By the time they had mapped out their details, they had reached Micronesia.

They spent less than an hour picking up the rest of Carienne's people. Aboard the Starlight, everyone laid back to rest in safety before traveling to Guatemala. After the long day and night they'd had, no one objected to resting. They set the Starlight for Guatemala.

Chapter Forty-Three: Confession

BY morning, they were back with Abuela. The old woman was so happy to see her son and granddaughters that she hugged them and wept for a long time. Finally able to let them go, she ordered the other women to begin preparing food for their guests. Introductions were made and the women headed off in a hurry to cook the meal. The newest members of the group were afraid of the wild cats lurking around them, but they were assured they would not be harmed.

Originally, Abuela and the others had left their homes in anticipation of the soldiers' arrival. However, after hearing of Esperanza's untimely death and the fact that no one came in the days that followed, they had returned.

Knowing they had a few hours before dinner would be ready, Daieh, Lanaia, Binah, Anjelita, Kafeel and Jahmil headed back to the house Lanaia had shared with her mother. She needed to retrieve her video camera and laptop. Lanaia had told them she could go alone, but they'd insisted. They claimed that after the trip in the Starlight they'd needed to move around, but she knew they were coming along to protect her.

She appreciated their concern, but wished they would stay behind. According to Abuela, Esperanza's body had been found two days after they'd left and so far, the investigators had no leads. She didn't know what would happen if she were discovered at the house. Surely her disappearance that night would cast suspicion on her and it would only be a matter of time before they discovered she was a murderess. The mission Anjelita and the others were on was much too important to have their lives and freedom jeopardized by her if she were to be caught, so she tried once more.

"Sisters," she began, looking up into the eyes of Anjelita and Daieh. "You must stay here and let me do this alone. If the authorities were to discover that I've returned I could be arrested. I've made peace with the Lord and I know He has forgiven me for what I've done. But if there are consequences to bear, I must bear them alone. I would happily spend the rest of my days in prison knowing that you were safe and doing His will. But I would die if I was the cause of any more hardship to you or the others!"

Her impassioned pleas touched their hearts, but they would not relent. "God has forgiven you and I have forgiven you as well. You risked your life for me more than once. It's only fair that I do the same for you," Daieh told her after giving her a strong hug.

"You are my sister, Lanaia. Your life is no less valuable than any of ours and you don't have to keep sacrificing it to prove you love us. We know that already. If you go; we go. And whatever we meet when we get there will be the will of Yahweh," Anjelita added, overjoyed because for the first time in her life, she truly understood what it meant to have a family; to have sisters and a father to always stand by her side.

Shaking her head at their stubbornness, Lanaia smiled and led them up the road. Upon their arrival, the small group went through the back door to avoid attracting attention. The first thing Lanaia noticed was that the kitchen was in worse condition than it had been in the night she'd left home.

She tried to avoid looking at the long-dried blood that stained the floor, and instead took in the broken bowls and crockery that were smashed during the struggle for the knife. The putrid odor of the milk that had been spilled still lingered. The neat, well-polished cabinets that once lined the wall and housed her mother's dishes and cooking utensils had been ripped from their place and stolen.

The small corner shelves that had held miniature figurines of Esperanza's saints were empty. The beautiful stove, refrigerator and microwave that had been imported from America were gone as well. The pantry door was hanging loosely on one hinge revealing the emptiness of the shelves. Gone were the sacks of flour, sugar, masa, rice, beans, coffee and canned foods her mother stored on them. The group looked on sadly as they watched Lanaia taking in the looted condition of the kitchen.

Lanaia was so caught up in her grief and memories of that night that Daieh had to pull her away. The living room had been trashed and the rest of the house looted as well. All of her mother's fine furnishings were gone. A quick inspection of the bedrooms showed that the beds had been taken, along with the television sets, clothes, books and shoes. Her mother's jewelry, the painted landscapes that once hung on the walls, the colorful rag rugs, the fine-gauge Egyptian cotton sheets Alejandro had given Esperanza as a gift were gone. All gone.

Lanaia felt sad and angry about the condition of her bedroom and the house in general. Though her room had not been spared, she dearly hoped they had not found her secret hiding spot. Inside the closet was a loose floorboard. Opening it carefully, she reached in and retrieved the metal box inside. The box resembled something a construction worker would carry his lunch in. Opening it, Lanaia found her diary and the matching gold earrings and necklace that she had accepted from one of the soldiers last year.

At the time, she knew her mother would not approve of her dating a soldier unless he was a highly ranking officer, but the handsome green-eyed serviceman had captured her attention. She'd snuck around seeing him for nearly a year, and for her birthday he'd gotten her the jewelry. Shaking off thoughts of him, she pulled out what she'd been seeking; her video camera.

When she and her soldier first began seeing each other, he'd given her the camera so she could videotape herself getting undressed. He'd told her at the time that since she wouldn't allow him to do more than kiss her, she should at least let him see her with her clothes off. It was a stupid thing to do, she knew now, but at the time it seemed fun and exciting. She'd felt powerful watching him beg her to see the tapes. She also remembered his frustration at finding she'd only stripped down to her undergarments. Even with his vehement promises of discretion, she knew she would die if anyone else ever saw them, so she'd played coy and shy.

In order to keep them from being discovered by her mother or their housekeeper, she'd kept these treasures hidden. Also hidden was the package of new tapes he'd given her. Holding on to the box, Lanaia and the others turned to leave the house. Her laptop was gone, but at least she had the camera.

As soon as they reached the living room, the sight of Alejandro staring around in confusion caught their attention. As his eyes settled on Lanaia, recognition and relief filled him. He rushed over to her and gathered her in his arms, crying silently.

He released her and repeated the move with Daieh. Though he was not as close to the younger girl as he'd been with her sister, it was clear that he loved her deeply. He seemed to notice the small group of onlookers for the first time and acknowledged them with a nod.

He continued to hold both girls hands as he whispered emotionally, "I was told you had been taken by the men who..." He couldn't bring himself to voice the horror that had befallen his sister. He'd returned from a four-week trip to Argentina this morning and found soldiers waiting for him. They told him that his sister had been viciously murdered and that it appeared his nieces were kidnapped.

Lanaia unconsciously jerked her hand back from her uncle. She couldn't bear to face him for fear that he would somehow see that she alone had been responsible for his sister's death. Knowing she had to say something, she quietly stated, "I'm fine Tio. I was with Daieh and Father." Still refusing to meet his eyes she added, "We must be getting back."

She turned to leave only to have him stay her with a gentle hand on her arm. "Lanaia," he began. "What happened? You never call Mmoju 'father' and you never stay with his people. Tell me. What happened?"

Not knowing what she should tell her uncle kept her silent for a long moment. How could she tell him that she'd killed Esperanza? And if she did, what would he do? Would he report her to the authorities? Would he hate her so much that he'd try to do her harm? And if he did try to tell the authorities, would Anjelita or Kafeel stop him? Would they be forced to kill him to keep the truth hidden? She had no answers; none for her uncle and none for herself.

Her eyes brushed across Anjelita's for a moment. *"And whatever we meet when we get there will be the will of Yahweh."* These were the words her sister had spoken to her earlier. Words of truth; words that strengthened her and showed her what she must do now. *Trust in the Lord.* Drawing in a deep, shaky breath, she turned and faced Alejandro.

Before she could begin to tell him what had happened, Jahmil interjected. "Not here. He can come with us if he wants to know all," he said.

Alejandro stared at the unknown man for a few moments. He wasn't sure why, but he felt he could trust the man. There was an open honesty in the man's gaze. *Besides,* he rationalized to himself; *they are only taking me to Mmoju's camp.* Alejandro had been 10 years old when his father died and Esperanza married Mmoju. During the first few years of their marriage, Mmoju had wanted Esperanza to live with him and had accepted Alejandro as a brother.

Alejandro had fond memories of his time among Mmoju's people. He could not compete with the other boys and girls his age in their games, but they were kind to him and still chose him first when picking teams. He remembered staying up all night in the men's house listening to stories about God and their ancestors. He learned quickly that the God they served was the same as the One he had been taught to worship. He also learned that their faith, devotion and understanding of and obedience to God was stronger, deeper and more profound than anyone he knew; including his priests.

Just as Alejandro was turning 15, Esperanza gave birth to Daieh. She insisted that Mmoju allow her to purchase a house in town and threatened to take the girls away if he refused. Once the house was built she'd forced him to go with her, although he'd protested strongly. For a while after they'd settled into the house, he would sneak back to the camp to spend time with Mmoju.

When Esperanza saw that he'd stopped praying to the saints and referred to God as Yahweh, Elohim, Elaha and many of the names she'd heard Him called by Mmoju's people, she'd been livid. In the weeks leading up to his 16th birthday he'd announced that he was going to go back and live with Mmoju. Not only had she forbidden him to do so, but a week later she'd sent him to Spain to be "educated properly," she'd said. He never knew where she had gotten the money for the housing and tuition, but he knew better than to ask; Esperanza had many secrets.

Moving as quickly and as quietly as they had come, the group returned to the others. Upon seeing Alejandro for the first time in years, Mmoju smiled broadly and gave him a welcoming embrace and manly slap on the back. "It is good seeing you again, Hermano," Mmoju said.

"Likewise," Alejandro replied. He wanted to spend time catching up with Mmoju, Abuela and the other smiling friends he'd once known, but there were other pressing matters to address first.

"Father, may we take Tio over to your house to talk privately?" Lanaia asked. Alejandro noticed the respect Lanaia showed Mmoju in her tone, her mannerisms and in her eyes. She was different, he realized, and his curiosity rose higher. The tall, smiling man granted his permission, but told them that the meal would be ready in an hour.

"You're not coming with us?" Daieh asked.

Sharing his smile with his youngest child, Mmoju answered softly. "No. This is something you and your sisters must do alone. I'll be here when you get back." Seeing the reluctance in their faces, he added, "Now hurry along; you know Abuela will take a switch to all of us if the food gets cold waiting for you!"

Though the girls giggled at Mmoju's threat, Alejandro's mind was spinning once more. He had said *sisters*; plural.

Having no answer to that question either, he followed quickly behind his nieces and the tall woman with them. The men who'd accompanied them back from town stayed behind.

They reached Mmoju's house quickly and took seats on the large pillows near the wooden, short-legged table. The house was much the same as he remembered it. The sleeping pallet was in the same corner, with its blankets and pillows arranged neatly. The table was still the only other furniture in the place except for the woven rug it sat upon. He also remembered how much Esperanza had hated the house with its lack of a stove, modern appliances, electricity, space or furnishings. She'd contemptuously called it 'Mmoju's savage-breeding hut.'

His reverie was short lived as a tense-looking Lanaia began speaking. She wasted no time and got straight to the point. "I killed Esperanza, Tio."

Alejandro's mind spun out of control. "What?" he shouted. She must be mistaken! He might have believed them if Daieh had claimed to have killed her because he knew the two didn't get along. He was well aware of the verbal insults Esperanza hurled at the young girl at every opportunity. But not Lanaia; Esperanza's favorite!

Lanaia gave her uncle a few moments to let what she'd just told him sink in. "It's true." To answer his question as to why she had done such a terrible thing, she told him she had to start at the beginning. She began with the arrival of Anjelita and the others. She told him how she'd rushed home and told her mother all she knew about the return of Mmoju's eldest child, leaving out her abilities for now.

"Sisters!" Alejandro exclaimed. He stared openly at Anjelita as if seeing her for the first time. Now, he could see the strong resemblance between her and his nieces. When he'd first come to live with Mmoju's people, he'd heard that Mmoju was married before. He also knew that a fight with the soldiers had caused the woman to flee carrying his unborn child. His sister had often cited her inability to compete with Mmoju's dead wife for his affections as the reason she could never love him, or give him her heart.

"Yes," she smiled affectionately at the tall woman. Her smile faded as she related the series of events that led up to Esperanza's demise. Though her voice was emotionless as she told him the details, the pain in her eyes revealed her sorrow. "Now that you know the truth, do you hate me?" she asked.

Alejandro moved to his niece and hugged her tightly. "Hate you? How could I, Sobrina? You did what had to be done." He held her close and rocked her gently as tears ran down both of their faces. For years he had listened as Esperanza berated Mmoju and his people. He'd watched silently as she would physically and verbally abuse Daieh until the girl grew old enough to stay away or to fight back.

He wept because during the years after his four-year stint in Spain, he'd said nothing as he watched the beautiful, light-hearted woman his sister had always been turn into a bitter, hate-filled shrew. He wept with the shame he felt because he'd known that the money to furnish the house and pay the bills had not come from Esperanza's catering business. Neither had the money to send him away to receive a fancy education or to stake him in his import business come from honest labor.

He'd blocked out the memory of the man who'd come to see her after their father was killed. The man who'd promised she would be taken care of if she married Mmoju. He'd also turned a blind eye to the men who came to visit her occasionally. Though they didn't come often and rarely stayed long, he knew what they were about. He couldn't stomach thinking about what his sister was doing, so he'd used his business as a reason to stay away.

But now, there was nowhere to run and hide. If he had been a strong man like Mmoju, he would have put a stop to it. Or if he'd been wiser, he would have gone to Mmoju and told him of his wife's infidelity and harlotry. But instead he had run like a coward. Just as he had run the day the man showed up and told Esperanza she was to marry. Even at 10 years old, he was the man of the house and should have refused to allow Esperanza agree to the man's terms. Now, his cowardice has cost his sister her life. For all her faults, he knew Esperanza had loved him and had done the best she could for him. And he'd repaid her sacrifices by running away. He'd failed her and he wept bitterly because of it now.

They sat in silence a few moments longer. When he released her, he asked her one more question. "You said that after you told Esperanza about Anjelita, she went to make a phone call. Do you know whom she called?" Lanaia shook her head that she didn't.

He was deep in thought for a few seconds and unintentionally said aloud, "I wouldn't be surprised if she was calling that Cilfure guy!" he spat bitterly.

Anjelita and the girls snapped their heads up at hearing his words. "How do you know that name," Anjelita asked brusquely. Her tone shocked him, as did the serious set of her face and the cold, hardness in her eyes.

Hoping her abrupt change in mood was not directed at him, he answered quickly and honestly. "I met him years ago. He's the man who arranged to have Mmoju marry my sister.

He'd promised to take care of us if she would spy on your people and report her findings to him." The thunderous look in the tall woman's eyes did not soften, so he continued, hoping to explain.

"You must understand, our father had just died in a war with your people," he addressed Anjelita. "Esperanza was barely 18 and had the sole responsibility of a 10-year-old boy. And even as beautiful as she was, none of the young men wanted to take a wife who came with a half-grown brother. We had no money to pay the rent or to buy food, so when the man came to see us and offered her money to do as he asked, she'd accepted. We were in a desperate situation, and her choices were to either accept his offer or to become a prostitute to feed me." He felt compelled to defend Esperanza and her decision. Right or wrong, she'd been his sister and he would remain loyal to her memory.

"I'm not interested in why she accepted the offer; I'm sure she had what she believed were good reasons," Anjelita said. Her voice had softened somewhat, and she chose words that would not disrespect her sisters' mother, but she wanted to know about the man.

Relieved that the woman's anger had seemed to dissipate some, Alejandro went on. "I only saw him once, and I was very young then. I remember he was very well-dressed and his voice was like music. He'd introduced himself as Mr. Tasan Cilfure and told us he had a proposition for Esperanza. Once he'd made his offer, he smiled and gave her a large envelope full of money. Then he turned to me as if he'd just noticed my presence. I swear, when he looked into my eyes I saw pure evil. I turned and ran from our little rented house with Esperanza calling for me to come back." Pulling himself away from the memory, he faced Anjelita.

"That's all I know about him. I do know that he must have had some connections with the militia because occasionally one would drop by and she would pass along information to them. She would usually send me on some errand so I wouldn't hear what she was telling them." He left out the part about her having these discussions in her bedroom, or that the visits came late at night.

Daieh looked out of the open door and saw they had been gone nearly an hour already. Even though the threat had been made in jest, no one wanted to have the others waiting on them to begin eating. "Come, we must hurry to get back before Abuela comes looking for us with her switches," she laughed, lightening the mood.

When they arrived, the platter of fried corn cakes was just being placed on the table. There was also a large, steaming bowl of rice, a crock filled with greens seasoned with onions and another of beans. Carienne and her kinsmen had offered to bring fish from the nearby lake, and their efforts were now lying on platters amongst the other offerings. Jafee, as the elder member, led them in a short prayer and they all began to fill their plates with the aromatic dishes.

As the meal wound down, the sisters related the condition of the house and the fact that Lanaia's laptop was gone. Riley told the girls they could use his android phone if they needed it. He explained that as long as he could connect to the internet aboard the Starlight, there should be no problem. Laqat assured them that they could either use Riley's device, or download their video to the internet directly from the Starlight. With that part of the plan in place, most of the group headed off to get some rest.

Chapter Forty-four: Get on your Mark...

B eing a pilot himself, Riley admitted to being awestruck by the Starlight and wanted an unobstructed look at the craft. Laqat had agreed to show him some of what the conveyance could do, so the two headed off in the direction of the hidden ship. Once aboard, Riley let out a long, low whistle. "This is amazing," he said in awe.

Now that the craft was empty, he looked around; puzzled at the small, open area for seating. The space appeared to be large enough to seat no more than six people comfortably. Yet, he knew there had been over 100 people aboard earlier. And since he'd been one of them, he knew they were all comfortable. Moving through the interior, he ran his hands along the smooth inner walls. Unable to contain his curiosity any longer, he asked, "How do the walls extend? And how far out do they go to accommodate more passengers? I don't see any seams."

He was rattling off his questions with such excitement that he dropped his head, smiling in embarrassment when he heard Laqat chuckling. He knew he looked like a new recruit stepping aboard his first plane, but he couldn't curb his enthusiasm. Never in his life had he seen something as sophisticated as this. He'd seen his share of top-secret aircraft with technology worthy of science fiction movies; but nothing in his wildest dreams could compare to this.

For his part, Laqat was thoroughly enjoying watching Riley. For the first time he was able to show the craft off to someone who truly understood how amazing the Starlight was. Kafeel, Jahmil and the other residents of Sanctuary were used to him flying around in Bridget's star-ship. And though they had been impressed by the changes made to it; their only interest was in its ability to get them where they needed to go with speed and safety.

But Riley, being a pilot and well versed in aviation technology, truly got it. Laqat allowed him to sit in the captain's seat, and reveled at the look on his face when the once-empty, smooth-looking dashboard came to life and revealed a plethora of buttons, levers and controls. The man actually squealed in delight and clapped his hands.

"You want to take it for a short ride?" Laqat asked. "We won't go far, and we can't stay long, but..." his never got to complete his sentence because Riley was nodding and saying "YES!" at the top of his lungs.

Smiling just as broadly, Laqat walked him through the basic operations. He wasn't worried about whether Riley was still in cahoots with the enemy and if he'd try to abscond with the craft after everyone was asleep. The Starlight was made from a living star and would only respond to someone whose intentions were in line with the Almighty.

After giving him the requisite commands, Laqat stepped back and watched Riley. The man was obviously nervous sitting at the controls, but no less excited. Once he'd given the commands, the craft started up. Laqat let out an inaudible sigh of relief; the man's intentions were true. He instructed Riley on how to maneuver the craft, and the two went on a short trip around the jungle. When they returned and settled back were they'd begun, Riley sat there beaming. "Wow!" was all he could say.

They spent a few more minutes talking about some of the capabilities of the vehicle, including the question Riley had asked earlier about passenger space.

To that, Laqat smiled. "Our Heavenly Father is the Great Provider. He knows what is needed and accommodates our needs accordingly. Just as Christ fed the multitudes with five small loaves of bread and two fish, so does He provide the space we need to do His work."

The answer both pleased Riley and filled him with a sense of awe and reverence for his God. After a few moments of basking in those feelings, he pulled out his cellular phone and asked Laqat to show him how to connect to the internet. Once the Unifiers had finished their recording, he'd want to be able to help them upload the footage. Laqat showed him how to connect, and once they were online, they both fell silent as they watched and listened to the latest reports.

"You heard it right folks," the announcer was saying. "The first 500,000 people to get their free, painless V-chip will be given an all-expenses paid trip to the biggest concert series in the world!" Riley's jaw tightened as the man continued.

"You and a chipped guest will choose from one of five cities to enjoy a non-stop, three-day, that's 72 straight hours; music extravaganza! The biggest names in Rock and Alternative music will play the Michigan Stadium in Ann Arbor. The best of the country music all-stars will be at the Darrell K. Royal Texas Memorial Auditorium in Austin, TX. Rhythm, blues and neo-soul greats will rock the Beaver Stadium in State College, Pennsylvania. An old-school 1970's and 80's concert like no other featuring the best artists of those two decades will rock the Ohio Stadium in Columbus. And last but certainly not least, for all you hip-hop and rap fans, the Sanford Stadium in Athens, Georgia will be the place to be!"

He went on to name at least two dozen super-stars in the music industry and promised that there would be at least 50 performers at each venue. "Live music daily from 8am until

2am, then highlights of the other concerts will be shown on the mega-screens from 2-8am! I tell you folks, this concert event will be so huge it'll make Woodstock look like a grammar school recital!" he laughed.

"Starting this Saturday morning, the first half-million people are going to one of these concerts! Check your area listings to find out where you can go to be first in line to receive your free, painless V-chip! But wait...there's more! If you miss out on the chance to be one of the first to get this revolutionary and life-saving implant and attend the mega-concert, don't fret; the next one million people will receive a tee-shirt signed by one of the performers and a 10-disc CD set of the concert's highlights!"

Riley knew that all of the venues he'd announced were sports stadiums and could hold over 100,000 people each with ease. He also knew that many of the people named were superstars in their genre. But what was worse, was that he knew many of them were devoted to the enemy and this concert business was nothing more than a ploy to make people rush to accept the mark.

He'd recognized several of the artists named and shook his head in disgust. He explained to Laqat, who hadn't known anything about the chip or the performers, why he was so upset by the broadcast. He began by explaining what the chip was and how it was to be implanted into the forefinger of a person's right hand. Laqat fully understood the implications of such a chip and was just as disturbed as Riley was.

As they headed back to the campsite to tell Bridget and the others what they had learned, Riley went on to tell his friend what he knew of the performers. "The entertainment industry has become so corrupt that in order to get a break, you have to sell your soul to the devil; literally. Radio stations, television stations, movie companies, you name it; they are all owned and operated by the enemy. They've gotten so bold with it that they wear clothes and jewelry covered in demonic signs. They constantly throw up signs with their hands and encourage their audiences to chant and throw them up as well. I've even seen interviews where they admit to allowing demons to take possession of them before they perform." Again, he shook his head sadly.

"And the worst part is that kids and young people are being targeted. They think it's all fun and games and that it doesn't mean anything when they recite the demonic incantations. And the adults and church leaders sit back scratching their heads wondering why suicide, disrespect, disobedience, disregard for human life, drug and alcohol addiction, sexual promiscuity, homosexuality and bisexuality are running rampant. People are opening themselves up to demonic forces and performing satanic rituals with the gods and idols they are worshiping disguised as celebrities!"

Riley's anger had peaked by the time they'd returned; his reddened face and tightened jaw was evidence of his feelings. After they told the others what they'd heard, Bridget shook her head sadly as well. "So it has begun," she stated quietly.

"What are we going to do? We could crash their sin-fest and stop the concert," Dakkar suggested.

"No, son. Our fight is not with the people attending the concert. And by then, they will have already accepted the mark. All we can do now is follow through with our plans, and pray. Tomorrow is Tuesday and the reports said they would begin implanting the chip on Saturday morning; 8am local time across the country. That gives us four days to spread the truth."

No one knew if their efforts would be enough, but it was all they could do. All of them had read and studied the scriptures and knew that time was drawing to a close on the evil of mankind. They hoped their messages of God's love and truth would make people turn their faces back to God, but they knew in their hearts that most would ignore them. For millennia, man had seen signs and wonders of His love, grace and mercy and had continued to harden their hearts against Him. Not even the death of His Son was enough for them to repent. The prophets and saints, the righteous leaders and preachers, the teachers, writers and singers who have devoted their lives and talents to sharing God's message have been dismissed as zealots, teased, mocked and abused.

Knowing how they were all feeling, Bridget spoke again. "Lift your heads and hearts, my friends! If only one person hears the truth and turns his life to Christ then we will have succeeded. Don't worry about the people who will not believe you, or those who will accept this mark. Trust that the people who will listen are the ones whom God has chosen." Smiling, she turned to Tehilla.

"I haven't heard your beautiful voice in a while, daughter. Sing praises unto the Lord!"

Chapter Forty-five: Make a Joyful Noise

Infected with a sense of renewed purpose, a smiling Tehilla stood and began the first verse of Amazing Grace. She wanted to sing a song that she hoped others would know, and chose the old standard for its beauty, and its timeless message of redemption. As she slid into the second verse, others had joined in. But to her ultimate delight, she realized they were each singing in their own language!

Anjelita's father, grandmother and the elders were singing in a language that sounded similar to Hebrew. Lanaia, Daieh and some of the younger people of Mmoju's tribe joined in in Spanish. Dakkar, Badee, Tookey and some of the other men from his clan were adding their voices in the Fulani language. However, Lark, Haku and some of the women sang in French. Mahi, Yanni, Nopere and the half of Carienne's kin sang the verses in Trukic-Ponapeic, one of the languages of the Micronesian islands. The other half, comprised mostly of elders, added Greek to the vocal mix.

To Tehilla, the sound of so many voices in several different languages blending together seamlessly in praise of God, was the single most beautiful thing she'd ever heard. By the time the song ended, everyone was joyfully praising God and crying and praying. Mahi, who had a beautiful soprano voice, sang a slow reverent song in her native tongue. No one needed to be told what the words meant; their hearts knew. They continued on in that manner with each group singing songs in their own languages until the late hours of the night.

"I need to speak with you privately," Badee whispered to Dakkar.

Seeing the serious set of his uncle's face in the firelight, Dakkar nodded, stood, and followed him away from the group.

Seated at the large table outside of Abuela's house, the two men sat and listened to the songs being sung by the group.

Dakkar knew better than to rush Badee, so he sat quietly and waited. After a few long moments, Badee turned to Dakkar. "I need you to do something for me," he began. He was unsure how his nephew would respond to what he was about to propose, but he felt the matter too urgent to ignore.

"Of course, Uncle. If I can, I will," Dakkar answered.

"It's Lark," he stated quietly.

Unconsciously, Dakkar turned his head and looked across the field to where she sat singing and praising with Haku and the others. "Is something wrong?" He wasn't sure what was troubling his uncle concerning his daughter.

"She's almost 20 summers now. I won't live forever and, well..." he stammered. "She needs a husband!" He blurted out.

Dakkar hadn't meant to, but he chuckled.

"You find this amusing?" Badee accused.

"No Uncle. I'm sorry I laughed. But... it's just that it seems to me she is already aware of that." Dakkar pointed to Haku sitting beside her.

"How can you even suggest something like that?" Badee asked, working to keep his temper under control. "He is not one of our people. I cannot allow it!" he stated vehemently.

Dakkar studied his uncle in the moonlight for a moment, but said nothing. For the first time, he noticed that his tall, strong uncle was beginning to show his true age. It dawned on him in that moment that Badee was nearly 65 years old. Hard work and his dedication to their people had kept his body in shape, but the laugh lines around his eyes that Dakkar remembered as a boy were gone. They had been replaced by lines of age, worry, grief and the difficulties of life on the run.

When Dakkar said nothing, Badee confessed his true desire. "I want you to marry her, Dakkar. You are her kinsman and I know you will protect her and provide for her." He slumped back against the edge of the table, apparently relieved that he'd said what needed to be said.

Dakkar shook his head sadly. "Uncle, I cannot marry Lark." Dakkar could see the sadness in the old man's eyes. When he'd been a boy, he'd learned the laws his people had concerning incest and marriage. If a man had more than one wife and children with each of them, the children could marry as long as they didn't have the same mother. Since Lark was only a cousin, none of those rules applied.

However, for many years the people of their clan would take only one wife, and usually it would be a distant relative. Back then, the people of his clan alone numbered in the hundreds and finding a suitable mate among their kinsmen had been an easy thing to do.

By rights, Dakkar should be flattered by Badee's suggestion to marry Lark; after all, she had grown into a beautiful young woman. Sometimes when he looked at her, it was hard for him to reconcile the skinny, bow-legged little girl who'd followed him and Tookey around in much the same way the two of them followed Tookey's older brother Nesom and his friends, with the curvaceous, chocolate-skinned beauty she'd become.

He thought back fondly on how Lark never played with the other little girls. She'd preferred to spend her time swimming and playing tree-tag with them. Some of the other boys teased Tookey about having his little sister tagging along everywhere we went, but no one really minded. She never cried foul if she fell or scraped her legs from the rough games, and everyone knew she was as good with a slingshot as the biblical David.

Her mother, Cassa, would often lament that she'd given birth to three boys instead of two and a girl because she'd have to threaten to beat Lark to get her to come help prepare the meals. Once, when Lark was about ten, she'd cried for a full day when she learned she wasn't going to grow up and be a boy. Dakkar and Tookey were preparing to leave with his father, Kalal, on the Journey to Manhood that all boys took as rite of passage in their twelfth year. She'd been okay with not being able to come along because of her age, but when Nesom inadvertently added the fact that it was only for boys, she'd become inconsolable.

"Why not?" Badee asked, his voice bringing Dakkar back to the present. "There is no one else!" The older man's frustration was plain; his deep voice a tear-choked, raspy whisper.

Speaking as calmly as he could, Dakkar tried to explain the myriad reasons he could not marry Lark. "Well, for one thing," he began; choosing his words carefully. "I'm on a quest for the Lord, Our God. And I have a responsibility to the others. I can't even think about taking a wife until this business is settled to His satisfaction. My life is not my own, but the Lord's. It would be unfair to any woman."

He hoped that would be reason enough to dissuade the man because he had no intentions of telling him or anyone else that a girl named Mahi had his interest. He barely even admitted it to himself because of his mission. Unfortunately, one look at the determination in Badee's eyes let Dakkar know that getting him to change his mind wouldn't be easy.

"Uncle, please understand. I *can't* marry Lark. Even if I didn't have this quest, she is in love with Haku and he is in love with her."

"But he is not of our people!" Badee continued to protest. "He'll teach her children to believe in silly superstitions. He'll have them bowing down to idols and worshipping false gods, men and money. No! I can't let that happen!" Badee stated, shaking his head vigorously. "She is a young girl and doesn't know her own mind!"

"Uncle, you taught Lark to be as strong and as confident as any man. Lark has never been one to follow anyone blindly. Even as a child she set her own course," Dakkar countered. "I've seen how men twice her age follow her leadership without question." Since the day he'd arrived, he'd watched her take charge of her people; dividing the chores equally, organizing the women into groups to cook and forage for food when they were back at the camp in Senegal, and leading the men into battle beside him when the time had come to fight.

"I know that we have always kept to ourselves and we don't marry outsiders; and for good reason. But Haku is not like many of the other outsiders, Uncle. Can't you see how he soaks up every bit of knowledge he can about God? Do you hear the questions he asks so sincerely?" Dakkar paused for a moment to gauge his elder's reaction to his words.

"No, Haku was not born to our people, but God has grafted him into our fold by his faith. Weren't you the one who taught me that *Jehovah-tsidkenu*, in all His glory chooses who He will as His people?" Dakkar's voice softened. "Are you willing to bear the responsibility of trying to pull asunder what He may be joining together?'

Badee sat quietly for a long moment, weighing the wise words of his young nephew. He had to admit that Lark was an exceptional young woman. She had proven herself to be a brave warrior and had earned the people's respect. He was still the elder of their small clan and was called upon to make decisions concerning their clan and to settle disputes, but it was Lark whom they followed into battle; not the tired old man he'd become. Even he respected her judgment and that she was not an addle-brained girl. Glancing over at Dakkar, he let a small smile show. "When did you get to be so wise, Mwanetu?"

Dakkar's heart swelled at hearing Badee address him in one of the languages spoken to the East. During the years of his imprisonment, Dakkar had refused to allow himself to remember the words of affection and terms of endearment used by his people. Words like *mwanetu* which is Swahili for my son; *neveu* which is the French word his people used for nephew, or the Spanish term *mijo* that Cassa often called him, Tookey and Nesom. His captors never referred to him by name, but rather with a series of pronouns usually reserved for inanimate objects. He'd been referred to as "it" and "that" so much he'd forgotten the sound of love in a familiar voice.

"Wisdom comes from the Lord. Occasionally He gives us glimpses of His plan and it is our responsibility to heed it," Dakkar answered. "Besides," he added, "I didn't want to have to remind you that Haku saved your life once and that deed alone should grant him enough favor with you to be considered as a suitable husband for your daughter."

Laughing loudly, Badee slapped Dakkar on his back affectionately as he stood to head back. "It seems to me that you just did!" The two shared broad grins as they headed back to the others. Shortly after they rejoined the group, the revelers tamped down the fires they'd built earlier and headed off to rest; content that the Lord's will would be done.

Early the next morning, Alejandro joined them in prayer and a meal. He'd intended to head back to town at sun-up, but he found he couldn't resist Abuela's fried corn cakes drizzled with honey. After breakfast, he and Mmoju sat and talked for a while as Lanaia, Anjelita and few of the others headed to the clearing. He saw the video camera his niece had and figured they were going to take videos of themselves in much the same way people do at weddings, family reunions and other gatherings.

Mmoju was asking him something, but he failed to respond because Anjelita had just turned into a tiger. "Did you just see that!" he exclaimed as he jumped to his feet. Right before his eyes the young woman changed into a series of other animals, birds, reptiles and rodents.

Chuckling at the younger man's wide-eyed disbelief, he told him to sit back down. "There are some things I need to explain to you, and you'll want to see what happens next," Mmoju assured him. For the rest of the morning and into the early evening, an astonished Alejandro watched and listened to Mmoju's daughter and her friends.

By the time supper was served, he had asked Mmoju and the others a million questions and felt like he had a million more. "Wow! This is really great," Alejandro said to Daieh, who was seated beside him. The smiling girl nodded her agreement. His fatigue from the excitement of the day was catching up to him. A few minutes later he stood and stretched. "I'd better be getting back. It's getting late," he told her through a long yawn.

"I thought you would be staying here with us?" she asked, the disappointment showing clearly on her face.

Smiling down at his niece, he bent and gave her a strong hug. "I would, but last night reminded me how hard and cold the ground is; even with a pallet," he chuckled. "And I've grown accustomed to sleeping in a bed."

Lanaia, who was also seated nearby with Binah reminded him of the condition of the house. "Robbers have taken everything; including all the beds and bedding, Tió. You don't have a bed to go home to."

"True," he conceded. "But Francesca does," he added, waggling his eyebrows. His nieces knew that Francesca Maria Gutierrez Gibron had been his paramour for over a decade. Shortly after he'd returned from school he'd met the beautiful, dark-brown, Dominican-born woman. In spite of the fact that at the time she'd been made a widow by the same war that had taken his father and was seven years his senior, he'd fallen for her immediately.

Of course, Esperanza had balked at the idea of him marrying her. She'd cited the woman's dark skin, foreign birth, widow status and age as reasons for him not to marry Francesca. When that didn't work and he was still bent on proposing, she reminded him that the woman he loved had worked for several years after her husband's death as a prostitute.

He'd finally agreed not to marry her, but that hadn't stopped him from buying her a small house on the other end of town once his business started to grow and expand. Now, her attentions were only for him, and after the day he'd had; he was in need of her comforting. Bidding them farewell, Alejandro headed the twenty-two miles back to town; he couldn't wait to share his news with his lady-love!

~~~~~~~~~~~~~~~~~~~~~~~~~~~~~~~~~~~~~~~

Half-way across the world in a small Italian city outside of Rome, Mr. Cilfure sat with a feral smile on his face. His plan was coming together and there was nothing anyone could do to stop it! No, he hadn't killed or captured the Unifiers yet, but that would come soon enough. His mind flashed momentarily on how the beast-woman had deceived him. He should have known better than to trust her; he should have stayed. But he hadn't; he'd needed to attend to other matters.

In hindsight, it was good that he'd left to make his other arrangements because as it stood now, his plans were back on track and stronger than ever. Setting aside thoughts of the shape-shifter for the time being, he did a mental checklist of his plan's other components. His plans to have everyone in the world accept the chip willingly was already in progress.

The leaders of the world's banking institutions, most of which were already aligned with him, had successfully convinced their board members to implement a policy that would make cash obsolete. In their vain attempts to "protect" themselves and their wealth, many were already willing to take the implant. Soon, his select, hand-picked followers would be able to control all of the world's economy; no one would be able to buy or sell anything without the implant, and without him getting a large piece of the profits.

Within a year, they would all be enslaved by him. The cost of bread would become so high that men would gladly offer their sons' and daughters' bodies for the price of a single slice. He knew that there would be a few who would refuse to accept the mark out of some misguided belief in conspiracy theories or for their blind devotion to Him, he thought ruefully; but in the end many of them would come out of starvation and desperation.

For those who had openly refused him in the beginning and accepted his offer later, he would set them up in fine houses and fine clothes for the others who'd refused to see. He will shine the lights on them to illuminate their wealth and apparent prosperity. He would show them that taking the chip was the only way to save themselves from poverty and destitution. They will come as well because they will be tired of the hardships of exclusion. Just as he'd made the world accept, then promote homosexuality and sexual immorality, so he would do with this.

His mind moved to the second phase of his plan; outlawing all forms of religion that did not have him at its center. The government leaders he already controlled agreed whole-heartedly that religion and religious differences were the main causes of civil and international wars and strife. Under his gentle prodding, public prayer had been banned in most places and God had been removed from all holiday observances and public celebrations. Those who openly declared a love for God were ridiculed and mocked. The leaders stood ready to follow his command to make all forms of worship illegal.

He laughed aloud as he thought of how the devout Christians would cry out in protest, but it would be too late. Many of their very leaders served him and those foolish people didn't even realize it! Many of them had made deals with him to ensure their ministries prospered. He'd set them up well; given them huge churches and beautiful buildings. The only thing he required is that they fill their parishioner's ears with half-truths, and they had done so marvelously!

Week after week people were being led to "spiritualism" instead of Christ. They were told to believe they could have whatever they wanted and it would be given to them whether they were obedient to God and followed His Son's teachings or not. Like sheep being led to the slaughter, the people followed the teachings and doctrines of men who publicly upheld all manner of unrighteousness in the name of a loving God; many of whom had already accepted his mark. How quickly they'd accepted a new-age Christianity that allowed them to do whatever they wanted; to follow every fleshly vice they craved without repentance. As long as they made the obligatory contributions to the church, all would be forgiven by a tolerant, passive god who understood that they all made mistakes, but as long as they were "good people," they were His friends.

In two days' time millions of people world-wide would run to accept the implant, and the majority of them would be young. By his estimate, he would have 90% of the people between 14 and 30 by Monday morning; and that was just in America! They will leave their schools, defy their parents and do whatever they have to do to get to one of the concerts. Already, advertisements featuring the most popular celebrities were filling the airwaves, encouraging them to "get chipped" because they had. He'd chosen the best, most beautiful, most popular people to appear in them because they were the gods the young people worshipped. Being the Prince of the Air and a musician certainly had its advantages!

In other parts of the world where such an event would only get him 20 to 30% of that demographic, he'd had to come up with a different plan. Food, land and water rights were of the utmost importance in some areas. He'd told the leaders in those countries to announce a land redistribution plan. All men over the age of 18 who have accepted the implant will be eligible for a tract of land, seed, and access to irrigation technology.

Many of the men whose forefathers had colonized areas in Africa and India had not wanted to offer up their land as bait, but once he assured them that they would still have total control, they relented. He'd explained that after everyone had the implant, they would control the prices of food.

"The people may own the land, but they have no granaries. They would also be indebted to you for the use of their irrigation systems, seed and supplies. Under his instruction, huge agricultural firms had already lobbied the politicians to make the use of any seed not sold by their companies illegal to use and anyone who did were fined or imprisoned. Small farmers were effectively locked out of being able to compete with the large farms because they couldn't afford the cost of seed. Most of them had lost their land in most cases, pleasing him further.

"Keep in mind, gentlemen," he went on to tell them, "that our primary goal is to rid the world of the useless people who suck up our resources." Over the past three decades, he had overseen their progress in genetically altering the majority of the world's food and water supplies. While most people were aware of the dangers associated with pesticides, they had no clue of just how far he had gone to ensure mass sterilization and the innumerable health problems connected to the poisons used in crops, animals and synthesized products. Even those who claimed to eat organically grown foods could not escape the fact that the seeds themselves have been genetically engineered or that the ground had been chemically treated.

"And of course," he'd added slyly, "they still have to pay taxes. Within 2-3 years you will have all of the land back when they can't make enough of a profit on their crops to pay the taxes."

He sat and gloated a few moments more at the ingeniousness of his plan before he allowed his mind to stray back to the last piece in his puzzle; the Unifiers. By broadcasting their abilities to the world, he'd been able to spark enough fear in the hearts and minds of people to make them steer clear of the Unifiers. Most of the television and radio stations were under his control, so having them spin stories of the trio being aliens from outer space coming to take over the planet, was a relatively easy task. People were so gullible that they would believe just about anything they saw on TV. Now with them exposed, it would only be a matter of time before someone would capture them for the 20 million dollar reward that was being offered for each one.

And when they do capture them, he smiled once more, *I'll be ready*! With that thought, he headed back to Senegal. He had to be sure everything was ready at the lab when the Unifiers were captured.

Chapter Forty-Six: Folly of the Heart

Alejandro walked quickly back through town. He didn't bother stopping by the house he'd shared with Esperanza because he knew there was nothing left to gather there. During his trek, he'd decided to have the house repaired and refurnished rather than selling it. Most of the damage he saw was cosmetic, and though it would cost a tidy sum to make it inhabitable again, he would do it so that Lanaia and Daieh could have a place of their own. He'd also decided that he was going to live with his sweet Francesca and that he would marry her.

He arrived at the neat, modest but well-appointed house late that evening. Using his key, he entered quietly and made his way to the bedroom in the still, dark house. Upon hearing him enter, Francesca stirred. "Al?" she inquired sleepily. Though it was only about 9pm, he knew she'd already be in bed; she was the epitome of a morning person, always rising well before dawn.

"Yes, Morenita. I'm back." He made his way over to the bed. She sat up and reached to turn on the lamp sitting atop her nightstand.

"What took you so long? You said you had to attend to that nasty business about your sister, and that you'd be back soon. That was yesterday morning," she pouted, glancing at clock. "I was worried."

Alejandro smiled down into her beautiful brown face. At 39 years old, she was still a beauty. Her petite frame was firm and lush, and the course, thick black hair that hung past her shoulders was free of gray and still as shiny as it was the day he'd met her.

Slowly drawing his finger across her cheek and jawline he whispered, "I'm sorry I worried you." When he'd arrived yesterday morning and found the authorities waiting for him with the tragic news of his sister, Francesca had been waiting for him as well. He'd sent her back to her house along with his luggage and a promise to return shortly.

Unable to resist, he pulled her to him and kissed her full lips passionately. Her arms came up to pull him closer, but he stopped her and drew back. She raised a delicately arched brow in confusion. In all of the years they'd been together, he'd never turned down her affections. Catching his breath he told her, "We need to talk."

Panic struck her instantly. Had he found someone else? Was she being pitched over for a younger model? Had he decided to seek a woman who could give him children? A thousand questions screamed in her head at once, but she fought to remain calm. "What is it?" she asked with as much calm as she could muster.

"You won't believe the wonderful news I have!" His excitement made her relax a bit. Surely if he'd been intent upon giving her the sack he wouldn't be so elated. She knew that Alejandro was a kind-hearted man and didn't have a cruel bone in his body.

"My nieces are both alive! They were with their father the night Esperanza was killed." He didn't dare tell her the truth about Esperanza's death; not because he was afraid to take her into his confidence, but because he didn't want her to think badly about his niece now that he planned for the two to become in-laws.

Upon hearing his news, Francesca let out an audible sigh of relief. "Oh, I'm so glad! I've been praying to the saints for their safe return!" She hoped he believed her reaction to his news was related to the safety of his nieces, and not to her relief that he wasn't breaking off their arrangement.

"And there's more," he continued, encouraged by her response. "They have an older sister!" He relayed. "Their father, Mmoju had a daughter by his first wife and now she has returned." He'd told Francesca about his sister's in-laws many times in the past. He knew that she felt the same way about them as Esperanza had, but he believed if she were given a chance to know them she wouldn't be so hostile.

"Alejandro, you know how I feel about those..." she caught herself before she said "savages." She knew the slur would upset him. "People," she completed the sentence. "I hold them personally responsible for killing my husband and for making me become so destitute I had to resort to..." she turned away from him. The anger she felt for the years she'd had to suffer as a result of their crimes made her cheeks burn and tears spill down her face.

Seeing the pain on his beloved's face nearly broke his heart. Pulling her back into his embrace, he wiped away her tears and whispered, "I know. I know." He held her for a long moment and when he released her, he continued. He had to make her see that she and Esperanza had been wrong about Mmoju and his people. It was too late for Esperanza, but he would do everything in his power to help Francesca accept the truth.

"I know how you feel about them," he began. "But you have to understand that things did not happen in the way we were led to believe. My father and your husband were casualties of a battle that should never have taken place. Mmoju and his people had lived in that area for decades, staying to themselves and not bothering anyone. What would you have done if people came and tried to evict you from your home?" He didn't wait for an answer.

"You would have fought to protect it," he stated quietly. "And when soldiers opened fire on you, you would have fought back to save your life and the lives of your family." Alejandro took her small hands in his. "And what you and Esperanza never understood is that they are not a bunch of wild, uncivilized savages. In fact, they are blessed of the Lord! The strength and speed that you fear is a gift to their people from God."

Francesca stared at him. She knew he'd spent some time among those people when his sister first married, and that he'd often spoke highly of them. She could never share his admiration for the people who lived in seclusion among the beasts, and doubted she ever would. She knew he could talk for hours about how strong and wise Mmoju is and how he'd never felt as close to God as he did when he was with them. To head off one of his long-winded stories, she sought to change the focus somewhat.

"So this new niece you have," she began. "Tell me about her. Is she like them, or did she grow up among us *common folk*?"

Alejandro chose to ignore the sarcasm in her voice. "She grew up in America. Her mother died giving birth to her after sneaking across the US border. She was granted citizenship, but little else. Poor girl grew up in an orphanage," he said sadly. His tone brightened once more as he told her, "But she is like her people; smart, strong and fast. In fact," he paused to make sure he had her complete attention. "She can do extraordinary things; she can change her form into any animal she chooses!" He blurted out excitedly.

323

Seeing her eyes widen, he told her more. "It's true; I saw it for myself. She can become any type of animal she wants to in the blink of an eye. And she'd not the only one," he rushed on. "There are people with her who can do other things that are just as amazing. Some can breathe under water and some can even fly!"

He was so enthusiastic in the telling of his story that it took him a few minutes to see how pale Francesca looked. Thinking that fear over the strange things he had told her was the cause of her silence, he sought to console her. "Oh, my sweet..., don't be afraid. They want to help us; everybody in the world, to reconnect with God. Don't you see?" His eyes were pleading. He desperately wanted her to believe him and to understand that she must give up praying to her Orichás and saints and offer her prayers and her life to the One who gave her life.

In the past Alejandro had spoken to her about her methods of worship and prayer, but he'd never pressed her about abandoning her faith before. She'd never told him that she was a high priestess of Santeria, or that the figurines of the saints displayed prominently and strategically around her home were in fact the Seven African Powers. Each one represented one of the gods of her people and she would never turn her back on them. Olodumare, the god of all creation had given them these seven lesser gods along with others, to help and protect her people because he had more important things to do. These people who Alejandro claimed to be connected to the Supreme God were liars!

Alejandro was a fool; a gullible, weak-minded, hopeless fool! Her Orichás had given her power over this weak man and caused him to take care of her all these years. When he'd purchased this house, he hadn't argued when she told him she

324

wanted only her name on the deed. At the time, she'd given him the excuse that since they were not married, sharing property with a woman in her previous line of work could be damaging to his business. The truth was, she'd been in her early 30s at the time and knew that her looks would not always provide for her and she'd need a place of her own when they faded.

It was visions of the saints who'd come to her during one of her trances that instructed her to take 20% of the monthly allowance Alejandro gave her and hide it in case he ever left her. Those same saints had also warned her not to stop seeing the two high-ranking officers or the police captain she'd had assignations with, so she'd continue to fatten her secret bank account with the funds she got from them as well.

She also knew that her devotion to her gods had led Alejandro to her this evening with this information. She'd seen and heard about these people all over the news. Every time she'd turned on the television or the radio, reports about these people filled her ears. She'd only half-listened to what was being said about them, but she remembered clearly that a reward of 20 million dollars was being offered for the capture of each one.

With that type of money, she could go home to her beloved Santo Domingo and take care of her ailing father and aging mother. They could all live out their days in wealth and comfort. She knew it would not be easy to capture any one of them, but with Alejandro's unwitting assistance, she knew she had a chance. And unlike him, she was no fool; she planned to seize this opportunity and hold on with all her strength.

Francesca sought to reassure him that she was alright, and was just shocked by the news. She had to act as if she believed him and was willing to learn more about these people in order to formulate a plan and not to arouse any suspicion. In her line of work, she'd always had to be a good actress in order to build a clientele and receive tips in addition to her price. Her looks and body may have gotten the men's attention, but it was her acting skills that made them come back; and now she would have to give her best performance ever because the stakes were very high.

"Oh, Alejandro! If what you're saying is true, then they *must* be divine of God! And if they are," she turned her head away as if she were ashamed. "Then my hatred for them all these years is the true cause of the pain I've suffered. I've been cursed by God!" She flung herself across the bed and began sobbing.

"No!" Alejandro objected. "That's not true at all," he countered as he stroked her back in an attempt to soothe her. "God loves all of us Francesca; no matter what we've done, He will forgive it. That's what they want people to know. They won't hate you or hold any hard feelings towards you." He continued to rub her back gently as her cries settled into sniffles.

Wiping away the tears she'd learned to bring to her eyes with ease, she sat up. "Are you certain?" she asked, deciding to play it for all it was worth.

"I'm positive," he assured her.

Smiling up at him, she wanted to know everything about these people she could, but wanted to start off slowly. It wouldn't do for her to ask him questions about their plans, weapons or numbers right away; she had the rest of the night to learn those details. She'd need to lure him into giving her the information, so she started with something simple. "Did I ask you what her name was; your new niece?"

Smiling brightly and excited by her interest, he answered cheerily; "Anjelita. Anjelita Azul; isn't that a fitting name? One of the nuns at the orphanage named her."

The hair on the back of her neck rose. *Anjelita Azul?* That was the name of the child her sister had helped raise in California. It was also the woman whose veterinary clinic Magali was visiting when she'd been savagely attacked by an animal last year. Francesca's head was spinning and her throat went dry. Alejandro said Anjelita was a shape-shifter! This had to be the same girl Magali would brag about in her letters home to her and their parents.

Her people lived among animals and she'd become a veterinarian. There were too many coincidences and now it all made sense. No animal had gotten loose in the clinic that day and killed her sister; she'd been murdered by this abomination! That's why the girl had disappeared and could not be questioned. It all made sense now, and it would make cashing in on their capture that much sweeter.

Alejandro had started telling her some of the animal forms he'd seen the woman take, when Francesca cut him off. "I'm sorry love, but this has been a very exhausting day. I think I need to lie down for a while. Do you mind?"

He was a bit disappointed that she didn't want to hear more tonight, but his spirits were still lifted that she'd finally come to accept what he'd been telling her. He also realized that he'd just challenged all of her religious beliefs and it would take time, strength and courage for her to move on. He supposed she did need her rest. "No. I don't mind. Get some rest," he told her as he stood to leave the room. He thought she wanted to be alone for a while with her thoughts, so he was going to rough-it over at Esperanza's house.

327

"Will you stay with me?" she asked, her voice sweet as honeysuckle.

The knowledge that she'd wanted him to stay with her made him happy. She needed him, and every man wanted to be needed by his woman. He knew that he provided well for her, but he'd never sensed that he was truly needed by her. Now he did, and that knowledge filled him with joy. He answered by stripping out of his soiled clothes and sliding under the covers next to her.

The fact that he'd not showered and smelled of sweat and animals didn't bother her as much as it would have ordinarily. With her financial future hanging in the balance, she would endure the stench for one night. The most important thing was that she keep him near until her plan was fully formed. The final act of her performance in tonight's play would be to scoot over and press her back to his chest and cuddle in for the night. They each settled into a contented and happy sleep, though for very different reasons.

Chapter Forty-Seven: "And the Award for Best Actress Goes to..."

Francesca awakened early that morning and slipped quietly from the bed. A few hours earlier, Alejandro had awakened and reached for her with soft caresses, intimating his desire for her. She'd consented because to refuse him would have aroused suspicion; something she could ill-afford at this stage in her plan. She also knew that once he'd been satisfied, he would sleep until at least 8am.

She moved through the familiar pre-dawn quiet of the house gathering up the things she would need and heading down to the small, dark cellar. She lit her candles and incense after arranging the gods in the correct order. She sat cross-legged on her ceremonial mat in front of them and rested her hands on her knees with her index finger and thumb touching and the remaining fingers outstretched.

She closed her eyes and began to chant softly to awaken the gods and ask them to hear her pleas. It didn't take long for the presence of their spirits to be felt. She sat, rocking slowly back and forth as she communed with the spirits. By the time they left her to return to their homes in the spirit world, she knew what had to be done. Francesca blew out the candles and headed upstairs to begin preparing breakfast.

By the time the sun was up, the camp was a bevy of activity; Mmoju and the men were sharpening their spears while Laqat, Jamil and Kafeel went exploring in the surrounding jungle for edible plants, berries and nuts. Carlos, Mahi and a few of Carienne's relatives went to fish and gather edible seaweed. Likewise, Lark, Tookey and few of their kinsmen armed themselves with their bows and arrows to bring back meat. With so many people to feed, the food grown in the small gardens tended by Abuela and the other women was not enough.

Carienne groaned at the fact that she and the other Unifiers would have to redo the video they'd spent all of yesterday filming because the tapes were no good. Lanaia felt particularly distressed when she and Carienne had tried to play them back on the Starlight's monitor. She confessed that she had never tried to play any of the tapes back before, and that she'd only allowed her soldier to see what she'd filmed twice and both times she'd used the playback feature on the digital recorder.

After assuring her that it wasn't her fault and that they could easily redo the video, Lanaia, Binah, Daieh, Kafeel and Anjelita headed to town to purchase new tapes for the camera. Anjelita also wanted to get a feel for the town and explore the area a bit more.

It was clear that Lanaia was uneasy about making the trip back into town. Anjelita picked up on her sister's apprehension and tried to comfort her by letting her know they would be there to protect her.

"Actually," Lanaia began, "I'm more worried about you being recognized or someone starting trouble with us because of Binah."

She had become very fond of the young man and didn't want the prejudices of small-minded bigots to cause him a problem. Throughout the years she had been something of a pariah in town because of who her father was; fueling her anger towards Mmoju when she was younger. One of the reasons she'd taken up with the soldier was because he hadn't been from their area and saw her for herself; not as the half-breed savage others often referred to her as when Esperanza wasn't around. She'd known that her mother's connections with the military and the police offered her physical protection, but it did little to stop he tormenting of her classmates and the townspeople when she'd been alone.

Taking a series of back roads as they made their way through town, Lanaia also considered the possibility that once recognized, she might be arrested or taken into custody for questioning about the events surrounding her mother's death. That scenario was the least of her worries because after a long conversation with Mmoju, Bridget and the Elders, she had memorized her alibi.

They entered the large super-store that carried everything from groceries to clothing and headed straight back to the electronics department. It took only a few minutes to make their purchase, but not before a few of the customers saw Binah. The angry looks on their faces were followed by nasty words and taunts. They moved quickly through the large store toward the exit, but by then a small group had gathered near the door, blocking their departure.

"What are you doing in here, monkey?" One of the men asked Binah. He knew better than to answer. No matter what he said, it would be seen as a challenge or as a sign of weakness. Either way, he wanted to avoid a confrontation if he could.

Anjelita was wearing a pair of jeans, tennis shoes and hooded sweatshirt sporting the picture of the American president, making her seem like a tourist. They glanced at her dismissively and refocused their eyes on Binah. Though they paid Anjelita scant attention, they did view Kafeel suspiciously. The tall, well-muscled White man looked as if he could protect himself easily, and one look at the fierceness in his eyes made them wary.

"What in the world is a White man like you doing keeping company with the likes of him?" Another man asked Kafeel. Anjelita was angry at the racist implications of the man's words, but she was also surprised by it because none of them were White. Though their colors ranged from golden-tan to brown, none of them could claim Caucasian heritage. Their position reminded her of the Black American children in school who'd attempted to taunt and berate her because of her color.

"Leaving," was the one-word answer he offered and moved towards the door. There were three men in front of the exit standing in a challenging posture.

"Sure, you and the ladies can go," he snarled in a thick accent, "but that one there knows better than to show his face in our town. He's got to be taught a lesson."

Kafeel remained calm, but his tone conveyed a deadliness they had little experience with. "Perhaps you misunderstood me. I mean that *we* are leaving; including my friend."

Before any of them could respond, four policemen walked through the door, shouting for the customers and workers to get back to whatever they'd been doing. They had no interest in whatever was going on, but they were focused on Lanaia. They asked her her name and when she answered, they instructed her to come with them. The four of them followed the officers outside the store but were told Lanaia was wanted for questioning, and that the four of them could not come.

They had hoped to avoid this situation, but had planned for it. The foursome quickly walked off in the opposite direction of the police, who were leading Lanaia to a squad car. Ducking around the side of the building, Anjelita told Kafeel to take Daieh and Binah and head back to the camp. She transformed into a bird and flew off behind the police car. Flying overhead, she watched as her sister was led inside a large building. The fact that she hadn't been handcuffed and wasn't being treated harshly made Anjelita relax a little, but she stayed sharp.

Circling the police station a few times to find where they had taken Lanaia, Anjelita was glad to see the girl being escorted into a small office. Perching on the ledge outside the open window, she listened intently as Lanaia was questioned by the detective who'd introduced himself as Luis Sanchez. When asked about her whereabouts that night, Lanaia told him that she had been away visiting her father and sister. She and the others had agreed that outright lying would not serve the kingdom of God, so she had agreed to tell the truth; just not all of it. She *had* been with her father that night, and though she'd killed Esperanza in self-defense, Carienne and Myla had healed all of the wounds that would have corroborated her claim.

"As you know," the detective began slowly, "I knew you mother very well. It has always been my understanding that you shared her dislike for your father and his people. Why the sudden change in attitude?" Anjelita knew Lanaia had been prepared for that question. Lanaia had confessed to them that through the years she had publicly denounced her father and had been known to refer to them as savages. She'd wept as she explained how she'd told people Mmoju's kinsmen ate raw meat and worshipped animals in hopes of being accepted.

"I had no choice. When Mmoju told us that I had to go with them on some stupid spirit quest, I begged my mother to tell him no, but she told me I had to go in order to keep an eye on them." Lanaia said the words with conviction, but convincing the detective that it had been Esperanza's idea wasn't difficult. Everyone knew the woman hated her husband, and it was no secret that Esperanza was feeding information about her husband's people to someone very high up in the military. Also known was the fact that she was under their protection.

"When you returned, why did you go back?" he asked. Even though he believed what the young woman was saying, he had to cover all his bases to be sure she was trustworthy. Her mother's loyalty notwithstanding, he had to be certain of her fealty.

Lanaia chuckled bitterly. "Where else could I go? My uncle was away on business; the house had been ransacked and looted; I don't have any other family; and I don't know anyone who would take me in." She desperately hoped her performance was being believed. Tehilla, who had minored in dramatic arts and music in college, had spent hours coaching her on how to deliver her "lines."

As she sat there answering the detective's questions, she focused on her mother's intentions to kill Daieh and the ugly words she'd said to her to make herself feel the anger. Though her words claimed she had no love for her father, her emotions were telling the real story.

The detective was watching her closely. It was clear to him that the girl hated her father, and he was glad to know it. Leaning back in his chair, he tapped his pen against his desk as he thought about how best to use the situation to his advantage. Smiling at the young woman, he told her bluntly, "You will continue to stay with your father. I need you to take your mother's place in keeping me aware of their activities."

Lanaia knew this was coming as well, but feigned shock and dismay. "No!" she cried out, shaking her head. "I can't! My uncle Alejandro is back now and I will stay with him. I can't go back to those people! I won't!" She set her mind to that horrible night once more. The rage she'd felt along with the horror and fear of what she'd had to do made tears well up in her eyes and spill down her golden cheeks. She allowed herself to be back inside that moment and protested the detective's suggestion with near hysteria.

The detective smiled inwardly at the young woman's distress. *"Yes,"* he thought to himself. *"She will go. She will report everything back to me and me only. If the military wants the intel, they'll have to pay me for it. Sure, she'll hate it at first, but after I become the only person she trusts, I'll own her. All of her; and I won't have to share her like I had to share her mother."*

He sat and allowed her to protest a moment longer before he stood and stopped her. "Pull yourself together!" he snapped. "You're a woman full grown now and I'm sure you are well aware of the relationships your mother forged to be able to afford that nice house and all the fine things you have. Those relationships need to continue through you. Esperanza's hatred for her husband was well known, even to him. He wouldn't tell her the things he would share with a loving daughter."

He wiped the tears from her cheeks as he spoke, but his tone was still very direct. "You will watch them and tell me what they are doing. And of course, you will be well compensated for your assistance."

Lanaia refused to look up at him for fear that he would see her true feelings. "And if you refuse," he said, tilting her head up so he could look into her lovely face. "You may find yourself sharing the same fate as Esperanza," he said with quiet force.

Snatching her face from his hand and taking a step back, she stammered, "Y-you had something to do with my mother's murder?" The disbelief in her voice was genuine; she couldn't believe he was actually implying that he'd killed Esperanza to scare her into doing his bidding.

"I'm just saying that certain relationships must be honored, and when they aren't..." he shrugged his shoulders to allow her to draw the only logical conclusion available; she'd be killed.

Sighing in feigned resignation, she slumped back into the chair. "Alright," she acquiesced.

Pleased, he nodded his head that they were in agreement. "You will be under my protection from now on. No one will harm you," he assured her. But smiling like the snake he was, he added, "unless I say so. You're free to go. We'll be in touch."

Lanaia hurriedly turned and snatched the door open to make her get-away. Her tear-blurry eyes and swift movement caused her to collide with a well-dressed, petite woman wearing a wide-brimmed hat with a black veil. "Excuse me, I'm so sorry," she said to the woman. Though the woman didn't reply and rushed past her into the office of the detective she'd just left, Lanaia had recognized the woman. What was Francesca doing at the police station, and why did she pretend not to know her? Lanaia had no answers and knew that standing in the police station trying to figure it out was risky. The thought that perhaps Alejandro had shared her secret with his girlfriend and that was the reason for her visit to the police crossed her mind as she exited the building and ran back to camp.

Chapter Forty-Eight: Frenemies

Anjelita sat listening to the man trying to intimidate her little sister and felt anger wash over her. She wanted to fly through the window, change into another animal and rip his throat out, but she knew unnecessary killing or violence was not the answer. She also reminded herself that they had discussed the possibility of the police trying to coerce Lanaia into taking up Esperanza's position as a spy.

Mmoju had told her that after the battle between the military and their people, soldiers continued to seek them out and attack them. Though they never lost anyone in those short skirmishes, he believed they were trying to gauge their strength. He'd also explained how he met Esperanza.

"Our people had to move constantly after that battle. For the next two years, we couldn't settle in any one place for more than a few weeks before soldiers would show up. One afternoon I had gone out to scout for a potential place to live when I heard a woman scream. Without thinking, I ran towards the sound and found a beautiful young woman being attacked by a soldier. I rushed to help her and knocked the soldier unconscious. The woman was Esperanza. She was shaken up, but she hadn't been injured. She cried and told me that since her father died, she'd been trying to earn money as a cook. She'd been working for the soldier's mother when she met him. He'd tried to offer her money to sleep with him but when she'd refused, he kidnapped her and dragged her out into the jungle. I'm not sure if it was due to my missing Anuka or because she was so beautiful, but I asked her to marry me. Since she had no father to protect her, I promised to take care of her and her brother."

Anjelita remembered seeing the pain on Mmoju's face as he continued. "Shortly after we were married, we settled in the area we live in now because the attacks stopped immediately. I didn't think it had anything to do with my new bride at first, but as it became clear how much she hated being amongst my people, I began to suspect that it did. At first I thought she was just uncomfortable being without the modern conveniences she'd grown accustomed to, but by the time Daieh was born, I knew it was much more than that. She refused to live in the house I'd built for her. She moved into town and purchased a house. I didn't have to ask where she'd gotten the money from because in my heart I knew. Abuela had a few confirming visions, but assured me that no attacks were coming. We watched and waited; always ready if the soldiers came back, but they never did. I know now that she was being paid to spy on us and that her marriage to me was simply a job to her; a job she hated."

Anjelita and the others had believed Lanaia would be asked to spy and they had planned accordingly. She saw Lanaia exit the building and was about to fly down to her, when a woman rushing into the detective's office caught her attention. Anjelita stared at the woman through the window for a moment, trying to identify her. She had seen the woman before, but where? As the woman removed her hat and Anjelita was able to see her full face, her heart leapt in her chest.

The woman was Sister Magali's sister! The woman had visited California nearly a decade ago when she still lived at the orphanage. She remembered how happy Magali had been to see her younger sister. At the time, the 15-year-old Anjelita was preoccupied with preparing for college and had not paid much attention to the woman. She'd listened through the years as Sister Magali would tell her stories about her family back in Santo Domingo and how much she missed her family; especially

338

her baby sister Francesca. When the woman in the office began to speak, Anjelita set aside her shock at finding Magali's sister in Guatemala, and concentrated on what was being said.

"What was she doing here?" Francesca demanded as she closed the door.

Luis had never liked nosy women who considered themselves to be intelligent. "None of your business, Franny," he answered coolly with his back to her. He watched silently as his last visitor left the building looking stricken. "The real question is what are you doing here?"

If Francesca hadn't needed his help to accomplish her goals, she would have walked out. But since she did, she sat down and suggested he do the same. "I have news. Very important news that will make us both very rich."

Luis knew that Francesca was an opportunistic whore and had never trusted her. However, she was the long-time girlfriend of Lanaia's uncle and might know something of interest. She had his attention so he urged her to go on.

"Alejandro returned recently from his business trip to find his niece was alive and well."

Before she could go on, he interrupted. "Obviously I know that already. She was just here," he snapped.

Again, Francesca was tempted to leave his office, but reminded herself that the greasy little man had the contacts she needed. "There is a time for talking and a time for listening, Luis. Now is the time for you to listen," she stated calmly. She knew he didn't like being put in his place by anyone; especially a woman.

She could see the muscles in his jaw tighten and anger flash across his face, but she wasn't scared of him. Raising a questioning eyebrow, she held his gaze; daring him to say more. Confident that his greed would overrule his anger, she went on. "As I was saying; when Alejandro reunited with his nieces he went with them to where the savages have been living for the past two decades."

"And," Luis asked.

"And," she paused for effect. "They were not alone. They were with those people from the news; the ones who can fly and change shape."

"WHAT!" Luis exclaimed, jumping from his seat. "How do you know? Are you sure?" His heart was pounding in his chest as he thought about the implications of her words.

"Of course I'm sure. Alejandro saw them with his own eyes, and tomorrow he's taking me to meet them," she stated triumphantly.

Eying her suspiciously, he asked, "And why would he do that? He knows how you feel about those savages."

"True. But Alejandro is not only a fool; he's a fool in love who believes I want to join him and those sub-human animals." She spent a few more minutes gleefully telling him how she'd pretended to accept his words about their god and was willing to convert to their religion. Once she was done, she outlined her plan to have Alejandro escort her to their camp. She told him that she wanted him to recruit men with speed and stealth, because it wasn't a battle they were after; just one or two of the special people.

The two sat for the next half an hour fleshing out their plan to abduct at least one of the people they'd seen on the

340

news. Pulling up images of them on his laptop computer, they were able to identify them from the rest of the people they were with. "As you know, each one is worth 20 million dollars. I'm prepared to offer you five for your help."

"Only five?" he asked. "The way I see it, you need me to make the contacts once we have them. You need me to recruit the men. You need me to handle the transport. In fact, my sweet; I don't really need *you* at all." He smiled devilishly at her. He had her over a barrel and there wasn't anything she could do about it. His contacts within the military as well as his own officers have known where they were camped for many years. With that in mind, he added, "So in reality, all you've done is alerted me to their presence, and I'd say that information is worth about fifty thousand dollars." He sat back and waited for her to scream at him; to call him vile names. He knew she could be a hot-head sometimes and he was ready for her to let him have it with both barrels.

Francesca's smile didn't reach her eyes as she told him calmly, "I thought you might try to pull something like this, so I brought along something to help you rethink your next move." Opening up her handbag, she removed a large manila envelope and tossed it onto his desk. Warily, he picked up the package and opened it. When he saw the two dozen pictures of himself and several of his associates, the color drained from his face.

"The pictures are nice, but the video is much better," she said, pointing to the USB flash drive that had fallen onto the desk when he'd pulled out the photos.

Trying to keep his hands from shaking, he connected the drive and opened the first of 10 files. It was a video of him, two highly ranked military officers and the owner of the largest coffee manufacturing company in the country. The four of them were discussing the next shipment of cocaine to be exported to the US via the coffee. For several years the illegal exportation of the drug had gone smoothly because of the sterling reputation of the coffee company. He knew that if this video were to get out, he'd be killed.

"I should kill you!" he spat venomously.

"Yes, I'm sure you want to, but there's something else you should know. If anything should happen to me; anything at all, I have friends around the world with sealed copies of this information and strict instructions to release it to every government official and news reporter from here to Columbia, Peru and the United States."

As she stood to leave his office she added, "And since you scoffed at my generous offer of 25%, now I'll make it 5%. And if I don't get my money, your life and the lives of everyone you know will be forfeit. We both know that your friends won't take kindly to their business being destroyed. They won't just kill you, they'll massacre everyone you know and love. Think about that before you do anything foolish." Glancing down at the pictures on his desk, she smiled sweetly, "You can keep those. I have plenty more."

Chapter Forty-nine: Love is the Answer

njelita flew from the police headquarters back to the camp as quickly as she could. A variety of emotions were running through her; anger at learning about this woman's plans to capture them for profit; sadness at how her new friend Alejandro was being manipulated by the woman he loved, and concern for the safety of her companions.

To keep herself from succumbing to any one of those feelings, she refocused her mind on what she knew about Sister Magali's younger sibling. At the time of her visit, Anjelita remembered the woman saying that she had been widowed during a battle in South America some years prior to her arrival in California. She recalled how angry and bitter the woman sounded as she told Magali that the people who'd murdered her husband were "savages from the jungle."

Anjelita wished that she had not asked to be excused from the women's visit so she could have learned more, but there was something about the woman that made Anjelita uncomfortable. At the time, she'd chalked it up to her aversion to the woman's profession. Magali had often prayed for her sister who had become a prostitute in order to feed herself after she'd been widowed.

The moment Anjelita landed in camp, she gathered Bridget and the Order along with Mmoju, Carlos, Badee, Carienne and Dakkar. Once the group was seated in the meeting house, Anjelita quickly told them all she knew. She hadn't wanted to alarm the others, but felt it was something Bridget and the elders needed to know. Lanaia had made it back to camp earlier had already told them of her encounter with the police so she didn't have to tell them how she'd come to be at the station.

343

"Lanaia told me that she saw Alejandro's lady-friend at the station and how the woman hurried past her in hopes that she wouldn't be recognized," Mmoju stated sadly. When he'd learned that his brother-in-law had taken up with the woman of ill repute, he'd shaken his head sadly. He'd hoped that Alejandro's interest in the woman was purely physical, but now he knew differently.

"Do you think he will bring her here?" Carlos asked. He too had come to like the man during his time with them in camp and wondered if his judgment could be swayed by this woman.

They all looked towards Mmoju for an answer since he knew the man better than anyone else in attendance. He shook his head and shrugged his shoulders. "I really don't know. I want to believe that Alejandro would not risk our safety to impress a woman, but there is no telling what a man might do if he thinks he's in love." He's stated the last part quietly because he knew from first-hand experience what a man might do for the affections of a beautiful woman. Abuela had tried to dissuade him from marrying Esperanza, but he'd argued that the lack of unmarried women old enough to marry among his own people was the reason he'd chosen an outsider. But he knew then, just as he knew now that a man's judgment can become cloudy where a beautiful woman was concerned.

They talked a while longer about the best strategies if they were attacked. Carlos thought it best if the women who were unable to fight, the elders and the children were sent to the Starlight. The rest of them would wait to see what tomorrow would bring and to prepare for another fight. In the meantime, they used the remainder of the day to reshoot the video.

As the large group of women and children were escorted to the Starlight, they were quiet and didn't ask what was going on. They had learned long ago that the Star Woman and their elders were trying to protect them, and that their job at this point was to pray. So they did.

Well before dawn, Carienne woke up. She'd noticed that lately she was becoming more like her mother Tehilla; rising before the sun. Finding that she enjoyed the calm solitude of the fresh day, she quietly slipped from her pallet in the meeting house and headed to the river. She needed to be alone with her thoughts, feelings and God; and for her there was no better place than the depths of the water to do so. Wearing the tee-shirt and shorts she'd slept in, she slid quickly into the water.

In a small house on the far edge of town, Alejandro awakened shortly after midnight. He knew that Mmoju and the others would be breaking camp and leaving Guatemala soon, so if he wanted to join them he would have to leave now to make the five-hour trip by foot. He gently shook Francesca's shoulder to wake her up because they needed to head out quickly. She sat up and shook off the last vestiges of sleep. Turning to him she smiled. She knew it was time.

Under the cover of darkness, Alejandro locked the door to Francesca's house and wondered if he was doing the right thing by taking her with him. Part of him wanted desperately to have her by his side for the rest of their lives, but there was another part that was filled with fear and trepidation about his decision. Shaking off the latter thought, he took Francesca's hand and led them away from town and into the jungle.

During the trip, she'd been uncharacteristically quiet. He assumed it was from fear of how she would be received. He didn't make any attempts to comfort her because he harbored his own misgivings. Deciding it was too late to turn back now, he led them deeper into the jungle.

Just as the dawn sky was turning pink, they reached the outskirts of the camp. Out of the darkness came Juba and Jalle, snarling and baring their teeth. Alejandro spoke to the large cats so they would know who he was. He'd never seen them act so agitated before.

The large male jaguar rushed him and knocked him down. Fear gripped him and he closed his eyes and covered his face. He'd let out a loud scream when he'd been knocked down, but he doubted anyone would hear him because they were still a mile away from camp. His heart was racing wildly, but when the animal did not attack him, he sat up and focused his eyes on Francesca. The two were circling her and growling.

"Francesca, don't move!" He warned her. He was going to try to get the animals to back down again. Before he could formulate a plan on how to do it, Francesca pulled a pistol from the bag she was carrying and shot one of the cats.

"No!" he screamed as the second cat pounced on the small woman. Alejandro was powerless to do anything more than watch as the woman he loved was mauled to death. So swift was her death that she hadn't had time to even scream.

Carienne ran up to them and got Juba to stop biting and slashing at the woman's dead body. Knowing there was nothing she could do for her, she turned her attention to Jalle. The female feline had been shot in the chest, but fortunately not in the heart. Carienne worked quickly to extract the bullet and repair the wound.

By then, Mmoju and the others had reached them. When he saw the woman's lifeless body lying in the dirt, he

346

turned to Alejandro to ask him what was going on. The man was apparently in shock after what he'd just witnessed, so Daieh went to his side to lead him back to camp to have him lie down.

The two had not taken more than a few steps when a swarm of soldiers descended on them from three sides. They were prepared for a battle and quickly began dispatching the attackers, but not before they saw Carienne being shot in the neck by a dart.

Dakkar screamed and flew over to protect her, but he was too late. The encroaching soldiers obscured his vision and were shooting at him. He made short work of clearing a path to get to Carienne, but as soon as he had, she was gone. The soldiers had been given the order to retreat and they did so quickly; scattering in different directions.

Realizing that his daughter had been abducted, Carlos screamed his rage. His feelings were shared by the rest of the group. Anjelita and Dakkar were about to take off to try and rescue the girl, but Bridget and Kafeel stopped them.

"It's more than likely a trap. They want to capture the two of you as well and we can't afford to lose you," Kafeel said, his voice thick with emotion.

"I don't care. I'm going! I can cover more ground from the air and see which way she was taken," Dakkar said.

It was clear to all of them that the young man meant business. They also knew just how determined he could be, but Kafeel was right; it was probably a trap and they couldn't lose him as well. Bridget placed a hand on his arm to calm him down. "No, son. You will stay here," she told him with firm gentleness.

Riley walked into the center of the group and laid down a map of the area he'd gotten from one of Mmoju's kinsmen a few days ago. At the time, the old pilot had just been interested in getting a fix on their location and an idea of the surrounding area, but he'd discovered a few things he believed might come in handy now.

"There are about six abandoned armories within a 50 mile radius of here." His tone held a hint of excitement as told them more. "Actually, they are little more than fortified warehouses." He could tell by their confused faces that they still didn't understand.

Speaking quickly, he gave them a brief lesson in the country's history. "Back in 1954 the American CIA wanted to overthrow the popular president of Guatemala. During his term, Jacobo Árbenz did a massive land reallocation in the country which gave small tracts of land to peasants. This included the land that had been given to the American-based United Fruit Company by one of his American-allied predecessors. Needless to say, our country wasn't happy that the land we'd been given in exchange for our support was being taken away and given to a bunch of locals," he chuckled cynically.

"Well that summer, the CIA set up a covert operation to overthrow the Guatemalan president. During that time, they needed someplace to store the weapons they were using against Árbenz and built a few concrete and steel bunkers. These bunkers were never destroyed because so few people knew they even existed. Their proximity to us would be an ideal place for a team to hold Carienne hostage until they could arrange transportation for her to be taken elsewhere."

They split up into two groups to aid in the search. Riley led Binah, Lark and Haku toward the western bunkers, while

Carlos, Kafeel, Tookey and Jahmil headed east. Bridget said a silent prayer as the groups took off.

****

Thirty minutes later, the soldiers arrived at the secret facility they had been instructed to take the prisoners to. The plan was to capture all three of their targets, but the commanding officer realized quickly they would not be able to do so. They had come with over 500 soldiers; a number that should have easily defeated less than 100 people, but within minutes over 100 of his soldiers had fallen. At that rate, they would have all been dead in less than a quarter of an hour. With that in mind, he'd snatched the one target; a young girl, and high-tailed it out of there.

Once they were inside the facility, the girl was secured to a gurney with thick leather straps on her wrists and ankles. Another was across her chest and handcuffs were added as an extra precaution on her upper wrists. No one wanted to risk the girl getting free. The building was a one-room, steel and concrete bunker used to store weapons in the past. It had been abandoned several years ago and no one would disturb them there.

The commander looked down at the unconscious girl and wondered about the true nature of her power. Until he'd see the carnage her group was capable of, he'd believed the news reports were some type of hoax. He stood and watched the girl who appeared no older than his own daughter and felt sadness creep over his heart. More than likely he would get the call from the higher-ups ordering that she be killed, and somehow that just didn't sit right with him. He'd killed many times before during battles and as a hired gun for members of the corporate elite who'd wanted to eliminate their

349

competition, but never had he been asked to kill a child in cold blood.

The longer he stood there, the more inclined he was to undo the straps, take her up in his arms and make a run for it. However, he knew that such action would get him killed; if not by his own men, then by the men who'd ordered her capture. Taking one last glance at the girl who appeared to be sleeping peacefully, he thought that it was good the girl had been given enough tranquilizers to keep a grown man twice her size sedated for several hours. That way, she wouldn't know or see what was sure to come.

He turned to walk outside to check on the two dozen men he had with him guarding their location when he heard a soft voice asking him to stay. Spinning around in disbelief, he stared into the lovely brown eyes of the girl strapped to the gurney.

"Please stay. I like the company," she told him. He almost fell back in shock. She'd only been unconscious for less than an hour and yet she was wide awake and looking at him with no fear in her eyes.

Panicking, he called for the guards and within seconds, several men rushed in to see what was going on. Seeing that the commander was not in any immediate danger, they too looked at the alert girl lying in the straps.

"How can she possibly be awake?" one of them asked.

Before anyone could come up with an answer, the commander's phone rang. It was the call he'd been expecting. He hesitated a moment before answering, and when he did, he received the order to kill her. He glanced over at the seven men who'd rushed in and gave them an almost imperceptible nod, confirming their orders.

Carienne looked around at each of the men who'd been sent to kill her. She didn't feel sadness or fear for her own life. Instead, she felt sad for them. They were moving through their lives without the help and guidance of God; an existence she knew had to be painful and lonely. Her voice was calm as she spoke to them.

"I know that the man you all serve wants me dead and I'm not afraid to die if that is my God's will. If I have served my purpose to Him then I will gladly leave this sin-sickened world to join my Heavenly Father. All I ask is that before you kill me you think about what He wants to do for you and through you. Each of you has killed for a government that you know is corrupt in order to preserve the wealth and status of the elite. You try to console yourselves with the belief that you are only doing your job and following orders. But you know in your hearts that it's a lie. It's that lie that keeps you awake at night. It blocks you from truly loving and living and being happy. You fear following those orders and you fear not following them. Fear is not an emotion that God wants you to have. He wants you to know peace, comfort and above all else; love."

She looked at each man in the eye and said softly, "I love you." The men began to tremble at her words but tried to stand firm. She said it again. "I love you." To each of the men she repeated the statement. And when she'd spoken to the last man, she said in a louder voice; "And God loves you even more."

She stared up at the ceiling of the building and let tears roll down the sides of her face until the wet stream tickled her ears. "God loves you and He forgives you. As do I. Do what you must." She closed her eyes and smiled. If they killed her, she was content knowing that she would be with her Father in Heaven. She would miss her mother and her friends and wanted to have more time with her newly found family; but God's will be done.

The men were overcome with feelings of love, joy and happiness. There was so much truth and power in the young woman's words that one of the soldiers dropped his gun and fell across her, clawing at the straps on her wrists. Within seconds, the others followed suit. They were all crying and begging her forgiveness.

Carienne, now free, sat up and reached out to each of the men. "You have my forgiveness, but the One you need to ask is God. Only He can forgive you for all of the sins you've committed in the past. Only the blood of His Son can wash away all of the guilt and pain you've suffered. Ask Him; He's waiting for each of you."

The sound of bullets firing outside made them all look up and rush to the door. Kafeel and his team of rescuers had tracked the soldiers back to this location with Riley's help. Of the three building they had been assigned to search, this was the second one they'd checked and they were happy that it hadn't taken much more than an hour.

They were busy fighting the several armed men when another group came out of the building. One of the men ordered the others to cease fire. Kafeel and his team stayed in battle positions in case this was a trap. The soldiers they had been fighting looked at their commander in confusion, but they stopped shooting; keeping their guns trained on their opposition, however.

Out of the building came two more soldiers and they were flanking a smiling Carienne. The commander stepped over to her, took her hand and began walking her over to where Kafeel stood. Jahmil and Carlos saw a sincere kindness in the man's eyes as he came abreast of them.

Seeing this, one of the soldiers who'd been outside fighting screamed, "No! You can't release her!" He'd been promised $50,000 of the reward money for capturing this demoness, and was not about to let his bewitched commander take that away from him.

He raised his gun and fired at Carienne, only to have his bullets turn back and strike him in his chest. The Kevlar vest he wore kept him from being wounded, but the pain from the bullet's force knocked him down. Carlos and Binah had nearly collided with each other as they both ran to push Carienne out of the bullet's path.

Everyone in their group looked up to see Dakkar hovering above the trees. He'd been responsible for redirecting the bullets. Upon seeing him, Jahmil shook his head.

"What?" Dakkar asked innocently. "You didn't really believe I'd let you have all the fun, did you?" He added with a smile to his friends.

To the surprise of everyone there, the Commander gave Carienne a hug in farewell. He then told the soldiers who'd been inside with him to disarm and restrain the others. Turning back to Kafeel he warned, "You have to leave your camp immediately. They know where you are and with the reward for your capture being so high, there's no telling how many people will come for you."

Heeding the man's words, Kafeel and the others headed for the Starlight. On the way, Jahmil asked Carienne if she'd used her mind-altering abilities on them. She smiled and told them no. She admitted to having considered that option, but as she laid there strapped to the table working the tranquilizers out of her system, she prayed that God would show her what to do. He'd told her to not pray for herself, but to pray for them.

"And when I started doing that, I felt His presence and His love pouring out of me. They felt it too and chose to help me."

Once they'd reached the Starlight and all the hugging was done, Bridget and the others wanted a report, so Carienne told them her story again. When she'd finished, Bridget smiled in wonder at the girl. "I've always known that you were an empath and could feel what others felt, but I had no idea that your gift was so strong that you could project your feelings out to others. God has truly blessed you."

Chapter Fifty: Go Tell it on the Mountain

S afely aboard the Starlight, Lanaia proudly announced that she'd completed the editing of their video and that she was ready to upload it to over fifty internet sites. "After you sent me and the others here, I thought it would give me a chance to make sure everything was in order. I didn't want to upload it until you all had a chance to approve it," she said.

Mmoju glanced briefly at Bridget and then back his middle daughter. The daughter who'd once openly despised him, their people and their ways was truly gone. In the past months she had transitioned from being a solemn, sad girl with a heart full of regret into a vibrant, considerate, God-fearing young woman who sought to please God and him. His heart swelled with pride as he praised God for her deliverance. "I know you've done your best, Lanaia. Your work is already approved," he told her through the tears streaming down his face.

Beaming with her father's approval, she quickly uploaded the footage. Once she had, she clicked onto one of the sites so that everyone could see the video. Laqat wanted to sit back and watch the video with his friends, so when he turned and asked Riley to take over piloting the craft, the old fly-boy grinned and jumped into the controller's seat. He'd assisted Lanaia for a while after everyone else had gone to sleep last night, so he didn't need to see it again.

The entire right side of the windshield filled with a clear image of the jungle clearing that Mmoju and his kin had called home for the past two decades. A second later, Bridget's smiling face came into view as the camera settled on her.

"I know that many of you have seen reports that there are people among you with strange abilities. Some of you believe that what you have seen are aliens from outer space. Others have been told that we are part of a top secret government project. We are here to explain to you exactly who we are, what we can do, and the how's and whys of these abilities. My name is Bridget, and of all of the people you will see today, I am the only one from another planet."

She paused briefly to gather her thoughts before continuing. "It is true that you are not alone in the universe. I am from a planet called Ehyeh Asher Ehyeh. The name of my planet means "I AM," out of respect for the divine Creator who made it. Yes, I am speaking of the one true living God." Bridget spent the next 15 minutes discussing how she came to Earth and why. She finished her telling by explaining the prophecy, and introducing the Unifiers.

Next up was Anjelita; as she was the eldest of the Unifiers. "My name is Anjelita Azul and I am a Unifier. My people are called the people of the Earth because they have lived in communion with the animals for several millennia. I have been given several gifts by the Almighty to carry out His plan of giving all mankind another chance to reconcile with Him. My gifts include strength; both mental and physical, speed, and the gift of sight. This means that I sometimes have visions about things that have happened long ago, as well as things that will happen. And finally, some of you have seen that I can change my form." Having said that, Anjelita shifted into the form of a tiger, then a buffalo, then an elephant, and finally an eagle before returning to her regular form. She finished her interview by changing into a field mouse and scurrying away.

Next was Dakkar. The young man stood in front of the camera and related his story. He began with his early childhood and his capture by the US military. He explained that as a Unifier, he too had been given gifts. "I was born to the people of the sky. I can soar across the skies by merely thinking about it. All of my people can."

He had Lanaia swing the camera across the sky to where Badee, Tookey, Lark and others from their clan were hovering. They chose a distance that would clearly show them in flight, but would not interfere with the interview. Dakkar went on to explain that he could rearrange the molecules in any matter be it metal or mineral. With that said, he pointed to the ground between him and Lanaia.

As she trained the camera on the spot he'd indicated, he proceeded to open a hole in the soft earth. As the camera recorded, he made the hole wider until it was nearly a foot wide and then a foot deep. Finally, he told the future viewers that he could also move matter. As if on cue, Lark and some of the others in the sky began firing arrows at him.

He could see that Lanaia was terrified, but he smiled her direction and told her not to worry. As arrows whizzed toward him, he stopped them in mid-air. Casually walking the six feet to where he'd stopped the dozen arrows, he reached out and grabbed them, held them up for all to see and carried them to where Lanaia stood holding the camera. His interview done, he flew away.

Finally, Carienne was to be interviewed. Before her turn, they decided to let Lanaia rest a bit. She'd admitted to being a little tired, but was far too excited to stop. A couple hours later, the group had reassembled near a small lake.

Unlike Anjelita and Dakkar, Carienne was right at home in front of the camera. As soon as Lanaia gave her the signal that she was recording, the young woman gave an exuberant hello and a sunny smile. "My name is Carienne Cotton and you can see, I'm the youngest of the Unifiers."

She spent a few brief moments talking about how her people were called the people of the sea and why. "I always knew I could do things in water that no one else seemed capable of, but I had no idea it was because of a decision made eons ago by my ancestors," the young woman said with a smile.

"Once I learned who I was and that my purpose was to help everybody in the world know that God is real and He's waiting for you to come to Him, I was floored! Seriously! But then, I learned that He gives us all gifts that He wants used to glorify His kingdom. One of my gifts happens to be the ability to control water."

With that, she motioned towards the lake and brought up a pillar of water 10 feet high. She then made the water bow to the left and then to the right. She made it spin around before letting it splash back down to the lake. "I can also heal people who are sick or have been wounded." Then she said in a more sober tone, "I am also an empath. That means I can feel what others feel. That is one of the hardest gifts because I can sense so much pain and despair in people. And to know that all it would take to heal each of you is for you to cast your cares upon Him; hurts more than anything." With that, the young woman raced to the lake and joined the half-dozen of her kinsmen in the water. Lanaia filmed a few more minutes of them ducking underwater for long periods of time and resurfacing.

To the surprise and delight of everyone watching, Johnathan Riley's face filled the screen. He spent a moment introducing himself and discussing his previous occupation within the US Air Force. "Who I am is really not that important because in the grand scheme of things, *I'm* not that important.

However, the things I have seen and yes, been a part of, needs to be shared."

Before he continued, he confessed his role in Dakkar's capture and how he'd been the one to draw attention to the young man's people. He also told them that because of his claims to have seen a man flying, he'd been labeled as being crazy by the military. Riley felt it was important to let people know that up front because he would undoubtedly be discredited and dismissed when his psychiatric records became public knowledge.

After he'd explained the circumstances that resulted in his being demoted, he went on to tell the viewers that once he'd captured Dakkar, he'd been vindicated and not only fully reinstated; but promoted as well. Turning his attention to the true purpose he was being interviewed, Riley exposed the real reasons for the genetic research being done at private labs around the world, including the one in Payar, Senegal.

Finally, he discussed the true nature of the "chip" being pushed by the financial institutions and the devastation it will lead to from an economic standpoint as well as a spiritual one. As he concluded his interview, the soft sound of Tehilla's voice singing Amazing Grace could be heard in the background as a teary-eyed Riley gave his personal testimony of salvation and redemption.

To cap off the piece, Bridget's face came back into the camera lens' focus. She knew that Lanaia had already captured nearly two hours of footage, but wanted to let the viewers know one more thing. "I know that with everything you've just seen and heard, it may be hard for you to decipher the truth. Ours has been a tale that, on the outside may seem like pure fiction; what with people flying and shape-shifting and breathing under water. But if you got nothing else from what

359

we have shared, know this; God is very real and is waiting for each and every one of you. You probably won't be able to fly or have super speed, but God has given each of us different gifts. Yours might be encouraging others. Or teaching. Or comforting others. Whatever that gift is, He wants you to use it to edify His kingdom. So don't look to us to save you because we can't. Saving you is the job of our Lord Jesus Christ. We can only tell you that God is real and He desperately wants you to get to know Him. Pick up His word and study it. Then pray and ask Him how He can use you. Whether you think our experiences are fact or fiction, know that the truth of God's love is the ONLY fact you need. We love you, and God loves you too."

With that, Lanaia clicked off the monitor to thunderous applause. The segment was two hours and eighteen minutes long, but it was engaging, uplifting and very informative. Bridget and the others showered Lanaia with praise for her efforts, which she accepted with a shy smile and soft thank-yous.

As the Starlight headed their expanded group of over 200 people towards Sanctuary, Anjelita asked what they planned to do about the concert series. "Shouldn't we try to stop them?" she wanted to know.

Bridget shook her head. "No. God gives us all free will and it is not up to us to take the choice from them. All we can do is keep spreading His message and pray for those who are still lost." She understood that Anjelita and the others were full of God's righteous fury and were eager to do battle against His enemies, but now was not the time.

She showed the frustrated young people a small smile as she told them, "There will come a time when we will have to fight. However, those people who are already lining up to accept the mark have hardened their hearts to God already and our fight is not with them. Right now, we are fighting for the people who have not accepted Christ but who are open to what they have heard about Him. And that fight will not take place on the battlefield; but on our knees."

Anjelita accepted the wisdom of Bridget's words and vowed to pray for the lost children of God. She remembered what Bridget had taught them about the Great Flood and how the wickedness of man was so rife that He decided to destroy everyone on Earth except Noah and his family. She realized that she and the Unifiers were like Noah; spreading the truth of God's love and His unhappiness with their wicked deeds. Jesus was like the Ark; the only safe place to be when God's wrath came down. She had been blessed to be able to reconnect with her family to bring them aboard as well. The condition of the world is just as it was in the days of Noah, and she counted it all joy that she was on the Ark.

****

Seated in the abandoned lab in Payar, Senegal, a furious Mr. Cilfure sat and watched the video of the Unifiers sharing their true purpose. He was extremely frustrated. Not only had he been unable to capture them and extract their DNA, but his plans to expose them as aliens or worse had backfired. In the three hours since their documentary had aired online, nearly two million people had already viewed it. His people had contacted him to alert him to the problem, but it was being shown on so many different sites that he couldn't shut them all down.

People were downloading it and adding it to their personal pages; blogs were exploding with comments, and chat rooms dedicated to discussing it were already up and running. In his rage he stood up and threw a chair across the room. "I am the prince of the air! Me! People watch and believe what I tell them!" He fumed.

Finally bringing himself to calm, he looked upward and said, "This changes nothing! You have only succeeded in telling them the same thing You have told them from the beginning of time!" Cilfure threw his head back and laughed cynically. "Not even Your precious Son dying for them would turn them from me to You. You stand back quietly offering them what? Peace? Your Love? Forgiveness? Ha! I show them all the things that money can buy. I show them how to get that money. How to have the power to not only control their own lives, but the lives of others. You may get a few more stragglers with heavy hearts to follow You, but in the end, most will follow me!"

The ominous roar of thunder and the shaking of the building cut his rant short. Still scowling, Cilfure left the lab but promised he would succeed at making man in his own image one way or another.

"A

njelita. Anjelita dear, wake up."

Slowly, the young woman opened her eyes. She had been jostled awake. "Yeah, yeah..." she began, but as her eyes focused and she recognized the voice speaking to her, she jumped straight up. "Wh-what are you doing here? How are you here?" she stammered.

Concern replaced the smile on Sister Magali's tan face. "What do you mean? I told you I was coming by and we were supposed to have lunch together." She peered into the young woman's face. "Are you alright, dear?"

Anjelita looked around her neat office. She was somehow back in Colorado in the animal clinic. Looking warily at Sister Magali and scanning her person for a dagger or weapon, she asked, "When did you get back from Rome?"

The woman looked truly puzzled then. "When did I ever get to go to Rome? You need to sit down. Do you want a glass of water?" Anjelita looked at the screen on her computer. The date, if correct was the same as the day she'd killed Sister Magali in self-defense.

It was a dream! She realized. Overwhelmed by that realization, she slumped back down into her chair. *Had everything she'd experienced over the past year and a half all been just a dream?* Anjelita relaxed in her office chair and laughed.

She laughed so long and so hard that tears were streaming down her face. Sister Magali didn't know what to make of the young woman's antics. When she could finally catch her breath and compose herself, she looked at her friend/ mentor. "Come, Sister; boy do I have a story to tell you!"

Still chuckling, Anjelita and Magali headed out to her car. Realizing that she had forgotten her keys in her desk, she ran back in. Walking around the desk, she spotted her keys next to her calendar. It was a spiritual daily word calendar and in beautiful italic font was the scripture:

> *Having then gifts differing according to the grace that is given to us, let us use them: if prophecy, let us prophesy in proportion to our faith; or ministry, let us use it in our ministering; he who teaches, in teaching; he who exhorts, in exhortation; he who gives, with liberality; he who leads, with diligence; he who shows mercy, with cheerfulness.*
> Romans 12:6-8.

Anjelita smiled, took up her keys, and headed out. Her steps slowed at the sight of Sister Magali speaking with a tall, handsome, muscular White man. "Anjelita, I want you to meet Mr. Davenport. The church had me interviewing for a new Chief of Security for the Home and I've hired him," Sister Magali told her.

Anjelita was so stunned that she could barely say a word. In an attempt to cover up the younger woman's social blunder, Sister added,

"That's why I had to come to Colorado. He's from here."

Finally finding her voice, Anjelita stuck out her hand. Pleased to meet you Mr. Davenport. Giving her a secretive smile as he shook the offered hand, he told her, "Please, call me Kafeel."

The

End

From the Author,

I hope you enjoyed reading the story about Anjelita, Dakkar and Carienne as much as I enjoyed writing it. I have always enjoyed fantasy and science-fiction stories about people who have extraordinary abilities, but have become increasingly dismayed at how so many of those tales involves witchcraft and sorcery. Imagine my delight when God gave me a story that featured many of the same themes in popular fantasy and sci-fi, but focused on Him as being the source of their fantastic abilities!

As Christians, we are taught through His Word to be aware of worldly entertainments that seek to corrupt the mind and the spirit. We all know that we are living in an age where all manner of perversion and evil are being upheld through the media in ways that desensitizes us to the corruption and wickedness permeating this beautiful world. Keeping that in mind, it was my intent to offer a tale that was fun and exciting, but devoid of the negative influences so prevalent in other stories of this genre.

Though I have said it throughout the story, I want to make this painstakingly clear; *this is a work of pure fiction.* While the characters are well-versed in the Word and they often share the Good News while trying to uphold the teachings of Christ, the story is purely the work of my overactive imagination. Theories about the Watchers and the Nephilim come from unsubstantiated works outside of the Bible and are only used to bring the story-line to life.

Having said that, the truths that you may have recognized throughout the story does come straight from the Bible and it is my most sincere desire that anyone who reads this and does not know Jesus Christ as their personal Lord and Savior, will stop and pick up the Bible right now. "For God so loved the world that He gave His only begotten Son that whosoever shall believe in Him shall not perish but have everlasting life"- John 3:16.

Again, while I hope you enjoyed the story, please disregard all non-Biblical story lines and comments as purely fiction. The one factual theme that I hope you will consider is that God loves you and is waiting for each of you to accept Him and His love.

Tara La Sean

God Bless!

www.ingramcontent.com/pod-product-compliance
Lightning Source LLC
Chambersburg PA
CBHW071507260626
47170CB00002B/297